THE APARA CHRONICLES BOOK 4:
GOING VIRAL

BY JEANNE RHODES-MOEN

DISCLAIMER:

Any similarities to actual persons living, dead, or otherwise is unintentional. I have used some actual place names from Asheville for realism.

Some characters occasionally utter words in other languages. See the last page of the book: Foreign Word List for definitions.

First published: 2024
E-Book ISBN 979-8-9885544-8-6
Print   ISBN 979-8-9885544-9-3
Cover design and book layout: Jeanne Rhodes-Moen

Published By:
Jeannius Designs
Asheville, NC 28805
www.Jeannius.com

Visit www.aparachronicles.com

Dedication and Thanks

To my parents, who both were in careers where science was key. My mom, who was a nurse, and dad, who worked for NASA when I was a child. I wish you could have seen these books come to fruition.

And thanks to Nicky Rea, who has acted as my editor through this book series, encouraging me to see it through and mentoring me to push my limits and make it better.

Books in Series

All books will be released during 2024-2025

ABOUT THE AUTHOR

 Jeanne Rhodes-Moen was born in Washington D.C. in 1966. She grew up in Maryland, and attended Hood College, where she received a B.A. Psychology and a second B.A. in Math, Secondary Education.

In 1991, she married a Norwegian and moved to Norway, where she made jewelry based in their traditional filigree fused with her own imaginative style. Her first book, Silver Threads: Making Wire Filigree Jewelry, was published in 2006 by Kalmbach Books, and is currently available as Print-on-Demand and eBook on Amazon.

She and her two daughters moved to Asheville, NC, in 2005 after her husband passed from diabetic complications. Since then, she has done a combination of jewelry, lapidary, and jewelry photography.

More recently, she has been using her creative skills toward this series: The Apara Chronicles. A science fantasy book series; of which Hidden in Broad Daylight is the first installment.

Jeanne and her daughters all deal with ADHD, but she finds it has a positive effect on her creative abilities.

TABLE OF CONTENTS

ALONE

It's late Autumn in western North Carolina, and a cold front has blown through, bringing early snow to the peaks along the North Carolina-Tennessee border; the last of the red and yellow autumn leaves are whipped to and fro by icy winds, torn from their tenuous hold on their branches, and mix with a light accumulation of snow on the ground. Hidden in a clearing in the forest on the North Carolina side is an isolated hunting cabin with solar cells for electricity. The windows are clouded over with dirt, and there's smoke coming out of the chimney. Inside sits an angry man. Jason is alone again. The other Apara have rescued or captured all the women he's turned to date, leaving him isolated; he slipped away once again when they ambushed him in Hot Springs, North Carolina. He's still puzzled by how they found him and Philipa, but his priority is to find and bring over other compatible women, so he won't be alone.

Ty Russo and his new partner, Val, secured the network servers containing all the information on who is and isn't compatible with the virus they all carry in their bone marrow. Jason left his laptop behind in the rush to flee the ambush, though he had some of his information backed up to a cloud account. Unfortunately for him, by the time he got to a computer and tried to log into the account, the password was not only changed, but had he been able to log in, he'd have found it wiped of all data.

He has one other possibility, but it's a major undertaking. Somewhere, he has a damaged flash drive Alice salvaged from the fallout shelter after they captured him. It doesn't include a copy of the actual database, but a collection of useful, compatible potentials, most of whom are far older than he prefers, and in most cases, farther away, in unfamiliar territory, but he deems them 'useful in a pinch'. Most are women, but not all. If he believes they might have some skill he could someday utilize, they're on that flash drive. When Tess kicked him across the room and into his computer, the flash drive was badly damaged by a power surge, and will no longer mount. He relegated it to a box of computer odds and ends and plans to salvage it eventually. He hid the box in this abandoned cabin that once belonged to a long-dead uncle of his, along with some other odds and ends.

For now, he'll fall back on observing Inspiration Inc. at a distance and stalk some of its Apara employees to see who they might be preparing to bring into their fold, as he had with Valyri. Recently, Jason put an e-Tag tracker on a car being used by a recent addition to their staff, Niall McFadden, who recently transferred in from the UK, along with his Apara sibling Katie. Tonight, he's been studying the tracking logs and discovers Niall has been frequently visiting a studio in the River District, as well as an apartment in West Asheville. After doing some research, he discovers the apartment belongs to a woman named Callista Xenos.

After some research, Jason Templeton feels the proverbial light bulb go on and realizes, *Ah! Ms. Xenos also has a studio where he's been parking in the River Arts District!* He searches and finds out anything he can about Callista Xenos, or Callie, as she prefers.

Callie's family is Greek, but her parents moved to the US long before she was born. She's slender, with medium-length, curly, black hair, dark eyes, and olive skin. She works at a local daycare three days a week, but her passion is for her jewelry work. She has a small studio where she designs, fabricates, and casts unique jewelry with stones she cuts. Between her part-time day job and her jewelry work, she manages to pay her bills with a little left over each month she often spends on new raw stones to cut.

Jason finds her Facebook page, reading her feed for the last couple of months, finding Niall visited her shop looking for a gift

2

for his sister, Katie, and struck up a conversation with her. Later, the two of them began dating, and her relationship status switched to 'in a relationship' about two weeks ago.

Jason thinks, *If she's a potential, especially one prioritized for turning, they will have those damn sensors and alarms set up in her home and car, and someone monitoring her otherwise! Fuck! I've got to find a time and place when they're only minimally monitoring her, so I can make my move!*

He ponders why he keeps stalking the same center for potentials. *Why not go to another city? One where they wouldn't expect me?* But his mind flicks back to his obsession with Tess, and his wish to stick it to the ones who have made his life miserable: Lissa Pederson for one, Amy, Marc, and others at Inspiration Inc. It has become personal to him he takes potentials away from them, even though his risk of getting caught is far greater than if he left the region.

He continues to read Callie's recent posts and sees one posted since he began perusing her page.

> **Niall and I are going out to dinner in Biltmore Village tonight, and then out to a movie I've been dying to see! I really need a fun night out. The kids in the daycare have been bouncing off the walls since this cold snap hit, and they can't play outside as much. My latest batch of castings went to Hell, 'cause the bottoms of two of my plaster molds blew out! I think I need to order new plaster.**

Jason grins maliciously. He heads to a gun safe in the corner and digs through it until he pulls out a small sniper rifle, complete with a silencer, and begins prepping it for use

WAKING THE DEAD

Apara don't die easily. Unless there's extreme damage to their brains, they merely *appear* dead if seriously injured. Their bodies need all the energy they have to heal the injuries, so they simply shut down, so they channel their energy into healing. This happens to their benefactors if they're injured. They transferred this trait genetically into the engineered Apara they created, as part of their healing and indefinite life span.

Unfortunately, from the time children understand the finality of death, it haunts them. The older one gets, the more it hangs over them; like a weight about to fall and crush them. Naturally, the Apara, being self-healing and self-resurrecting, have a unique view about death. Earlier, most have seen it as a temporary nuisance, should they be 'killed' in the line of duty. They know they'll eventually heal and wake up from the dead with renewed life. That changed after the Jerusalem nuclear bomb obliterated around 3000 of their fellows. They still know they'll rise again from gunshots or falls, but now, even they have a shadow hanging over them; the possibility of a permanent death.

Once one joins the Apara, their first 'death', or stasis, is a turbulent hurdle to jump. Humans have it ingrained that their existence is finite and even fragile; subject to illness, accidents, old age, and crime. Yes, some humans believe in an afterlife or reincarnation, but no one really knows. An Apara knows they'll come back...usually.

Tess Waterford never expected to die at 30. However, after watching the man she loves 'die' in a pool of blood, after barely escaping the nuclear tempest in Jerusalem, she knows, consciously, Apara *can* come back from some *very serious* injuries. Still, one may know they'll come back, but until one experiences it, that event is still a big question, psychologically.

Marc told her one is oblivious to everything during stasis. There's no pain, no thought, no dreams, no awareness. Tess, however, never does things the normal way, and went on an out-of-body jaunt shortly after taking her last breath, lying at the bottom of a deep mineshaft. She unconsciously followed the last person she wanted to spend eternity haunting, Jason Templeton.

She astrally followed him to a cabin in the mountains but had no idea where it was. She was drawn back into her body with the usual thud, but didn't wake up this time, but rather, 'turned off', as Marc had described stasis to her.

PRESENT DAY:

The first thing she's aware of after that, is a loud, rushing sound, a burst of bright light, and she's out of her body again, this time in medical, looking down at her body. Sara's checking her over, and Marc's there too, looking worried and impatient. Oddly, she can't hear what they're saying. She has no idea how much time has passed. Slowly, she drifts toward the ceiling. Before she knows it, she's zipping away at warp speed again, and is back at the cabin, now cleaned up. The solar panels are cleared and working, and there's smoke coming out of the chimney. She phases through a dust-caked window, and into a much cleaner version of the shit-hole cabin she was in before. It's still rustic, but it's been cleaned up, the electricity is working, and Jason's sitting at a new laptop. She feels a multitude of emotions coming from him, from frustration and anger to loneliness, fear, and an odd yearning for Philipa's company. The thought: *She's a crazy-assed bitch, but she did WANT to be with me, and she was company...* echoes as if he'd said it out loud. Once again, some part of her sees the small, frightened boy he'd once been, desperate to have someone around him to keep his mom from abusing him. 'Safety in numbers.' is taking on a whole new meaning.

Tess gets the oddest sensation in her Astral chest. She can almost feel her heart make a sudden, hard thump, she feels a sharp 'tug', flies back across the land, collides with her body, and wakes up sputtering and coughing.

"*Damn*, child! I've never seen anyone wake up so quickly after they've come out of stasis! You weren't breathing for more than about two minutes when you snapped out of it. Are you feeling alright?" Sara asks, running a scanner over Tess to check her vitals.

Tess lets herself sag into the pillow behind her, noticing her heart's pounding harder than she can ever remember, or at least since the night she stumbled onto Marc feeding on some woman in an alley, and discovered what he really is. "Honestly, I don't know. I think I was somewhere else, out-of-body again. I woke up because I crashed into my body like a meteor!"

Sara looks pensive. "So, you were out of body while you were in stasis?"

"Yeah. I think I was. Not the whole time, but I remember fragments. Marc and Amy in the mine shaft, crashing into my body, then darkness, and being out now and crashing back.... But I can't, for the life of me, remember anything else! I know there's more, but it's gone, just like a dream!" Tess says, frustrated, as Sara checks her over to make sure she's healed enough to move around, or if she should sedate her again. Tess picks up on Sara's thought about sedation, reaches up, and puts a hand on Sara's arm. "Don't you *dare*! I don't want to be knocked out again! I'll lie here if I must, but don't *freaking* sedate me!" She snipes at Sara.

Sara stands up straight, hands on her hips; her lips are twisted into a quirky expression until she lets out a slight chuckle. "Well, if you can order *me* around, you must be doing okay." She puts the scanner on the table by the bed. "So, you don't remember anything else? I'm just curious. I can't remember anyone else having out-of-body experiences during stasis. It's quite fascinating. I'd have hooked an EEG up to you if I'd known what was going on."

Before Tess can reply, there's a knock on the door, and Marc sticks his head in. "*Tess!*" He blurts out, comes in, leans down, and hugs her before Sara can chastise him for being too rough with her patient.

"Now, Marc, I know you haven't had Tess's company for the last eight days, but I need to check her over *before* I let you take her home." Sara stares him down, he nods, and walks back out to the waiting area, leaving Sara to her duties.

"I've been out for eight days?" Tess asks, somewhat overwhelmed by the revelation.

"*Yes*! You *don't* want to know how many bone fractures I had to align in your arms, legs, and back! You were quite a mess, *child*! And you did have to have some time for your brain to recover as well. Luckily, we don't get brain damage like humans do. Thank the Benefactors for *that*!" Sara runs her hands along Tess's legs and arms, both feeling and sensing the bones, torn muscles, and tendons have all healed properly. "Wiggle your toes." Sara tells her as she gets down to her feet, and Tess obliges.

Sara puts her hands on her hips again. "You're almost as good as new. I'd suggest you and Marc hold off on anything too strenuous for a couple more days, but I know you *won't* listen!" She chuckles and gives her a mischievous glance. She hands Tess a stack of clothing to change into, as she's currently only in a hospital gown.

Tess gets dressed while she talks to Sara, "I'm not sure I'm up to *that* yet. Not quite sure what's up. Things feel a bit off." Tess admits.

Sara sits on the edge of Tess's bed. "You've been through a major life milestone. By human standards, you *died*! And a rather *rough* death at *that*. At heart, you're still psychologically human, and you're going to react to that death, even if it was only temporary. Not to mention, it happened because of *yet* another confrontation with Jason!"

"I guess it hasn't quite hit me yet. I mean, I knew I'd wake up again..." Tess trails off, trying to get a grip on what she's feeling.

"It could come any time. It could hit you today, next week, next month, or next year, though I suspect it will be sooner rather than later. When it does, there are people you can reach out to. You're not alone; you're part of a very large family now." Sara gives her a warm smile.

"Yeah, and there's always Sue! Resident shrink." Tess quips.

"*Yes*, I'm sure she'll help you, just don't hold it in. You'll need to grieve your death, just like you would any other death. In some ways, it's a rite of passage for us. Even though you've been one of us for a year, your first

8

stasis is the symbolic death of your human existence. You'll find your perspective changes. The world will seem different now." Sara hugs Tess. "Now go find that man of yours! I can hear him wearing a rut in the carpet pacing from here!" She chuckles and nudges Tess toward the door.

Tess walks down the hallway, sees Marc, and gives him a soft smile. She feels a bit odd after her conversation with Sara, but walks rapidly over to Marc, and gives him a big hug. After a minute, she pulls back, looks up, and says, "Let's go home!"

He gives her another hug, and the two of them vanish, reappearing at home. They spend the evening talking and watching a movie together, and soon, Tess is asleep against his shoulder, still exhausted, as her body is still healing. He ports her into bed where she can get the rest she needs.

He gets up in the morning, and quietly leaves her to sleep, while he works from his home office downstairs. At about 12:45 PM, he senses her stirring, and fixes some food. He feels a distant gasp of terror and hears a thud. He immediately takes the pan of eggs off the stove, and ports to her side, finding her curled up in the fetal position, trembling, at the top of the stairs.

"What is it, *love*?" He asks as he reaches down and tries to get her to face him, but her body is frozen in the fetal position.

After a few seconds, she stammers out, "I stumbled near the top of the steps, looked down, everything suddenly went dark, and I was back in the shaft, *falling*! It was so real!"

He puts his hand on her hip, and ports her back to bed, pulling the covers over her still curled-up form, sending her soothing, reassuring emotional energy. His empathy can work both ways, not only receiving emotions, but sending ones that can alter one's mental state, such as reducing the terror and near shock Tess's flashback caused. He gently rubs her back until she relaxes, and her breathing and heart rate return to normal. Eventually, her body unclenches, and she rolls over onto her back to look at him.

"Marc? I was so sure.... It felt like I was back there, *falling* again, waiting to crash into the stone ground." She sobs lightly.

"I know, love. I could see the images in your mind. You're safe, though. Must have been some sort of flashback." He leans over and kisses her forehead to comfort her.

She recounts, almost as much for her own sake, as to explain to Marc what happened, "I was on my way down the hall, and kind of tripped over my own feet near the stairs, and it was like the fall was replaying, but it kept going! Like I was falling without end!" She grips his hand.

"Stay here! I'll bring you something to eat, and blood, naturally. Sara told me your *need* may be higher than normal, as your body is still healing. If you need me, path! I'll come to you." He ports back to the kitchen, returning a few minutes later with a tray of her favorite pancakes with hazelnut-chocolate spread, two fried eggs, several strips of bacon, a glass of chocolate milk, and a bag of blood on the side. "Do you need me to feed you, or do you think you can manage?" He says, grinning mischievously. He knows how much Tess hates feeling helpless, so his comment should encourage her to feed herself.

She raises one eyebrow in annoyance, glaring at him. She pulls herself into a seated position, dragging the tray onto her lap with a sharp tug, then grabs a slice of bacon. "I *can* manage!" She snipes, but then her expression softens. "Thanks, I honestly don't know how long I'd have lain there if you hadn't come and pulled me out of it." She admits.

"Not like I'd ignore your panic, *love*! Do you want me to stay here while you eat, or are you okay?" He asks, stroking her leg.

"I'll be okay. I'm still tired, so I may just eat, and then sleep some more, if that's okay?" She admits, yawning.

"Do that. *Path* if you need anything." He gives her a lopsided smile, knowing her stubborn streak, and leaves the room on foot, leaving the door slightly ajar in case she has another panic attack, and doesn't path.

He lets her sleep for a few hours, but ports in to her in the early evening, gently nudging her to awaken. "Tess, can you get up? You've got a visitor."

"*Visitor?*" She asks with a stretch and a yawn. "*Who?* Sara checking in on me?"

"*No,* Sue's here." He admits, picking up her robe from a nearby chair and handing it to her.

"You *told* Sara what happened, didn't you?" She glares at him as though he's betrayed her.

He raises an eyebrow, giving her a look she knows as his 'cut-it-out' expression. He explains, "Sara warned me; you might be healed physically, but there could be some psychological fallout, especially knowing how you've reacted to confrontations with Jason in the past, and this being your first stasis." He sits next to her on the bed, and swipes a piece of leftover bacon from her plate, nibbling on it as she glares at him. "She made me promise to contact her at any sign of a PTSD-like reaction, and *that* was *definitely* a big one!"

"I'm sure it was just a one-time thing from tripping so close to the stairs. *Honestly,* I'm fine!" She insists.

He reaches over, cups her face, and makes her look at him. "Humor me. Sara sent Sue over because she thinks you'll be more comfortable talking to her, since you two have been working together so much."

"As *colleagues!* Not as a client-patient thing! Makes me feel like I'm back at the community clinic, in *therapy* after Digital Danger." She complains.

"That was a *long* time ago. You've come so far since then, both in becoming Apara, and as a person. Get ready. I'll send her up in about ten minutes. And *no porting out* in the meantime!" He scolds her, picking up on the thought in the back of her mind.

Annoyed, Tess throws a spare pillow at him, but he ports out, and it hits the door instead.

HUMAN ON THE INSIDE

Tess hears a light rap on the bedroom door a few minutes later, and grabs her robe from the chair next to the bed, slipping it on, and sitting on the edge of the bed before saying, "Come on in, Sue." without the usual enthusiasm she's had in the past when her friend visited.

Sue opens the door and gives Tess a lopsided smile. "I hear you're not in the mood to be *shrunk*?"

"I'm just *tired* of it always coming back to this! I should be able to deal with it all without crashing and burning every time Jason throws me a curve-ball!" Tess whines.

Sue joins her on the bed, gently putting her hand on Tess's arm. "You know as well as I do, this is different! Not only did you have an all-out brawl with that jackass, Marc thinks he intended for you to fall down the shaft!"

Tess looks at her with wide eyes. "I just *fell* in, didn't I? He didn't *push* me!"

"He didn't *have* to. Marc saw it from a distance, but couldn't get there in time. That shaft was Jason's project down there; he knew the shaft's location, and how close you were to it. He believes that's why Jason took those sudden, lunging steps toward you. He knew you'd instinctively back away from him, straight into that hole, and I think, on some level, you know that, but blame yourself for *taking* the bait." Sue suggests.

"Maybe, I mean, I did feel *stupid* reacting like that. I should have *stood* my ground and fought him, but I reacted like a *scared* kid!" Tess admits, relenting in her opposition to being 'shrunk'.

Sue scoots farther onto the bed, sitting cross-legged, and Tess does the same, facing her. "I know you have mixed feelings about facing Jason.

In one way, you dread it, and in another, part of you wants to finally best that asshole, so you can *take back* that part of your life, *right?*"

Tess sighs dramatically, "Yeah, he ramps up my anxiety something awful, but I feel like until I really beat him, as I did in the fallout shelter, only for good, he'll always be a shadow hovering over my life; like he'll always have a hold over me. As long as he's free, I feel like he'll always be just around the corner, waiting to get me despite all my abilities, and Amy's combat training!" She gives a halfhearted grin.

"But there's *more*, isn't there? Especially this time." Sue asks, sensing guilt lurking deep within Tess.

"Yeah, if I hadn't gotten spooked and fallen down that shaft, maybe he'd be in custody now; but since Marc was more concerned about me falling down the shaft, Jason got away again! And now, if he goes out and tortures other women, it's *my fault!*" Tess is breathing heavily, and tears flow down her cheeks.

"*Nonsense!* You can't control *how* you react to everything! Even if you'd stayed in the shed and hollered for Marc, he'd still have gotten away, because he'd have gotten to the tunnels well before they could have caught up. You did what you had to at the time, and from what the satellite replays show, you gave him a few good lumps as well!" She grins. "Something I don't think he expected from you."

"I did, didn't I?" She cracks a wavering smile through her tears.

"I know you can't turn off your guilt with the flip of a switch, but you need to remember something..." Sue trails off.

"What?" Tess asks.

"You've been Apara for only about a year. *Underneath* it all, your *emotions*, *personality*, and *psychology* are basically human; and honestly, it's best it stays that way. Yes, you'll change as you get used to being Apara, but at the core, you're still who you've always been, so, you react human, be it how you react to Jason, from anger, to fear, to feeling vulnerable, or triumphant. That's not going to change just because you're now an Apara *superhero!*" She grins, knowing Tess's love of Marvel movies.

"I *feel* like I should be stronger. I shouldn't let him affect me. But when it comes down to it, he can still trip me up with a glare and a lunge!" She leans back against the headboard of her bed with a thunk, feeling defeated and deflated.

"You'll have to work through those feelings, but there's something else we need to look at, your first stasis. When Sara put me into stasis during my transformation, Colin was in my mind with me, reassuring me when my heart stopped, but you had a terrifying push into stasis! One of the biggest, instinctive fears is the fear of heights, and falling. Even as babies, we instinctively move away from a perceived precipice. It's an instinctive fear. You not only fell, but you fell because of Jason, even if you didn't think of it that way consciously before now. How many times has he come after you now?" Sue inquires with a raised eyebrow.

"Let's see, copy room, parkway, fallout shelter. Oh, yeah! And then there was when I ran into him telepathically in the restaurant in town!" She lists off.

"And of course, the *brawl* led to a violent stasis-event." Sue reminds her.

"Yeah, but I knew I wouldn't *stay* dead! I told myself to relax, and everything would be fine in a few days!" She declares, rejecting any human weakness in her passing into stasis.

"*Tess*! By *human* standards, you *died* a violent and painful death! Did you *really* think you wouldn't have a psychological reaction to that?" Sue's frustration comes across in her voice and makes Tess flinch slightly.

"I just figured... well, it's like that song about getting knocked down and getting up again! If I knew I'd be alright, I would be, physically and mentally, and I could pick up where I left off, right?" Tess postures.

"You may not be a psychologist, but as Kari's said many times, you're one of the best, intuitive, people readers here! You've even caught stuff I missed! The problem is, with yourself, you've got built-in blinders! Remember how Sara told you never to lose your humanity?" Tess nods, so Sue continues. "There's a cost to keeping that core;

you react like a human, and always will in some ways; but losing your humanity would make you cold and uncaring, so you'll have to deal with your human reactions. You may have superpowers, by human standards, but you're not a comic-book *superhero!* You're a *person*, and you're going to react and have to deal with those reactions. There's nothing *shameful* about that. It's not a *weakness!* Your internal human-ity is a *strength*. But said strength comes at a cost. Understand?"

After a pause, Tess admits, "Yeah, I get it. I just feel like I should be able to..." but Sue cuts her off.

"No more *'should haves'!* You're going to react. The only thing you can do is *deal* with it! So, stop ignoring it and accept it! Dying by falling down a 200-foot-deep mine shaft is traumatic! Not re-acting, would be rejecting your core humanity. *Get it*?" Sue stares her down until Tess replies.

"Got it! But how do I keep from having more flashbacks?" She asks in frustration.

"There are techniques, and it's going to take time. You'll have fewer as time passes. You also need to deal with the symbolic part of your death." She explains.

"Sara mentioned something about that when I came out of it." She admits.

"Sara's seen a lot of Apara go through their first stasis. Even though we wake up, and go back to 'normal', it's a figurative death. Death is the *end* of your human life, even if you haven't been human for a year. More if you count the limbo time you told me about where you were more than human, but not Apara. *Yes*, you're still Tess Waterford and not officially 'dead to the world', but this is the first time you've died by human standards. Don't discount the psychological effects of this, just because you *knew*, intellectually, you'd be fine in a few days. If it were that simple, you wouldn't be having the flashbacks!" She tells her firmly.

Tess is quiet, and lost in thought. Sue gives her the room to run it all through her mind. "I *guess* you're right. I *knew*, but I guess part of me wasn't certain, and part of me still saw it as an end. Part of me was afraid I might not come out of it."

"But you did, and the next time you end up in stasis, it will be easier, psychologically. You need to take some time to deal with this, and *for God's sake*, cut out the guilt! We'll get Jason, sooner or later! *Hell*! You and Val should get together! She's having similar issues. I won't go into them, but seriously, you're both tearing yourselves up over Jason getting away. Take things *one* day at a time, and if you feel another flashback coming on, reach out to Marc telepathically; use him as an anchor to keep you in the here and now. We'll work on this more next time." Sue tells her.

"*Next* time? Does this mean I'm *officially* in therapy again?" Tess asks sarcastically.

"*Yep*! And if you *don't* behave, Sara and I will double team ya!" Sue grins at her as she watches Tess contemplate that scenario.

"Oh, *God*! *Anything* but that!" She groans.

"Keep a journal. Note what *triggers* reactions. If you know what triggers your PTSD and flashbacks, you can avoid the triggers, or at least prepare yourself, and maybe even cut off the flashbacks. There's no magic cure for this, my friend. You'll have to work through it like any person; human or Apara." She tells her.

Tess gets a pouty expression. "I think I'd rather be a comic book superhero with no weaknesses! But I get your point."

"Hey! Even Superman has his *kryptonite*! Now, get some rest. Sara's orders! If you need me, you certainly know how to reach me." She stands and extends her arms in an invitation for a hug. Tess relents, letting Sue give her a long embrace."

"Call me, *anytime*!" Sue says, and leaves the room. She goes downstairs and Marc looks concerned and impatient, while Sara has a Yoda-esque expression, as if she's watched the entire session and approved.

Sue joins them in the living room, and Sara pushes a mug of one of her homemade teas toward her. She takes a sip and sighs. "She'll have to work through this like anyone else. She's strong, which has its advantages and disadvantages. She'll get through it eventually, but sometimes, inner strength can get in the way. She feels like she needs to be invulnerable, which makes her ignore her very real vulnerabilities. Marc, keep your eyes open, watch her mood, and behavior. She may withdraw, or she may do the opposite, and start taking unusual risks to reinforce her need to feel invulnerable. We'll set up times for sessions, but a lot depends on Tess."

"Got it. And the first-time stasis issue?" He asks.

"She gets it intellectually. But don't be surprised if you see typical grieving patterns. Look up the stages of grief; understanding those will help you put her reactions into perspective, and be patient with her. I need to get back to Colin. I've been so swamped with stuff at Medical lately, I promised him a little 'us time' tonight. She nods to Marc and Sara, and vanishes.

PROGRESS

A couple of weeks pass; Tess and Sue have been working on her PTSD, and stasis issues. Tess resumes some of her usual duties. They're still short-staffed globally, and need to find more strong potentials who are suitable for joining the Apara. Tess and Kari review the status of the recent Lost Mission Potentials they've found and evaluated. There are quite a few living in the region, as Asheville is a potent, psychic hot-spot that attracts people with psychic tendencies, especially potential Apara. All potentials have it instilled in them to be drawn to such energies unconsciously; so, many centers, like Inspiration, Inc, are built on hot-spots, while others are set up in major cities. It makes it much simpler to recruit when potentials settle nearby.

"So, I heard from our office in Atlanta, and they've coordinated the ones in their area into Apara circles. They've only turned one of eight they've tracked down so far, but the other seven are all either in work or personal contact with our people down there." Kari grabs another of Marc's homemade, chocolate éclairs Tess brought with her, and takes a large bite, savoring the rich, custard filling, and the decadent, Belgian chocolate Marc insists on using.

Tess stretches in her chair and yawns. "*Sorry*, I'm wiped out today. I've been on another binge of nocturnal astral trips for some reason! I keep finding myself flying over the mountains, but I've no idea why!" She yawns, and picks up her tablet, pushing a button, and its contents transfer to the computer screen. "We currently have seven in the Asheville area queue. Unfortunately, only two of them can be brought in here on the pretense of job recruitment. We've maneuvered one woman into a job down at Li's restaurant in Arden. Three we're still observing, and then there's Callista Xenos, the jewelry artist in the

River Arts District. Niall contacted her shortly after transferring in from the UK, and they've hit it off nicely, so I'd suggest Liz get an update from him about where things stand."

"I'll tell her when we're done. You know, you can borrow one of Sara's damping generators if these astral trips are taking so much out of you." Kari suggests, licking the last of the chocolate and custard off her fingers.

"I *know*! But earlier, it felt like I was having them for a reason. Like with Annie, or when I'd home in on Jason." Tess looks like she could curl up and take a nap with her head on the desk in front of her.

"I know, but you won't be able to do much if you're so worn out. Have you at least told Marc about your latest *excursions*?" Kari raises one eyebrow and stares Tess down, knowing she tends to hide such things from Marc, so he won't worry and dote on her.

Tess rolls her eyes, then looks away, but doesn't say anything.

"I'm going to take that as a no! *Tess*! You need to let him, and us know these things! Maybe we can help you figure them out, or at least keep you from walking around like a sleepwalking zombie." Kari reaches over and puts her hand on Tess's arm sympathetically.

Tess turns around, feigning annoyance, but sighs. "I know! And you're right, but I hate feeling like I can't fight my own battles and personal demons."

Kari lets out a long sigh, purses her lips, and says, "No one thinks you're incompetent! You're handling a lot of power and abilities far better than many would, but you have to get over this need to take everything on by yourself. We're all more than willing to help you manage! Even if you don't technically need the help; we *want* to help!"

"All right! I'll tell Marc about them when I get done here! He's been in with Peder since we got here, so I don't want to interrupt them." Tess busies herself putting printouts and information for their local potentials back in their respective folders.

"Tess, is there any chance you're *subconsciously* trying to find Jason again?" Kari asks, concerned how it could affect Tess.

20

Tess gives her a disgruntled look. "Honestly, part of me hopes I never see him again! I know you all think otherwise, but part of me still feels guilty for letting him get away."

"You couldn't help it! You know he triggers your old PTSD." Kari leans back in her chair, frustrated, because they've been over this many times, and despite all her work with Sue, Tess still feels guilty they didn't catch Jason in Hot Springs.

"Kari, will that ever go away? I mean, the thought of reacting like this for decades to come makes me want to crawl under the covers and hide!" Tess sounds emotionally worn out.

"Eventually, his hold over you should weaken, and when we catch and contain him, you'll be able to forget about him!" Kari suggests.

"I'm so *tired* of him and wish I could stop thinking about him and worrying about what he'll do next!" Tess complains.

"Got it, but that being said, is there *any* chance you were homing in on him again?" Kari closes her laptop and stacks her tablet on top of it, focusing solely on Tess.

"It's possible, but in the past, I usually homed right in on him. All I'm seeing now is freaking trees and an occasional bear or deer!" Tess spews out in a huff.

"You know he's surely cloaking himself extra well since our ambush. Maybe he's shutting you out?" Kari grabs one last éclair and pushes the plate with the last one toward Tess, who chomps it down halfheartedly.

"*Maybe*, I really wouldn't know." Hints of her old self-image demons seep into her voice and demeanor like pollution in a clear, mountain stream.

"I'll tell you what..." Kari gets up, pulls out a small, journaling notebook out of a nearby closet. "Take this. Keep it with you, and write every detail you can remember from your jaunts, assuming you don't plan to ask Sara for a dampener?" Tess shakes her head. "Keep a record of anything like potential landmarks, or hints to where this place is. And for the *Benefactor's* sake! Stop tearing yourself up over his escape!"

"I'll try." Is all Tess utters in response.

"Will you *please* talk to Sue about your jaunts and your fears when you see her again? Kari's worried about Tess's mood swings, and knows how stubborn she can be.

After a minute of silently staring down at her fingernails, Tess replies, "I'm meeting with her tomorrow about the latest batch of names Jasamin sent over for evaluation. I'll *try* to remember to bring it up when we get through all this!" She taps on a thick folder of printouts that came in from Jasamin early this morning.

"Don't try, only do, as Sara is fond of quoting. And do it first, not after, or you'll end up putting it off! And please, tell Marc about your jaunts!" Kari scolds her.

"Aye, aye, Captain Kari!" Tess says with a lopsided grin. Tess glances toward the door as she hears Marc's all too familiar footsteps coming down the hall toward the lobby. "Guess that's my cue to get my shit together!" She grins halfheartedly as Marc sticks his head in to Kari's office.

"Guess I need to make a bigger batch of éclairs next time?" He chuckles. "Come on, Tess, we need to go home and make some long-distance calls!" He smirks at their euphemism for their latest exercises. He has Tess home in on people from her past and read their thoughts. He piggy-backs along her telepathic linkage and confirms her accuracy, which annoys her, even though she knows it's necessary.

Tess picks up her things, hands them to Marc, and ports out without him, but he rapidly follows her home.

THE STATUS GO

Niall knocks on Liz's door frame. "You wanted to see me?"

"Hey, Niall. Come on in." She tells him with a gentle smile. She stands and closes the door, motioning for him to sit. She pours some sweetened Sassafras tea for the two of them.

"Kari said you wanted me to stop by." Niall says.

"Yes, I need a status update on how it's going with Callie?" She takes a careful sip of her hot tea.

"Oh, *fine*! Things are progressing between us quite nicely." He grins lopsidedly.

"That sounds promising. Last time she came by here to meet you, she was in a *very* good mood." Liz hints.

"Yeah. We've reached a more *intimate* stage of our relationship." He grins subtly, thinking of Callie.

"Any idea when you'll breech the subject of what we are, and of her joining us?" Liz pours a little more tea for herself, adding a twist of lemon, and some fresh honey.

"Liz, I *really* don't want to rush her, especially considering my own history, but I'm hoping within the next month. I'm playing it by ear! It's not like she's had the subconscious preconditioning to keep her from freaking out if I show off my fangs!" He grabs a couple of homemade chocolate chip cookies Kari baked the night before.

"There's no need to get *defensive*! I'm just trying to get a feel for where everyone is these days! Oh, sorry, I forgot about your own rough start. Have you ever recovered any of the memories from your human years? I understand the rogue woman who turned you wiped out most of your memories to keep you under her control?"

He regards Liz a bit uncomfortably, nearly gagging on the tea he's drinking, mid-sip. "Unfortunately, I've never recovered more than some random images and flashbacks. Irena was quite a piece of work, and my first year as an Apara was beyond miserable. She thought eliminating my past, and any connections to friends or family from my mind would make me want to stay with her, but it didn't. I hope you can understand why it's important to me Callie *chooses* to become one of us of her own volition."

"*Yeah*, I get it, but with Jason on the loose, and likely more desperate now that he's alone, I'm not sure I can promise you that luxury. We never know when he'll go after someone, but we've currently got seven LM potentials in our area; three of which are at risk of identification by association. The two we have working in Martin's department, and then Callie, by association with you. We believe that's why he went after Val; he saw Ty with her and assumed she was a potential. I hope you're keeping a mental ear out for any signs he might be stalking you or Callie." Liz gives him a questioning look.

"Always! Irena did give me one useful gift. I'm constantly on alert." He takes a long sip of his tea, puts the mug down in front of him, and leans back in his chair.

Liz looks at him sympathetically. "Since you two have reached a more intimate stage, have you had a chance to implant the tracker Kari provided? With Jason still in the wind, I'd really hate for him to get hold of any of the potentials, least of all an LM potential!

"I'll do it tonight. We're going out for dinner in Biltmore Village, then seeing a movie. Afterward, home to either her place or mine. I'll pack the tracker in case we end up at her place tonight. She was saying something about a special dessert she has in mind tonight, but I'm not sure if she's talking about food, or *herself!*" He gives her a sly look.

"Luckily, she and the other LMs were identified after we discovered and blocked his network hack, but the sooner we can find and change the suitable ones, the better." Liz grabs one of Kari's cookies for herself.

"I know, but I want to ease her into this. She's already hesitant to think long term about any relationship, let alone committing to decades or centuries, but I'll tag her while she sleeps tonight. She should be *plenty* relaxed, so I'll only need to lightly cloud her mind." He grins. "I need to get back to my office and call her to finalize plans for tonight."

"Good luck! Make sure you have the transformation kit Sara gave you, including the Cent-opal bracelet, just in case; and don't forget to check with Tess as things look more concrete. She's gotten quite good at predicting how our new potentials will react, and what's the best way to approach telling and turning them." Liz reminds him.

"Will do!" He says, grabbing one last cookie and heading back to his office to call her.

He settles in at his desk and calls her from his cell. "Hey, Callie. Ready for tonight?" He says in a suggestive tone.

"Which part of tonight?" She asks, daydreaming, and almost dropping a newly made casting flask she plans to burn out and cast the next day.

"Well, my thought is, we go down to the restaurant in Biltmore Village, then head to the theater to see your movie at 8:30. Afterwards, maybe we can head back to town for a walk, or a drink before we..." he trails off, letting her imagination take over.

"Head somewhere more comfortable and private?" She purrs.

"My thoughts exactly! Assuming you aren't tired of me already?" He jokes, smirking to himself.

"*Nah*, I think I'll keep you around a *little* longer!" She says sarcastically. "Your car or mine?"

"I'll pick you up at five at your studio, and we'll head to dinner. Parking is always tight on Friday nights, so I'd like to get there in good time." He reminds her.

"Good thing I brought a change of clothes and some shampoo! I had two blowouts while casting today, and I'm absolutely covered with plaster dust! I'll be ready for you by five, though!" She laughs.

"Can't wait!" He replies enthusiastically. He settles in to do a little more work before taking out the tracker and transformation kit and sticking them in his jacket pocket.

GUESS WHO'S COMING
AFTER DINNER

Niall gathers up a few things, and leaves for the day. Unlike some Apara, he enjoys driving from place to place. He heads home, showers, and gets ready to pick up Callie for the evening. He arrives at Callie's studio promptly at five, and she's waiting outside. She's medium height, with very curly, black hair, and dark eyes to match. She isn't classically beautiful, but most would consider her cute. She's slender and clearly works with her hands. Short, worn away fingernails from lapidary and jewelry work. Her long fingers showing nicks and small scars from working with tools. She's wearing a flowing, mid-length dress in a sheer white fabric, with fine flower print, white, medium heels, and a hand-dyed silk scarf Niall recently bought her at the craft guild shop on the Blue Ridge Parkway.

She gets in the car and they share a brief kiss. He flips on a playlist of vintage music by Jefferson Starship, more recently known as just "Starship". He introduced her to their music, and she hasn't been able to get enough of it. They drive about ten minutes, find parking in Biltmore Village, and walk to an upscale, local restaurant. They have dinner, then share a slice of freshly made, pecan pie, and top it off with a final glass of wine.

Callie stares at him as the waiter refills his glass. "You sure you should be drinking more wine and driving?" She asks, already feeling a tad buzzed by her indulgence.

"No problem, wine doesn't really hit me until I've had *several* glasses, and I'm only having these two, but feel free to have more if you want." He says with a grin, as he takes a sip.

"Not like you have to get me *tipsy*, you know! Besides, I don't want to fall asleep mid-movie!" She jokes with a sparkle in her eyes.

"*Oh*, that reminds me! I double-checked the time, and the movie is a little later than it said yesterday. I was thinking, it's a really nice night, do you want to go walk along the river?" He asks.

"*Sure*! I could stand to walk off the calories from the pie! If you keep feeding me like this, we're gonna have to do a lot more than walk along the river to keep me slim!" She says with a suggestive grin.

"No problem!" He smirks and pays the check, then theatrically takes her hand in his, leading her out of the restaurant. They head a couple of blocks back to Biltmore Avenue, walking past some galleries. She stops in front of a gallery that specializes in jewelry, and points out a few of her pieces in the window display, before moving on down to the river, along Thompson Street. They start walking along a new green-way park along the Swannanoa River. There's been a bit of rain lately, so the water is high. They stop to feed wild geese some left-over bread from dinner, and Callie is amused by how they all race to get each piece before another one can.

Niall gets a prickling feeling in his mind and starts to look around anxiously. "We should probably head back to the car. If we cut through this parking lot, it'll be quicker." His unease grows rapidly and he feels like someone's watching them; someone *like* him.

He leans down and helps her up off a low bench and they hasten back to the car. They cross Thompson Street, passing through a parking area with closed shops. They walk toward the railroad tracks, and he increases his pace, pulling her along quickly, but without alerting her to potential danger by running. He hears a rapid heartbeat, and footsteps in the distance keeping pace with them, but can't see anyone when he looks back.

"*Hey*! *Slow* down! Keeping up in these heels is no easy task!" She rebukes.

"*Sorry*, underestimated how long we'd be out. We'll be late for the movie if we don't hurry!" He has a strong grip on her hand, mentally nudging her to speed up. Before they can get to the active heart of Biltmore village, he hears a gunshot with a silencer in the distance. Before he can react, a bullet tears through his femoral artery, and he goes down to the ground! His blood is gushing out quickly. He doesn't let go of Callie's hand, so she looks back to see why he's stopped and is dragging her down, only to see his other hand on his leg and blood everywhere. She rushes to him, bending down to help him put pressure on the wound, blood splattering all over her dress, but she ignores it.

"What the *Hell*?! What happened?!" She panics, as blood presses out from the wound through her fingers.

"*Sniper.*" He says weakly. She tries to get her phone out and call 911, but fumbles with it due to her wet, blood-soaked hands. She feels him pull her down suddenly, bend her head back, and sink something into her throat. There's momentary pain, followed by numbness, and an inability to speak or move.

The world's spinning, and her stomach turns. In her head, she hears his voice saying. *SORRY! SO SORRY! Only way to protect you!* She feels an odd sense of movement, the area around them is suddenly brighter, and she's somewhere else, pinned to the floor, his mouth still on her neck. She's unable to move, but instead of the dark, starry sky, she sees a white ceiling with dark wooden beams and elaborate molding around a hanging lamp; a ceiling she knows well, Niall's living room ceiling. The image blurs and all fades to black.

***

Several hours pass, sunlight peaks through the nearby window, causing Callie to stir. Her eyes slowly flutter open. Everything's fuzzy and her thoughts feel like they're pushing through molasses; slow and requiring major effort. She stares up at the ceiling for what seems like forever, though it's only been a minute or two, mentally tracing the patterns in the molding. Slowly, she realizes she's in Niall's living room, and a nagging feeling something's wrong starts to cut through the mental molasses. *Shot? Sniper? Bleeding? Pain? What the Hell?* is her stream of thought. She brings her hands up to rub the sand out of her eyes, and they're covered in dried blood. Her heart races, her stomach clenches with panic, but her head clears as adrenaline kicks in. She's too weak to sit up easily and wonders if the blood is her own, but she doesn't have any pain, just some minor itching on her neck. She feels what she assumes is Niall's arm laying across her leg, and attempts to roll in his direction. She rocks back and forth, eventually rolling toward him, and full panic sets in. Not only is he covered in blood, but there's a drying *pool* of blood in the carpet under his right leg that makes her heart sink.

"*Niall!*" She gasps, but it comes out nearly unrecognizable due to weakness. "*NIALL!* ARE YOU *OKAY?!*" She demands as loudly as she can, thinking, *considering all the blood, that's a dumb question!* She digs her fingers into the plush carpet fibers and, with major effort, pulls herself closer to him. With relief, she notices he's still breathing, shallowly, but breathing. She looks around for her iPhone, but when she finds it, the battery's dead, and the screen's covered in dried blood. She reaches for him clumsily, trying to rouse him. "*NIALL! Please* wake up!" She implores. He gives a quiet groan, but doesn't wake. Callie forces herself into a seated position to get a better look at his leg.

There's a visible hole in his pants leg where the bullet hit, and lots of blood soaked into the fabric, staining his skin. She carefully sticks her finger tips into the hole and rips it wider to look for the wound to determine how bad it is, but there's no visible wound, only a slightly raised, discolored welt, more like a scar. She uses the edge of a nearby coffee table to pull herself up. *I've got to find a phone and call 911!* She thinks, but as soon as she gets halfway to a standing position, dizziness hits, and blobs swim in her vision. She feels her butt hit the floor again, followed by the sensation of falling backward; a dull ache spreads across the back of her skull as everything fades to black once again.

SETTING THE STAGE

Time passes, but she's unaware of how much. She flits in and out of consciousness, unable to fully awaken. She stirs again as she feels a warm, soft, wet cloth wiping her face, arms, and hands; carefully wiping between her fingers and up the undersides of her arms. She groans.

"Don't try to move. Lie still. You're going to be fine." She hears and recognizes Niall's calm, soothing voice. First, there's a feeling of relief, and then confusion. She wonders if maybe she's been wounded too, and a vague feeling flits through her mind, something about her neck, but she can't resolve the memory. She knows she wasn't shot, but something made her incredibly weak.

"Niall...." She whispers.

"Shh, rest. You're fine, a little weak, but fine. It's nothing a little rest and time won't fix." He reassures her calmly.

Callie struggles to get the words out. "Were you shot? *Hospital*?" She asks.

"Don't worry about that now. Right now, you need to rest. I'm okay, but I need to wash your clothes. Let's get them off, clean you up, put a t-shirt on you, and get you somewhere you can rest comfortably." He reassures her. The words echo in her mind, soothing her, making her not want to question or fight anything he's doing. She's so sleepy. "That's right, sleep Callie. Everything will be fine when you wake up." He says, evenly, reassuringly, until she slips back into slumber.

When Callie wakes again, she still feels sluggish, but feels clean and comfortable, with a mattress and pillow under her. The curtains in the room are light tight so she doesn't know what time of day it is. There's a soft comforter on her, and she realizes Niall's warm hand is holding hers.

"Hey there, sleepyhead." He says, in soft-spoken tones. "How're you feeling?"

"Tired, like my brain's wrapped in cotton, but okay, I think." She still sounds very weak, but a little more coherent.

"*Good.* I'll get you some food. Don't get up without me. I'll help you to the bathroom after you eat." He leans over and kisses her on the forehead.

Callie can't even fathom getting up, and halfway dozes again, until she smells pancakes and bacon. She rouses and tries to sit up, and hears him put the plate and silverware down, feels him lift her upper body, putting extra pillows behind her back. Her vision clears as he puts a wooden tray with legs in front of her, along with the plate, silverware, and some milk on the tray.

"Hmmm, how long have I been asleep?" She picks at a pancake with a fork, but has trouble hitting her target.

"Long enough, you should be famished. Do you need help with your food?" He sits next to her on the edge of the bed.

Callie struggles to cut the pancakes, skewer the pieces with her fork, and steer it to her mouth without them falling off, and landing on the comforter or on her t-shirt. "Looks that way..." She clumsily hands him the fork.

He picks up some pancake with ease and pops it in her mouth. "Take it slowly, not sure how much your stomach's ready for." He suggests.

"Ready for?" She feels a minor wave of nausea and dizziness hit her. "What the *hell* is wrong with me? What happened? How did we get here? I don't remember."

"Eat and regain your strength. I'll fill you in on everything when you're ready for it." He hopes she doesn't push the topic any further.

"Huh?" She says, and pauses, hand on forehead, clenching her eyelids closed, trying to remember something, anything. "Something happened, but I can't remember what, only flashes." She tells him, and he shovels another helping of pancake into her mouth.

"Don't force it. The memories will come back when it's time and not before." He tells her.

"Sounds ominous." She says, craving the salty, savory taste of bacon. Her fingers feel uncoordinated and she fumbles, but eventually grasps a piece, brings it to her mouth, and slowly eases it in, savoring the flavor.

"Callie, you trust me, don't you?" He asks, putting a slight telempathic spin on the words, hoping that will reinforce said trust.

"Yeah, of course... course I do." She stammers out.

He lifts the glass of milk to her lips, and she drinks it down like she hasn't had anything to drink for a long time. "More?" She asks; the cool, wet milk soothes the dryness in her throat.

"In a minute, Callie. I need you to trust me, and let me take care of you, alright? I'll explain everything to you, but right now, you're not thinking clearly enough, and I'm afraid you may not process things too well." He hopes he's influenced her enough that she'll accept his reassurances.

She glares at him for a second, concentration and a bit of frustration in her gaze. "Okay, but *better* be soon... *ugh...* still so... tired." She yawns.

When she finishes her meal, he helps her up and takes her to the bathroom. "Think you can manage this part on your own while I go get your milk?"

"Mmm... hm, probably..." She tries to focus on his face, but her vision blurs, shifts, and has a dream-like air of non-reality.

"*Wait* here! *Don't* try to get back to bed on your own! I don't want you falling!" He insists. He leaves the bathroom and partially closes the door so she can have some privacy. Once he's out of the bedroom, he ports to the kitchen and fills another glass. He reaches out telepathically to Sara, their equivalent of a doctor. *Sara! She woke up and ate, and is taking care of nature's call. How much more should I give her? She's still rather anemic.* He paths.

Sara paths, *Give her another 5 ml of the mixture I gave you. Once she's asleep, infuse her with the trinaline in the pre-measured infuser. That should speed up her red blood cell regeneration. How's your leg?*

As good as new, thanks. And thanks for putting the memory inhibitor in the mix. I don't want her to remember until she's stronger;

this is going to be hard on her as it is. He paths, as he laces the milk with the drugs in proportions recommended by Sara.

Yes, and she'll likely experience some trauma symptoms, both from your being shot, and you biting her, once she regains awareness of the events. Tess and Sue are on call if you need them, and there's an ampoule of seda-tive if she gets completely inconsolable. Sara paths, showing him the im-age of an infuser ampoule with a green band around it.

Thanks, I'd hoped to draw this out another month before break-ing all this to her, but if Jason's got his mind set on her, this can't wait! He says, worried, as he ponders how he's going to explain everything without completely freaking her out, and her hating him for being some kind of monster.

No, but don't rush her either. Explain what happened, release her memories carefully, and give her the illusion of choice, even if there isn't much of one. Sara explains.

I know. I need to get back up to her before she gets stubborn, and tries to crawl back to bed from the bathroom! He paths, grabbing the glass of med-icated milk, and tucking the infuser ampoules and infuser in his pocket. He ports in right outside the door, walks in, and puts the milk down on the nightstand. He opens the bathroom door fully, and she's half-asleep on the toilet, leaning with her head against a wall.

"Okay, Callie, all done?" He asks, gently steadying her, keep-ing her from tipping over, and falling off the toilet.

"Yeah, waiting on you." She mumbles.

"I'm gonna help you up and to bed, or would you rather I carry you?" He asks.

"You shouldn't lift me! Might hurt your back!" She feels drunk.

"My back's fine." He slips an arm under her legs and lifts her, carrying her to the bed, and sitting her on the edge. "I brought your milk. Drink it, and then get some more sleep." He hands her the glass, making sure she has a good grip on it before letting go. He telepathically encourages her to drink it all down. He helps her into bed, under the covers, and gently strokes her cheek and forehead. "Just sleep." He tells her.

She's nearly asleep when she starts awake, blurting out, "Oh, *Shit!* What about work? Missed work!" She stammers out, trying to sit up.

He gently pushes her back down onto the mattress. "Yes, but it's okay. The doctor let the daycare know you're not well." He mentally pushes her to accept it.

She stares at him for a second, trying to unravel whatever's on the tip of her tongue. She wants to say or ask him something, but can't remember what, so she closes her eyes, and succumbs to the sedative in the milk. After she's fully settled, Niall takes out the infuser, and gives her a dose of Trinaline; the compound released when they feed which promotes healing and red blood cell regeneration in humans. He also pulls out the tracker kit and injects it near a vertebra, just in case Jason somehow finds her before Colin can turn her.

Niall checks her blood count periodically and painlessly, using a handheld scanner reminiscent of some sort of Star Trek device. He doses her again, and Sara stops by to set up an IV with a nutrient bag. "When this is empty, remove the line and heal the insertion point. The nutrient solution should last until she wakes up. It should also stop her need for another trip to the bathroom for now. Have you thought about how to break it all to her?" Sara asks, making piercing eye contact with Niall.

"I *think* so. I hope she doesn't lose it when she finds out the truth, and hate or fear me too much when she remembers what I had to do." He gently strokes Callie's arm.

"You'll have to present it to her so she'll understand; you had to either feed from her, and save her life, or go into stasis, and hand her over to a sadistic madman. Apologize for biting her, and taking as much as you did. If you weren't likely turning her shortly, we could have given her a transfusion, but incompatible blood mingling with compatible tends to make the transition much rougher than usual, as the virus consumes any non-compatible blood to help fuel the transition, rather than transforming it." She packs up her things in a leather case. "Again, Tess, Sue and I are all on call, so if you need reinforcements, *HOLLER!*" She ports away.

MEMORIES AND MAYHEM

Callie sleeps two full days after her brief awakening. When she finally opens her eyes again, Niall's asleep next to her, their foreheads touching, and his arm is loosely curled around her protectively.

"*Niall*?" She mentally notes her own voice sounds weak. She reaches over and touches his shoulder, and he starts awake.

"*Callie!* You're *awake!* How do you feel?" He tries to read her and get a hint of what's going through her mind telempathically.

"I guess I'm ok. Though I can't say I remember how I got to your place. Everything after dinner is fuzzy or missing." She searches his eyes pleadingly to fill in the blanks in her memory.

"Yeah, about that, something happened, we were both in rough shape afterwards, and the doctor was worried about how you might handle everything, so gave you a sedative that's temporarily affected your memory." He grasps her hand, folding her fingers in between his, and gripping her hand reassuringly.

"What the *hell* happened that I needed sedation? Were we in an accident or something? And if it was that serious, why are we here, and not in the hospital?" She tries to sit up, but is still unsteady, loses her balance, and nearly falls backwards off the bed. Niall's reflexes are lightning fast, and he reaches out, catching her, and pulling her back up. "Thanks!" She says, heart pounding.

"It wasn't something the hospital could help with, but we need to talk about what happened. I'm afraid this may be difficult for you to deal with, my sweet. The doctor told me to tell you what happened, and see if your memories come back." He explains calmly.

She glares at him, brows furrowed, and forehead creased with concern. "This sounds serious. *Come* on! Tell me what the *Hell* happened?" She barks out, exasperated. Her head thuds with a dull ache.

"*Okay,* but I really need you to trust me and promise to hear me out; preferably without freaking out." Once again, he uses telepathic suggestions and reassurances to calm her, and prepare her for the rough ride to come.

"*Alright*! I *promise,* now *OUT WITH IT!*" She demands impatiently.

He reaches behind and grabs a small bottle from his nightstand. "First, *drink* this. The doctor said it will help clear some of the haze, and help bring your memories back." He opens the bottle of orange juice, and hands it to her.

"Orange juice?" She looks at it, and then him, askew.

"There's a medication in it that helps flush the sedative out of your system." He pushes it into her hands. She sighs and drinks it down.

He gives it a few minutes to hit her system before recounting his tale. "Okay, do you remember taking a walk along the Swannanoa after dinner?" He asks.

"Vaguely, I remember ducks, I think? No, *geese*! You rushed us back toward the car, and then nothing! From there, it's *blank!*" She's flustered by the gaping hole in her memory.

"Yeah, well, *plenty* happened. Sometimes, I can feel when I'm being watched, and I felt it strongly, which is why I rushed us back to the car. I was afraid we were in danger. We cut through the nearby lot, but before we came out into the main shopping area, someone shot me in the leg, and I was *bleeding* out." He recounts calmly, as though describing a plot in a script, disconnected.

"*What*?! *Shot*? *Bleeding* out?" She gets flashes of him on the ground and blood everywhere, including on her hands and all over her formerly pristine dress. Her heart rate spikes as the memories spark a spurt of adrenaline into her bloodstream.

"Do you remember something?" He asks.

"*Yeah*! I think so, unless it's just a suggestion. You're right leg? About a foot below your hip?" She remembers trying to staunch the bleeding with her hands. Her voice is strained with rising anxiety.

"Yes, *exactly*. The man who shot me is someone who used to work for Inspiration Inc. but went... *freelance*. He's been targeting some of the women associated with us. The reason he shot me, was to get to you. He must have assumed you were with Inspiration Inc. because we were together." He waits anxiously for her reaction.

"I *never* saw anyone else...you said something about a sniper and then...." She lets out a loud gasp as a look of terror crosses appears in her eyes. She grasps the left side of her neck, and looks at Niall like he's a *stranger* with a knife, two of them, in fact.

"I'm guessing you remember me grabbing you and..." He swallows anxiously.

"*BITING ME! What the fuck, Niall?*" She shouts, beginning to hyperventilate.

"Callie, *remember*, I know this is hard, but I'm begging you to please hear me out, and preferably *not* freak out. I promise you, you're as safe as you can be here." He sends her calming energy.

"*Safe*? If I'm remembering *correctly*, you *bit* me, and somehow were...no...can't be...drinking my blood like some *Goddamn vampire!*" She shakes her head like she wants to make the images and sensations go away, as though she were wiping an old etch-a-sketch by shaking it.

"Callie, *please*, don't judge me before you've heard me out. I had *no* choice. It was the only way I could save you from Jason." He forces himself to speak calmly, his hand is on her knee, hoping the physical contact might help him get through to her.

She looks around the room uncertainly. "Then we were here! No, in your living room!" She demands, "How's that even possible?!"

"It almost wasn't. Jason shot me in the femoral artery because he knew I would bleed out, and *appear* to die. Then he could swoop in and grab you without any resistance from me. *Callie*, I was *bleeding out*, and close to losing consciousness. The only way I could stop that was to replace the blood, and the only source *available* was *you*. I'm *so* very *sorry*, but it was the *only* way to keep him from getting you!" He apologizes, waiting for a response; holding his breath, wondering what her reaction will be.

She pulls away, watching him closely, and is quiet for a few seconds, then asks timidly, "Niall, are you a...a...oh, *God*...a *vampire*?" She asks, knowing it sounds insane, but it's the only thing that makes *any* sense.

He hesitates as he searches for the words that will make sense without sending her into a full-blown panic attack. "In so much as I have *fangs*, need to drink *blood,* and am a lot *older* than I look, then yes; but I promise you, the rest of the mythology's bullshit! I'm *alive*, I *breathe*, my heart *beats*! I don't hurt anyone, nor do others of my kind, but *Jason* is another matter entirely. After he became one of us, he went after women and tried to change them. At first, he even killed some of them, but eventually found some he could transform. We eventually rescued them from him, but now, he wants to make you one of *his*; to *replace* the ones we rescued! I was trying to *protect* you by bringing you here, but I couldn't have done it without an infusion of blood, as mine was running out on the street. It was the only way I could keep you *out* of his hands.

Callie stares, wide-eyed, and trembling. She sits there for a couple minutes, saying nothing, trying to calm herself and regulate her breathing so she doesn't pass out. "*Explain* to me the improbable fact that two *vampires* are showing an interest in me. Surely, he could have found someone else? Why me? There must be some reason both of you chose *me* to *pick on!*" She huffs out, trying hard to stay in control of her words and emotions, but her nose is running, and tears are trickling down her cheeks. Niall's heart breaks, as her fear of him takes a leap forward, instead of diminishing.

He pulls himself together, and calmly tells her, "Yes, there *is* a reason. Only a tiny percentage of people are susceptible to the virus that transformed me, and others of my kind. The virus depends on a key genetic sequence that bonds with the virus, activating it, and bringing it out of a dormant state. If one of us feeds from a compatible human, the virus becomes keyed to the human's DNA and activates for about an hour, and if the human then ingests, or somehow gets infected through blood transfer, the virus will change the compatible person, making them one of us." He waits anxiously for her reaction.

"*So*, let me get this *straight*! He's after me because he *knows* I'm compatible? That he could *turn* me into a... oh, *God*! I can't believe I'm saying this! He could turn me into a *vampire*?" She asks, carefully, like she's trying to solve an intricate puzzle.

"*Yes*, that, and you are *female* and *attractive*. That's what matters to him." Niall explains.

She pauses, giving him a long, concerned look before speaking. "And *you*? Are you *planning* to change *me* into a vampire, too?" She asks. The pit of her stomach drops as she awaits his answer, and she holds her breath, suspecting she already knows what he's going to say.

He pauses, and then looks her in the eye, his expression softening. "If you hadn't been compatible, I'd *never* have let myself get close to you. One of the worst things for one of us is to get emotionally wrapped up in someone, only to find they can't become one of us; we'll have to watch that person grow old, or sick, and die. Even if we 'break up' before it becomes obvious I'm not aging, I'd still check in on you from time to time, and it's so *painful* to watch someone you care about age, or sicken, and eventually die when you know you'll be around long past their demise. So, most of us won't let ourselves connect, unless there's at least a *chance* the one we love might *choose* to stay with us; to become *one* of us." He explains.

"When were you planning to break this important tidbit about yourself to me? It would have been nice to know before we started *sleeping together!*" She snaps, angrily.

"*Honestly*, I planned to tell you in about another month." He pauses, holding his hand up to pause her impending outburst. "I *wanted* to wait until I felt you could accept me for what and who I am, and still feel for me as you do, or at least did. I wanted to wait until we were close enough, emotionally, that you could see beyond the mythology, and see me as a person, not a monster, or you *might* even entertain *letting* me change you." He looks her in the eye, waiting to see how she reacts.

"I'm not sure I'll ever be *ready* to make that decision." Her voice shakes thinking about it.

He nods in acknowledgment, but says, "I know this is unfathomably hard for you, but the problem is, because of Jason, you may have even less of a choice than you would have, had it only been me." He tentatively reaches out and takes her hand. She flinches but lets him hold it.

"*What* do you mean?" She asks, confused.

"Jason *won't* ask. He *won't* be gentle about it. From what we know of his patterns, he uses multiple forms of abuse and assault to break the women he transforms. He wants them obedient and subservient. The women we rescued from his clutches are dealing with major psychological trauma, and I don't want to see you, or anyone go through *that!*" Niall explains, knowing she's already been traumatized.

"And... how... would *you* do it?" She asks, her eyes tearing up again, making his heart ache. He wishes he could just reach out, and hold her, but knows it's too soon for that.

"Eventually, I'd have told you about myself, my people, and the life we can have together, then ask you to join me. I'd do my best to convince you, but in the end, if you still refuse, I'd make you forget about me and what I am and only have a short-term relationship, eventually parting ways with you. It would tear me apart to do so, but I'd do it if I must." He adds.

She pauses, and after a minute, he senses her shoulders and back relax, as she lets herself collapse back onto the bed, sinking into the luxuriously soft, down pillows, exhausted physically and emotionally. "Niall, I *do* care about you, even now, though part of me feels like my heart's *breaking!* Part of me *loves* you and wants to continue to see you, but this is some *scary shit*, especially after you *bit* me!" She sniffles and wipes her eyes with her free hand.

"I only did that because there was *no* other way! If I hadn't, I would have succumbed to my injuries and appeared to die in the street, and he'd have you now. Trust me! You don't want *that*! He doesn't care about anyone; he only cares that he can *make* them *his* and make them do as *he* wishes!" He explains.

"Now that he knows I know about him, maybe he won't try it again?" She asks, knowing her logic is beyond faulty.

He cautiously reaches over and cups her cheek with one hand, saying, "Jason's an *obsessive*. Once he sets his mind on someone, there's only two things that can make him lose interest." He waits for her to ask him the inevitable question.

"And that is?" She dreads the answer.

"Either the person dies or is turned by someone else. Until one of those happens, anytime you're where he can sense your mental signature, you risk him popping in, and grabbing you!"

"What do you mean, mental signature, and popping in?" She asks, the terms not making sense to her.

He explains, "Remember us going from the parking lot to my living room in the blink of an eye?" She nods tentatively. "That's what we call porting. It's not true teleportation, but we're able to travel nearly instantaneously anywhere in the world, and as soon as you re-emerge from such a port into your home, or on the street, or even across the world, he'll be able to sense you, follow your mind, and *grab* you." He notes her look of shock and dread at the thought of that *monster* showing up, invading her life, her home, and even her body.

"Then why hasn't he popped up here to grab me? Is he afraid of you?" She shivers. He lets go of her hand, walks around the bed, grabs a quilt, and drapes it around her shoulders. *If I can't hold her, at least she can feel some comfort.* He thinks.

"I'm sure he'd rather avoid a direct confrontation, which is why he shot me, but it's a bit more complicated than that." He tells her.

"Oh? *Explain* it to me then!" She's getting frustrated by the slow dispensation of information, and the agitation is noticeable in her tone.

"We're not where he can sense you *here*." He hopes she'll leave it at that.

"But you said he could sense me *anywhere*! My home, or across the world! Which is it?" She feels a stress headache brewing.

"Yeah, about that, we're not *technically* on *your* Earth, but in a *parallel* reality, where humans never evolved, we call it Sanctuary." He hopes she'll accept that, and not freak out even more, but those hopes are dashed quickly.

"WHAT THE *ACTUAL FUCK* DO YOU MEAN WE ARE *NOT* ON *MY* EARTH?!" She shouts.

He recoils from her empathic and vocal outburst, but tells her, "You're a sci-fi person! Think Multiverse Theory! *Parallel* to *your* Earth, are an infinite number of Earths with different histories. Some, the differences are minor, like whether or not you had coffee or tea with breakfast, and some are nearly unrecognizable; or they could be anywhere along a vast continuum between the two extremes. This one happens to be one where humans never evolved beyond basic primates, but is otherwise very similar." He explains.

"And *HOW* can I get *back* to my *own* reality? I've *had enough* of this *bullshit*!" She says, frustrated.

"I'm afraid you can't. Not if Jason's free, and has his sights on you; at least not alone." She's about to open her mouth to object again, so holds up his hand to silence her. "*Hear* me out, *please*! I'm *not* kidding! If I take you home right now, and leave you there, he can be there within *minutes*, if not *seconds*, because he'll *sense* you. He was never taught to traverse the realities, and come to Sanctuary, which is why you're safe here." He explains.

"*So*, are you telling me I can *never* go *home*?" She asks, wide-eyed.

"I can escort you there to get your things, but it would be better if you tell me what you want, and I'll go get your things, or have someone else collect them. As to *never*? We've been trying to catch him, but he can cloak; which means, he can mask his mental signature, making it hard for us to locate him, or anyone with him he may choose to mask. He could hide you from us, cloaking you, and make it *damn* near impossible to find and rescue you quickly. You *see*, my options were truly limited. I had no choice but to reveal my secret by feeding on you, so I had enough strength to transport you to safety. *Unfortunately*, I had to take more than I normally would because of my injury. That's why you've been here for several days, convalescing. Your body needed to replenish your blood levels." He explains.

Her jaw drops open, and she lets out a huff. "Ever heard of a transfusion? With *human* blood, that is!" She snaps, her arms crossed defensively in front of her chest, trying to look angry. However, part of her comprehends that he really did what was necessary to save her from a horrific nightmare, but her feeling of helplessness makes her lash out.

"Yeah, but that brings me to your other option. You're safe *here*, and welcome to stay here as long as necessary. However, there's one other way to make you safe." He pauses to see if she connects the dots.

After a pensive pause, she looks him in the eye, opens her mouth, and takes controlled, deep breaths. "You're talking about changing me, aren't you? You said he'd *stop* if I'm *changed* by someone *else*?"

"Yes, that's the *other* option, and if you choose to be turned, having non-compatible blood in your system can make the transition much more difficult. Jason only wants women he can turn, break, and mold to his needs. If I turn you, you'll never *truly* be *his*, so he'll lose interest in you." He bites his lip and waits for her reaction.

Again, there's a prolonged silence, but then she says, "So, you're saying I could go back, hide somewhere in the real world, and risk him getting me, or hide out here in some kind of indefinite, protective custody, or become one of you?" She's visibly disconcerted by her lack of options. "None of those are exactly what

I'd call *acceptable!*" She blurts out, breathing rapidly, as her anxiety rises to new heights.

"You only have two choices. Neither I, nor others of my kind, will let you take the risk of going back to your reality and becoming one of his handmaidens, or whatever you want to call them! *So*, you'll either be my human guest, *here*, until such a time as he, and anyone else he may turn, are in custody, or you'll have to become one of us." His voice grows softer toward the end, and he looks at her with genuine sympathy, telepathically pleading for her to see reason.

"I can't decide this like I'm deciding whether to have eggs or cereal for breakfast!" Her stomach rumbles with hunger at the very thought of breakfast, but nausea stops those thoughts in their tracks. "You're asking me to give up my humanity and become some kind of *blood-sucking monster?* It's *not* fair! I want my *regular* life back!" She pouts.

He slowly edges closer to her, looking her in the eye. "Sweetheart, there's no way back to your old life. Even if you stay here, as a human, you know about us now, and will always have a tie to us." He explains.

She looks up at him, confused. "But you said you can make me forget about it all if I reject your wish to change me!" She argues.

"*Unfortunately*, that's only possible if it's within a short time after you find out. If you know more than a couple of days, *max*! I can't redact that much memory without causing other issues; if I can do it at all, that is." He explains calmly, knowing all of this is overwhelming her, and difficult for her to accept.

"This really *sucks*! *Why* did you have to take me out on that date? If you hadn't, none of this would have happened! *Hell*! Why did you even come into my studio that day?" She pouts, and tears run in torrents down her cheeks.

"Most likely, he planned to go after you one way or another, and saw our date as a convenient option to, not only get you, but hurt one of us. In this case, me, who he sees as his rival or enemy. As to my coming into your studio and your life, had I not, then no one would have been there to stand in his way." He twists the truth, knowing Jason would never have realized she's compatible, had it not been for her association with him. He hopes if she thinks it would have been inevitable, maybe she'll relent and choose him.

Callie grabs her head with both hands, and closes her eyes. She feels a roll of nausea building. Sensing this, Niall hands her a basin from the nightstand. Since she hasn't eaten in a couple of days, only bile comes up. "Ugh, I hate puking!" She whines. "And my head feels like it's going to explode!" She cries harder, and curls up on the bed, sobbing frantically. Niall grabs the comforter, and lies down behind her, cautiously curling himself around her protectively, and pulls it over them both. She shifts a bit anxiously, but gives in to the much-needed comforting, and relaxes into his embrace.

"Rest. You don't have to decide now, but until you do, you'll have to stay here where you'll be safe. Sleep. I'll be here with you, and no, I won't do anything else unless you want me to." He says, as he senses her concern he might bite her again, or even change her. He hears stifled sobs, and tries to ease her pain, pushing her over into slumber.

YOU'RE NOT ALONE

A few hours pass, Callie stirs, rolls over, and is alone in bed. A robe is lying conveniently on a chair nearby. As she lies there, she hears voices in the house; one's Niall and another's female, but she can't hear what they're saying through the closed bedroom door. She cautiously stands and is more stable on her feet than she expected. She puts on the robe, ties the sash, and walks toward the door. She opens it and hears the voices more clearly, occasionally hearing her name mentioned.

She grips the handrail on the stairs and slowly descends to the living room, listening in surreptitiously on the conversation. She sees Niall, a woman with long brownish hair with a kind face, and a dark-haired woman with olive skin wearing medical scrubs, sitting around the coffee table with a few snacks on a tray. Niall notices Callie as she gets about halfway down. He ports over to her; afraid she might fall in her weakened condition.

"How are you feeling? Headache gone?" He asks and extends his hand to her.

She pauses, sighs, and takes his hand, allowing him to help her over to the others. "Mostly, as to how I am, I'm not really sure about that one." She says as they reach the bottom step, and move into the living room. "Callie, we've got a couple of visitors. This is Tess from work, and this is Vanessa Manheim. She works in our Hendersonville office."

Callie nods to both women, not sure what the situation is, or whether or not they're human. Niall guides her over to the sofa and sits with her. Turning to her, he says, "The answer to your unspoken question is yes, they're both like me."

She makes a visible gulp. "You're *both* vampires?" She asks, shocked to find out these women who she gets nothing but good vibes from are both like Colin.

"Yeah, though I guess he hasn't filled you in on everything. We call ourselves Apara, meaning 'others'." Tess gives her a genuinely, warm smile. Callie can't help but relax a bit, as Tess puts her at ease. "Callie, Vanessa, and I share something in common. We've both been on the receiving end of Jason's wrath." She says, waiting for her reaction.

Callie looks from Tess to Vanessa, then asks, "Did he change you two into vam..., *Apara*?" Callie asks.

"*No*, but we've both dealt with him. He began at Inspiration Inc. at the same time I did and was a bastard as a human too! As soon as our boss was away, he decided to be an ass, cornered me in the copy room, and made advances. He and I were both human at the time." Tess clarifies.

"Copy room? Then you haven't been like this very long?" Callie asks.

"No, not long at all. A little over a year. So, I know very much what you're going through right now. I found out about my *partner*, Marc, in a similar way as you did Colin. Not through a violent situation, but by literally stumbling upon his little secret. I needed his help, so I followed him into an alley, and caught him having a snack, if you get my drift?" She grins.

She stops to count. "So, with you three, Jason, and your partner, there are at least five Apara, in Asheville." She starts to feel very outnumbered.

"Yes, and there are others as well, but you don't have to worry about them. None of us, besides Jason, will ever hurt you, in fact, we *want* to *help* you." Tess says.

Callie asks, "How, exactly, would you help me?" She asks warily.

"I thought, perhaps, if you could talk to someone who's dealt with Jason, you'd understand this is exceedingly serious. I'm guessing, you've been teetering between whether this is real or a set up by Niall; as in, a way to convince you to let him change you?" Tess asks with a sympathetic half-smile.

Callie shrugs, then says, "The thought had crossed my mind. It kind of seems like the lesser of two evils kind of choice." She gives an apologetic glance at Niall.

"I get that, and it's true. He hopes to eventually turn you because he does care about you a lot, but Jason's nothing to *joke* about, or use as a pretend *boogie*-man! If he gets you, he'll do his best to break you psychologically before he turns you. I was lucky, he never went that far with me as I was literally turned a short time before him, but he did try to run me off the road and kill me while still human! Later, he kidnapped me to force me to 'choose him'. You see, he doesn't take rejection at all well, and I was probably the first one who'd ever rejected his advances. Luckily, I turned the tables on him and rescued myself from his clutches. Vanessa *here* wasn't so lucky, but I'll let her tell you what happened in her own words." Tess nods to Vanessa to continue.

Vanessa gives Callie a nervous smile, then tells her story. "I got off work one night at Mission Hospital; I'm a nurse. I went downtown to grab some carryout food before going home. I was exhausted, as I'd worked a double shift. I got my food, and was out the door, when I got an urge to walk a completely different direction than where my car was parked. I was kinda on some weird autopilot. Next thing I knew, the back door to a building being renovated opened, and I walked on in! I had no control whatsoever! After that, the sequence of events gets unclear, as he repeatedly fed on me, and abused me for two days. However, I stayed defiant and wouldn't break. He must have decided I was too much trouble, so brought another woman in, and they both fed on me, and then tossed me in a construction dumpster to die." She pauses, her eyes haunted by the painful memories.

"That's awful!" Callie feels sympathy welling up for the woman.

"They left me to die among old boards, concrete, and drywall scraps. Nails poked into my flesh when they threw me in. I was still vaguely aware and could hear the two of them laughing as they walked away." She trembles as she recounts her tale. "I must have blacked out, but someone must have heard me sobbing, and got me help. The ambulance took me to Mission, where they knew me well. From what I understand, the 'bite marks' referenced in the intake exam raised instant flags, and an Apara team was sent in to get me out of there. They had to do damage control, like wiping memories, and records. They took me to their medical center, but the damage was too severe. The only way they could save me was to finish what Jason intended, and turn me." She explains.

Callie reflects on her story, realizing something similar may have awaited her, had Niall not gotten her out of there in time. "That must have been traumatic. I'm sorry they couldn't fix you. Is it… what's it like? How do you feel now? Do you wish you were still human?" She asks.

"At first, I was in shock, and distraught. It's like they say about any death, real or figurative, there's a grieving process. Once I got over the shock of it, I discovered it's not a bad life! I now work at the med center in Sanctuary part-time, do some volunteer work at Pardee in Hendersonville, and I've been able to do a little healing on the sly when traditional medicine isn't quite doing the trick! I work at the Hendersonville office, as Niall said, but mostly for training purposes, learning to use these new abilities, but medicine's where my heart is." She explains, less shaky now she's gotten beyond the horror story.

"So, you're saying you're happy?" Callie asks, making certain she's reading the situation correctly.

"Yes, though I still have some flashbacks I'm dealing with, and when I heard Jason got away again, I had a week-long meltdown, and hid at the Med center in Sanctuary, where I felt safe!" Vanessa explains.

"Because he can't get to Sanctuary?" Callie asks.

"*Yes*! And I hope to *God* he never learns how to get here! However, if he comes after me again, Tess's friend Amy's teaching hand-to-hand and self-defense to some of us!" She glances at Tess.

Callie shifts a little uneasily and frowns. "Niall said he wouldn't come after me if he turns me first." She says, curious Vanessa is preparing for a possible attack.

Tess chimes in. "He likely won't; he wants to 'create' his own, but in cases like Vanessa's, we over prepare victims, so they'll feel confident they *could* beat the shit out of him, or anyone like him, if they're ever in a similar situation again. Empowerment helps a lot when PTSD is involved."

Callie lets out a 'hmmm', and turns to Tess, hesitating briefly before asking something she needs to know, but is uncertain she wants to know the answer. "And you Tess? Are you *happy*?" She suspects she already knows the answer, and realizes both women are systematically disassembling any arguments she might have against Niall turning her.

"Yes, I found a wonderful partner, and my life has purpose now, a good purpose." She tells her.

"What kind of purpose?" Callie asks.

"We try to make a difference in the world. When you become one of us, you gain certain psychic-based abilities. Some, everyone has, and some will be stronger in some than others. I'm a people reader. I help people like you and Vanessa through all of this, but I also help determine if someone will transition well." She explains.

"And me? How do you think I will transition? Assuming, I do..." She asks softly, knowing Tess's answer may be the nail in her proverbial coffin, pun intended, negating any excuses she has left.

"I think, once you get over the shock of everything that's happened, learn about us, and accept that we, and you, aren't monsters, you'll do just fine." Tess tells her reassuringly.

"I need... I need some time to process all this, so if you'll excuse me." She heads back to the steps.

"Callie, do you need me to help you up the stairs?" Niall asks.

"*No*, I can make it, and I need a little me time. Think I'll take a hot bath if that's okay?" She grabs the handrail and carefully walks up the steps.

"Go ahead, you know where the towels are; yell if you need me. I'll be up in a few." He tells her as he watches her ascend. Once she goes back in the bedroom and closes the door, he asks Tess: "*Well? Impressions?*"

"She knows what needs to happen; that even if she waits, and hides out here, being turned is inevitable. She just needs to make peace with it. It wouldn't hurt to remind her how much you care about her, and I'm *not* talking about *telling* her. You need to show her, be what she needs right now. Be there for her, but wait until she's done with her bath! Part of her knows she should stop fighting you on this, and a warm bath is always a good place to ponder things." Tess tells him as she reads Callie at a distance.

"Thanks, you two." He says aloud. Tess and Vanessa get up, Vanessa grabs a couple of snacks from the table before the two women port out.

RESIGNATION, RESILIENCE, AND REBIRTH

Niall makes some food to take up to Callie. He fixes grilled chicken and tortellini, and carries up two plates to the bedroom. He opens the door and finds Callie lying on the bed, staring at the ceiling. "Thought you might be hungry." He sits on the edge of the bed, offering her a plate of food. "How was your bath?" He tries to read her empathically, but her emotions are a turbulent jumble.

"Good. It's nice to feel clean again. My hair was all greasy and stringy." She takes the plate and picks at her food.

"Sorry to broadside you with all this Callie. I planned to ease you into it all. Believe *me*, the last thing I would ever want to do, is force this on you. You see, I went through that myself when I was transformed. In this case, the rogue was a woman named Irena. She was mad with grief and loneliness after her longtime partner was killed in an avalanche, and she chose me as her new partner. I was later told that I already had a family, and she took me away from them." He plays with his food absentmindedly as he tells his tale.

"You *don't* remember if you had a family or not?" Callie inquires.

He sighs, then explains. "Remember how I mentioned trying to wipe too much memory can have complications?" She nods. "I was inconsolable when she changed me, I couldn't go back to my family, so she tried to make me forget them. But they were such a large part of my life, I forgot everything from my human life! *Poof!* Memories gone! I was a blank slate. It worked for a while, but eventually, I had enough, and took off while she was out feeding. That's when I met Katie." He explains.

"Your sister? I guess you didn't remember her?" Callie asks, curious.

"Katie isn't my *biological* sister. She was already Apara long before I was born, but she felt my anguish from a distance, and tracked me down. When I told her what happened, she took me to the woman who took her in as a *daughter*. Not all partners are lovers, you see! Her *mother* took me in as well. Tanith is one of the oldest of our kind I ever met, on par with our doctor, Sara. She was kind, and hid me from Irena, while other Apara found Irena and dealt with her for what she had done. We don't break up families just because we want someone, or take a parent away from their children. Irena did that, and tried to take away all I was, so she wouldn't be lonely."

Callie is quiet for a minute, then says, "I'm sorry, Niall, that must have been really hard on you." She reaches out and takes his hand, initiating contact for the first time since she discovered his true nature.

He squeezes her hand, and continues. "That's why it's important to me you *choose* to be with me; why I was going to wait until you were ready to tell you what I am. I know you feel pressured, but I hope you'll still want to be with me when the dust settles."

"That makes a lot of sense, I guess; and I'm sorry for the lesser of two evils thing. I don't think you're evil. I... it's just, the thought of becoming something other than human... taking that step into the unknown, is a bit much to handle. If I'm going to become one of you, I'd rather have you do it than a sadistic bastard this Jason must be. At least with you, I think, perhaps, I could be *happy*." She says anxiously, knowing it's probably going to happen sooner or later.

"I'd like to think we could be *happy* together!" He rubs her leg gently through her robe.

"*So*, it's not *just* that I'm *compatible*? You really care about me as a person?" She holds her breath waiting for his reply.

"Yes, *very* much so!" He forces eye contact with her, and tells her, "I'm in *love* with you, Callie!"

She turns away briefly, and stuffs a larger piece of chicken in her mouth, as she realizes she's a hair's breadth from giving in.

He continues, "I need you in my life! I don't want to lose you, but I'm not the only one that needs you. My people need you as well."

She sniffles, then replies, "What do you mean, *they* need me?" She asks, putting her plate on the nightstand, and crossing her arms defensively in front of her chest.

"We've got a network of people like us around the world, and we do various things to try to help, *not* hurt humanity. Jerusalem is a prominent example. Some of us have strong, precognitive abilities, and many sensed something was imminent. We figured it out last minute, unfortunately. Nearly 5000 of us were over there, either searching for the *damn* bomb or helping with evacuations. Others were in cities around the world stopping their accomplices from completing similar devices. Originally, they were all to go off simultaneously. We were able to stop all but the one." He explains.

She lets out a loud gasp when he mentions about the world timer, and says, "*Damn!* I had no idea! They mentioned it but then just stopped talking about there being other bombs."

"*Here's* the thing, we may live indefinitely, and heal quickly and completely, but apparently, being in the wake of an exploding nuclear device is one of our *weaknesses*. We lost thousands of our people, and hundreds more were injured. Some are *still* recovering. I guess you could say we're rather *short-staffed*, and we're actively looking for new people, *good people*, to join us. They turned Jason right after Jerusalem. He wasn't supposed to be, but the people who turned him never got the message he was psychologically unstable. Since he was very intelligent and psychically gifted, they prioritized his transformation." He tells her, holding eye contact; her arms slacken as defensiveness wanes.

"But why in the world would they need me? I'm *just* an *artist*! Not like I have any skills that might someday *save* the world!" She asks, swallowing hard.

"Every single one of us can do some part in protecting this world, even you. You're intelligent, have the right psychological makeup, and are likely psychically gifted. We believe you can help us make a difference in the world, but also, you'll make a difference to *me* and *my* life. I *love* you and want to spend as long as I can with you. I know you have the same feelings for me." He leans in, puts his hands up to her face, and gently holds her gaze. When she says nothing and her heart rate rises, he leans in and gives her a gentle kiss. At first, she just lets it happen, but soon, she returns the kisses with fervor. She realizes she can literally feel his love for her washing over her mind in waves of empathy.

She pulls away briefly, taking a gasp of air, and juggling the on-slaught of emotions, she says, "Niall, *wait*, I'm not sure we should...."

"*Callie*, I'm the *same* person I've been this whole time. My *feelings are genuine*, as are *yours*. Let me *prove* that to you! I know part of you is afraid of me, and I get that. I'm so sorry I had to feed from you the way I did; the last thing I ever wanted to do is hurt or frighten you. Please, let me earn back your trust." He continues sending her waves of emotions.

"No biting, *okay?*" She relaxes a touch and lets the distance between them dwindle.

"I promise, but maybe someday you'll let me show you how it feels under the right circumstances?" He grins with a hint of fang. Instead of a feeling of dread or fear, it sends shivers of excitement and anticipation she does her best to ignore. She leans in and joins him in a passionate kiss, bringing back memories of other nights spent together. She gets wrapped up in the waves of love and desire as they make love. He keeps his promise not to bite, though he does occasionally tease up the excitement by dragging his fangs lightly across her skin. He opens his mind and emotions to her, pulling her in so they almost think and feel as one.

Afterward, she lies with her head on his chest, listening to his heart thumping away, nearly in time with her own. He dozes off to sleep before she does, and she's left to contemplate her imminent future.

She thinks, *I guess I know where this is going. I can't risk that asshole getting me, and sooner or later, even if I choose 'protective custody', my resolve will wane and I'll let him turn me. At least if I'm like him, I'm safe, and maybe I can make something of my life, make a real difference. The question is, do I wake him and get it over with, or wait until morning and risk chickening out?* She tries to work up her courage to take that leap sooner rather than later, but her nerves make her stomach knot, and she trembles, not with fear, but with the momentous decision she must make and a bit of anticipation. She realizes it's a kind of death and rebirth; uncertainty can be both terrifying and exciting. She quietly gets up, careful not to wake him, goes into the bathroom, and looks at herself in the mirror

Slowly and methodically, she brushes out her hair, washes her face, and takes care of nature's call. Realizing this is likely the last time she'll see herself as a human, she memorizes all the little details, including some early creases around her eyes and a few early gray hairs. She notes some scars and wonders if they'll remain or fade away. Callie gathers her courage and goes back to the bedroom where Niall's sitting up, his light on, watching her return to bed.

"Are you *okay*?" He senses her tumultuous mood.

"Yeah, I think I *am*." She leans down as she reaches the bed and kisses him before crawling in.

"Has something changed? Something feels different with your emotions, your energy...." He hopes what he senses isn't just a projection of his own desires.

She settles on the bed, making herself comfortable, and pulls her hair back behind her so her neck is exposed. "I guess it's time." She stares him in the eye.

"*Time*?" He hopes but wants to be absolutely certain he's interpreting her intentions correctly.

"We *belong* together. I think I've *known* that since before things got intimate. It's like we were part of the same *stuff*; two parts of a whole, and even when you bit me, part of me registered what you were and still knew we belonged together, and what that might mean. Part of me even longed for it, like it's something I'm supposed to do or become, but it scared me *shitless* when I started really thinking about it."

He listens intently, waiting for her to gather her words, and say the ones he's been waiting to hear.

"*Even* if you guys were to catch that asshole tomorrow, and I'd be free to go home or wherever, I don't think I could leave you. Tonight, it was like we were almost one person for a while, it was so *right*. So, go ahead, turn me. I *won't* fight you on this." She tips her head back for him to get better access.

He takes her chin and tips her head to meet his eyes. "You know this can never be undone, right? Once you're like me, there's no cure."

"I know, but I think there's been no turning back for a while now, but between the shock and fear of the change it will mean, and feeling like I had no real choice, I *balked*. You *know* me! Tell me I can't do something or that I must, and part of me gets *pigheaded*!" She gives him a nervous grin. "I just have one question before we do this."

He looks at her, amazed at her turn around, and the way she's facing it all. "I'd say *shoot*, but that's probably not a good expression under the circumstances!" He grins.

"Can I *keep* my studio and continue making jewelry?" Her eyes plead with him.

"*Of course*! We'll set one up here. Tell me what you need and I'll make it happen!" He says and stands. "You know, your stubborn streak will see you through this! I need to run downstairs for a minute. Get comfortable and relax." He vanishes from the bed beside her, startling her.

She tries to get comfortable, not sure if she should get dressed, or stay naked. She makes one more nervous run to the bathroom, comes back, and lies on her side, with her head propped up on one arm as he re-materializes with a shot glass with a blue, swirly liquid, and some kind of cylindrical device. "What's that? Are we drinking a toast to me losing my humanity?" She asks.

He chuckles, "Not exactly. *You*, my dear, are *very* special. It's a long story, but your genetic makeup is unique, and may produce some powerful variations on our normal gifts." He says.

"What makes *me* so special?" She asks.

"You were born during a period when some unusually strong, cosmic radiation bombarded the earth. Children, especially girls conceived and carried in that period have some unique mutations. While they don't seem to manifest much while human, they've produced some unexpected skills in others we've turned from your 'generation'. This medication will help those abilities come forth with ease. And this..." holds up the device "will dampen your body's immune response, hopefully giving you an easier transformation with fewer viral symptoms." He explains.

"How long will the transformation take?" She asks.

"Normally, most people make the transformation anywhere from a few hours to a day; occasionally, it may last up to two days. With others like you, it's still too early to know. A couple of people have taken as long as 3-5 days, which is why I'm giving you the immunosuppressant. It should prevent your body from fighting and let the virus work." He hands her the glass.

"Out of curiosity, what happens if I drink this and then change my mind?" She swirls it around in the glass, watching the slightly pearlescent swirls in it shift as she does.

"That's not going to happen. If you drink it, abilities will surface you'll be unable to handle as a human, it would likely drive you *mad*! Call this the point of no return!" He emphasizes.

She takes a deep breath, and slowly brings it up to her lips, sniffing it. There's an odd, almost mesmerizing odor to it, and after a few seconds, she opens her mouth, and tosses it down. Niall's practically holding his breath waiting for her to drink it down, and breathes an audible sigh of relief when she knocks it back like a shot.

"Had ya *worried* for a sec, didn't I?!" She looks at him with that old twinkle in her eye he hadn't seen since this began.

"That, you *did*! Now, lie down. I'm going to take even more than I did in the parking lot. You may feel like you're dying, but you won't." He pushes her hair out of the way, and puts his arm behind her neck to support her head as he tips it back. He starts to bend down and kisses her. "Thank you." He grins, showing his fangs.

Callie braces herself for the sudden burst of pain she felt when he bit her before, but when he sinks his fangs into her pulsing artery, it's painless. She loses all of her earlier fear, only feeling this is meant to be, and lets it happen, not that she could fight now, even if she wanted to. Niall senses her psychological surrender and savors the warm liquid more than he has any other time he's fed. This time, there's true meaning, not just feeding, but a bonding.

Callie feels her awareness wax and wane as she loses more blood. She's barely aware when he slides his fangs from her neck and kisses the wounds. He pulls his arm out from behind her. "Still with me?" He caresses one cooling cheek with his hand.

"Mmm… hm…" She murmurs, her eyes flutter open with effort to look at him.

"Your *turn*. Open your mouth." He whispers.

She opens it and feels something warm, salty, sweet, and metallic drip onto her tongue. After a minute, she becomes more coherent, and instinctively grabs his bleeding wrist, pulling it to her mouth and suckling like a hungry baby at a breast. A few minutes pass and so does her urgency. She lets his wrist go, going limp, but not slipping into unconsciousness yet. She feels pressure on her arm as he infuses the immunosuppressant. "There's also a sedative in this, so you should sleep through much of this. It'll be easier on you." He tells her.

All she can say is: "O…Okay…night" and she loses consciousness.

DESPERATION

Jason watches Niall fall from his precise shot and feels triumph rise, knowing, with him out of the way, he can port in, drag the desperate young Callie from his side, and port out with her to the hunting cabin, where he can break her spirit, and bind her to him. His smile broadens into a wicked grin as he watches and gloats.

He gloats just a little too long, and his grin drains away as he sees Niall reach up, drag Callie down, and sink his fangs into her throat. Jason rushes to port to them before Niall can regain his strength and port them to safety, but he takes a little too long to react. When he ports across the parking lot, he's standing in a pool of Niall's blood, but both Niall and Callie are long gone.

"*Fucking Hell!*" He curses under his breath, not wanting to draw attention to himself. He looks down and there's a small pouch lying in the blood. He picks it up. There are infusers like he'd seen while in Apara custody, and a velvet bag with a lockable opal bracelet. He looks in the pouch and finds written instructions. The pouch gets stuffed into an ammo pocket in his jacket to examine later. Jason paces back and forth across the pool of blood, trying to sense them, thinking *he couldn't have gotten very far! Not as weak as he was! Why the fuck can't I sense them?* His internal tirade is interrupted when he senses others are about to port in.

He ports back to where his rifle lies, cloaking himself as well as possible, and watches. *That's that bitch, Liz!* He thinks, and watches as several other Apara port in, including Amy, and several large, male Apara who move like they've had military training. *Shit!* He thinks, tempted to load his rifle with one of the high-capacity magazines he has in his bag, and take out Liz, Amy, and the men out of frustration, but knows he'll have to be quick and accurate or they'll be on him immediately. Instead, he quietly gathers up his rifle and ammo bag, and discretely walks away like a human would until he's half a mile up the river, at which point, he ports back to the cabin, bouncing to three other cities on the way in case they try to track his port.

Once there, he lets out a roar of frustration. "There *has* to be an easier way!" He shouts and kicks a wastebasket in anger, projecting it across the main room of the cabin and into a freestanding closet where he keeps some of his personal items. One of the doors creaks open, and he stomps over to close it again, not being particularly proficient in telekinesis.

When the door is halfway shut, he grabs it again and opens it slowly. A box with various DVDs, computer cables, flash drives, and some printouts from earlier searches for compatible women catches his attention. He grabs it, drags it out, and kicks the door closed again. He dumps it out on a rustic coffee table and digs through the pile. He spots what he's looking for, a purple flash drive with some scorching and a partially melted casing. He grabs it and his laptop. The flash drive is a backup of some of Kari's precious database.

When Tess knocked Jason across the fallout shelter, and into his computer table, destroying most of the equipment in the process, the flash drive was hit with a power surge before skittering across the room, and into a crevice between two old cinder blocks in the wall where the mortar between them had crumbled years earlier. Liz's clean-up team had missed the flash drive when they cleared out the fallout shelter. When Alice Thompson and Philipa Ball, the two women he'd turned and bound to him returned to the shelter to report on some of the women he'd been considering turning, they found the shelter empty, but Alice, whose skills are generally mediocre, is gifted at finding things. She found the flash drive and took it with them. This drive contains individual profiles of people who could be useful for various reasons, even if he doesn't turn them. He puts it in his USB port, and it blinks a couple of times and goes out. "*Fuck*! It's fried! He makes note of the model of the flash drive and ports out to a Walmart in Waynesville, west of Asheville, and finds an identical drive. Knowing Walmart has too many cameras to port out from the store floor, he pays for it and some other supplies with cash, leaves the center, and ports back to the cabin in the mountains.

He carefully pries the old drive open, pulls out his micro-soldering iron, and delicately removes the flash memory chip. Then he opens the new one and replaces the chip in the new one with the one from the damaged drive, holding his breath while soldering it in place. He reassembles it and puts duct tape around it to keep it from falling apart. He practically holds his breath as he slides the *Frankensteined* drive into his USB port. After a few seconds, the drive mounts on his desktop, and Jason breathes a sigh of relief. *Fantastic! Now, to salvage the files before it can crash again!* He thinks and drags all the files over to his hard drive. It gives him an error saying certain files are damaged and cannot be read. He stops himself from ripping it out and throwing it into the burning fire in the fireplace. He uses a rescue utility to rescue what he can, and salvages about 70% of the individual database files he'd saved as pdfs.

Okay, now to see if her file is among that 70%! He thinks. There were 517 of them, but all the original file names were lost as the utility rebuilt the salvaged files and named them with sequential numeric identifiers, so he must open each file to check it. After about three hours, he finds the file he's looking for.

The file is for a 48-year-old woman, Thaddea Price. He skims her file, noting she has two children, but is divorced. *Hmm, two daughters, 20 and 22...Not compatible themselves, unfortunately, but could be used for leverage!* He thinks. He skims a bio for her he'd found online and saved, and finds the information he remembered. He sinks down in his chair with a pensive look and a lopsided grin. He says aloud, as though he were talking to the woman, "Well, well! Ms. Thaddea Price! Hm, *Dr Price, PhD* in genetics! Specializing in genetic engineering and gene therapy! I'll just bet you know a thing or two about engineering viruses!" He makes plans, scribbling notes in a notebook he grabbed when he bought the new flash drive.

THADDEA

Dr Thaddea Price, a geneticist, lives in Frederick, Maryland, and works at a research facility at Fort Detrick, on a joint project for the U.S. Army Medical Research Institute of Infectious Diseases (USAMRIID) and the National Cancer Institute (NCI). Fort Detrick was a center for controversial bio-warfare in the 1970s, but now focuses on medical research, including cancer studies. She is currently running a study attempting to use genetically manipulated viruses to attack and destroy tumor cells without chemotherapy or radiation. She moved to Frederick when her daughters Lynda and Celia both graduated high school. They currently live in California, officially with their father, a UCLA professor. He pulled some strings to get their daughters discounted, in-state tuition at UCLA with a waiver on the one-year residency requirement, if they live with him once they enrolled.

Thaddea, who goes by Dee to her friends, wrote a research proposal and was one of five who was chosen by the CDC to receive a grant to do their research at USAMRIID and NCI. She lives in a town home in downtown Frederick.

She usually takes the bus to Fort Detrick every day, but has had an odd feeling recently while riding the bus. She gets an odd tingling on her scalp, and the distinct feeling she's being observed. This has been going on for about a week. She's also had the feeling like someone's in the house with her, even though her doors and windows are all locked, and she never finds any sign anyone has been inside her home. One night, she gets a call from a Fort Detrick number about 11 pm.

"Hello?" She answers groggily, having gone to bed early after a very busy week at work.

"Hello? Dr. Price? This is security over at Detrick. An alarm went off in your lab about 20 minutes ago, and when we went to investigate, your lab rats were loose and it looks like some of your equipment's missing. Can you come in and see if you can determine what may be missing?"

"Oh, *God*! Yes! I'll be over as soon as I can. I was sleeping, but should be over there in about fifteen minutes!" She grabs her clothes from earlier that day, throws them on, makes sure her base ID is on her, grabs her bag, and heads out the door.

She gets in her car and drives but swears she sees movement in the seat behind her in the rear-view mirror. She slams on the brakes before she gets ten feet from her front door, grabs a small bottle of pepper spray she keeps handy, and turns around to spray anyone back there, but the back seat is empty. *Oh Hell!* She thinks. *I'm getting paranoid!* She puts her pepper spray in the cup holder on the dash for quick access, and drives on, turning left onto Chapel Alley, and then again onto 4th Street, which becomes Rosemont Avenue. She passes Hood College on her right, continues down past the exit for Route 15, pulls into the front gate of Fort Detrick, shows her ID, and drives to her lab. She parks and sees a light on in her lab. She assumes it's because security was inside, and probably are waiting for her.

Dee walks rapidly down a hallway and enters an already unlocked lab. A red-headed guard she's never seen before is sitting there waiting for her, and several pieces of equipment appear to be missing.

"Dr Price?" He stands and approaches her, and something makes her intuitively step backwards.

She feels uneasy about being alone with this man. "Yes, that's me! What the hell happened?" She steps back as a couple of rats skitter past her on the floor. She grabs a wastebasket and promptly puts it over one of them, trapping it, while the other runs under a cabinet. She thinks, *I really didn't need this shit this week!*

The man in the guard's uniform continues. "Dr Price, we got an alarm at our post and came to investigate. Seeing as how the rats are free, we believe it may be some sort of animal rights stunt; however, some equipment appears to be missing, so you need to tell us what's missing and if any of your equipment can be used to make weaponized bio-materials."

She looks at him, shocked, and wonders if he's accusing her of doing something wrong. "We do *cancer* research here! Genetic manipulation to find alternative treatments to chemo and radiation! We *don't* do bio-weapon research!" She says, aghast at the thought she might be suspected of doing that kind of research on the side.

"Yes ma'am! I realize that, but we've had reports of chatter suggesting a potential terrorist cell may exist across the Potomac River in Virginia which may be seeking to weaponize bacteria and viruses for a possible terrorist attack on the D.C. Metro area. Your lab doesn't have very high security since you're doing medical research, and since some equipment is missing, I was told to ask you what, if anything, can be used to genetically engineer viruses, and if any of *that* is missing?"

Dee sits in an swivel chair and puts her hands up to her face in frustration. "Well, if you look at it *that* way, yes, several pieces of equipment could be used for illicit purposes. Let me think!" She concentrates, and then starts at one end of the room, going over each piece of equipment, present and missing, telling him if it can be used in creating a potential bio-hazard.

The guard takes detailed notes and appears to call it in to base on his cell phone. When he hangs up, he tells her. "Dr Price, my supervisor says one of the other guards found several pieces of lab equipment in a dumpster nearby. We think maybe they panicked, tossed the equipment, and got out through a hole in the fence. They'll recover the equipment and put it in here for your inspection first thing in the morning. I'm sure if anything is damaged beyond repair you can file an insurance claim through the CDC."

He tries to bluff his way through and walks out of the building, holding his cell phone as if he's still talking to headquarters.

Dee looks around at the mess in her lab and wants to cry. She manages to catch the escaped rats and matches their tags to their cages. She notices something odd, the small locks on each cage are all warped, as if someone twisted them to rip them loose. "That's odd, those are solid locks! I would have expected them to use bolt cutters." She comments aloud. She creates makeshift locks out of paper clips until she can get new locks during the day.

She picks up her phone and calls her supervisor to report the break-in, explaining the equipment may have been found and she'll come in the next day to check over whatever security might leave for her. After cleaning up broken glass and scattered rat food, she checks all the cages one last time and heads out, noting there is no damage to the main door or locks. *I know I locked the doors myself! Either I'm going crazy, or whoever broke in, must have had a key or some way of breaking in without breaking the locks!* She thinks. By the time she leaves her lab, it's 3:25 am, and she's wiped out.

NIGHTMARE

Dee is so tired she goes home to get a few hours of sleep before coming in on her day off to inventory recovered equipment. She drives home, parks out front, and sits there for a minute, exhausted to the core. She feels a creeping feeling of being watched again, so grabs her pepper spray and keys, and heads for her front door, warily looking around for any threats. She gets inside and locks the door. It's light inside, as she'd left the lights on when she left in haste. Once inside, she lets her guard down, puts her jacket, pepper spray, and keys down on a table in her living room. She stretches and yawns.

The room goes black and she feels someone grab her from behind, pull her head back and to one side using her hair to get a painful grip. A sudden, sharp pain burns through her neck as she feels herself being pulled against someone. She lets out a brief whimper, then can no longer speak or move. After a couple minutes, she feels lightheaded, and then the world around her spins and sways in the dark. Her foe releases her and she falls, pain radiating from the back of her skull as she hits the floor.

There's a faint, dull red glow in the room. She looks up and sees a nightmare bathed in red from the dying embers in a nearby fireplace; she feels faint heat radiating from it and hear the crackling of the wood. The nightmare has a face she's seen before; it's the guard she met in her lab. He stares down at her malevolently, mouth open, unusually long canine teeth extending down from his upper teeth, and she sees something around his mouth.

She focuses but is not certain of what she's seeing as everything's bathed by the faint red glow from the fireplace, but she

71

could swear it was blood and she has the sinking feeling it's hers. Darkness clouds her vision as unconsciousness overtakes her.

When Dee comes to, it's daylight out. She's disoriented but can tell it's light out, and she's lying on a cold, wooden floor. She cautiously looks around the room without moving or making any noise, but can't see any sign of her captor.

She attempts to sit up, but when she tries to move her feet in front of her, one is chained to a support pillar nearby. She tugs at the chain, but it's heavy and tightly secured to her ankle. *What the hell happened? How did I get wherever here is?* She thinks. She looks at the windows, but they're crusted with dirt and dust as if they hadn't been cleaned in years. She notices shadows of trees swaying in the wind outside, but can't tell where she is, or what the landscape might be like outside.

She looks around the room. The fire's out now, but she hears a space heater nearby. She looks at the walls and sees a mounted deer's head with huge antlers, as well as old, dust-covered rifles hanging on the walls, and cobwebs everywhere. She sees a tanned deerskin thrown over the back of a ratty, old sofa and goes with her supposition she must be in some old hunting cabin. Hmm, *this doesn't look good! I'm guessing this is a hunting cabin, which means I'm probably somewhere isolated in the woods.*

She's distracted by the wind rattling the rustic, old windows in their frames. She feels hints of ice-cold wind leaking through them, and from under the door across the room. She's dizzy from sitting up too long, and lies down again, flashing back on the night before. Images and sensations bombard her almost too rapidly to process.

She reaches up with one hand to feel her throat where she remembers the pain. Her fingertips slide over the two welts on the left side of her neck. She looks at her hand; glittery flakes of dried blood litter her fingertips, and she gasps, as the memory of the long, sharp *fangs* in the supposed security guard's face flashes through her mind. *That's not possible! Vampires are a scientific impossibility!* She thinks, and closes her eyes again, trying to run through the details of her memory. No matter how hard she tries though, she can only interpret what she saw as some sort of fangs; though her leading hypothesis is he must be a mentally ill man with delusions of being a vampire, or possibly one with a vampire fetish. *There's no such thing as the undead! There must be a logical explanation! Unfortunately, no matter what he is, I'm in trouble!* She thinks.

She takes a deep breath, opens her eyes again, sees tennis shoe-clad feet and jeans in front of her, and starts with panic as she looks up from the feet and focuses on the face of her attacker from the night before, staring and sneering down at her. She instinctively pulls away from him, but he grabs her by her shoulder-length, black and silver hair, pulls her into a sitting position, and crouches down before her, looking her in the eye.

"So, Ms. Price, you don't *believe* what you see? You think you can explain it all away through science?" He laughs. "I'm going to make it quite clear to you what I am." He opens his mouth and drops down his fangs so she sees them clearly in the daylight-flooded room. "I'm very much what I appear to be, Ms. Price, and *yes*, you *are* in trouble!" He sneers, yanks her forward by her hair, and bites her neck again.

Not only does he not numb the pain, but he's figured out how to amplify it several-fold in the minds of his victims. He finds the epinephrine surge in their blood and the energy from their fear intoxicating. After a minute, he releases her, throws her down on the floor, and kicks her in the stomach. She lies there, stunned, and in pain, her mind reeling with the scientific impossibility of what she's experiencing; though science would tell her real-life observations and logic would suggest her original hypothesis was somehow, unimaginably flawed.

Jason walks away from her to the table with his computer on it. He picks up several pages from his color printer and walks back over to Dee. He throws them down in front of her, laughs wickedly, walks of, and settles in front of his computer. When Dee's mind stops spinning long enough to look at the papers scattered in front of her, her heart clenches, and her stomach turns queasy. The printouts are photographs of her daughters at UCLA: walking to class, hanging out with friends, sitting in the library, and eating lunch. These are the kind of pictures a stalker might take from a distance, with a zoom lens.

He couldn't have taken these pictures himself! Not when they're out in California! He must have a partner or something! What the hell is he? She thinks as she shivers from a combination of cold air, fear, pain, and blood loss. She fears for her daughters and sobs quietly, curling up into the fetal position, worrying about what this man has planned for her. Emotionally exhausted, she drifts off into a light, numb sleep.

She's awakened sometime later when he grabs her hair again, twists it in his hand, and pulls her into a seated position. She gasps in pain and lets out a scream of anguish.

"Scream all you like, Ms. Price! No one's going to hear you here." He narrows his eyes and gives her a lopsided smirk. She sees the tip of one fang, real or not, and shudders.

She pulls herself together enough to stammer out. "Wh... who are you? What...what do you want with me?" She holds her chin down defensively but stares him in the eye as if he were some wild animal she must glare into submission.

He laughs. "That will become clear to you soon enough! Let's just say I need your expertise for a project."

She glances down at her shirt and sees drops of dried blood. Her scientific mind kicks in and she thinks, *If he'd actually pierced my carotid, as it felt like, then I should be dead! There should be a lot more than a few drops of dried blood! It should have spurted out everywhere! While it felt like he actually...oh, God! Drank my blood, it must have been a shallow wound from his prosthetics.* She watches as his expression changes to one of amusement.

"Still don't *believe*? You *will* when you're *just... like... me!*" He sneers at her a couple of seconds, allowing understanding to sink in, and then lunges for her, pinning her down, sinking his fangs in painfully, and drinking her blood until she knows it's real because she feels like she's dying.

Tears cascade down her cheeks and onto the wooden floor. He bites into his own wrist while forcing her mouth open painfully with his other hand. She fights to keep it shut, trying to turn away, but he's too strong. Dee feels and tastes the first drops of his blood on her tongue, and promptly spits it out, hitting him in the face with blood splatter, but more fall from his wrist. Faster than she can react, he reaches down and breaks her wrist for spitting in his face. She lets out a muffled scream as the pain cuts through her body and mind like a knife, shaking her resolve to fight. Suddenly, she has an undeniable urge to drink his blood, and her mind spins and gives up as she sucks at his wrist on autopilot until she loses consciousness from pain and blood loss.

Dee's transformation is rough. It takes nearly thirty-two hours. She runs a high fever and hallucinates terrifying visions of him attacking her daughters. Her body is wracked with pain as internal signs of aging regress. External de-aging takes longer; usually, a month or two for every five years one regresses.

She suffers several rounds of seizures as her psychic abilities activate. The neurons in her brain take time to regress age wise, and the increased energy levels rip through her aging neurons like a 220-volt charge through 110-volt wires. When she finally comes to, the rancid smell of vomit rips through her nostrils. She opens her eyes, looks down at herself, and at the surrounding floor. There's blood and vomit all over her shirt and more vomit on the floor. The room is dark, but she can still see every detail. She's weak, and something inside her feels like anxiety, desperation, and a need welling up and gaining strength. She's alone in the cabin, her new hunger grows, and her body shakes.

THREAT AND COMPLIANCE

Jason's hunting in Atlanta, a city he's familiar with from earlier in life. Even from a distance, Jason senses his new protégé has awoken, but intentionally draws out his return to her. He takes his time finding someone to terrorize and feed from, then wipes their mind, sending them on their way, weak, and confused. He senses Dee's hunger grow and become desperation. He wanders the streets of downtown Atlanta, looking for just the right person for Dee's first feed.

After a couple of hours, he spots a young woman who bears a striking resemblance to her youngest daughter, Lynda. He commandeers her mind at a distance, forcing her to come to him in the shadows of an alley. When she enters the alley, he lets the control drop just enough she realizes she's in peril, and her adrenaline level and heart rate skyrocket. He grabs her from behind with a headlock as she turns to run out of the alley and ports back to the cabin with the terrified and fully conscious young woman.

He maintains his hold on her neck until he's sure Dee notices the young woman, whose long, curly black hair hangs over her face, so Dee sees the resemblance to her daughter, but can't tell if it's her. Jason bites the young woman's ear with a fang, causing a trail of blood to run down her neck, sending Dee into a desperate state. Dee's still tethered to the support post by the chain. She lunges toward the potential food source in desperation, shaking the dust from the rafters as her increased strength rattles the support and the beams above it. She falls forward, landing a few feet from the terrified woman. Dee's intellect, emotions, and hunger war within her. She's terrified the woman may somehow *be* her daughter, but is desperate for her first feed as Jason nearly drained her dry in the process of turning her. He'd also fed from her as she was turning, so she would be starving when she awoke.

Dee lies there, sobbing, her new fangs cutting into her lower lip as she fights her instincts. She doesn't want to hurt anyone, and the mere thought he might have Lynda in his arms is pure torture.

Jason laughs at her inner struggle, holding the woman until he notices Dee gaining a modicum of control over her hunger. He throws the young woman down on the floor with Dee. Before she can stop herself, she's at the woman's throat, feeding. Still afraid she may be Lynda; she finds the will to stop before it's too late. She lifts her head, brushes the black curls out of the young woman's face, inhales, and shudders with relief.

Not only is the woman still alive, but she's *not* her daughter! She flings herself away, and back into the fetal position, still trembling from the experience, and nauseated by what she was forced to do.

Jason grabs the young woman and ports out with her. He slowly and erotically licks her wounds, closing them while she shivers in terror. "Don't worry, you'll live this time! I don't need anyone looking into an unexplained death by draining."

He runs his fingers down her neck, inside her jacket, and shirt, tempted to do more than fondle her, but he wipes her mind, puts a mental order in her mind to dispose of her bloody clothes in a dumpster when she gets home, and forget everything that's happened. He reaches into her mind and finds out where 'home' is, porting her there, and watches her follow through with his instructions. He returns to Dee.

"Do you believe, now?" He gloats over the woman lying in shambles on the floor, covered in blood and vomit.

Dee rolls over, a bit stronger after feeding, and stares at him. "How is ...this...*possible*?" She stammers out, breathless. When she realizes the woman's gone, she looks around, worried. "*Where* is she? Is she *alive*? Did I *kill* her?" She blurts out desperately.

He stands over her, then crouches down, and grabs her by the jaw, forcing her to look at him. "She's alive, but if you ever give me trouble, I might just use the real thing rather than a stand-in! *Understand*?"

Tears cascade down her cheeks, making pink lines in the blood smeared there from her first feed. She looks up at him, swallows, and gives a curt nod.

Jason reaches his limit of the stench of vomit on Dee. He associates that smell with his abusive, alcoholic mother, and has very little tolerance for it. He leans over, unlocks the chain around her ankle, and drags her up into a standing position. He looks her up and down, reaches over, and rips off her clothes rapidly, leaving her feeling shock, humiliation, and dread he might take things even further. She covers her breasts with her arms out of embarrassment. Jason throws her soiled and ruined clothes into the fireplace, lights a match, and tosses it in.

Jason looks at her, disgusted. *Stupid bitch! Why would I want to do anything with someone as old as her?* He thinks. His intent, in her case, is humiliation and the use of her daughters' safety as leverage. Otherwise, her age reminds him too much of his mother. "The shower's through that door! Clean yourself up! You *reek*!" He points to a closed door, on the wall, opposite the fireplace. "When you're done, clean up this mess!" He looks down at the vomit and blood on the floor, turns, and walks out the door to get some fresh air.

Dee waits until he's out of the cabin, goes into the rustic bathroom, turns on the water in the shower, and is relieved to find warm water. There's shampoo, soap, and a washcloth on the counter, and a towel hanging on a hook near a small window, high up on the wall. She gets in, and lets the hot water wash over her, wishing it would take this nightmare with it! She thinks of her daughters and wishes she could warn her ex-husband to get them into hiding. She realizes she may never see them again, and she probably shouldn't, as she may lose control, and hurt them.

Tears stream down her cheeks, but blend with the water from the shower, and wash away. *What have I become?* She thinks, and feels her teeth with her fingers, but her fangs have retracted. She forces them down, and she examines them cautiously. *Oh God! They're real! It's all real!* She realizes, as she looks down and sees the last traces of pink from the blood on her washing down the drain. She grasps her left wrist with her fingers and is relieved. *I have a pulse! I'm alive! I don't know how the hell any of this is possible, but there must be a way to reverse the process!* She ponders.

She washes her hair and realizes her wrist, which he'd broken, is healed. *Whoa! I know he broke it! How could it have healed so quickly?* Somewhere in the back of her mind, the scientist part of her thinks, *if only that factor could be isolated! We could heal people easily!*

She gets out of the shower, grabs the towel, and dries herself off. She stands in front of a small mirror hanging over the sink. It's semi-clouded as the silvering on the backside has begun to separate from the glass, but she looks at herself and sees all the bite marks he made on her neck are gone. She runs her fingers over her neck in disbelief, but the skin's smooth. She wraps the towel around her, but it's barely large enough to cover both her breasts and her buttocks.

She carefully opens the door a sliver, but her captor is nowhere to be seen. She opens it up enough to see there's a pair of sweat pants and a sweatshirt lying on the arm of the sofa, but no underwear or a bra. She grabs them and goes back into the bathroom to put them on. They're baggy, but at this point, she's relieved to have clean clothing. She comes out of the bathroom and walks over to the fireplace where her old clothing is burning along with a couple of fresh logs. Her badge from the base is halfway melted, and she watches it burn through the ID photo of herself. She stands there, feeling the warmth.

She backs up, nearly falling over a bucket of water and a mop her captor left for her to 'clean up the mess'. She does so, and dumps the filthy, blood and vomit laden water down the toilet. She goes back in and curls up on the sofa, halfway in shock as it all begins to sink in. The incongruity of what's happened, what she's become, and the normality of things like showering and mopping the floor make her mind practically shut down, unable to process the new reality she's found herself in.

WHY?

Dee floats in and out of sleep. Her body feels heavy and somewhat weak, like she'd felt after having a long bout of the flu. She wakes when she hears the front door open and close and a McDonald's food bag is dropped in front of her. Dee's confused, and thinks, *Do vampires eat real food too?*

Jason snorts and sits in a nearby armchair. "Yes, we do eat real food, but you'll have to feed on blood at least every couple of days for a while. For now, you'll feed from me, or from bagged blood. When I know I can trust you not to run away or give me any shit, then I'll teach you how to feed yourself." He leans forward, a menacing look in his eye. "If you so much as try to escape or give me any problems, your next meal could be one of your daughters." He smirks malevolently. "Or, I might take a liking to one or both of them, if you get my drift?"

"Her mouth drops open thinking of what he might do to her beloved daughters, and she silently nods, and takes her cold burger out to eat.

Jason is at his computer, focused on whatever he's reading online. Once Dee's finished with her food, she quietly asks, "Why me? Why have you done this to *me*?" Tears threaten to fall once again.

Jason stops what he's doing and goes back to the armchair. "Ms. Price, hm, *Dr.* Price. I know that your expertise is in genetic manipulation. Our..." He grins, showing his fangs. "condition, is caused by a virus. I need you to extract said virus and find a way to alter it."

She sits silently, pondering what to say, worrying she might upset him if she says the wrong thing. When she speaks, she inquires, "Do you want me to find a cure?" She thinks, *that would make sense, at least! Changing me to be like him would certainly give me an incentive to find one.*

He laughs loudly. "Oh, *no*! *Not* at all! I like being this way. The problem is, the virus only works on a small number of people! Most people can't be transformed by it. It requires a small, specific genetic sequence to be present in the transformee for the virus to work. If there's no sequence, a person can't be changed! I *want you*, my *dear* doctor, to alter the virus and remove that little requirement! I want to be able to change whomever I choose!" He glares at her, waiting for a look of comprehension.

"You *like* being a...*vampire*? You want to change *more* people?" Her expression is akin to someone who's been told to inject school children with a new strain of COVID!

"Yes, doctor. You see, I *had* women like me as companions, but others like me took them away. *They* know who's compatible with the virus, and are keeping that information from me, *forcing* me to be alone! I want to change anyone I choose to, independent of any genetic requirement." Jason sits back in the armchair, waiting for her reaction.

"I... see. But that means I'm *compatible*?" She looks at him, confused.

"Yes, you *were* compatible, or you wouldn't have transformed. I stumbled on you when I still had access to a database over compatible people. Not exactly on my A-list, but with your skills, I saved your info as 'good to know'. *Now*, I have a use for you, *Doc!*" Jason folds his fingers together, clasping his hands together as he watches Dee.

"I'm not sure I can do what you want. Not only technically, but I'm assuming you wouldn't be asking someone's permission when you infect them? You certainly didn't me!" Her outrage at what he wants overrides her fear momentarily, allowing her to speak her mind.

"Why *should* I? Let's just say I've always had a way with women, and *get* what I want! Except, I can't physically change those I choose now! I changed you, Doc, because you have the skills to make this happen, and the motivation." He grins and makes sure his fangs show.

"You mean my daughters?" She cringes, but inside, red-hot anger burns.

"*Of course*! They're *not* compatible, even though *you* were, but I can certainly *imagine* a few *creative* things to do to, or with them, if you don't cooperate...." He walks behind the sofa, leans in, and whispers in her ear. "And I'll make you *watch*! If *worse* comes to *worst*, I'll starve you for blood and put you in a room with them! *Got* it?" He sneers at her, feeling triumphant as she nervously swallows.

"Yes, *got* it. I *can't* do it here though! I *need* a lab! I need *equipment*!" She trembles as his mouth lingers close to her throat.

He comes around and sits on the arm of the sofa; still too close for comfort. "Already taken care of." He smirks.

Dee looks pensive, remembering the night she first met her captor. "You *stole* my equipment?" She struggles to control her anger, but he feels it lashing out at him, and laughs.

"*Yep*! I'd only hidden a few pieces in a closet! I *needed* you to tell me what I should take! Of course, you showing up to your lab late at night, equipment disappeared, and so did you...well, let's just say they have the impression *you took* the equipment and ran off with it!" He laughs again as he sees her expression shift to horror.

She blanches as she realizes it was all a setup to not only take her and her equipment for his own purposes but to make her the scapegoat. "I see. So, even if I get out of here and go back...."

"They think *you're* a bio-terrorist! I left some additional *evidence* in your town home down on 3rd! A rather *elaborate* manifesto on your home computer, as well as some vials of anthrax and stuff in a bio-hazard case under your bed! You won't be going anywhere, *Dr. Price*, because no one will help you!" He gets up and stokes the fire.

Dee's at a loss for words. She's been mutated into some sort of monster. Her career's been destroyed, her reputation completely ruined, and the authorities *believe* she's a bio-terrorist! All of this, and the threats to her daughters, and she wishes, for the first time in her life, she could just die. She almost laughs out loud when she realizes the irony, as vampires supposedly live forever.

SCIENCE MEETS FANTASY

During the first week of Dee's new Apara life, Jason has little to do with her. She sleeps a lot. Her body's still changing because of the age factor. Most of the initial de-aging begins on an internal, cellular level. The Benefactors designed it to make the external de-aging lag to give older transformees time to put their affairs in order before having to either relocate or fake their deaths. Most of the time, it's usually only a matter of about five years or so when someone de-ages, and that can often be written off as improved health, makeup, or cosmetic surgery. It would be harder to explain a nearly 50-year-old regressing to the appearance of a 25 to 30-year-old practically overnight.

Jason makes her wait to feed until her hunger rises to an unbearable level, making her dependent on him, and reminding her, frequently, that if she doesn't comply, the next time she's starving, it could be one of her daughters in a locked room with her.

Jason doesn't teach her to use any of her new abilities, especially porting. He discovers the opal bracelet can be programmed to limit someone's abilities and puts it on her one night while she sleeps and locks it in place, and programs it for the maximum to keep her from being able to flee or use her new abilities against him. Jason wants Dee to feel powerless, so she will lose the will to fight him.

In most newly turned Apara, a certain amount of their preconditioning and subliminal education manifests when they're turned. Some of it surfaces as instinct, such as with feeding or control of their base abilities. Other things, like the knowledge of their Benefactors, can be brought out using subliminal triggers, if necessary. The older the transformee, the more such subliminals are often necessary to bring early teaching to the surface. In Dee's case, very little has surfaced, apart from knowing how to feed. She also doesn't have conscious knowledge of the origin of the Apara beyond a virus causes their transformation.

The morning after he put the bracelet on her, he wakes her up by kicking the sofa she's sleeping on. "*Get up!* Time to start working!" He glares down at her impatiently.

She stares at him, annoyed, but holds her tongue. She stretches and feels the opal bangle move on her wrist. She looks down at it and asks, "What the *Hell* is this?" She holds up her arm with the bracelet on it.

"Call it a mark of *ownership*. You *belong to me* now, and will do as told!" He grabs a duffle bag, pulls out some clean clothes for her, and throws them at her feet on the floor.

Her anger simmers, but she holds it in check for the sake of her daughters. She picks up the clothes, showers, and changes. *Well, what do you know? The jerk actually brought me underwear and a bra this time!* She thinks, drying herself, and getting dressed. She brushes out her hair and returns to the living room. A pair of old sneakers and socks are sitting on the sofa for her. She slips them on. He's sitting at his computer, as usual. She looks at the screen, noting he's reading up on viruses and genetic manipulation. She sits on the sofa, waiting for him to tell her what's next.

He walks over to the sofa, looming over her menacingly. "Get up! We're going to your new lab."

She stands, and he grabs her by the arm. The room swirls to darkness, and when her vision clears, they're standing in a nondescript room with white walls, fluorescent lighting, no windows, and her stolen lab equipment. "I want you to go through everything and make a list of anything you need for this project. I'll get it and bring it back here."

Still a bit disoriented from being ported, she asks, "How did we get here?"

He tells her, but lies. "We teleported, and no, you can't do that. It's something I can do, but not everyone can, so don't even think about trying it, or I'll know, and your daughters will pay the price!" He gives her a lascivious smile to convey what that fate may be.

He sits in a rolling office chair, watching her go through everything, and making her list. After about an hour, she hands it to him. Most of the equipment is here, but I'll need certain chemicals, and a CRISPR Enzyme kit. This is crucial to editing genetic sequences. I can't do it without that. I'm assuming we're talking about a virus no one's studied before, so I'll need tools to purify and gene sequence the virus from scratch. My equipment isn't that advanced. And, it will all take time." She stands in front of him, not sure how he'll react, especially to the latter, as he clearly lacks patience.

He reads down the list, looks up at her, not angry, but his eyebrows are furrowed in thought. "Where can I get these things?" He looks at her expectantly.

"We can order some of the kits online, though they aren't cheap. As to the equipment, I'll have to have access to the Internet to find one that will do the job." She pulls up a rolling desk chair, thinking, *Maybe I can get a message out somehow?*

He scowls at her. "Haven't you learned yet, Doc? I *know* what you're *thinking*! There's no way in Hell, I'll let you get online unsupervised. We can search together and you can tell me which one you need. You might as well forget about... hm...'getting a message out somehow'." His lips part a little, and his fangs show. "Dr. Price, just to stop any future issues, I'll let you in on a little secret." He narrows his eyes and sneers. "I'm *telepathic*. I can *hear* your thoughts before you can act!"

Dee gets a deflated expression, knowing her chances of escaping are nearing zero, as is the probability of warning her family. "*Fine.*" She stomps over to the equipment she has, and begins setting things up. She turns around to look when she hears the door open, close, and lock. She lets out a sigh of relief now that he's out of the room. She gets to her microscope and checks the lenses, noticing it's out of alignment and needs calibrating after being moved.

She goes through the process and finds a slide. She looks for a syringe to take a sample of her blood, but can't find any. "Another *damn* thing to add to the list." She mutters aloud. She realizes what she can use, brings down her fangs, jabs her index finger on the tip of one of them, and rapidly moves it down to the slide before it can heal up.

She puts on the slip to spread out the blood for viewing and places it under the microscope. She checks at all magnifications but is disappointed to see it looks like ordinary, human blood. She does, however, notice one odd thing. Her blood is completely devoid of foreign pathogens! *No viruses, no bacteria! Not even any leukocytes! Very odd!* She thinks. She continues to watch the cells on the slide and notices that the red blood cells are dying more rapidly than normal. They practically disintegrate before her eyes.

Jason returns with his laptop. "What are you doing?"

Dee jumps anxiously at his sudden return. "I'm testing my microscope after recalibrating it! It's quite curious, but I think you may be wrong about a virus! There are absolutely no pathogens, viral or bacterium, in this sample I took from myself!" She continues to watch the cells break down rapidly in fascination. "And the red blood cells are dying much faster than in normal samples.

"Yeah, they told me something about that after I was turned. It's some kind of survival thing. If I were to cut you, and you bled on the floor, it would leave a bloodstain, but all the DNA would degrade within a few hours, making it untraceable. Why do you think no one's ever proven our existence? At least not *scientifically.*" He puts his laptop down and opens it up to a search page where various genetic sequencing machines are listed.

"That *quickly*? I'm not sure how I'll be able to properly study it if it degrades so quickly! We'll need a fast sequencer, for one thing!" She stands there, hands on her hips, looking perplexed.

"It's the virus you need to examine, though it, too, has a limited lifespan in its active form." He shoves her out of the way to look into the microscope.

"*Active* form?" She's confused.

"Yeah, the virus lives in our bone marrow most of the time. It stops normal red blood cell production. I was told our marrow can only convert whole human blood for our own use, not make it from scratch." He explains, knowing it, but not fully understanding it himself. When we feed on someone compatible, it activates the virus or something, flooding our blood with it. That's why you don't see any viruses, I guess. There aren't any unless you feed on a compatible person!"

Her scientist persona kicks in full force. "*Fascinating!* There's another virus that resides in the bone marrow, often causing short-term anemia! I wonder if it's related to Parvovirus?"

Jason looks at her like she's crazy. "The *dog* virus?"

She shakes her head emphatically. "That's one type of parvovirus. Just like COVID-19 is one of many Corona viruses! Humans don't get that one, but there's a variant, B19, that's usually a childhood virus, but adults can get it. When they do, it often causes anemia, rashes, and sometimes joint pain." He stares at her blankly, not understanding her excitement.

"It's a place to start a hypothesis. But if it's only in the bone marrow, we're going to need bone marrow needles, and unfortunately, getting a sample will be quite painful. Do anesthetics work on... on... vampires?" She still finds it hard to use a term for something that shouldn't exist.

"I wouldn't know, but we can block pain when we feed." He remarks, bored by her technical talk.

She scowls at him, again having to bridle back her anger. "Then *why* did it always hurt so much when you bit me?"

He gets an amused expression. "Because I *wanted* it to, Doc."

Her anger swells to a crescendo, and she balls up her fists up tight, her fingernails cutting into her palms until they bleed. Jason senses her anger and smells her blood and says, "*Temper,* temper, Doc! *Focus* on your work!"

Dee takes several slow, deep breaths, trying to diffuse her fury. She pulls herself back on track. "Is there any way to collect a sample of the active virus?"

"I guess we'd have to feed on a compatible subject, something I'm having trouble getting a hold of, besides you, and unfortunately, biting you now won't create that reaction!" He turns back to his computer and looks at the pages on his laptop.

"Marrow biopsy needles it is, I *guess*." She pauses. "Do you know exactly what happens when someone feeds on a compatible person? Technically speaking?"

He looks up impatiently, having been halfway watching a video on his phone. "I really didn't pay that close attention to the technical details, Doc, but it's like I told you already, that little genetic code compatible people carry activates the virus, and floods our bloodstream with it, making it active and capable of transforming the compatible person if we give them our blood in return. I was told the active period is only about an hour, and then the active virus either dies, or goes back into dormancy, or something. So, after that time, it won't transform anyone, 'cause you'll just be giving them blood, not the virus."

"What happens if you give the activated blood to someone who doesn't have that genetic sequence?" She asks.

"Is all this necessary, Doc? They told me only compatible people will change because the virus must latch on to the genetic sequence to work, okay? I'm going out to feed, but I'll come back by and get you in a while, so update your list, and get things ready. We need to get moving on this as soon as possible." He grabs his laptop, walks out the door, and locks it from the outside. There is no locking mechanism on the inside doorknob.

Dee sits, frustrated by her dilemma, but also curious about the medical aspects of what she's become. She updates her list and finishes setting up her equipment. He leaves her sitting there for hours, finally collecting her and taking her back to the cabin. He knows she's feeling the early signs of hunger, but doesn't offer her a chance to feed until she becomes desperate two days later when she's shaking and unfocused.

GOING THROUGH THE MOTIONS

It's been about two weeks since Jason took Dee, and stress has worn on her. She's locked in the cabin most of the time. She's seriously tempted to break out and run away, even though she doesn't know where she is, but ultimately decides she can't risk it when he reminds her that, with *his* ability to port, he could get to her daughters instantly, even if she warns them. After that, she becomes increasingly despondent and depressed. She spends a couple of days lying on the sofa, barely moving, or even thinking, afraid he might be listening in telepathically.

One morning, she wakes and is alone in the cabin, but after an hour, Jason ports in carrying several packages. "Your supplies have come. The sequencer came a couple of days ago. It's already at the lab. Clean yourself up. It's time to work." He tells her.

She sits up slowly, feeling hopeless, grabs a clean set of work clothes, and gets ready. She comes back into the main room of the cabin, letting out a slow, deep sigh of resignation. "Ready." Is all she says.

Jason hands her the packages and ports her to the lab. Her reaction time has slowed due to depression, and she nearly drops the boxes when they phase in. "*Stupid bitch!*" Jason mumbles, taking the packages and putting them on the table. Get to work! I'm tired of waiting and want results!" He sneers and ports out.

She slowly, half-heartedly, opens the packages, takes out the various kits and supplies, and sets up to take a sample when he comes back. With nothing better to do, she takes a standard syringe, and takes a new sample of her own blood, preparing it for sequencing to test the equipment. She initiates the process, goes back to sitting, and not doing much of anything, as it takes almost twelve hours for it to process. Then, she must analyze it.

A couple of hours later, a very impatient Jason comes back in. "Have you found anything yet?"

She looks up at him, expressionless. "How *could* I? You haven't let me take a bone marrow sample yet?"

"Then *what's* running in the machine?" He asks impatiently.

"I didn't have anything else I could do, so I ran my own blood through sequencing to test it. Hopefully, the DNA will remain intact long enough to get some results. I must make sure the machine will be able to process it!"

"Why didn't you take a bone marrow sample from yourself? You carry the virus; you don't *need* me!" He sneers.

She looks at him, mouth open, and says, "I *can't* perform that operation on *myself*! It's extremely delicate and painful and I don't know how to numb the pain! You haven't *taught* me how!"

"Well, you're *not* gonna get it from me, so you'll just have to suck it up!" He gives her a purely evil grin and pulls out his smartphone. "By the way, I thought you might like to see this." He puts the phone down in front of her and plays a video of her daughters with her ex-husband being questioned by police outside his home. Her daughters are crying and her ex-husband looks angry.

"You were there? Why are the police there? Did you *hurt* them?" She feels an emotion other than despair for the first time in about a week. She feels panic and anger, thinking maybe he'd done something to frighten or hurt her family.

"No, I haven't *hurt* them. The police were there questioning them about you! *Ah!* But of course, you haven't seen the *news* in a couple of weeks." He pulls out a ripped-out article from the Frederick News-Post and gives it to her. "*Congratulations*! They think you're working with right-wing extremists!" He walks away; laughing and ports out before she can say anything.

She sits in an office chair, the only sound in the room, coming from the sequencer. She feels broken inside. Her will to fight is nearly extinguished except for an ember when she thinks about trying to protect her daughters. She reads the article a couple of times. Tears fall from her eyes and soak into the newspaper article in her lap. She looks up at the bone marrow biopsy tools and knows what she must do. She knows there's no hope for her, but the only hope she has for her daughters is to do what he wants, and hope he doesn't go after them anyway. Too emotionally exhausted to even walk over to the tray of tools, she rolls the office chair over to that station. She stares at the special extraction needles, steeling herself up to do what she must. She takes a needle by the hand grip and positions the tip on her hip, where the back pelvic bone is. She wills herself not to feel any pain and pushes it in. It still hurts, and she screams as she pushes it into the bone marrow, continuing with the extraction, and pulling out the sample. The extraction wound heals quickly, and the pain stops, but she's visibly shaking from the experience.

She knows she must work quickly, and puts the sample into a machine that will separate out the virus from the marrow cells, purifying it for sequencing. Her sequencer can run up to ten samples at the same time, so she sticks the purified virus sample into the second slot and starts the process. She takes a sample of the virus and puts it under the microscope. It's unlike any virus she's ever seen. She takes photos using the microscope's built-in camera for later study. The virus has an unusual shape and structure, and appears to have some organelles that could be used for propulsion, like a paramecium does. Where some viruses have spikes used for infecting cells, this one has an oddly shaped protrusion. She theorizes that this might be what locks onto the genetic key sequence in compatible cells. She makes a culture dish to see if she can grow the virus artificially, and puts it in a containment unit. Lastly, she takes the purified sample of her own bone marrow and examines it under the scope. Its structure is abnormal and lacks any sign of nascent red blood cells forming. She takes more photos. They're automatically transferred to a computer via Bluetooth, where she can enlarge them and study them.

Jason pops in briefly, leaving a few slices of days' old pizza for her, and leaves her to work. She eats like she's going through the motions, and then checks the remaining time on the sequencer. As there are at least four more hours to go, she ends up curling up in a corner, on the hard, vinyl floor, and sleeping.

She wakes up when the sequencer beeps. She gets up slowly, takes the memory card out, and puts it into her computer. An image of sequenced DNA comes up on the screen, and she uses the cursor to zoom in and out on the different chromosomes. She tries to identify what type of virus it is, but it doesn't fit any one category. It contains both DNA and RNA, and its visible structure is unlike any virus she's familiar with. She runs a program on her computer that will analyze the sequences, hopefully giving her more insight.

Jason returns two days later and she's pacing the floor anxiously. She looks up when he comes in, and he perceives the literal pain of unfulfilled hunger. He tosses her a bag of blood, and she sinks her fangs into the plastic, draining it quickly.

When she's done, she looks up at him, and says, "I'm doing everything you've asked, can't you at least give me something in return?! Even something to sleep on if you're going to leave me here to work?"

He's surprised she's making demands after all he's put her through, but he does need her, at least for now. "Tell me what you've found so far, and I'll consider your request!"

"The computer's having trouble identifying some of the sequences. Some of it doesn't match any of the known elements of any viruses in the sequencing database. Some of the amino acid pairings don't make sense either. There's something off about them! It's like some brand new form of virus. It has both DNA and RNA in it, as well as…, if I had to guess, it almost looks more bio-mechanical! Like

94

it was built as a nano-gene-splicer! I wish I could study it in action, but I know that's not an option." She realizes a lot of what she said went over his head, even though he'll never admit it. "To put it simply, this virus is like nothing I've seen before. But considering what it does, I guess that shouldn't be surprising."

"Will you be able to do what I want you to do?" He asks, wondering if this woman has been a waste of his time.

"I don't know. Maybe. I need more time to analyze it, and I need...a sample of your DNA to compare to mine and see if I can find that sequence! I really need more samples, but I'm guessing that's not possible?" She regards him expectantly.

"Unlikely doctor, unless..." He ports out.

She shakes her head and goes back to work. A few hours later, Jason returns with two older people, a man and a woman, who are in a trance-like state.

She looks up and asks. "Who are they?"

"They are compatible, that's all you need to know!" He sits them down along a wall.

"You're not going to change them too, are you?" She wouldn't want to put anyone else through what she's been through.

"Not unless I have to, Doc. I don't have a use for two old farts that I'd have to feed as well! Especially since I doubt they have anything to contribute! Can you use samples from them to find your answers?" He motions to them.

"Will you release them, unharmed, after I take samples?" She asks.

He looks at her, sighs, and furrows his brow. "Yes, I will, *IF* you continue to work, and produce some results. If you don't, then I'll bring them back in and turn them in front of you, or make *you* turn them, then release them with no supervision!" He raises an eyebrow and gives her a sadistic grin.

"*Okay!* Okay! I need blood from each of them. I'll manage with half a pint each, plus cheek swabs." She pauses. "How much blood would you have to ingest to trigger the active virus?"

"Don't know, but probably not much." He tells her, off-handedly.

"I need to see what happens when it's active. I don't want you to turn them, but once I set up sequencing for both of them, I want to trigger the active virus and apply it to a sample of their blood so I can watch what it does." She holds her breath, waiting for his reply.

"Take the samples, Doc, so I can get them back where they belong." He moves to the side to allow her access to his catatonic guests.

Dee brings over syringes for taking blood samples and several laboratory type tubes, filling several from each of them. She gets a DNA swab kit and swabs each of their cheeks. "Can you heal the spots where I drew blood? You don't want them to notice they've had blood drawn, right?"

Impatiently, Jason leans down and heals each track where their blood's been drawn.

"Okay, please return them, unharmed, to where they belong. I promise I'll set things in motion here." She reassures him, and he ports out with the two people. First, she prepares small samples for DNA sequencing and then puts most of the remaining blood into a refrigeration unit to keep it stable.

She keeps one flask out, pouring half into a culturing dish, and drinking the rest. She hopes she might feel something when it triggers the virus to activate, but doesn't, so after ten minutes, she draws a vial of her own blood, puts the culture under the scope, and sets it to record video. She puts half a milliliter of her blood into the culture and watches on the monitor attached to the scope. Dee's mesmerized by what she sees. The virus moves from cell to cell, bonding with it, taking it over, and actively splices copies of DNA from the virus into the chromosomes of each cell almost mechanically. When it's colonized all the cells, and activity slows, she extracts a sample and puts it in for sequencing. She leaves the culture under the scope, recording, while the sequencing runs.

She hears a noise and spins around toward it. An old twin mattress and a blanket are now lying in the corner of the lab, along with some fast food, but Jason's long gone. Knowing the sequencing will take time, she gets some long-overdue rest.

EUREKA!

It's taken several days of analyzing both the sequences of the virus, the two 'compatible' donors, the changed blood, and the videos of the process, but Dee makes some headway. While still depressed about her situation, her curiosity boosts her energy and focus. Somewhere in the back of her mind, she hopes by understanding the virus and what it does, she might find a cure for herself, no matter what her captor's goal is.

Jason periodically leaves her bags of blood he's been acquiring from blood banks or hospitals, as well as occasional regular food. Sometimes he comes in and watches her work, then leaves without warning.

A few days later, her computer lets out a ping, as it's found one identical sequence between the two donors, and it nearly matches a sequence in her own, except for one gene. Hm, he said biting me would no longer trigger a reaction by the virus. *My sequence is one gene away from the ones that are common between the two donors. Perhaps the virus removes or changes a link in the key sequence when it changes someone?* She thinks.

She analyzes the suspect sequence, and looks for an inverse sequence in the virus, that might match up with it, acting like a key. After hours of searching, she finds it. "Oh! My *God!!* The protrusion on the virus fits like a lock to a key!" She exclaims to the walls in the room, almost wishing one of her colleagues could be there to appreciate her discovery.

She tests it in a simulation in another program, and the protrusion and the common sequence from the two donors theoretically line up and bond to each other. She's excited by the discovery, but something bothers her. There are elements of the virus the sequencing software doesn't recognize. She looks at those sequences herself on the computer, zooming in and discovering there's an unknown amino acid base bonded to some of the sequences. *A fifth base?* She reacts with surprise.

Her mind feels like something's slapping her synapses awake; she gets dizzy, and has flashes of strange people. No, they weren't regular people. She thinks, *Aliens?* Suddenly, a chunk of subconscious knowledge floods her mind, making her head throb. She lies down on the mattress sorting through the thoughts, images, concepts, and ideas flooding her mind. As everything begins to settle, she has a proverbial "Eureka!" moment, and knows the virus is not only *alien*, but *engineered*.

She not only knows that it works more like an engineered retrovirus similar to those used in gene therapy, only about a thousand times more complex, but that it was created by an alien race to transform humans into a long-lived subspecies of humanity that became their liaisons on Earth.

She thinks, *That's crazy! But somehow, I know it's true, like I know my own name! What the hell is going on?* She lies there, mind reeling, trying to work her way through some of the ideas and information that's flooded her mind. She sleeps and has vivid dreams, comprehending that, despite how she's come to be this way, she was meant to be what she's become. A word comes to mind, *Apara? The others?* She thinks.

She also knows the reason compatible people contain the gene sequence; it's a safety measure to prevent the virus from spreading to people who are not suitable. *I've got to talk him out of this! Find some way to dissuade him from this.* She rolls over, closes her eyes, and tries to take in everything she now understands. She realizes that the way he behaves goes against everything that she had ingrained in her from *Their* teachings.

Jason senses something's off with her and ports in. "What's going on?" He demands.

She stands rapidly. "Nothing! I'm just tired." She isn't sure how to dissuade him, as he's clearly not stable, and will be unlikely to be convinces by rational arguments."

"He narrows his eyes trying to peer into her mind, but gets nothing other than her normal anxiety. He looks down and notes that the bracelet is still securely in place, so assumes that not reading anything means there's nothing to read. "Have you found anything yet?" He barks out impatiently.

She's slow to answer, not wanting to upset him. "Yes, but there are some things the software still hasn't been able to analyze. I looked myself and found some unusual amino acid bonds not normally seen in DNA. This may make it very hard to edit, at least without potentially unforeseen results."

"So, have you found the gene sequence or do I have to bring our...donors back and experiment on them directly?" He sneers, and she knows he's talking about making her turn one or both.

"I *found* the sequence, but I'm not sure how the CRISPR enzymes will work on the virus with these extra factors! I'm trying to explain that tinkering with it could make the virus worse!" She's surprised she suddenly knows how to instinctively shield her mind, but she can't read him for some reason.

He's only halfway paying attention to her, but turns to her and says, "I don't want your opinion; I *want* it *done! Soon!* I'm so tired of waiting, and I'm growing *tired* of your *excuses!*" He tells her before porting out in a huff.

She sits at her computer and stares at the image of the mystery base. She reviews the various unidentified segments of the virus, and all of them contain an atypical base. No matter what she does, she can't identify it. *Maybe it's not found on Earth? That would certainly be reason to believe it's extraterrestrial, and with that, I can't possibly predict how the CRISPR enzymes will work on it.* She looks at her own, sequenced DNA, starting with the suspect segment, and sure enough, the replaced gene contains an atypical base. She scans the rest of her own DNA, and finds several locations containing what she decides must be non-terrestrial bases.

A RECIPE FOR DISASTER

Dee continues to search for a way to edit the virus safely, and possibly neutralize it in him, or even find a way to use it against him, but it always comes back to one thing: the unidentifiable sequences and the unknown elements make doing any editing on such a virus risky at best, and potentially disastrous should she get it wrong. She's always had an intuitive knack for genetics, but knows she's in way over her head considering the virus was clearly created with genetic science far beyond even the most cutting-edge techniques she's read about. She concludes that there are two separate, atypical bases, and the logical conclusion is they must come from sampled, alien DNA.

After about two weeks of studying the viral sequences, Jason ports in, and she hears a thud and a whimper behind her. She jumps and turns around, only to see her oldest daughter, Celia, sprawled on the floor with bite marks on her neck. Celia looks up in shock and the word "*Mom*?" escapes her lips, sounding halfway between a cry of anguish and a question.

"*Celia!*" Dee runs over to her daughter, but before she can reach her, Jason pulls her up and puts his arm around her from behind. Dee stops short, knowing her daughter's life is very much in danger.

"Shall I finish what I started Doc, or will you complete my project?" Jason's fangs are bared and poised to sink into Celia's neck, and his hand meanders toward Celia's breast, implying other consequences should Dee refuse. "I promise, it won't be a quick or painless death!"

"*Alright! Please! Don't* hurt her! I've been *trying* to explain! What you *want* me to do could have serious ramifications if it goes wrong!" Dee's eyes plead with him, both on behalf of her daughter, and to listen to her about the potentially disastrous consequences of attempting to alter such a complex, alien virus using relatively primitive genetic tools, compared to whatever was used to create this masterpiece of a non-mutating virus.

Jason puts his fangs away, but holds on to Celia, who's visibly terrified, but unable to scream or struggle. "Are you going to do it or not Doc? This is your, and *her* last chance!" He grips her tighter, and licks her neck, making Dee feel sick thinking of what he has in mind.

"I'll do it! I think I know how. It will take a few days to culture it. Then we'll have to inject it into your bone marrow. It'll take a few more days before it colonizes your bone marrow before you can test it out. That's just how it is! There's no way to speed up the process! You'll still have the original virus in your system. I can't change that, but I can splice in the needed sequence like our donors carried, turning it on permanently; and I can splice in the DNA to create a spike, which should make it infectious to the general population. However, I can't be 100% sure about anything with those *unknown* factors! You'll probably still need to feed first to trigger its release into the bloodstream, but if I'm right, the spike will inject the virus without needing to match up to the target's DNA! Now, please! Let Celia go! Make her forget all of this! Including seeing *me* like this!" She pleads.

Jason tries to read her, but can't perceive any deception, only fear. He smirks malevolently, then heals Celia's bite wound by once again, lasciviously licking it. Celia goes into the same state the two unknown donors were in. "Dr. Price, this *is* your last chance. If this *fails*, let's just say both of your daughters and I will have a night *you'll* never forget!" He ports out, taking Celia home and sending her on her way, taking a video of her walking, almost mechanically, back in her front door. He ports back to Dee and puts the video on for her to see. "I've returned her, safe and sound, and with no memory of her visit here. Exactly how long will this take?" He stands there, arms crossed, scowling impatiently.

"If it goes well, and cultures like the original virus, I can have it ready in five days. Then, you should wait a few days before testing it to allow it to colonize your bone marrow. She thinks, *Please don't choose my daughters as your guinea pigs!*

"I'll hold you to that, Doc! For your and your daughters' sake, you better be right!" He ports out, leaving her to work.

After he departs, Dee goes into the small bathroom in her lab to wash her face after crying. She looks at her reflection and notices that there's less silver in her black hair. It's been salt and pepper since she turned 45, but now, it looks more like when she was in her early 40s. She looks closer, and notices there are fewer age lines around her eyes. She pulls up the sleeve on her right arm, examining her skin closely. "It's *gone!*" She exclaims aloud, realizing that a work-related burn scar on the underside of her arm has healed and the skin is now not only unblemished, but is softer and more elastic. Is it possible? *Am I getting younger? I've been so busy, not to mention depressed, to notice the changes before now. Oh, God! Did Celia notice? No, Celia was certainly too terrified.* She finishes up and goes back to her work, preparing to do something she was certain she shouldn't, but her family's safety overrides her instincts to protect the 'greater good'.

***

Five days later, she has the cultured, edited virus ready. She's tested it on some of the blood from a bag he'd brought her to feed on, and it attacks the non-keyed blood.

She thinks, *it appears to work, and the viral culture should be sufficient to inject now. It's just to do it and hope he'll leave my girls alone, and perhaps even free me.* She lies down to get some rest while she waits for him to show up for his infusion of the altered virus. While she sleeps, she has odd dreams about other people like herself, being with them, and being oddly happy, though she does miss her daughters in the dream.

She wakes up to her mattress shuttering from him kicking the side of it. "Get up! I assume you're ready or you wouldn't be napping!" He reaches down and grabs her by the hair with one hand, as he had in the first days, while his other pulls her up by her arm.

She gasps in pain, but once he releases her in a standing position, she glares at him, wishing she could smack the sneer off his freckled face. "Yes, it's as ready as it can be. It appears to work on general blood, though there's no way to be sure of the final effects it will have on a live subject."

She goes over to a storage box for keeping viruses alive, pulls out a bone marrow syringe, and fills it with the purified version of the virus. "You should sit or lie down. This is going to hurt. He pulls up a chair and sits. *I'm so tempted to jam this thing into his skull and take my chances, but I can't risk the girls!* She thinks.

"*Well*?" He asks impatiently.

"I need you to pull your pants down below your hip on this side so I can find the best spot to infuse it." She has the bone marrow needle by a hand-grip, and waits for him to comply, or blurt out another smart-ass remark.

Jason stands and sneers. "Curious, Doc? How long's it been since you've seen a man's *junk*?" He pulls down his pants all the way, giving her threatening emotional waves and an undesired viewing.

"I need to be able to see what I'm doing so I can insert it into your pelvic bone in the proper location! I don't *want*, or *need* a peep show!" She snaps, fed up with his arrogance. She feels the skin and tissue along his back pelvic bone region, and realizes she can intuitively sense the best angle to insert the needle, though part of her strays to wanting to put it where it'll hurt most and rip it around after the threats he's made to her daughters. She controls her impulses, and does her job, sinking it into his bone until she feels it sink into the softer bone marrow. She pushes the plunger, and infuses his bone marrow with the altered virus.

Jason grunts with pain as she infuses him, and she feels a little satisfaction. "Damn, Doc! You *weren't* kidding!" He says, as she pulls the wide needle back out, watching the track heal rapidly after removing it.

"You should probably lie still for a few minutes. Even though you heal quickly, I can't be sure you won't have some internal bleeding or clotting from this. You must wait a few days so the virus has time to spread to the rest of your bone marrow before you...test it." She walks away and throws the marrow needle into a bio-hazard disposal box. When she turns around, Jason is standing there, still naked from the waist down, obviously aroused. She tries not to let it fluster her, and walks away from him, busying herself with her equipment.

"Don't *like* what you see, Doc? Don't worry! It's *not* for you! I'm thinking about the women I'm gonna turn now that I'll be able to choose whichever ones I want." He laughs, and it makes ice water go through her veins.

She hopes her daughters will be safe now, but part of her weeps inside for the women she may have enabled him to transform and torment; she still worries he may go after Lynda and Celia to spite her. She feels guilt welling up for putting her own daughters over other women's safety. *Stop it! You did what you had to!* She thinks. She turns to face Jason, quiet at first, but steels herself up to ask what must. "What happens to me if this works? Once you get what you want?"

He gives her a surprised look. His pants are now back on, though she can still see an obvious bulge. "Haven't thought about it, Doc! I certainly don't want you in the same way as I want some luscious young flesh to play with, but you've been *useful*, albeit slow."

"So, you're not going to let me go?" She asks quietly.

"And where would you *go*? You can't exactly go back to your family, or your work! The police and FBI are still looking for you. What do you think they'll do when they figure out you're no longer human?" He walks over to her to gloat, and cocks his head to one side, staring at her, examining her face, and noticing something has changed, but not quite what. He laughs. "Too bad I didn't find you when you were younger! I'll bet you were quite a piece of ass back then!"

Her face turns red, not only out of embarrassment for what he just implied, but out of anger for all that he's put her through, and how there is no foreseeable end. She thinks, *As long as he keeps me with him, my daughters will be in danger anytime he wants something! I shouldn't have complied, but I couldn't sacrifice them! Now, I know it may never be over for me or them!* She pauses in thought for a second, as a new realization hits her, *If I continue to grow younger physically, I may have to deal with yet another, and more unthinkable form of abuse by that monster!* As her anger grows, she feels an odd sensation from her wrist, where the opal bangle rests. She unconsciously puts her hand on her wrist, rubbing it like she might if she'd had a strong static shock.

"Get everything cleaned up and do what you have to keep the cultured virus thriving in case we need to try again." He tells her, but the tone of his voice implies that she would be better off if that didn't end up the case! I figure you can sleep at the cabin tonight. May even let you use one of the bunk beds in the other room, if you don't give me any trouble between now and then!" He laughs and ports out. She hears in her mind, *I'll be back in two hours. Be ready!* While he's occasionally sent her telepathic messages to check on her progress, this time it's much louder than usual.

CRISIS MEETING

After Jason's attack on Niall, and Callie's subsequent turning, Liz calls a crisis meeting in her office. Callie is there too, transformed, coherent, but just sitting close to Niall, still overwhelmed by everything. Liz, Kari, Marc, Amy, and Tess are also present.

Once everyone's settled in, Liz says, "Seems Jason's gotten desperate. His attack on you, Niall, in a public venue certainly proves that! I'm worried he may escalate."

"I was surprised myself! Especially his use of a rifle to take me down; though, as I understand it, he had some special ops training somewhere along the line, so knows how to shoot. I can certainly vouch for that!" Niall says, leaning back to reassure Callie with a gentle hand rubbing her leg.

Tess chimes in. "He's never been stable, not since day one with us!" She blurts out.

Liz gives Tess a glance at her outburst, but continues. "Have any of our precogs, or anyone, reported any impressions that could tell us where he might be or what he might be up to?"

"No one's reported anything so far", Marc says, but nudges Tess, giving her a look. She glares at him and pulls her hand out of his with an implied 'traitor!' admonishment in her gaze. "Alright! It's probably nothing, and Kari knows about it, but I've been going astral again. But I haven't seen him so I don't know if it has anything to do with Jason or not! For all I know, my brain's just joyriding!" She quips.

"What, exactly, have you been seeing?" Niall leans forward so he can regard Tess's face from where he's sitting.

"That's just it! Not a hell of a lot that seems important! *All* I've been seeing are mountains, woods, bears, deer, elk, and some snow! I'm honestly beginning to think my brain's telling me to take a *freaking* vacation away from it all!" Tess crosses her arms tightly across her chest and gives Marc an annoyed look for outing her.

"Kari mentioned your little jaunts to me after you told her. Have you been keeping a journal of them as she suggested?" Liz leans on the edge of her desk and tilts her head to one side while watching Tess expectantly.

"Yes! *Yes!* I've been writing them down every time I have them and remember enough to *bother!* Nothing specific to see! Just kind of gliding through the mountains..." She trails off and Liz can tell she's holding something back.

"What is it, Tess? I sense there's *more*?" Liz asks, a bit frustrated that Tess still doesn't always trust herself.

"Last night was different, though it was probably just a dream. I was over a city, but I don't know where! I just know it's also in the mountains, but not Asheville, and there's a military base of some sort, but I can't say where it is. It could be almost anywhere!" She closes her eyes, drudging up the memories from her out-of-body jaunt. "I take that back. The mountains weren't huge like the Rockies or anything. They looked like the Smokies, kind of rounded and forested, rather than stark and rocky. I'd say the season is about the same, as there was snow on some of the peaks, so it's at least the Northern Hemisphere." She scowls. "I saw flags flying on the base. One was the US flag, and the other I couldn't make out any details other than it had yellow and red on it." She rambles out, like once she turned it on, she couldn't turn it off.

Liz makes a note of Tess's 'dream', or astral impressions, and after a few quiet moments of thought, suggests, "From the mountains and the season, I'm guessing it may be on the east coast somewhere. If you are subconsciously connecting to Jason again, I really doubt it would be in another country." Liz turns to the others. "Has anyone else heard anything?"

108

Niall shakes his head. "Sorry! I've been so busy with Callie's transformation and all, I haven't kept up with anyone but Katie lately. The only thing her people are seeing is they think there's going to be a bad flu or virus outbreak, maybe even a new pandemic, but it's all still quite vague."

Liz notes that down and scans the room, waiting for someone else to chime in. "How about *Val*? Has she seen anything? She's our big precog now?" Tess suggests.

"Val and Ty have been setting up the new server interface at the LA office, but I'll check with them. Hopefully, she's seen something, and if not, maybe telling her about this will trigger a vision." Liz pauses. "I guess, unless we get some kind of precognitive, clairvoyant, or astral input..." She glances at Tess, "we'll have to play it by ear. I'll have Peder keep scanning police reports for missing persons and suspicious deaths. Maybe, considering Tess's latest impression, we should expand our radius and look beyond Jason's normal comfort zone of the Southeast?"

Marc nods in agreement. "I'll get my precog network to focus on him, too, and Niall, please touch base with Katie to bring it up with the Atlanta crowd as well."

With that, they all part and do what they can, frustrated, and feeling helpless.

Liz puts a hand on Tess's shoulder before she can leave. "Can you give Sue and Colin a call? Sara wants to consult with her about her cousin, Philipa, and what to do with her. They've moved her to Sanctuary, under Sara's care, but before allowing her to come out of stasis, she wants Sue's input on her redeemability."

Tess says, "Sure, Liz. Sue's coming over tonight to help me with another batch of LM evaluations. I'll talk to her then." Tess rushes to get out of Liz's office. She hasn't had time to catch up with Amy lately, as she's been working so much with her security guys outside the office that she wants to catch up with her before she could port away again.

HE'S BACK...

Tess leaves Liz's office, but Amy is long gone. Amy's office is on the second floor, two doors down from Ty and Val's office. She zips through the lobby and takes the stairs two at a time, glad there are no humans coming down them or she might knock them down the stairs. She enters the hallway as Amy turns into her office and closes the door behind her. Tess trots quickly down to Amy's door and raps on it lightly. "Amy, it's Tess! Got a few?"

The door quickly opens showing Amy with arms wide open for a big hug. "Hey, girl! You're a sight for sore eyes! Come on in!"

The two women settle in the meeting area in Amy's office. "Wow! Like what you've done with your office! It sure beats our old cubicles." Tess says, making small talk.

"Sure does! Not as big as yours, but then again, I've got a *whole* training facility for working with my guys!" She gives Tess a wide grin.

"Speaking of guys, how're things going with you and Dave?" Tess smirks, knowingly, enjoying a bit of 'normal' gossip for a change. It makes her feel human again.

"Oh, pretty *good!* He's out in Denver for a few days, running training ops for me. I needed a break after Hot Springs; not from him, but from all the training and *shit*! Now that I've got him and the others up to speed, I'm delegating and sending my best out to train similar teams in other centers." She explains.

"Is Marc still being super overprotective after your accident?" Amy asks.

"*More or less*! That's why I high-tailed it up here after the meeting to see you! I love him dearly, but sometimes he still acts like

I'm a *frail* human!" Tess chuckles, but the emotional tone behind the laugh is far more serious.

"*Don't* tell me there's *trouble* in paradise?" She quips.

"Nah, I guess I'm still dealing with the whole symbolic death crap, and little things irk me. Sue says I'm hypersensitive and over-react, but that that's normal under the circumstances." Tess explains.

Amy sighs, "Speaking of little things irking, guess who sent me another email."

"*Charlie*? What's he *want*?" Tess inquires skeptically.

"He'll be in town next week and wants to get together for *old time's sake*. You know, I really did like the guy, but I'm so *over* him, but he's pretty insistent." Amy shakes her head in dismay.

"You don't suppose he wants to pick up where you two left off, do you?" Tess gives her a skeptical glance.

Amy lets out a guffaw. "That's too bad for him! After becoming Apara, I'm just not into Charlie! *Not* even as a *snack*!" She jokes with a wicked grin.

"So, are you gonna see him or not?" Tess asks.

"Haven't decided yet. I want to show you something." Amy grabs her tablet and pulls up the email. Read his email and tell me what *you think*." She hands it to Tess and waits expectantly.

After reading it, Tess's expression is troubled. "He's sure curious about Inspiration, Inc, isn't he?"

"Yep, and specifically about Liz and Marc." Amy says.

"I noticed that. Maybe he's hoping you'll get him a job here?" Tess suggests.

"*Doubt* it. Charlie's a nice guy and all, but not exactly a techie or an intellectual type. He'd never want to work in an office like this. He gets restless if he can't burn off some energy. Even the School Resource Officer position got to him because there wasn't enough *action*!" Amy elucidates.

"Maybe he's hoping you'll leave here and go off with him somewhere? I mean, maybe he misses you and hopes you'll follow him back to Israel or something?" Tess suggests.

"I doubt that! If he missed me so much, how come I've only gotten a handful of emails since he left, and it went a couple of months before I got that first one and now, suddenly, he's coming home on leave. I'm not sure what's up, but I...well, I'm not getting a good feeling about it, if ya know what I mean, girl?" Amy gives her a knowing glance.

"Are you thinking it's a precog trying to get out?" Tess leans forward in concern.

"I don't *know*. It leaves me with a general sense of unease. I'm think'n I should give Liz a heads up. Maybe you should tell Marc that he asked about him, too?" Amy suggests.

"Will do. Have you answered him yet?" Tess wonders.

"No, not yet. I'll do that after I speak to Liz." She tells her.

Tess's stomach lets out a huge growl and the two friends laugh. "How about we go down to the deli like we used to and grab some lunch!" Tess suggests.

"Deal!" Amy grabs her wallet and the two friends head out for lunch.

CONFIRMATION

Charlie waits anxiously for a reply from Amy, but knows that it may take a while. Not only have they not kept in touch, but he left rather abruptly without talking to her about it first, so she was rather pissed off when he left. Even if she'll answer him, there are several hours' time difference, and at the time he wrote the email, she was probably asleep.

Still, he checks his email frequently, and when the reply comes, he reads it carefully. Amy agrees to meet with him at a brewery in South Slope he isn't familiar with. She confirms that she still works for Inspiration, Inc, and that her bosses, Liz and Marc, are still there, but that she's no longer working directly under Marc. She tells him she got a promotion, and even has her own office now, though she does not say what her new position is. Charlie reads the reply three times to make sure he's read not only the words, but between the lines. Then he prints a copy and heads out of his quarters and down to Uri the spook's office, knocking hesitantly.

Uri comes to the door with an eyebrow raised. "What can I do for you, Sgt. Abrams?" He asks, curious why he's knocking on his office door without getting permission by email first.

"Sorry to bother you, sir, but my ex replied." He explains and hands Uri the print out.

Uri gruffly motions for him to have a seat in his very utilitarian office, in an uncomfortable metal chair. He reads through the email and eyes Charlie pensively. "You're going to meet up with her then? Do you think you'll be able to get any information on her bosses? Especially their phone numbers so we can confirm if they match those in our *guest's* device?" He says sarcastically.

"I'll do my best, sir. If I know Amy, she's probably still using one of three passcodes on her phone. Hopefully, she'll leave it alone with me at some point, then I can get into it with the cloner, and get her contact list." Charlie explains.

Uri looks contemplative, then asks, "Abrams, are you sure your ex is *human*?"

Charlie looks taken aback and almost insulted. "Sir, I'm sure! We were together for quite a while, Sir. I think I'd have noticed something was off!"

"None the less, if there's any way to get a DNA sample from her; a hair, or a glass she drinks from, secure it and get us a sample. Our guest's DNA breaks down rapidly, so I'll have Zelkind provide you with a special storage container that will preserve DNA." He says.

"If I may, sir, have you had any luck with your project?" Charlie asks cautiously.

"*Very* little. We've now tested a controlled blood exchange with over 125 subjects. Only one has gone through the transformation. We need to figure out why it only worked on that one person. What makes him so *special*? If we're going to face these beings, we need some of their kind on our side or I suspect they could slaughter us like flies." Uri explains offhandedly.

"*Sir*, are you sure that's *wise*? I mean, what if you can't control those you transform?" Charlie inquires.

"We've made certain that all our subjects are thoroughly prepped and *obedient* before testing. Their loyalty *shouldn't* be an issue. I understand you've inquired about taking part?" Uri asks.

"Yes, sir. I thought it might be wise in case I have to infiltrate them."

"When we know more, Abrams. You're valuable as you are right now." Uri tells him cryptically.

"Sir, *if*, by some chance, my ex is one of them, how will I know?" Charlie inquires, wondering if Amy's promotion might have been more than a new job position.

"We're working on a device that scans for a certain energy frequency both our prisoner and our one successful transformee give off. We'll fit your cell phone with the sensor before you leave. If you're...Amy, wasn't it?" Charlie nods "is one of them, the sensor should go off when you're near her." He confirms.

"If she *is* one, should I capture her and *bring* her back?" Charlie asks, wondering if there might be any way Uri's team may be able to cure her.

"*No! Absolutely* not! We must not let on that you have *any* suspicions about any of this! This is an information reconnaissance mission only! Besides, *if* she is one of them, and she figures out you know, not only could she tip off the others, but she could probably rip you to shreds!" Uri reminds him.

Charlie narrows his eyes and lets out a long 'Hm' sound.

"What is it?" Uri reacts to Charlie's utterance.

"You've got me wondering about Amy now. She's a small woman. Five foot one, and yet, when I took her martial arts training, she threw me with little effort! I'm wondering if maybe she is one of them and has been all along!" Charlie ponders.

"Perhaps, but I've seen some of our own female soldiers do that myself. Don't get paranoid, but pay attention." Uri tells him.

"I will, sir. Question, sir. What's the plan if we do confirm that this Lissa Pederson and Marc Girard are the two in our prisoner's contacts?" Charlie inquires, curious about the endgame, considering these beings are quite strong and have unusual abilities, including teleportation.

"Don't try anything on your own, Abrams! We're working on ways to capture and contain them like our guest; we'll need to interrogate them, and if warranted, find some way to punish them for the destruction of Jerusalem."

"Sir, they're *blood-sucking vampires*! That, on its own, should warrant capturing, if not *eliminating* them! They *prey* on humanity. God knows how many people they've *killed* for blood over the years!" Charlie rambles out, sounding more paranoid.

"*Abrams*, until we know more, we're just *observing*. We don't even know how many of them there are or where they are in the world! Are they a small, local cell of these creatures, or are they found everywhere, living among us? If there are many, and we take out one nest, what will the others do? *Perhaps*, if we can find a *weakness* in their biology, we can find a way to eliminate *all* of them." Uri says, but thinks: *Though they certainly would make useful soldiers if we could somehow control them!*

"I see, Sir. I'll do my best to play it cool when I see Amy, just in case." Charlie concedes.

"*Good*! We'll have a briefing before you leave to let you know what we've learned and give you any tools we've developed by then, such as the detector." Uri tells him and then waves Charlie out the door as though he were some frivolous pest.

***

A few days pass and Charlie's called in for a briefing before he travels back to the US. He reports to a briefing room where Uri, Dr. Zelkind, and a soldier he doesn't recognize are waiting. There's a small, metal briefcase sitting on the table.

Dr. Zelkind motions for Charlie to take a seat on the opposite side of the table from them. "Sgt. Abrams, before you leave for North Carolina, there are a few things you should know about these *vampires*. I understand that Uri has told you about the detector we've created?"

"Yes, ma'am. May I ask how it works?" Charlie inquires curiously.

Dr. Zelkind gives his curiosity an approving look. "As a matter of fact, that's what part of this briefing is about. This..." She motions toward the soldier. "Is Elias. He's the one subject that has transformed to what our prisoner is. There are several things you should know. Unlike the mythology, Elias is very much alive. He heals quickly and has grown slightly younger in appearance since he was transformed. He is physically much stronger than the average human male, as well as faster. His fangs retract, so unless they are down, it will be hard to recognize one of them visually. Being alive, they are also not pale, nor does he have any sensitivity to sunlight, and they do cast reflections."

Charlie looks unsettled. "That means they can be just about anyone, doesn't it?"

"Indeed. Which is why we've created this detector. While we've kept our guest subdued, Elias here has been helping us learn more about these beings. He has intuitive access to various abilities which come with the transformation. One of said abilities is telepathy." Dr. Zelkind tells him and watches Charlie shift uneasily as he considers the implications. "We've monitored him and the energies from him, and discovered a frequency common to both him and our prisoner, which we believe is a native telepathic channel. They can communicate with each other telepathically; and yes, they can definitely read human minds."

Charlie notices a bemused grin on Elias's face as he wonders if Elias can really read his mind.

"Charlie, I want you to think of a number between one and one hundred." Zelkind orders.

He does, and Elias plucks it out of his mind like he might a bug out of a glass of water. They repeat this several times, and try it with other things such as colors, animals, and even an innocuous memory of a place Charlie has been, which Elias describes, in detail. This unsettles Charlie, as he is a more "feet-on-the-ground" personality. That someone could read his mind upends his concept of reality. He's come to accept Amy's 'intuitions' as nothing more than her mind processing clues more efficiently than most, but this is the first time he believes someone has true paranormal powers.

"We've created two tools using this discovery. The first is the detector. No humans we've tested emanate this energy frequency, and the sensor should detect any of them within about a ten-foot radius. It's installed on this phone." Dr. Zelkind explains and Uri takes out a normal-looking smartphone from the small metal suitcase and slides it across the table to Charlie. "It's set up with your old telephone number from America.

Should you pass someone giving off that frequency, it will generate a seemingly innocuous text message: 'proximity'. If you are within three feet of one of them, the message will be 'target'." She explains.

Uri chimes in. "You won't need to wait for her to leave her phone alone. There's an app on here which will use Bluetooth to access her phone. Enter the likely pass codes before you meet with her. Activate the app, it will try those first, and if they don't work, it will start going through possible codes systematically. Once it connects, it will clone her contacts, GPS history, emails, and text messages. It will also install a spyware app that will let us remotely access her phone in the future." Uri explains, knowing it would be too risky to wait for her to leave the phone alone with Charlie.

"And the other device?" Charlie inquires.

"The other device is a telepathic dampener. The frequency changes somewhat when Elias here reads a human. We have created the telepathic equivalent of 'noise cancelling' technology that blocks people like him from reading one of us. The last thing we need is one of them reading your mind and finding out you know about them!" She says, looking toward Uri, who takes a kind of large, syringe-looking device out of the suitcase and hands it to her. Dr. Zelkind walks behind Charlie. "Lean your head down."

Charlie does and feels an odd numbness followed by a warm, prickly sensation as the device activates once implanted subcutaneously.

"This generates an inverse frequency to their telepathic reading frequency, nullifying it." Zelkind explains as she sits back down across from Charlie.

Charlie reaches behind his head and feels the small object under his skin. "So, this will protect me from having my mind read? Even by *him*?" Charlie nods at Elias.

"Give it a try. Think of a number as before." Uri tells him with a grin.

Charlie thinks of a number, but Elias can't read it. They try several times, but Elias is completely blocked by the device.

"That's *amazing*! Are you sure it will work with other ones?" Charlie asks.

"*Unfortunately*, we only have him to test it on as the other subject is non-cooperative. Now, get what you need and Elias will be providing your transportation." Uri orders.

"Elias? Is he a *pilot*?" Charlie asks.

Uri let's out an amused chuckle. "Why fly when you can teleport? It's quite safe! We've been testing how far he can teleport, and if he can take people with him. You may feel a bit disoriented, or nauseous at first, but it beats sitting in a plane for at least 16 hours! Plus, there will be no record of your leaving Israel or entering the United States!"

Charlie is uncertain how he feels about this new revelation, but it's not his place to question as a soldier. He returns to his quarters, packs a small bag, and returns to the briefing room. "Ready, Sir." He says.

Uri gives him one more device. "Pin this on to your lapel." He says as he gives him a small, American Flag pin. If you need to photograph any potential targets, push the button on the right side of your phone twice and your pin, a remote camera, will take a picture, and relay it to your phone's memory. A bit less obvious than using your cell phone directly!"

"Got it, Sir." He says and feels uneasy as Elias comes over to him and puts his hand on Charlie's back. The room fades away and his senses are overwhelmed as Elias takes him through the membrane outside our reality. When they 'land' in an alley near a parking deck in downtown Asheville, he nearly vomits.

"You'll get used to it." Elias says in a somewhat thick dialect. He hands Charlie a set of keys. "There's a rental car waiting for you on the top floor, in slot 37. When you're ready, dial #8686 and I'll collect you for the return trip."

"Okay, sounds simple enough. Where am I staying? I lived with Amy before, so it's not like I can stay there." Charlie wonders.

"You've got a reservation at the Glo Hotel in East Asheville. It's set for two nights, so if you need that extended, text Uri at #9999." Elias vanishes before Charlie can ask any more questions.

DINNER WITH THE ENEMY

Amy gets ready to leave work to meet Charlie at a brewery in South Slope. She stops to check in with Liz before leaving.

"Hey, I'm on my way to meet Charlie. I'm probably being overly paranoid. He probably just wants to hang out." Amy says, trying to quell her potentially-precognitive unease.

"Hopefully, that's all it is, but I, too, find it a bit odd that he would ask about Marc and I by name. Didn't you say his earlier email urged you to quit?" Liz asks, motioning for Amy to come in and have a seat.

"Yep, and I'm really not sure what's up with him. I don't think he'd ever do anything to hurt anyone outside of combat, but something is nagging at me horribly." Amy elucidates.

"Follow your intuition; it's served you well in the past. I understand Dave is going to be your backup?" She inquires.

"Yes, but I think part of it is he's a bit worried Charlie might make a move on me!" She laughs. "He's been getting kinda protective lately!"

"Well, he won't be alone. I suggested that brewery for a reason. An Apara friend of Ty's works there as a bartender. His name is Vince. Tell Dave to introduce himself and stay at the bar as backup. Vince will make sure you two get a table nearby." Liz instructs.

Amy breathes a little easier knowing that Liz is taking her intuition seriously. "I'll let you know how things go tonight."

Amy heads out to her car. She's been porting in lately, but since she's meeting Charlie in South Slope, she drove to work today.

She arrives a few minutes early and enters the bar. Dave's already sitting there drinking some wine while Vince does the stereotypical cleaning of glasses as he watches the room. The bar isn't that busy as it's a weeknight, and there's some big rodeo at the Fairgrounds tonight that has a lot of the regulars occupied. She paths to Dave. *Wish me luck!*

You've got this, Ames! But I'm here if you need me, as is Vince. He paths.

Amy sits at a table about fifteen feet from the bar and waits. Vince brings her a glass of her favorite craft brew, thanks to a telepathic tip from Dave.

Thanks, wish this would help relax my anxiety. She paths to the bartender, a slender man with sandy blond hair, a matching beard, and stark blue eyes. She perceives what she would describe as a reassuring, mental smile as Vince goes back to his bar and strikes up a random conversation with Dave.

Amy assumes she'll sense when Charlie arrives. After all, they were together for a good while, and even though she was human then, she can easily picture his mental signature. However, she's caught off-guard when she hears a message tone right behind her, and turns around to see Charlie grinning awkwardly, but something is off, like his smile is forced.

"*Charlie!*" She stands and gives him a hug, but feels him flinch as she puts her head against his shoulder. She tries to read him and get an idea of what's wrong, but she can't get anything, at least not thoughts. There are a few anxious, emotional overtones, but no thoughts. She thinks, *That's odd. Hopefully, it's just a mental block on my part, because it would be very odd if he's blocking me telepathically.*

She pulls back and looks him straight in the eye. "Join me! Tell me what's new with you!" She feigns good-willed interest, as she should when meeting with an old friend, but her intuition tells her something's off.

"Thought I could sneak up on you, but my phone had other ideas!" He jokes as he sits in the adjacent chair. Charlie motions to the bartender, as there doesn't seem to be a waitress around, and Vince comes over, smiling gregariously. As he approaches, Charlie gets another text. He glances down, and the preview says 'target', the same as it did when he approached Amy. He thinks, *Shit! Two of them? Amy and the Bartender? What the hell?*

"What can I get you, sir?" Vince asks politely.

Charlie stumbles mentally as he copes with this development. "Whatever the house's favorite craft brew is, thanks." He says and stares at the bartender as he walks back to the bar. Again, the text beeps when the bartender approaches again, so Charlie puts his phone on vibrate only.

"Here you go, sir. This is one of our newest brews. Hope you enjoy it." Vince says and goes behind the bar again.

"So, you must have been awfully busy! Big gap between emails and suddenly, you're back in town?" Amy asks, gauging his reactions.

"Things have been crazy over there. I'm on debris clearing duty and I'm usually so dead by the end of the day, I don't feel like doing much other than crawling into bed." He says, though his thoughts drift to Janna joining him there, the emotional overtones come across to Amy, and she knows he's got someone in his life.

"So, *meet* anyone over there? Or aren't there many women working on the reclamation project?" She asks, hoping to confirm what she sensed.

He looks a bit sheepish, but admits, "Yeah, there's one gal, Janna. We've been working closely on the project for a while, and well..." he trails off.

Amy smiles subtly, thankful he's likely not interested in resuming things with her if he's got someone else in his life. "Yeah, me too. A guy I work with named Dave. He's not too thrilled about me meeting you tonight, but I told him it's *just* a visit and we needed to kind of tie up some loose ends after you left so suddenly." She gives him a lopsided grin and takes a pull on her beer.

"So, tell me about this *big* promotion you got! You're certainly looking good! Really healthy! Hell, you almost look younger! So must be good for you there?" He inquires.

"Yeah, I finally feel like I'm in a job where I belong. The company has projects besides web work. Things have been kinda crazy, thanks to an ex-coworker who's been causing trouble, so I'm in charge of a security team connected with that crap. So, I'm still doing my thing with the martial arts!" She forces a smile.

"Still knock'n guys on their asses?" He asks.

"That too! But I enjoy what I do, it feels like I belong there, and can maybe even make a difference!" She admits, cryptically, but truthfully.

Charlie looks down; a symbol lights up on his smart phone indicating it's connected to hers and is doing its job. He makes a small, unconscious sigh of relief, as that is a large part of his mission, getting access to her phone for its contacts and other data. "Well, that's good. I wasn't sure that place was for you; It's hard picturing you settling for a desk job after the military." He rambles.

"We do good work there. At first, it was creating websites for charities, and I still do some of that when not working with my team. We're also building up an advertising, print, and publishing department, specifically to provide services to those same charities at discount rates. Kari and Tess are working on developing a job placement service, as well." She explains, relaxing as she falls into a rhythm in their conversation that feels more comfortable and familiar.

"Your bosses treat you well? The gal from Scandinavia and what's his name...Marc?" He asks, pretending he doesn't really know their names.

"Yeah, Liz is cool. And my best friend at work hooked up with Marc, so if he gives me any flack, she'll give him an earful!" She jokes.

Charlie wonders if Amy's friend is also one of them if she 'hooked up' with Marc Girard, or if he might be keeping her as a handy snack. The idea infuriates him that someone might use a woman that way. As he's chatting with Amy, someone walks past him and his phone vibrates with a text saying 'proximity'. He looks up and the bartender is too far away for it to have been him. It's registered Amy as stationary, so wouldn't go off again for her. He thinks, *That makes three! How many of these bloodsuckers are there in Asheville? Always knew it was a weird town, but having a population of vampires?*

126

Dave walks back past him, trying to read his mind, as Amy had relayed that she couldn't, and the sensor goes off again, allowing Charlie to realize that both the man at the bar and the bartender are both like Amy, bloodsuckers. His heart aches at the thought that she, too, might have to be 'put down' eventually, if there isn't any cure for her condition.

"You sure keep looking at your phone a lot. Is everything *okay*?" She asks, suspicious of his frequent glances.

"Oh, yeah, just a friend who wants me to meet up with them while I'm in the country; a friend in Charlotte. No one you know!" He smiles nervously. "Let me answer him and tell him I'll call him later." He tells her and opens his phone, pretending to reply, but pushes the pound sign twice while facing in the direction of the bar. He does this a few times to try to get a better look at the bar patron's face. The man glances briefly at him, and he manages to get a shot of his face. "There!" He tells her, and turns the phone face down so he can ignore any future warnings. He was already feeling very anxious knowing there are three *vampires* around him. He thinks, *Maybe this is where they come to find dinner? I can't imagine Amy would have brought them with her. She couldn't know what I'm up to!*

He shifts the subject to talk about old friends, the fun times they had, but eventually, he yawns, and says: "It's been a blast seeing you! But I'm still a bit jet lagged. I think I need to get back to my hotel room and crash."

"Charlie, you never did say why you came home for a few days?" Amy inquires, wondering what excuse he'll give her.

"*Oh!* My sister just had another kid! Had to come home and spoil the little guy rotten!" He says, anxiously, and somehow, even though Amy can't read his thoughts, she knows he's improvising as his anxiety level spikes.

"Oh, *okay*. Say hi from me. Do you need a ride back to the hotel?" She asks, and senses Dave tense up at the thought of her alone with Charlie in the car.

Charlies stands. "Nah, I've got a rental. How about another hug?" He suggests. She stands and he gives her a bear hug, intentionally catching his high school ring in her hair, pulling out a few strands with roots. "Oh! Sorry about that!" He tells her, while stuffing the strands into a pocket. He reaches down, picks up their glasses, and takes them up to the bar, carefully wiping off any residual DNA from her saliva onto a special cloth he'd gotten from his bosses. It will absorb and preserve any DNA until he can get it to them. He pays the bill for both of them and heads out.

Once Charlie's out of the bar, Dave and Vince join her at the table. "Are you alright, Ames?" Dave asks trying to keep down his temper as he feels like going after the guy for causing Amy pain, even inadvertently.

"Yeah, *yeah*! He just caught his ring in my hair! Not the first time that's happened! So, you're *impressions*?" She looks from Dave to Vince.

"He's hiding something. I couldn't read him at all, and it was weird, when I tried, it was like sticking a hand in mud, if that makes sense." Dave tells her.

"Yeah, I agree. It felt like something was stopping me from reaching his mind, like my attempts were being eroded somehow." She admits.

"Amy, is he a potential?" Vince asks.

"*Hell* no!" Amy replies abruptly.

"Then I doubt he should be able to shield his mind naturally. Either he's had some experience or training in mind resistance, like how to resist torture, or something on him was preventing us from reading him." Vince ponders.

"What? Some kind of psychic blocker or something?" She asks.

"It's a thought. Probably wrong, but keep it in mind." He suggests and stands as a small party of patrons wander in wearing rodeo gear for post-rodeo festivities.

"We should update Liz." Dave tells her and gives her a hand up.

"We shouldn't leave together in case he's watching." Amy suggests. "Meet me there?"

"Gotcha!"

Amy leaves, and Dave heads for the restroom, porting out from a stall. Vince is busy with patrons, but sends a rapid path to Liz that something was definitely 'squirrelly' about Amy's ex, that the others will meet her at the office shortly, and he will catch up with her the next day as he has to stay on until closing.

Liz, Amy, and Dave all arrive at the office and sit in Liz's meeting area.

Liz crosses her legs and anxiously bounces the top one. "Well, is there anything to be concerned about?"

Dave makes a move to interject, but Amy stops him with a look, and then turns back to Liz. "Something was off. He asked about you and Marc again. Liz, I couldn't read his mind; *none* of us could!"

Liz sits quietly for a minute, and her bouncing foot stills as she gets a look of consternation. "Considering he's not a potential, that is rather disturbing. You couldn't get anything from him?"

"Some emotional overtones, including anxiety, nervousness, or maybe fear?" Amy tries to put the amorphous emotions she'd gleaned from him into words.

Dave chimes in. "I couldn't get anything from him, not even emotions."

"I'm not surprised. Amy had an actual relationship with him, so would naturally be more in touch with him psychologically. Did he do anything concrete to make you concerned?" Liz inquires.

"No, I have to admit it was mostly just two old friends meeting for old time's sake, but he seemed *off*." Amy admits.

Liz sits there, thinking, her foot bobbing up and down again, then replies. "For now, stay aware and keep me in the loop if he contacts you again. Get me any general information on Charlie you can and I'll get some of our research guys to see if they can track his recent movements, contacts and so on."

Amy nods and says, "Alright, you're the boss! I'll let you know as soon as I hear from him again."

Vince reiterates the same impression that, while things seemed relatively normal visually, that Charlie's energy was off, like he was hiding something.

***

A few miles away, Charlie unlocks his hotel room door, coming down from the adrenaline high of his mission with shades of dismay and guilt about Amy being one of the 'monsters'. He thinks, *It's my fault! If I hadn't gone over to Israel, she'd probably still be human! I'd have known something was up and somehow prevented her from becoming one of them.*

He wants to go to sleep, but knows he has one last task to do before he can. He reaches into his bag and pulls out a laptop and his cell phone from his pocket. He holds it up to his face so the phone wakes to his retina ID. Once he's in, he pushes an icon that looks like two hands about to shake and then moves over to his laptop, finding the same icon. The phone and the computer sync, and a secure, satellite connection to the computer is made. The purloined data from Amy's phone is transferred to a secure cloud hosted on a top-secret server at the base in Israel.

His work done, he showers and tries to sleep, but keeps waking from nightmares of nights with Amy biting him and draining his blood. Since he can't sleep well, he checks out early, and drives the rental back to the parking deck. He pushes the code Elias gave him, and a few minutes later, he appears.

"Ready to head back? They got your data and are already going over it." Elias says. "I'll pop back and return the rental." He extends a hand to Charlie, who cautiously takes it. Even though he knows Elias is on their side, he still feels awkward being so close to someone who could, in theory, rip is throat out. Especially after his dreams about Amy. The two men vanish and reappear in the subterranean base, where Uri and Dr Zelkind spend a couple of hours debriefing him.

PUZZLE PIECES

A few days later, Peder pops his head into Liz's office. "Do you have a few?"

"Of course, Peder! For you, always!" Liz grins, but her smile fades quickly as he doesn't smile back. "What's up?" Her tone shifts to something more serious.

"You know how I've been monitoring missing persons reports?" Peder sits, still getting weak faster than usual.

"Yes, have you found any unusual ones? Perhaps someone that fits Jason's usual profile?" Liz asks, sitting up a bit straighter.

"*Unusual*, yes, but I doubt it has anything to do with Jason." Peder debates how to explain his findings and why they're throwing up an intuitive red flag.

"Okay, *what* then?" Liz taps her pencil on her desk anxiously, feeling anxiety rolling off Peder.

"I had our system run an automated search on any female missing persons and match them to any known potentials. I got a hit on one of them, but she's definitely not Jason's type. However, she works at a military base in a mountain city." Peder explains.

"*Oh*? Go *on*....", Liz says, taking her tablet out to make notes.

"Did you hear the news about a woman who worked at Fort Detrick in Maryland who went missing?" Peder asks.

Liz focuses and then asks, "Do you mean the scientist who disappeared along with a bunch of her equipment? Weren't they thinking she was involved with bio-terrorism?"

"Yes, her. She's not Jason's type at all, she's nearly 50, and a mother. She worked with bioengineering on a cancer project up at Detrick, but if you remember, they have a history of bio-weapons research. They're looking at her in that light. The thing is, she threw a flag in our system. She is, or at least was, a potential, but was married and had children in her prime transformation years, so wasn't considered. She was pretty gifted and quite brilliant." Peder watches for signs Liz grasps his concern.

"*And?*" Liz asks expectantly.

"She was a *promising* potential, which I wouldn't expect, with all the pre-conditioning in ethics, to lead someone like her to become a bio-terrorist. It feels *wrong*! Katie told me the Atlanta precogs are foreseeing an outbreak of some kind." Peder stops when he notices Liz has one of those expressions meaning she hopes Peder is wrong, but is probably right.

"Oh, Peder! Why am I afraid you're onto something? Touch base with Katie, Niall, Marc and Tess to see if they get any impressions of a connection. I'll put a general alert out for her. You're right, she wouldn't be Jason's type, but she could be connected with what Tess has been seeing in her Astral outings, or what the Atlanta area precogs are anxious about. Do you know if there have been any other precogs about illnesses?" Liz looks worried and drafts a quick alert on her tablet to go out to all centers.

"As a matter of fact, one of our contacts working at the CDC has been getting calls from other Apara, saying something bad is coming, but it won't be as widespread or deadly as COVID, but still a health crisis."

"Get your ball rolling and I'll get mine. I think we need to up our alert to all the precogs to have them report any impressions to a centralized database. Get Marc on that one. He coordinated it pre-Jerusalem." Liz sends Peder out. She works on an alert to send out to centers worldwide to report on anything related to potential illnesses or bio-terrorism.

A GLIMPSE OF CHAOS

Val and Ty have finished updating the database server connections in LA, and return to their home in the Sanctuary equivalent of the Italian Alps. "God, Ty! I'm looking forward to a break from so many people! LA can be fun, but when you have that many people in one city, I honestly don't know how any Apara can stand that much telepathic chatter-static!" She says after they port into his sunken living room. "I'm going to take a long, hot bath and enjoy the quietness of Sanctuary!"

He laughs. "You get used to it after a while. You'll learn to tune it all out with practice!"

"Yeah, well, I'm not sure I can afford to tune it all out! If I'd tuned you out when I bumped into you at the bookstore, I'd never have seen you coming!" She smirks, and he wraps his arms around her and gives her a kiss. I'm looking forward to a few days' rest, love, just you and me!"

"Hm, me too! Though I wouldn't mind a quick trip out to the Social, in Asheville, for Open Mic night this Sunday?" She looks at him pleadingly.

He laughs. "I'm sure we can make time for that! It's been a while, hasn't it?"

She nods, then says, "It's also been a while since we've had time for each other!" She gives him a look that tells him exactly what's on her mind.

"Go take your bath! I *predict* we'll have that time very soon." He jokes, as she's the one who's always seeing the future.

Val heads down the hallway toward the master bathroom by the bedroom. She runs a hot bath and fills it with fragrant bath salts. She puts on some relaxing music, undresses, sinks into the hot water, and lets her muscles unknot. She almost falls asleep, when she sits bolt upright as she sees flashes of images too fast to process.

Ty feels her reaction, ports to the bedroom, and puts her sketchpad and drawing supplies on a desk near the bed. He opens the bathroom door without knocking, as Val won't hear him anyway, mid-vision. Since she transformed, she doesn't have the extreme pain she'd had with her visions as a human, but she often gets information overload. She doesn't see or hear anything around her when the visions hit, and the images often flow too rapidly for her to process them until she can sketch them. Ty waits until she snaps out of her REM-state and helps her out of the tub. He quickly wraps an oversized towel around her, rushes her to the desk before the details of her visions can fade, and she gives him a grateful glance. The visions also short-circuit her speech center, so she has no choice but to sketch it out, as she often has difficulty stringing sentences together right after a vision attack. He guides her to the desk in the bedroom, where her drawing supplies await. She nods to him, but doesn't smile.

She winces slightly, as a small burst of pain hits her, then begins to sketch. As always, she sketches from left to right, and fills in the focal point with color. She draws three images. When she snaps out of autopilot, she looks them over. The first one shows a red-haired man and a black-haired woman in a club somewhere. There's a group of four young women standing together who are also in color: a blonde, two with brown or black hair, the latter possibly Asian; and one African American with long twist braids.

Sarah recently made some upgrades to her centauri-opal bracelet, and now, even though she can't speak during or right after her vision, her voice usually comes back once she's put them down on paper. Her voice is still a bit gravelly, but she says, "Uh oh!" as she sees that familiar figure with red hair. "I think I know who these are about!"

"Liz did send out that general alert and Marc sent out the precog alert! I guess it was only a matter of time before your brain kicked in and did its thing!" Ty says, gently rubbing her back to help with the post-vision muscle tension. "What about the other ones?"

The next one is similar, but Jason, and whoever the other woman is, appear to be at odds. Jason gives her a threatening sneer on, while the woman looks upset, and points toward the group. This time, only the blonde woman is in color.

"What do you think it means?" Ty asks.

"I think it means *that's* his victim." She says, pointing to the young, blonde woman." Val feels sadness welling up from within. "I've definitely got a bad feeling with this one!"

"And who's the woman with Jason? And what's going on there?" Ty asks Val questions to help her interpret her visions and sketches. They often work as a team, both on computer security and on her visions.

"No idea." Val says, hesitantly turning the page to the final *vetch* and gasps. The two women are sprawled on the ground in an alley. The black-haired woman has a wound in her chest. The blonde is lying on the ground with bite marks in her neck, and Jason is falling backwards, an intense, red wound in his chest. "Oh *God*! I don't think this is going to end well!" Val slumps down in her chair from exhaustion.

"Val, stay with me now! We need to look at these for clues to time or place, and we need to get Marc and Liz in on this as soon as possible!" He says, encouraging her to keep going a little longer.

Val sighs and starts from the beginning. The two of them scrutinize the images of the club, looking for clues as to when or where the vision takes place. Val examines the pictures or posters on the club walls. There's one that looks like a stylized peach tree. She sees one with Olympic rings and a tower that looks like a giant torch. A third poster shows a building, a shark, and a blue, stylized G with a fish tail on it. A band is playing on a stage I the background, and there are Christmas decorations up. There's one more poster, and she has to look carefully, but it says "TONIGHT!" and has the name of a very popular k-pop artist and his band.

Val gets excited. "That's *it*! That's *them* in the background! We need to find out where and when they'll be playing! Let's see, Olympics, Aquarium, and a peach tree? It's *got* to be Atlanta! I went down there once for a sci-fi convention! I attended the young adult lit track for my book store's chain! Half the city streets are named peach tree this or that, and if I remember correctly..." She picks up her cell phone she'd left in her room before bathing, and looks up the Georgia Aquarium, and the G logo is a match. She looks up at Ty and grins. "We've *got* him!" She exclaims, and then frowns, "*but* I'm afraid we may have collateral damage to deal with." She pulls up the third sketch and points to the two women on the ground.

"Get dressed. I'll get Liz and Marc over here so we can coordinate. You *did great,* love!" Ty rubs her shoulders to relieve the tension, leans over, kisses her on the head, then vanishes, leaving Val to get ready for company.

STRATEGY

Ty waits in the living room for Liz and Marc to port in, while Val consolidates her information and impressions into a coherent presentation. Liz ports in first, followed by Marc and Tess. Val hastens down the hallway, and into the sunken living room with her sketchbook in hand.

Liz watches Val come into the room. "I hear you've got *something*?" They all sit around a coffee table, and Val sits on the arm of Ty's sturdy arm chair.

"Yep, I did. We're pretty sure we have it narrowed down to a place and a date and within a short time period!" Val looks at Liz and opens her now infamous sketchbook to the first drawing. We've analyzed the posters and pictures on the wall, and it's Atlanta. This shows who's performing, and it's late November or December from all the Christmas stuff. When we googled the band's tour schedule, they'll be performing at the Peach Tree Pagoda, a club and concert venue in downtown Atlanta on the evening of December 12th. They're supposed to start playing at 7 pm, so we know this is happening between then, and maybe 10-11 pm."

Marc leans over and looks on with amazement at the details in Val's sketch. "That's a *truly* impressive gift you've got Val! What are the other sketches?"

"Unfortunately, it looks like there may be casualties. Kind of depends on whether we can alter it." Val glances over to Ty and he rubs the small of her back to reassure her.

Marc looks at the next two pictures as Tess peeks over his shoulder. He passes the sketchbook to Liz. "It looks like we may have two casualties besides Jason."

"I can't tell if they're just injured or dead. I'd say the young blonde is his target. I think Jason and the dark-haired woman are together, though my impression is she's not there willingly." Val takes the sketchbook back and looks at the second image. "Something's missing." She whispers hoarsely, getting a twinge of pain. "Ty?" She says, her intonation rising.

Ty knows what she wants and ports out and back with her pencil box. Val spaces out and draws a small area on her second picture that looks like two young women in a fog, and the fog trails from the black-haired woman. "That's weird..." She gasps out as she looks at her addition.

Ty pulls her closer to him. "What do you think it means?"

Val looks at the two girls and the rest of the image. She draws something, then erases one of the woman's arms and redraws it in a protective gesture in front of the two new women. "I think she's protecting them." She focuses, closing her eyes like she can almost watch a playback of the scene. "They're arguing. I think Jason told this woman to choose one of the four there, or he'd take the two she's protecting? I'm not sure. This vision feels different. It's like I've got more information than what I sketched. That could be why I can actually speak...it's not a new vision, but information coming to the surface from earlier."

Tess looks the picture over. "Could he have picked up a new protégé?"

"We've got the system locked down, so not unless it's someone he had info on from before, but she could be a human victim he's keeping around as a convenient feeder?" Liz looks perplexed. "I supposed he could have gotten lucky and found someone by chance, though that's a stretch. Tess, are all the LM potentials in Atlanta accounted for?"

"I spoke to Michelle in Atlanta, and all were as of earlier today!" Tess focuses on the woman in the sketch, then says, "She must be a strong woman though, if she's standing up to that bastard!"

Liz turns back to Val. "Maybe you'll get some more visions before December 12th? In the meantime, we'll plan to have people at the venue. We can't have people he knows, which rules out all of us. Tess, can you ask Amy if any of her team that wasn't in on the raid in Hot Springs can go down to Atlanta, then?"

Tess grins. "Yeah! I'm sure she's got some she can send! Her guys have been setting up teams in other cities. We can bring some of them in!" Tess suggests.

"We'll have to plant them at the venue earlier in the day. If they're already there and using Sara's masking agent, we may catch him off guard. We don't want anyone porting in, even in the area, or he might sense them." Liz speaks to Val, "You're certain on the date, location, and approximate time?"

"One hundred percent!" She nods emphatically, and then yawns. She leans against Ty and he hugs her close, then releases her. She stands and goes into the kitchen, coming out with a bag of blood, sipping from a corner she'd cut open. She yawns again. "Sorry, if I don't feed and get some sleep, I'll crash!" She ports out.

"Those visions really take it out of her, don't they?" Liz asks Ty.

"Yeah. She was already tired after our trip in LA, and was looking forward to relaxing when they hit. Give her a couple of days and maybe she can give it another try." Ty reassures Liz.

"We have a location and a time window. We can start with that and get planning. Scan those and send me copies. And all the details about when, where, and so on?" Liz stands, looking tired as well.

"Will do, Liz. Keep us updated, please. Val's not in the pictures, so I don't expect us to be there, but she'll want to be kept in the loop; it may stimulate more visions, and more details." Ty yawns, and Liz senses he wants to be with his partner and gets some much-needed rest. Everyone ports out except for Ty, who walks off down the hallway, and joins Val for the night.

IN THE WILD

Dee isolates herself in the bunk room as much as possible; anything to avoid her captor. Her depression has deepened as she realizes that she and her daughters' peril has no end in sight. She worries about what she's created. *I have to find a way to stop, or at least delay him! That virus needs more testing before he tests it in the wild! For all I know, I've created the virus from the Walking Dead!* She thinks, sighing. She goes through what she might say to convince him to delay testing the virus on a real person over and over in her head.

She hopes she can find some way to stop him altogether, or perhaps the virus won't work at all; but she also *dreads* that option, as she knows he'll likely follow through with his threats with at least one of her daughters. If he were to follow through with both of them, he'd lose his leverage. She thinks, *He'll probably make me choose between them!* She crawls into the rickety old bunk bed and sleeps. She sleeps a lot in the next few days, though has nightmares of Jason and her daughters. He ignores her other than tossing her occasional pouches of blood and real food, but otherwise, leaves her alone.

Dee's asleep and dreaming of her daughters when she's startled awake by loud banging on the bunkroom door. "*Get up! It's time!*" Jason shouts through the door.

She puts her pillow over her head, ignoring him, but he continues to bang loudly until she gets up and comes to the door. "*What?!*" She snipes at him.

He shoves a bag in her hands. "Get *dressed!* It's time to see if your tinkering worked."

She peeks in the bag and sees something more like what her daughters might wear out with friends on a Saturday night. "*Really*? Not exactly my *style*...."

"Too *fucking* bad! We're going to a club tonight. It's time I find something new to..." He grins lustily. "*play* with! *Hell*! It's been so long, even *you're* starting to look *tempting*!"

Dee swallows, remembering her thought about her appearance getting younger, and closes the door. She leans against it, as though she can keep him out, thoughts of that man using her for sex make fear, disgust, and anger rise in the core of her soul.

Again, she feels an odd, spark-like pain where her bracelet lies, and rubs her wrist. She looks and notes that the stone has fine fractures in it, like crazed China.

She changes into the skimpy clothes even though she thinks she's way too old for them. However, when she looks at herself in an old, full-length mirror, she notices that even more of the silver in her hair has gone away, her weight has clearly redistributed to a more youthful shape, and she cringes at the thought that her captor might notice. *Damn! If I go out in this thing, he's bound to realize I don't look 48 any longer!* She sighs. *Then again, if I have to sacrifice myself to save others, maybe that's what I'll have to do?* The thought of him touching her makes her shiver, not with desire or longing, but with revulsion.

She grabs a dusty old coat from a closet, more like a hunting jacket, and puts it on over the revealing outfit, peaks through a crack in the door to see if he's there, and makes a dash for the bathroom when she's sure he isn't. She washes up, brushes her hair, and reluctantly sits on the sofa in the main room waiting for him.

Jason comes back in, covered in snowflakes as it's snowing on the mountain, but he must periodically clean the solar panels. She stands as he comes in the door and barks at her, "That coat looks *ridiculous*. *Lose* it! It's bad enough I have to take you to a club, I'm not gonna be seen with you in *that*!"

"But it's *cold* outside!" Dee holds the coat closed against her.

"It's not like you're going to catch a cold or *die* of exposure!" He yanks it off her, then stares at her, quipping, "Hm. I've definitely been *without* too long! Let's go!"

Dee shudders, but says, "Maybe we should wait! We really should do more testing before using this virus in the wild. We just don't know what could go wrong."

"We're in the wild now! We're going to the city, to Atlanta." He says, clearly not grasping her reference.

"No, 'in the wild' refers to using or releasing a pathogen or substance in the real world as opposed to a controlled, lab situation! I *told* you; I have no idea how those *mystery sequences* might be affected! We could be starting a zombie apocalypse!" She rants.

"Well, *that would* be interesting, at least! Now *come* on!" He raises his voice and indicates she should come over to him.

Resigned, she joins him, and he grabs her arm. They port to an alley near a club, The Peach Tree Pagoda, a club that specializes in Asian musical artists. Tonight, one of the more recently popular K-pop boy bands is playing, so the venue is packed with many young, female fans. Even though the venue specializes in acts from all over Asia, the audience is surprisingly diverse since K-pop has gone nearly as mainstream as country music in Atlanta. The music and flashing lights overwhelm Dee's heightened senses, and she becomes disoriented.

"*Damp* down your senses." He tells her.

"And *just how the Hell* do I do that?" She shouts over the music.

"You don't need to shout for *me* to hear you! As to how, try *focusing* for once! Focus, and imagine turning down the 'volume' on the sound, color, brightness, and so on." He explains as though she's a simpleton and not a PhD scientist.

She closes her eyes, takes a few deep breaths, imagines the sound and other stimuli becoming less intense, until her ears stop throbbing, and she feels like she can open her eyes without verging on a seizure. When she does, he shoves a drink in her hand.

"Take it! The alcohol won't have any effect on you, but if you don't have a drink, you'll look out of place; not that you don't at your *age*! I'm going to look around and find something I *like*!" He grins. Dee feels sorry for whoever he chooses and guilty for making it possible. She withdraws to the edge of the room, near a poster of a stylized peach tree with a pagoda at its base, watches the room, wishes she could just disappear, port out as he does, and escape.

Another 'spark' arcs between her skin and the bracelet. Dee looks at it again as her skin stings. A crack now runs *through* the stone, not just surface crazing. She glances at the people in the room and is nearly overwhelmed by random emotions inundating her mind. Looking from person to person, her empathic impressions change. She focuses on a girl on the dance floor gyrating and bouncing to the music, and gets a manic, buzzed feeling from her.

Then she glances at a guy sitting alone on a bench against the wall and feels despondent. She watches the bartender, knows he has a headache, and wants to be anywhere but there. *Whoa! What the hell? This is new! Could I really be feeling what they're feeling?* Dee wonders.

She searches the room for her captor. Jason never told her his name to keep her feeling isolated and disconnected. She spots him, tries the same thing, and gets an overwhelming impression of a black pit of emotions swirling within him. There's an impression of a hunger that can never be filled, but it isn't for blood. Dee forces herself to look away, and shakes her head, trying to shake it off. Mentally, it feels like she walked into an emotional spider web and wants to scrape it off.

She gets an odd tingling on her scalp and looks back at the bar again, but there's a different bartender. She works her way through the people between herself and the bar and sits to catch her breath. The new bartender catches Dee's eye. He's wearing a name tag that says Vince. He looks back at her with an odd expression, but comes over and asks, "What're you having?"

"I'm fine with what I've got. I'm waiting on someone to come back from the dance floor." Dee says, but thinks, *I wouldn't mind if he never did, but I don't think I will be so lucky!*

"All right, but if you *change* your mind, my name's Vince!" He heads down the bar and strikes up a conversation with some guy that looks like he's probably in the military from his build and mannerisms. Dee feels an odd tingling on her scalp and shivers.

***

Back in Asheville, Liz and her usual inner circle, including Val and Ty, are in her office, monitoring the situation at The Peach Tree Pagoda. Liz gets an impressed look. "Interesting... Ty, your buddy Vince is coming in handy. He says an Apara woman who fits the general description of the dark-haired woman from Val's sketches is at the bar. She's waiting on someone to come back from the dance floor. He said he's alerted one of our security guys that she might be one of the focal points to watch."

"Jason turned someone *new*?" Marc inquires, giving Tess a side hug as they wait for news.

"I can't imagine any of our established people taking up with him!" Liz stares off again. "Vince *says* she's wearing a *Cent-opal* bracelet, but I think it's malfunctioning or damaged as he's getting variable energy levels from the woman."

"But how would Jason *get* one of those?" Tess wonders, grabbing a pastry from the table in front of her.

"That's an excellent question! Maybe she isn't with *him*? It's not like Sara would *issue* him one." Liz joins them on the sofa, feeling like their first potential lead has fizzled.

Niall clears his throat and everyone looks at him. "I *completely* forgot until now! I lost my kit for Callie when he *shot* me. I assumed one of you all picked it up when you cleared the area, but never confirmed it. What if he *found* it? There were instructions on using it in the transformation pack."

Liz shakes her head, frustrated. "No, none of us picked it up. Jason must have found it before we arrived, which makes it much more likely she's the one in Val's vision." Liz sighs, then addresses Val. "On the *bright* side, that means that she's likely in stasis in your vision, and not actually dead, meaning only his target is in question now. The important question is, *who* is this new transformee, and how the hell did he find her?" Everyone hears and feels Liz's frustration.

***

Back at the Peachtree Pagoda, Dee glances at the wall behind the bar. Glass shelves with various bottles lie in front of a large mirror. She looks at her reflection and is shocked to see that she could almost pass as Lynda's older sister. Celia looks more like her father, but other than her hair being straight and Lynda's being curly, they no longer could pass as mother and daughter, but could pass as siblings. *Damn! If I have to guess, I now look like I'm in my mid-thirties! Even if I can get away and get to my family, they wouldn't believe it's me.* She thinks, feeling despair as it looks progressively more like her family life is over.

She looks up and sees Jason returning from the dance floor and heading straight for her. She feels his mood has shifted, he's clearly spotted some women he likes and is considering. He comes up beside her and orders a drink from Vince. Dee faces the bar, ignoring him while she sips her drink.

"Not gonna ask me if I *found* anyone?" He jeers at her.

"I'd *rather* you didn't. I *told* you, it's too soon to try this! I can't help feeling It's a disaster waiting to happen." She turns and stares him in the eye.

"Whatever happens, happens! But if I don't turn someone tonight, I might just have to find a new *use* for you." He smirks and looks her up and down, knowing it makes her very uncomfortable. He gets an odd expression, noticing something is off with her energy, but assumes she's merely reacting to his comments. "Come on! I *want* you to look at my options." He grabs her by her upper arm, which is bare in this outfit, and slaps a $20 bill down on the bar for their drinks. He drags her off in the direction of a group of four young women taking a break from dancing. They're standing near some posters along one wall, closer to the entrance. He pushes Dee into a small booth where they can observe his potential targets.

"Now *what*?" Dee asks. Her patience running out for his bullshit. Somehow, she doesn't feel as helpless as she has up until now. She feels like she can even fight him if she has to, but does her best to keep those feelings to herself.

"I'm going for *one* of them." He nods toward the four women. There's a thin, blonde woman with long, wavy hair in a simple, black dress, a brown-haired woman with green eyes and way too much makeup on, A black haired woman who looks like she's part Asian, and an African-American woman with long twist-braids in a short, sparkly dress. "And you get to choose our guinea pig." He turns to her and grins malevolently. Since she's close to him, she notices the tips of his fangs in the narrow gap between his lips.

"*Hell no*! *This* is on you! I already told you we need more controlled tests before you try this." She glares at him with shock and loathing.

Jason leans back in the booth. "If you *don't* choose, I can always grab a *guinea pig* in LA?" He leans forward and puts his elbows on the table so he can stare her in the eye.

Dee blanches. "You mean one of my daughters?" She tenses up.

Jason raises one eyebrow, and paraphrases Darth Vader. "You'd prefer I choose another woman? An *unrelated* one?! Then *pick* one!" He leans menacingly closer to her across the table. "*This* is your *last* chance! *Choose*, or I'll *experiment* on one of your daughters!

Dee feels horrible. She doesn't want anyone to be his victim, but she can't bear the thought of one of her daughters in his evil clutches. She looks over at the four young women; they're laughing. chatting, and full of life. "The blonde." She tells him, looking him in the eye, figuring she would be more his type. Having chosen, she's hit with a wave of nausea as she looks up at him and sees a pleased and maliciously triumphant expression.

Jason saunters over to the young women, flirts with the group, and eventually focuses on the blonde. The other three wander of to the dance floor like they've forgotten their friend, and the blonde woman follows Jason back to the table like a puppy.

Meet your new sister! Jason paths to Dee. She hears his mental laughter echoing in her mind as he flirts with the young woman next to him in front of her.

Dee thinks about how she wishes she could snap the young woman out of whatever influence he has on her. After a minute, the girl gets a confused expression, stands, and runs back to her friends. Jason's expression is one of stunned disbelief as he watches her run off and start dancing with her friends again. He turns and glares at Dee. "Did you do that?"

Dee feigns her own look of shock. "How could I have done that? I don't know *how* to do stuff! You haven't taught me how to do *anything*!"

He shakes his head, thinking, *What the hell am I thinking? Even if she knew how, she couldn't overpower me!* He stands and saunters back out to the dance floor, begins to dance with the blonde woman again, and soon her friends drift away.

Dee watches, feeling helpless to stop him from going through with his attempt to turn her. She's sitting in the booth, feeling despondent, when she sees someone approaching from the bar. She realizes it's Vince, the bartender, drinks in hand.

"Ma'am, you *left* your drink at the bar!" He says, smiling pleasantly as he talks to her.

Dee looks at the drink. "Thanks, but I'm really not in the mood for a drink right now."

"*Oh*, but I brought *this* one out just for *you!*" He says, and something in his intonation catches her attention, making her look at him closely. His lips are slightly parted and she tell that he, too, has fangs. *Relax! I'm here to help you. I know you're here against your will.* He paths, sending reassuring waves of emotions.

Dee lets out a long sigh and thinks. *Thank God!*

Vince reacts to her not replying telepathically. He says aloud, "Did you *hear* what I *said*?"

She stares at him and says uncertainly, "*Yes*, I...I *think* so."

He nods in return, then asks. "What's your name? I want to make sure I put that $20 on the right bill."

"Dee", she says, and checks to makes sure Jason is still dancing up a storm.

"And *this* is for your companion. What's *his* name?" Vince puts a drink down on the table.

Dee shakes her head. "He's *never* told me." She gives him a sarcastic smile.

Vince says out loud, "Here's your change." And gives her a Susan B. Anthony dollar, pathing, *Keep that on you, it will prevent him from reading your mind!*

She nods, and not having any pockets in the clothes he got for her, sticks it in her bra.

Vince pretends to wipe up a spill and tells her, "That drink is for him, *don't* drink it! It's *going* to be okay!" He reassures her and walks away back to the bar.

For the first time in weeks, Dee feels like there's hope, even though her guardian angel is another *vampire. I did dream about others like this, being with them, even being happy.* She thinks and pats the underside of her bra to reassure herself that the coin is there.

Jason comes back to the table with his lost puppy in tow. He looks at the drinks on the table. "Where'd those come from?"

She looks up. "The bartender saw that I'd left mine, and brought it out to me, and brought you a fresh one."

Jason, one arm around his target, takes his glass, and takes a large gulp, but puts it back down. "Stay here! I'll be busy for a while, but will be back for *you* when I'm done!" He gives her a lopsided smile with a hint of fang and takes the young blonde girl outside.

Dee's anxious, so looks around for Vince to tell him the girl's in danger, but when she looks around, she sees the large man who's been standing by the door, working as the bouncer, walk toward her. He looks down at Jason's drink with a look of irritation.

"Didn't he drink *any*?" He stares Dee right in the eye.

"A big gulp, that's it!" She says, startled. "Are you *also*?"

"Yes, ma'am. I need to notify others he didn't finish his drink." He stands and motions for Vince to come back.

Vince trots over and sits next to her. "We'll deal with him from here. Let me see your wrist; the one with the bracelet."

She holds her wrist out to him. "Are you sure you can catch him? He's going to go after my daughters if you don't!" She asks frantically.

"We hope so. They're waiting until he's distracted to grab him in the alley. They won't let him hurt the girl." Vince reaches a finger under the seam in the bracelet and it pops open. He removes it and looks at the stone. "*Wow*! Did you *bang* it on something?" He looks at Dee and she's clearly disoriented. He extends his own shields around her. "Didn't he teach you how to deal with your abilities?"

When she can focus again, she explains, "He never *told* me I had *any*, but I've had some things happen the last week or two. He hasn't been able to read me as easily, and that thing kept giving me a static-shock! Thanks for taking it off!"

"It *wasn't* giving *you* a shock; *you* were *zapping* it!" He smirks. "That's why the stone is crazed and cracked. Did your abilities come out after that?"

"More or less. I got the shocks when I got angry, so thought it was some kind of negative reinforcement for being angry and less submissive." Dee massages her wrist now that the bracelet's gone.

He looks toward the door as he hears a skirmish. He paths to Liz. *Something's up. I hear a commotion and yelling outside, but his captive is fine. By the way, her name's Dee.*

He heads for the door but is hit by it flying open, and knocked into the wall. Jason rushes in and heads for the crowd to lose several large men chasing him. Dee is terrified he'll get away. She wants to stop him, and instinctively ports, phasing in to tackle him just as a guy in an old QAnon "Q Sent Me" t-shirt pulls out his concealed gun, and shoots five times. One hits Dee in the neck, two hit Jason in the chest. One of those goes through him and into some random man's shoulder. The last two shots hit Jason in the abdomen and leg as some of the Apara security guys tackle him, pulling him down. There's blood everywhere, including on some of the clubbers on the dance floor. Jason appears dead, but is really in stasis.

Vince is standing by the booth where Dee had been, frantic that Dee had shot, and that she *ported* in public. He paths Liz. *We're gonna need damage control!* He paths what happened and senses exasperation from Liz, but she replies, **Already on their way!**

He runs through the crowd to reach Dee. He puts pressure on her wound, but paths, **It's okay. You won't die, not really. We got him, and we'll take care of you. Don't be afraid!** He feels her slipping away as her heart stops and her body gives way to stasis.

An ambulance and a police car pull up outside. Paramedics come in. Vince nods to one of them. It's Sara, with Vanessa Manheim. They go straight to Jason and Dee, pretend to do CPR, and have them carried into the Ambulance. They drive off before another Ambulance shows up, this one containing human paramedics, and they deal with the human injuries.

The police, who are Apara, lock down the venue, and interview witnesses. Luckily, only one saw Dee port, and he was so drunk, that it was easy to convince him he'd imagined it. Everyone else, however, had to have their memories redacted to be fuzzy, and that the incident wasn't as serious as it was. There would be no official police report on this one. One of the Apara police officers works with the Atlanta PD and is tempted to take the man in the QAnon t-shirt in for reckless endangerment for shooting his weapon in a crowded venue. However, she gives a telepathic compulsion to leave his gun at home in the future, and burn his shirt.

The blonde woman in the alley, while fed upon, has had her wounds healed, her mind redacted, and is sent on her way.

MYSTERY WOMAN

Jason's body is taken to a holding facility. They implant a small device where his damaged heart is. His body is currently healing in stasis, and would eventually heal him completely, except that this small device prevents his heart from completely healing and beating again. He won't be aware of anything, but he also won't revive until the Apara decide what to do with him.

In the meantime, Dee is taken to Medical in Sanctuary and allowed to heal. She's still in stasis when Liz finally has time to check on her. She arrives at Medical two days after Dee's rescue, and Sara meets her in the lobby.

"How's our mystery transformee doing?" Liz asks, walking up a flight of stairs with Sara.

"As well as can be expected. From what I understand, her abilities were suppressed and were freed up at the club, which is why she unconsciously ported when she tried to stop Jason. We're letting her heal at her own pace, but have fitted her with a new bracelet that's not set on maximum. It will allow her to ease into her abilities once she's conscious again." Sara stops to talk to one of her staff briefly, and then continues to walk down a hall with Liz.

"Do we have an ID on her *yet*? I know Vince said her name is Dee." Liz takes out her tablet, ready to type in any new information.

"*Yes*! And I'm quite *eager to* talk to her once she's awake! She's a medical scientist! Her name's Thaddea Price." Sara rambles off as if it's not a big deal.

Liz stops in her tracks, making Sara look back at her curiously. "Thaddea Price? As in Dr Thaddea Price from Frederick, Maryland?"

Sara chuckles. "*Yes*, one and the same! *Why*? Do you know her?"

"Yes, give me a second Sara." Liz takes her cell out and calls her brother, Peder.

Peder answers. "*Javel?*"

"Hey, Peder, I'm with Sara, visiting our latest transformee. Guess who it is." Liz glances at Sara and rolls her eyes.

"I heard her name is Dee? But I don't know anyone by that name." Peder replies.

"She goes by Dee, but you know her by her real name, Peder— *Dr Thaddea Price!*"

"*Helvete*! No kidding? So, Jason turned her?" Peder sounds surprised.

"Yes, he did. The question is, *why*? Especially if there really is a connection with what the Atlanta precogs have been seeing. Keep your ears open. As soon as she's revived, Tess and I will have a talk with her. I have a *bad* feeling this isn't over yet!"

"As she's wanted by authorities who believe she's a bio-terrorist, we need to wrap that up, so they stop looking for her. If she was 48 when turned, assuming she was turned right after she was taken, she's not going to *look* 48 now!" He suggests.

"*True*. Didn't she have a family?" Liz types on her tablet and the search for Dr Thaddea Price comes up. "Hmm, two adult daughters and an ex-husband. Well, at least it's not *small* children. We need to think this through and make it easier on her family. Can you work on that?"

"Sure, does Sara have any idea how long she'll be out?" Peder asks.

Liz knows Sara certainly heard her brother's question and raises one eyebrow expectantly.

"I'd like to keep her out about another month to let her de-aging wrap up. It often speeds up when a stasis is involved, so what might usually take two months may speed up and be done in three weeks; but if you need her awake sooner, probably ten to fourteen days would be best." Sara estimates.

"Probably at least two weeks, maybe longer. Does that give you time?" Liz asks.

"It's a start. Any idea where they've been all this time? If we knew where he'd held her, we could set up something to fake her death and pin it on someone else. It will be best if we can put her family's minds at ease about the whole bio-terrorism mess." Liz hears Peder typing on a keyboard in the background, making notes.

"No idea yet. We'll know more when she comes out of stasis. They won't find her as long as she's in Sanctuary, but it would be good to give her family some closure as soon as possible. I'll call you as soon as I know more." Liz hangs up and sighs, giving Sara a somewhat frustrated look.

Sara looks uneasy. "What's this about bio-terrorism?"

"Our latest addition is suspected by authorities of bio-terrorism. It's a long story, and one we must get to the bottom of, but, right now, we must focus on her recovery. From the articles I read, she and some of her equipment disappeared simultaneously, and other evidence was found at her home in downtown Frederick. However, since Jason's responsible for her disappearance, we can't make any assumptions or take any 'evidence' at face value! I'd still like to see her and see if I can pick anything up. I *know*! She's still in stasis, but I'd like to try anyway." Liz follows Sara to the room where Dee's laid out in a bed, still in stasis, her neck bandaged to hide the still-healing gunshot wound. A monitor shows her heart's not beating, she's not breathing, and no current brain activity is detectable displays silently above her head on the wall.

Sara flips a switch on the display and a field pops up showing an estimate for Dee's regeneration and revival. "Looks like about two weeks. I can speed it up, but I wouldn't recommend it." Sara raises an eyebrow and looks at Liz seriously. "Bringing her out too soon could be traumatic, since the last thing she likely remembers is being shot and dying on the floor, and that her daughters were in danger from Jason. Allowing time to heal, also means allowing her nervous system and mind time to heal. The shock will fade the longer she can rest."

"Yeah, I can certainly understand that. Jason's one sadistic piece of work! I don't know if there's any hope of redeeming him after all this, or even if he'd be accepted or trusted if we can." She pauses, gently stroking Dee's hand and trying to get any impressions or residual energy that might suggests where she's been or what she's been through the last few weeks, but doesn't get anything. She sighs. "*Nothing*! We'll just have to *wait*! Keep me in the loop. Any changes whatsoever, call me!" Liz nods and ports out, leaving Sara to check over their latest patient in Medical.

***

Two days later, Liz, Kari, Tess, and Sue meet in Liz's office.

"So, Kari knows all about this, can't keep much from her!" Liz jokes and puts her hand on her partner's shoulder, but Jason's latest victim comes with some *complications*." Liz joins the others in the meeting area after closing her door.

"What kind of complications?" Tess's own unease and anger build, wondering if Jason may have physically or sexually abused Dee.

Liz catches Tess's thought. "I don't know about physical abuse, but I have my doubts about sexual abuse in her case, Tess. Dee is, by far, not Jason's usual type, considering her age and appearance when turned. We don't know why he chose her, other than that she was obviously compatible, but she doesn't fit his usual target profile. Considering her age, and his history with an abusive mother, it makes it even more of a mystery."

"Maybe he misses his mommy?" Tess grins, but then suppresses her humor. "Sorry, you know me! I joke when I'm anxious."

Liz nods courtly to Tess and continues, "Anyway, our latest transformee disappeared from Frederick, Maryland a few weeks ago. Tess, I thought you might be interested to know that she worked at a military base there. If you're not familiar with Frederick, the terrain there is very much like here in Asheville. It's in a valley in the Appalachians in Western Maryland." Liz watches Tess's expression shift as she makes the connection.

"Oh, *holy crap*! My astrals were about *her*? But I don't even know her! Didn't even bump into the woman like I did with Annie!" Tess rolls her eyes, annoyed at her somewhat uncontrolled abilities.

"I know, but all of these things have one thing in common, don't they?" Liz gives her a knowing look.

"*Yup*! Captain *Asshole*! AKA Jason! *Please* tell me I'm *not* going to spend centuries linked to his *bullshit*?" Tess frowns.

Liz regards Tess sympathetically. "Hopefully, we've got him for good this time. As soon as Thaddea… Dee is out of stasis and revived, we'll know more, but I doubt if he transformed anyone else, as she's the only missing person that matches a known potential. In which case, no one is going to *rescue* him! At this point, if he can't be redeemed, he may be kept in stasis indefinitely, or…" Liz lets out a long breath. "We may turn him over to our Benefactors to see what they can do with him. I don't like the idea of ending his life, even if he is a bastard. He's also a victim of his upbringing, and it was *our* mistake that brought him into the fold. If they can do something with him, I'd prefer to go that route. Hopefully, he won't be *your* problem anymore!"

Sue chimes in. "The more I hear about Jason, the more I'm thankful Colin got to me *first*! I've counseled too many *victims* of abusers like him, and I wouldn't want to be on the receiving end!"

Tess relaxes a tad. "Thank God! Anyway, you started to say there are complications?"

"We probably won't know the full extent of them until Dee revives and can tell us her side of things, but she's wanted by the authorities, including the FBI for bio-terrorism!" Liz pours herself a cup of fresh, Sassafras tea with a hint of honeysuckle nectar, something Kari recently concocted for her.

Tess puts her hand up to her mouth. "Holy *shit*! That's a *major* complication! What do we do if she's *guilty*?"

Liz takes a sip of her tea. "I was talking about her with Peder weeks ago. He discovered she was a missing potential, or, more specifically, a former potential, due to her age and family status. He also discovered the bio-terrorism angle, and reminded me that, based on her ratings and psych profile, it's highly unlikely someone like her would *ever* lean in that direction. I suspect this may be something Jason came up with to pressure her into staying with him. Even if she is cleared of wrongdoing, her career and reputation are damaged beyond repair! Add to that she's 48 and has clearly de-aged into her 30s already. It's impossible for her to go back to her family and find any closure there, even briefly."

Kari leans over and rubs her partner's thigh. "To put it simply, we've got a mess to clean up, and we still don't know *why* Jason went after her in the first place! It feels like we're in the dark, waiting for a ticking time bomb while we wait for answers!"

"Tess, Sue, whatever the situation turns out to be, we're going to need you to help her make her psychological transition to Apara life. She'll be dealing with whatever trauma Jason put her through, her professional losses, as well as losing contact with her family. We're going to have to do some sort of death scenario to give her family some closure and get the authorities off her case, because no matter what the basis for the bio-terrorism issues, she's *one of us* now, and we don't need anyone tracing her to us. I'm working on getting a new identity created for her. You'll have to make it clear she mustn't contact her family! Never! We may find some way to get a 'last message' to them, but contacting them after they think she's dead is off the table!"

Sue takes notes. She's still a little uneasy in her new life, but suggests, "Did she have any life insurance? If we can officially clear her, I see her daughters are both going to UCLA? The insurance would go a long way to help them with tuition and getting started with their lives after losing their mom."

Liz grins, appreciating Sue's efforts to contribute. "Good point! I'll get that researched! And you're right, they probably won't pay out if they think she's a terrorist, so we need to clear her for multiple reasons! Keep thinking that way, Sue! That was very helpful!"

Tess gets a worried expression. "Liz, why do they think she might be involved in bio-terrorism? Didn't you say she's a doctor?"

"Yes, she is. She has a PhD in genetics, though she has basic medical education as well. She was working on new treatments for cancer before Jason took her." Something about what Liz tells her makes Tess uneasy, but she can't quite put her finger on it.

"I'll do some research on her online, but please send me what you already have, Liz! The more I know, the more I'll be able to help her!" Tess makes several notes on her tablet, and zones out for a second. "*Oops! Sorry guys! Marc wasn't home when I left! He just path-yelled at me for not letting him know I was going out! He's still a bit overprotective; even with Jason on ice! If that's all you have for now, I'd better port home before I'm grounded!*" She grins at Liz and rolls her eyes.

Liz nods. "Go on! I'd like you and Sue to work on a strategy for helping Dee! It's going to be a mess to deal with no matter what! Sara thinks she'll come out of it in about another ten to twelve days"

Tess ports out, they wrap up the meeting, and Liz and Kari leave early, porting off to Norway for a *julebord* celebration, which is a traditional, pre-Christmas party many businesses have for their employees. They meet about three dozen other Apara from Norway at one of the larger hotels in Kristiansand, on the southern coast. Liz makes a half-hearted effort to enjoy the evening, but something nags at her precognitive senses all night. When Kari notices that Liz isn't her usual gregarious self with her other Norwegian, Apara friends, she corners her privately.

"Liz, what's going on? I know you too well! There's something you haven't told me about the situation with Dee and Jason, isn't there?"

Liz sighs and looks at Kari with worried eyes. "Should've known you'd notice eventually, *love*! Yes, there is. When Peder first discovered she was a missing potential, we assumed she wasn't likely connected to Jason, but considering the bio-terrorism angle, she might be connected to some health-related precogs coming out of the Atlanta area that Katie told Niall about. No specifics, only that there were health concerns popping up among the precogs down there. Our guy at the CDC has also had some reports from various precogs about something brewing."

Kari can't mask her concern, both for what Liz is telling her and for her partner, who is clearly anxious about this. "And now that you know Jason's involved? Do you still think there may be a connection with the precogs?"

"*More* than ever! The more I think about it, the more I wonder why he would turn a 48-year-old scientist. Jason thinks with his groin when he goes for women, and that doesn't fit with Dee! There must have been something else he wanted from her. Something only *she* could do for *him*, and it sure as *hell* wasn't sex!"

"Are you *sure* he didn't grab her because he knew we wouldn't be watching older potentials, and that she'd get physically younger over time?" Kari asks, taking her partner's hand in hers.

"I don't know, but I doubt he even realized she'd de-age! We so rarely turn anyone over 30-35, that it's not common knowledge, at least among the more recent transformees! But what would he *want* from *her*?" Liz shakes her head, concerned by this mystery.

"Maybe he wanted a cure? Maybe he thought she could make him human again?" Kari hazards a guess.

Liz laughs. "Not likely! He *enjoys* the *power* being one of us gives him! He was bad enough while human with enough telepathic and telempathic persuasion skills to get women to sleep with him, but once he became one of us, his powers really went to his head! I have a terrible feeling about this, and there's nothing we can do until she's awake again!"

Kari leans over and gives her partner of 600 plus years a long, rocking hug. "Come on! I hear they've got one hell of a *karamellpudding* this year!. The two of them try to enjoy the rest of the evening with their fellow Norwegian Apara. It helps Liz to know that Kari now knows the truth, and why she is so worried.

CLUES

As everyone waits for Dee to come out of stasis and wake up, everyone has their tasks to do. Tess and Sue are creating a plan to help Dee through her difficult life-transition. Peder researches Dee and the bio-terrorism investigation, using various tools and Apara contacts to search for confidential law enforcement and FBI information.

Marc, Katie, and Val are all keeping their precognitive ears to the ground, and Liz and Kari are researching some of the practical elements, such as working on a new identity for her, and on ways to help her family, which will also help put Dee's mind at ease about not being there for them.

Amy also plays a part. Considering the entire event where both Jason and Dee were gunned down by a semi-drunk, over-eager gun carrier, and a lot of memories had to be altered, Amy's tasked with monitoring the media for any signs of exposure for the Apara. An event like this would normally have made national headlines, but because of the Apara damage control team, it never even made the local news.

A couple of days before Dee is expected to emerge from stasis, Amy swings by Liz's office. Liz is hit by her anxiety even before she knocks, and says, "Come on in Amy! What's got you so anxious?"

"Felt me coming, huh?" Amy sticks her head in the door, giving an anxious, half smile.

"You need to work on not broadcasting your emotions. It comes with time, but when you're dealing with a lot of empathic people around you, it becomes the courteous thing to do, but otherwise, I get the feeling this is something that you *feel* is *important*?"

"I'm not sure. If it were only the one article, considering it's in a tabloid, I might've ignored it." Amy sits on the edge of Liz's desk.

"I'm guessing it's not the only source?" Liz puts down her tablet and focuses on Amy.

"Two *different* sources, and two separate *incidents*, but both centered in the Atlanta area. One's a tabloid, paranormal-type story, and one's a local public interest, feel-good story." Amy explains, and hands her the tabloid.

Before looking at the story, Liz shivers; her own precognitive senses giving her a subtle warning. She looks at the article: "Witnesses Report Woman Disappearing into thin air!" Liz leans back in her chair without reading the article, and looks up at Amy. "We *missed* witnesses at the Peach Tree Pagoda?"

"*No, read* the article! This happened a few days *later*. A woman was crossing the street when a car swerved to miss a dog, and lost control, heading straight for her. Several witnesses report that she suddenly disappeared and appeared again across the street!" Amy points out the underlined sections of the article.

"*Faen i helvete!* Which one of our people was so careless?" Liz asks, looking annoyed.

"I don't *believe* it was one of *ours*! I checked with Michelle, and no one admits to it, at least. And even worse, someone got it on cell phone video!" Amy pulls out her tablet, loads the tabloid's website. and plays the video.

"*Faen!* See if Ty and Val can do anything about scrubbing that off the net! If not, have them contact Dennis Villa at Google! He'll do a search engine bypass on it. What's the *other* one?" Liz looks like she has a migraine brewing, though Apara rarely get headaches outside of psychic overloads.

Amy pulls up a link to a local, Atlanta TV station. "It's under public interest stories. A woman in her late 30s, with five kids claims she woke up the other day knowing the lottery numbers for the state game all this week. She hit five days in a row, winning $136,024 in total. She was about to lose her home because she couldn't pay her mortgage. They're calling it a Christmas miracle."

Liz looks thoughtful. "So, we have people witnessing someone mysteriously porting, but so far, we haven't found any of our own to be responsible, and a woman in desperate need has an unbelievable run on the lottery? Precognition? I'm less worried about that than the porting, especially with the video! Maybe we can get someone to claim to have analyzed it and debunk it? In the meantime, see if you can find anything else odd down in that area. *Oh!* Watch for any stories on local health issues!"

Amy gets an uneasy expression. Liz puts her head down in her palm before looking up and saying, "*What?*"

"It's *probably* nothing! But the woman claims she'd felt sick for a few days, fever and severe headaches before this happened." Amy explains.

"If it's nothing, why did I just get a sinking feeling that this is only the beginning?" Liz notes the two incidents in her tablet. "Keep searching. I know it's only two incidents, but my intuition is screaming up a storm right now!"

Amy heads off to do more research, focusing on strange or paranormal happenings, miracles, and illness in Atlanta. By the next day, she returns, this time trying to damp down her anxiety, but Liz feels her none-the-less.

"Come on in, Amy!" Liz is already sitting in a chair around the meeting table. "What did you find?"

Amy sits in the chair next to Liz, looking exhausted and disturbed. "Too much! There's been an increase in...well, weird stuff. I checked the news, social media and, with Kari's help, into police reports and ER psychiatric admissions. I found several cases of people having strange experiences. There was a report of a haunting or poltergeist at a school in Duluth right before Christmas break began. There was a pretty disturbing incident in Decatur. A man claimed he dreamed his wife was having an affair with her ex and went after the ex with a shotgun. Luckily, the man got away, but it turned out his dream was *correct!*" She scrolls down. "In Atlanta, someone call 911, saying they dreamed someone was going to set fire to a church, but they didn't know where. They described it, and the next day, a church that matched the description burned to the ground. All over Georgia, there's been an increase in cases where people are reporting hearing voices."

"What about *illnesses*?" Liz asks, her expression solemn.

"I couldn't get an answer in all cases, but some reported a cold or flu like event prior to, or during, their experience. There's also been a general increase in some sort of mild bug. Mostly fever and aches, but none of the typical sinus or respiratory issues. What do you suspect?"

"I'm not sure, but keep watching for stories like those and keep a record of them. *Oh*, if you get names, find their addresses, just in case..." Liz says, chewing on her lower lip. "Thanks, Amy." She goes back to her desk, lost in thought. Amy heads back to her own office and continues to research.

AWAKENING AND ENLIGHTENMENT

Liz gets a path from Sara that Dee has come out of stasis, is restless, so should wake soon, but she could keep her sedated until Liz and Tess can get there. She suggests that her 'guardian angel', Vince, might be a friendly face for her to wake up to as she'd picked up dreams about him from Dee, and noticed that he makes her feel safe.

Liz and Tess port in to Medical, and Ty's friend Vince is waiting for them in the atrium. He approaches the women and bows slightly, smiling. "Nice to see you again, Liz. And you must be Tess?"

"Yes, I'm Tess. Amy was telling me about you after her meetup with Charlie. Sara's waiting for us in Dee's room. She says she got the impression Dee trusts you; she sees you as her guardian angel, albeit with fangs!" Tess motions for the other Vince to precede her up the stairs, and points the way to Dee's room.

Sara meets them outside. "Okay, you three. I think maybe it would be best if Vince is there when she comes to, then he can tell her you two aren't going to *eat* her for dinner!" Sara grins. "I've given her something to help wake her. It will take about five minutes to work, so go on in. Pretty sure *your* presence will put her at ease!" Sara winks at Vince, and he rolls his eyes at her.

Tess paths to Sara. *Are you matchmaking again?*

Hush, girl! Dee feels comfortable with him! He helped her out, and she sees him as her proverbial knight in shining armor! Plus, while Vince and his partner went separate ways a couple of centuries ago, she was one of those lost in Jerusalem last year, so it may do them both some good!

Tess rolls her eyes at Sara, knowing firsthand how she likes to match make.

***

Vince sits next to Dee's bed. The overhead light is off, and a smaller, dimmer light on the nightstand is on, so the light doesn't overwhelm Dee's senses since her eyes have been closed and non-functional for about two weeks. Dee makes a gasping intake of air and scrunches up her shoulders while her eyes start to move under her lids. Slowly, her eyes open part way, then slowly close. Everything's a blur after two weeks of disuse.

She's aware that she's somewhere soft, warm and comfortable, and for the first time in weeks, she honestly feels safe. She stretches and rubs her eyes, blinking again, and sees a pair of piercing blue eyes that she recognizes, but can't immediately place. She studies Vince; his blue eyes have a kindness behind their intensity, and a sparkling intelligence. The familiar face comes with a kind smile, sandy, blonde hair, as well as a well-kept beard and mustache. She lets out a gasp that becomes the word "Hi", drawn out, her voice weak from disuse. "I remember you. *Vince*?" She still sounds a little groggy.

"Yes, Dee, it's me. You're safe now, and they caught your captor, so your *family's* safe too!" He reassures her.

Dee takes a deep breath, slowly letting it out, and visibly relaxes. "When can I *see* them?" Dee asks, not realizing how complicated that would be.

"Right now, we must focus on you. A couple of friends of mine need to speak with you. They won't hurt you. Their names are Liz and Tess." He tells her, holding her hand gently while sending calming thoughts at her. The fact it's two women puts her somewhat at ease.

Her expression is tentative, and her voice still rough, but she asks, "Are they like you?"

"Yes, *they* are like *us*, and they want to help you, but they have some questions they must ask you. I'll stay here if you wish?" He says, sensing that she feels uneasy about any other 'vampires' but him. Vince looks up at the door and nods. Tess and Liz come in, pulling up chairs on the other side of her bed.

Liz and Tess agree it's best if Tess talks to her first, being a more recent transformee, and having personally dealt with Jason before. Tess flashes a reassuring smile. "Hi, I'm Tess."

"H-hello." The words come out breathy and she clenches Vince's hand a little tighter. He squeezes it back to reassure her. She looks up at him, and he nods.

"Dee, we're all here for you and are going to help you through this. I've personally dealt with Jason first hand, so have an idea what he may have put you through." Tess says sympathetically.

"Jason?" Dee asks.

Vince chimed in. "He was your captor. You told me he never told you his name. It's Jason Templeton."

Dee looks at Tess with comprehension. "Did he do the same to you?"

"Not exactly. He didn't transform me. I was turned by someone I actually really care about, but I've known Jason since he and I were both still human. I can honestly say that he's a self-obsessed, arrogant bastard, and I know he can be very abusive, so if you need to talk to someone, I'm here, and a friend of mine, Sue, who's a therapist, are on call any time you need to talk. I don't know what he did to you besides transform you, but he does have a history of psychological, physical, and sexual abuse."

Dee closes her eyes slowly, then opens them again. "I got the impression he could be sexually abusive, but with me, he was physically ..." She pauses to catch her breath and coughs to clear her throat. "and very psychologically abusive."

"I heard he threatened your family?" Tess asks.

"*Frequently!*" She coughs, and takes a few careful breaths before continuing. "When can I see them? My daughters?"

It's difficult for Tess to be blunt and tell her the truth, even though she ran through this with Sue multiple times. None-the-less, she tries. "Dee, your daughters are fine. They're clear out in California. We're far away from there right now, and we want to focus on you getting over the trauma first."

Dee interrupts. "Seeing daughters...would...help!"

Tess pauses, knowing Dee is going to continue insisting she sees her girls.

"Dee, when was the last time you looked in a mirror?" Tess asks, gently taking her other hand.

Dee's mind flashes on the gunshot to her throat, and pulls her hands away from Vince and Tess, feeling her throat and face, afraid she might be horribly disfigured or scarred from the wound. She breathes a sigh of relief when she can't find any irregular tissue or scabs.

"Dee, you *look* fine. You're totally healed. That's part of our condition, but I need to know if you noticed any changes in your appearance after you changed?" Tess asks cautiously.

Understanding shows in her expression. "I looked younger. Maybe 35-38?" Dee admits, her voice getting stronger with use.

Tess nods to Sara, who's standing across the room, pathing *Mirror, please!*

Sara hands her a medium-sized hand mirror, and Tess holds it face down, away from Dee. "You *looked* about 35-38, but, well, take a look." She holds up the mirror and Dee's mouth drops open. Her hair doesn't have a bit of gray, and she now looks like she's around 28 to 30 years old. "*Holy cow!* My kids won't recognize me! *Hell!* I could pass for their sister!" As Dee says this, her rational side comprehends the dilemma. "They *can't* see me like this, can they? I *can't* tell them *what* I am, what I've *become*! Not sure I want them to know! I almost *killed* a girl that looks like my youngest, Lynda. He starved me and brought this young woman to me and I *thought* it *was* Lynda!" She cries. "Oh, *God!* I can't face them knowing...." She pauses, as the whole virus mess comes to mind, and her face goes pale. "knowing what I've done..."

Tess feels Liz's hand on her shoulder, gripping it. *Did you catch that, Tess? Something about a virus?*

Yeah, she's pretty distraught. Let me reassure her, then you can talk to her if she's up to it. Tess paths.

"Dee, *whatever* Jason made you do, it's *his* doing, *not* yours!" Tess reassures her, and again takes her hand, trying to comfort her.

Dee shakes her head, tears flowing. "*No*, I should have said *no*! But I couldn't let him hurt my girls, so I did what he wanted!" She asks Vince, "Didn't you say the girl's okay? In the *alley*?" Sobs making her words come out in bursts.

"Yes, Dee. The girl's fine! They stopped him right after he bit her. We healed her, made her forget it all, and sent her home! She's fine!" He reassures her.

"He didn't transform her?" She asks.

"No." Vince looks at Liz and paths. *Was his victim in the alley compatible? No one said anything about it?*

No, she's not. I checked the database myself. Liz replies.

Vince strokes Dee's hand gently. "I don't know if he told you this or not, but you must be *compatible* with the virus we carry to become like us. The girl's not. She lost a deciliter or so of blood, but should be fine!"

Dee looks distraught and all three of them feel powerful waves of guilt coming from her before she asks, "Are you *sure* she's fine?" When Vince nods, she visibly relaxes. "Maybe it *didn't* work?"

Sara picks up on Dee's thoughts and comes over. "*What* didn't work?"

Dee's startled by the latest voice in the conversation, but answers. "He... forced me to alter the virus. He wanted me to make it *compatible* with *anyone*!"

Sara walks out of the room abruptly, but everyone hears her rambling off harsh words in some long dead language. Liz gently nudges Tess aside.

Liz maintains a calm facade, but her mind is already making connections to Amy's findings and a disturbing possibility. "Did you successfully alter the virus that transforms us?"

"Altered it, yes, but if she's still human, it didn't work. You *must* understand! I had *no* choice! He threatened both of my daughters! I *know* I should have put the bigger picture first. But I *couldn't* sacrifice them! I tried to make it do what he wanted, and in a couple of tests on general blood, it attacked the non-compatible cells in the lab. I told him, there were sequences and bases I couldn't identify, and I didn't know if it would work! The tools we used to edit genetic sequences are built for the normal 4 bases all DNA on *Earth* is based on, but there are two more in this virus!" She rambles.

Sara returns and walks around Liz, surreptitiously adding a mild sedative to Dee's IV, helping her calm down. Liz nods an unspoken 'thanks' to Sara, but senses Sara's concern as well.

Liz takes a controlled, deep breath and asks, "Do you *understand* why the virus has those *extra* bases?"

Dee looks up at her and nods slowly. "Yes, it came to me while I was analyzing it." She laughs. "Out of the blue, I understood it contains sampled, *extraterrestrial* DNA! It's a genetic engineering *masterpiece*! And I *corrupted* it for that *monster*!" She sounds a bit loopy and her eyes blink slowly.

Sara quietly says, "Sedative's kicking in for real now. You two should set things in motion. *Vince*, if you want to stay for a while in case she comes to, that's fine, otherwise, I can holler if she does." Sara tells him. He remains by Dee's side while Sara walks out with Liz and Tess.

Liz walks into the hallway and practically drops onto a bench in stunned disbelief. "*Helvete!*"

Sara sits next to her. "You said it! I need to take some blood samples from Jason. I'll let you know when she's conscious and hopefully calmer. I assume she has a lab somewhere, so we need to find it, and deal with whatever samples are there before someone stumbles upon it. I assume she made records of what she did, as any good scientist would." Sara walks off, again rambling off ancient curses. She ports out, but Tess can still hear telepathic echoes of Sara's cursing in the ether.

"Liz, what does all this mean? I get that she *somehow* changed the virus, but...." Tess is at a loss for words.

"Oh, Tess, I'm not sure you *want* to know! If I'm *right*, that virus may be on the loose now, and may be changing people." Liz says, feeling overwhelmed by the weight of this revelation.

"*What?* Do you mean people out there are *changing* into *Apara*?" Tess looks at her in disbelief.

"I *don't* know! I haven't gotten any reports of 'bite' attacks or blood loss deaths, though there have been reports of *unusual* phenomena, possibly following a mild, virus-like illness around Atlanta and surrounding areas. Amy's been researching it." Liz is too overwhelmed to move.

Suddenly, Kari pops in, sensing Liz's state. "*Liz!* What is it?" Liz paths the situation to Kari without words.

"*Herre Gud!* We need to get this contained fast!" Kari says.

Liz looks at her. "We don't *know* enough yet, and it's probably been on the loose since the night at the Peach Tree Pagoda! Love, talk to Amy. She's been making a list of those she's found who're experiencing unusual phenomena. Run the lists through our database. We need to know if they are all potentials or if it's hitting the general population. Then, we must figure out exactly what this altered virus is doing! Sara went off to get blood and viral samples from Jason."

"I hate to bring this up, but we should inform our Benefactors." Kari sits next to Liz and rubs her lower back without thinking.

"I *know*. I'll contact them as soon as we know enough." She holds up her hand to stop Kari's objection. "Just waiting until Sara confirms the altered virus. Hopefully, we'll get more information from Dee when she's calmer. What a way to end the year!" Liz hugs Kari and the two of them port out, leaving Tess alone on the bench.

Tess sticks her head back in to Vince. "Are you going to stick around?"

"For a while. You?" He asks, looking tired from the emotional hurricane that blew through in the last few minutes.

"I'm heading home, but here..." She hands him a piece of paper with her cell number on it. "Call me if you need me to come back. I suspect we're in for a long and wild ride if what Liz suggests is true!" Tess ports out, but Vince remains, holding vigil like a good guardian angel.

GUILT BY DISSOCIATION

Sara urgently summons Liz, Tess, and Sue to Medical later that afternoon. The three women arrive quickly, as it's unusual for Sara to summon people without some sort of explanation. Liz and Tess assume it's related to the altered virus, but when they enter a small conference room, and find Sara pacing anxiously, they know that's just the tip of the proverbial iceberg.

When Sara notices their arrival, she motions them in urgently. "Come in and take a seat. We have a lot to deal with!"

Liz and Tess look at each other, quite familiar with the normally unflappable Sara. "Did you get a sample from Jason?" Liz asks.

Sara glances at Liz and raises one eyebrow. "Yes, but that's only part of our problem." Sara takes a seat with the other women at the table. "But we can start with the virus! I took both marrow and blood samples from Jason, and it's not good! There's only one virus, but it's NOT the same one the rest of us carry! When Dee told us about altering the virus, I got a flash from her mind that she infused the altered virus, but the original *should* still exist! However, the original is *gone*, and I can't explain that without seeing her research or comparing a sample of the created virus to the current one!" She rubs her eyes, and Tess senses a high level of stress emanating from Sara.

Tess is confused. "Can't we *ask* Dee about it?"

Sara stands anxiously and paces again. "*No!* She's *currently* in no shape to tell us *anything!*"

"Did she slip back into stasis?" Liz asks.

"No, the situation is more complicated than that. When she came out of the sedative, she crashed psychologically. She refused to speak, eat, or feed, and curled up into a ball in her bed! I'm having trouble reaching her telepathically. She's locked herself in a bubble and blocked out the world!" Sara pounds her fist on the table in frustration. "Unless we can get through to her, find out where the lab is, get her research, and the information on *how* she altered the virus, as well as her samples, we're pretty much screwed!"

Liz and Tess stare at her, unaccustomed to her using modern slang, outside of her frequent, Star Wars references.

Sue's hesitant at first, but speaks up. "It sounds like something made her withdraw and disassociate from the world around her, but it's hard to know without talking to her."

Tess turns to Sue. "She *was* pretty distraught when we were here, at least toward the end. Sara had to sedate her."

Sue nods. "Do you *know* what was upsetting her? Did she indicate what it might be?"

Tess focuses on what Dee said, and summarizes it for Sue. "I think it was a *combination* of things. At first, she was doing okay because she knew she was safe from Jason, but then she wanted to see her kids, but we explained why she couldn't. In fact, she'd already concluded that she doesn't want them to know what she's become, but I don't think it was that, in itself, that upset her. She rambled out something about almost killing a girl Jason brought her to feed on. I think she resembled one of her daughters. Then, she got very upset about having altered the virus. I think she suspected it might do more than let Jason turn non-compatible women."

Sue ponders that while Sara addresses them, "Tess, I *believe* you're right! Her anxiety and emotional turmoil were increasing rapidly, which is why I sedated her! I thought she'd be calmer after the sedation, but she completely shut down instead." Sara turns to Sue. "I'm wondering if you can reach her through your talent. Perhaps you can discover what's at the core of it all and somehow coax her out? Unless I can get that information from her, I won't be able to predict much about this new version of the virus, at least not until it is likely too late."

After a tentative pause, Sue says, "I can try. I've mostly worked with willing patients, and it doesn't sound like she's willing! If she's blocking you out, she may not *let me* in either! Perhaps, if Tess helps me read her objectively, I can slip into her dreams."

Liz takes notes on her tablet, while Tess looks Sue in the eye to reassure her and agrees, "We can start together, but I think your ability to go into her mind, and walk through her unconscious or dreams is what may do the trick! I'll do my best to read her, and give you feedback, however."

Sue nods, then looks back at Sara and Liz. "I'll do my best!"

Sara lets out a sigh of relief. "Thank you both. This is why I called you two in. Liz, you should know the virus is active in his bloodstream, even in stasis, as well as in his marrow."

"*Faen i helvete!* If I remember correctly from the reports, there was blood splatter everywhere thanks to the trigger-happy shooter?"

"Yes, Dee was hit once, but Jason was hit four times. I'm still waiting on a report from Kari and Amy on whether those who've manifested abilities are potentials, or normal humans, but either way, I'm guessing many people were exposed at the venue, and it's no doubt spreading in ever-widening circles from Atlanta. Unfortunately, Atlanta is a major travel and business hub. Depending on how it spreads, who can get it, or even carry it, the virus is likely far beyond a simple quarantine situation. It may *not* be *containable*, but we must know more about it. I'll have to test Dee to see what her strain looks like! She could have been exposed in her lab, though I suspect she took precautions, or by Jason's blood when they were shot, or if he made her drink from him." Sara looks worn and worried.

Liz runs her fingers through her blonde hair in frustration. "I'll need whatever information you have Sara and keep me up to date! I don't see any way to avoid it; I'm going to have to contact our Benefactors."

"I agree. I know they prefer us to handle things ourselves as much as possible, as they've left the situation with Jason up to us, but if it's spread to the human population, we could be looking at one hell of a pandemic, and a major disruption of human evolution. If normal people start exhibiting strong psychic abilities, or, Heaven forbid, the virus actually *turns* people, there *will* be chaos! We don't have the technology, or the manpower to keep up with millions of infections worldwide. We'll need their advanced knowledge and technology to stop something on this scale." Sara stands and opens the door. "Tess, you know where Dee is; take Sue down there and see what you two can do. Give poor Vince a break! He's been there since this morning!"

Tess and Sue walk down the hall, and Tess knocks on the door. Vince responds with an exhausted "Come in."

They enter and immediately see concern in his eyes. Tess puts her hand on his shoulder. "We'll try to help her. Sara said you should take a break."

He nods, freeing up his chair for Tess. "Call me if you need me." Vince leaves the room.

Sue closes the door and sits in a chair on the other side of the bed. "If you don't mind, Tess, see what you can sense first, maybe that will give me somewhere to start."

Dee is curled up on her side, facing Sue. Tess gently puts one hand on Dee's back and closes her eyes. She immediately withdraws her hand and sits back, eyes wide in surprise.

"What is it? Did you get *anything*?" Sue asks anxiously.

"Not exactly. It's like Sara said, she's blocking me out. It was like reaching for something, trying to touch it, getting an electric shock, or running into a mental thorn bush." Tess says, trying to describe it.

"Was it *painful*?" Sue looks worried.

"Not physically, but in a way, it was. It's like she's created a shell out of her own pain to keep everyone out. Let me clear my head and try again." Tess relaxes and grounds off all the negative energy. This time, she doesn't try to breach the mental briar patch, but passively read what's leaking through. She shakes her head as an emotional wave hits her. "*Guilt! Lots* of guilt! She sees *herself* as a *monster. No*, that's not the word; a *malignant* parasite? She feels *contaminated* by Jason, like *she's evil* because he is? Does that make sense? She feels like it's all her fault, which is *bullshit!* He made her do this!" Tess is growing increasingly angry at the damage Jason's done to so many people! Not only Dee, but herself, Annie, the other women he turned, and those he killed. A light panel behind Tess flashes bright and goes dark with scorching. "*Oops! Sorry!* That's on me!" She gives Sue an awkward grin as Sue stares at the smoking light panel. Tess finds some paper on a nearby bench and uses it to fan the smoke away.

When Tess settles in her chair again, she notices Sue's deep in thought. She nods to Tess. "Makes perfect sense! It's not uncommon for abuse victims to blame themselves, no matter how much their abuser pressured, threatened, or even physically abused them! The abuser forces the victim to take the blame onto themselves. He or she makes the victim at fault, not themselves. Dee lost herself. Her perception of who she is, or at least was, prior to Jason, was shattered, and she's taken on his guilt and malevolence as part of who she is. Everything she was in her human life: a research scientist, independent woman, human, and perhaps most importantly, a mom has been stripped away." Sue doesn't realize she's slipping through Dee's barriers and reading her unconsciously. I need to go in, but I need to get comfortable. She looks around the room and there's a reclining chair in the corner. She pulls it away from the wall so she can recline it fully.

Sara comes by to check on them, and notices a burnt odor. She looks around and spots the burnt-out panel, and glares at Tess, shaking her head. "How's it going? Have you made any progress?" She asks.

We've got a good idea of the root of the problem, but I need to go into her dreams and make her understand she's not some kind of monster! She instructs Tess. "Monitor us from the outside. Grab a chair, 'cause I don't know how long this will actually take, and turn off the overhead light."

Tess opens the door and grabs a chair. "Do you want me to find you a pillow?"

"No! If I have a pillow, I'll probably fall asleep. It's better if I stay in conscious control." She leans back in the recliner, and Tess turns off the overhead light. A small strip of soft light appears around the room, about halfway up the wall. Sue forces herself to relax, but stay awake and aware. She reaches out with her old, unconscious psychologist senses she used while still human. She pictures herself moving through a thick, black, billowing fog. Ahead of her, she sees a faint, red glow. She follows that glow through the fog and ends up in an old cabin. The red glow is a fire in a jagged, stone fireplace, yet the room is ice cold. She surveys the room and sees a deer head with exaggeratedly large antlers mounted on the wall, but the tips of the antlers look more like fangs, stained with blood on the tips.

There are old rifles and cobwebs on the walls, and a ratty sofa in front of her. She feels fear and anxiety nearly overwhelm her, but continues to look around the room. The windows are crusted over, so she can't see out, but they aren't crusted over with dirt, but with dried blood. She stops and listens, and hears quiet sobbing coming from the other side of the sofa. She goes around it expecting to find Dee lying on it, but is shocked by the scene; Dee's lying on the floor, sobbing, covered in blood and vomit. She's fastened by an oversized chain to a support post, her ankle worn raw where the manacle binds her. Her clothes are in shreds. Sue approaches her slowly, and stops about three feet away. "Dee?" She says, softly.

Dee faces her, exaggerated fangs in her mouth, blood all over her face, and she snarls at Sue in a defensive attempt to warn her away. Red tears run from her eyes. When the snarl doesn't work, she pulls away into a corner, and hides her face.

Sue doesn't push it, but looks around her for symbols of Dee's emotional turmoil. She notices the body of a young woman with black, curly hair and realizes she looks a lot like Dee. A pile of test tubes and Petri dishes overflowing with an oozing goo lie on an open window sill, perched precariously, ready to spill into the outside world. A glowing 'bio-hazard' symbol pulses eerily above them. The ooze drips out the window and she hears wails of anguish from female voices outside, and a man's laughter, distorted and echoing. She assumes it must be some distorted version of Jason's laughter. She looks back at Dee, who's staring at the fire in horror. Sue watches the fire burn, and sees an image of Dee, older, silver in her hair, on an ID tag burning in the fire, turning to ash, and wafting up the chimney.

178

Sue sits on the old sofa, facing her patient. She sees a shattered woman, hidden under filth, shaking with fear, guilt, and self-loathing. Sue knows what she must to do. *I have to reach out to her, and help her see that this is not what she is. While she's no longer the woman who she literally just watched go up in smoke, she's not this cursed soul either. I've got to show her that I'm not afraid of her and that she shouldn't be afraid of herself.*

Sue slowly lowers herself to the floor to be on the same level as Dee. She carefully, calmly, and without fear, calls her name again. "Dee, Thaddea? I'm Sue."

Dee faces her, and snarls like some rabid animal.

"You're not going to scare me away! I know you're not going to hurt me. I'm here to help you." She says gently, and knows that she's in control and Dee can't hurt her in this therascape, even if it's essentially a self-imposed version of Hell for her patient. Dee doesn't snarl at her again, but keeps her distance, hiding her face.

"I know this isn't you, Dee. Jason forced all this on you. This place, your fangs, your hunger, and *your* guilt." She pauses, waiting to see if Dee reacts.

Dee slowly turns toward her, listening tentatively.

"I know you think you've lost yourself, that the good person, the healer is nothing but ashes in the wind, but *this* is not you either!"

Dee closes her eyes, and opens them again, speaking with a slight lisp through her over-sized fangs. "Yess it isss..."

"No, Dee, I *feel* you! Under all the blood, vomit, and filth, there's a woman who loves her daughters so much that she broke her own heart to save them!" Sue looks at her kindly, and gently reaches out to stroke her matted and blood-stained hair compassionately, and without fear.

Tears fall from Dee's eyes, but they're no longer tears of blood, but clear. The room's lost its ice-box chill and is a little less dark. Dee turns and sees the body on the floor. Sue knows it's not the woman Jason brought her that looked like her daughter, but her perception that Dee had attacked and killed her own daughter;

that her hunger made her a monster that she couldn't control, not even to save her own child.

Sue sees her stare at the dream body of her daughter, throat bloody, skin pale, and hazel eyes staring blankly back at her mother. She feels Dee slipping backwards, falling back into the abyss of her self-imposed hell. "*Dee*! Your daughter's *fine*, and so's the woman Jason *forced* you to feed on! Try to remember! She was alive after you fed on her, wasn't she?"

Dee looks away from the body and back at Sue, her fangs have become normal sized, though still down in feeding position. "Alive, at least he said she was."

"I doubt Jason stopped you from killing her, did he? You stopped yourself, Dee, right?" Sue asks, repeatedly addressing her patient by her name to reinforce her identity and individuality.

She nods.

"Dee, if you were a monster, you *wouldn't* have stopped! And you wouldn't feel guilty for feeding on her, or what you *might* have done! Jason *is* the monster! He feels no guilt! He's a *sociopath. Incapable* of feeling guilt for his actions, and he shoves his guilt off onto those he torments! Makes them take the blame!

Dee looks back toward the body and it fades away. She regards Sue, and looks less bloody, less filthy, and the room warms a little more. She hears the screams of women Jason might turn and his haunting laughter coming in through the cracked open window, and a new wave of guilt weighs her down, and she sinks to the floor as though she were weighted down by lead in her soul.

Sue reaches out telepathically for Tess and somehow drags her in with her. Tess is rather shocked to be standing in the middle of Dee's backwoods, dungeon hellscape, and notices Dee lying on the floor, chained. She's even more surprised that the cabin, despite its warped, nightmarish distortions, seems oddly familiar.

She sees a glowing key hanging on the wall, just out of Dee's reach. Tess grabs it and unlocks the chain. She leans down and heals her leg instinctively, as though she were healing a bite wound. Dee carefully lifts herself from the floor. Sue grabs the test tubes and Petri dishes, tossing them into the fire. She closes the window, silencing the screams and near demonic laughter that represents Jason's tormenting. She sits on the floor by Dee and Tess joins them. A hand mirror appears in Sue's hands, face down.

"Dee, I'm going to show you how we see you, and what you can become with us." Tess and Sue reach down and help Dee into a seated position now that she's no longer bound. "We're both like you, Dee. We share the same path as you, and we want you to walk with us, to help this world." Dee's appearance changes, still in rags, looking worn, but no longer covered in blood and filth. "We *care* about you Dee, and will help you through all of this."

"But the virus! I can't forgive myself for *that*!" She says, fangs now shorter, nearing normal human canines.

"You *can help* us stop it or at least undo or limit the damage! The fault's *Jason's*, not yours! No one *blames* you for not sacrificing your daughters. That's the part of you that's still *human*, no matter what you physically are. Dee, we're *not* monsters, and *neither* are you! We welcome you! You're one of us now, and we *embrace* you!" They literally reach over and hug her. When Sue feels Dee's mood shift, they release her, and ask, "are you ready to see yourself as we see you?" Sue asks, and grips the handle on the mirror. Dee nods, now looking more human and less disheveled. Sue lifts the mirror, showing Dee that she has the glowing, inner light of a healer, and that she's a beautiful soul.

The Cabin lightens inside, and nearly glows, then fades and dissolves into a white, boundless space as the three of them awaken, back in medical. Sara's standing in a corner of the room. She observed Dee's rescue from psychological hell, and monitored the women's energy levels and patterns as well.

Dee stretches as she opens and rubs her eyes, feeling the dampness of tears on her cheeks. Sara turns the light back on, briefly overwhelming Dee, but as her vision adjusts, she focuses on Tess and Sue. She inhales through her nose, clearing it from crying and says. "Thank you, both of you. I'll do what I can. Just tell me what you need!"

Tess takes one of Dee's hands in hers. "I know Sara has a lot of questions about the virus, and needs information only you can provide, but if you need us later, we'll be back, just *ask* for us."

Dee looks at Sue. "Were you really in my dreams? It felt like it!"

Sue gently puts her hand on Dee's arm. "Yes, it's an ability I'm still learning to use, and one most people like us don't have, but it let me go into a dreamscape of sorts, showed me what was wrong in your mind, and helped to heal you psychologically. Jason destroyed your sense of self and dumped his unfelt guilt on you like a ton of bricks. He made you feel like an *aberration*! What was the term you used, Tess, a *malignant parasite*?" Tess nods.

"*Yes*! That's exactly how I saw myself! Like a *cancer*, feeding off people; off life itself! I thought I couldn't control it, like the difficult to cure cancers I study!" Dee's relieved that someone understands her perspective.

Sue sits on the edge of her hospital bed. "By seeing how you saw yourself, and knowing none of it was true, I was able to help disprove what you believed about yourself by talking you through it logically, and like a *good* scientist, you *couldn't* reject the evidence!" She gives her a knowing smirk.

Dee chuckles weakly. "I feel better, but still feel bad about the virus." She turns to Sara. "What do you need from me?"

Sara brings Dee a bag of blood, sending Tess and Sue packing with a grateful path, *Go get some rest. Will call you all soon! Thank you!* Sara tells Dee, "First, we take care of you, so you can help us!"

SCIENTIFIC METHOD

Once Dee's fed, eaten some actual food, showered, and gotten some clean clothes, Sara examines her, taking both blood and a bone marrow sample from her. She teaches Dee to block pain, both in herself and others, then tells her, "Relax for a few. I need to go check these samples, and then I have a *lot* of questions for you." Sara leaves the room, and Dee finally has a few minutes to herself. She curls up in her hospital bed, hugs her pillow, and thinks about her daughters.

She knows she can never see them again, at least not where *they* can see her as well! She wonders if they believe what's been said about her, or if they think she's even still alive. In the end, she realizes that the important thing is that they're both safe, and that Jason can never go through with his threats. She slips into the first comfortable sleep she's had since this total nightmare began.

About an hour passes, and a gentle knock on the door awakens Dee. Tess enters. "Hi, Dee. Sara's done with your tests and asked me to come get you."

Dee puts on some slippers and a robe Sara left for her. "You're Tess, right?"

"Yup! That's me!" Tess stands ready to help her if she's at all unsteady, but feeding and proper food have restored her equilibrium.

"So, how did you get involved in all this?" Dee inquires, as they walk down the hall toward the conference room where Sara and Liz await. They've decided that it was best to stick to all women, feeling it would make Dee feel more comfortable after her experiences with Jason. Even though he did not sexually assault her, he held that threat over her daughters to get her to comply.

"*Long* story! The important thing is that I, like most of us, are happy with this life, and do what we can to make a difference in the world, and hope this can be the case for you too."

Dee's quiet as they walk into the conference room. She knows Sara, of course, and Liz looks familiar, but she's only dealt with her briefly before her psychological crisis. Tess guides her in and motions for her to take a seat next to her around a table. She looks around at the other women. "So, I guess this means you're all vampires too?" Dee asks, uncomfortably.

Liz nods. "Yes, but, as you can imagine, the negative connotations of that term have become somewhat unpalatable to us. We prefer to call ourselves Apara, which is an ancient word for 'others'."

Dee reacts to the word, remembering it from when the subconscious pre-conditioning surfaced from her conscious mind. "Yes, *Sanskrit*, isn't it? I suddenly knew that and a lot of other things, including... well, I still have trouble saying it out loud; the virus was created by *extraterrestrials* adept in genetic engineering. That's mind-boggling!"

"So, you *know* about that?" Liz is surprised.

"When I was trying to analyze the virus after I gene sequenced it, I couldn't figure out certain elements, including some which don't exist in any life on Earth. It suddenly hit me and...well, that's when I knew I had to dissuade Jason from going through with it." Dee admits, still angry when she thinks about it.

Tess senses Dees anger and twinges of guilt. "It's okay! No one here's angry with you. We need to deal with this situation as soon as possible, and we *need* your help to do so." She reassures her.

"I kept copious notes in the lab, but I honestly don't know where the lab is. He always teleported me there and to the cabin." She explains.

Tess makes the connection between the cabin in her hellscape and the one she's talking about. "Is that where you were? In your *nightmare?*"

"*Yes!* That's the cabin, albeit, worse than it actually was. Unfortunately, I can't tell you where it is either. It's a hunting cabin, as far as I could tell, and I never heard any sounds of traffic. I

184

heard occasional flyovers of planes, but otherwise, only sounds from nature, and Jason." Dee wishes she could help more.

Sara clears her throat. "We'll get back to the location, but let's start with the virus itself. You did alter it, but I get the impression there should be two strains in Jason's system?"

"Yes, I had no way to eliminate the original strain. I used a sample from myself; the bastard wouldn't let me take a sample from him or even help me with the pain! After studying it, I spliced a copy of the key sequence into the inverse sequence of the virus to activate it, and then used RNA from a common corona virus spike protein to bypass the key sequence. I didn't *want* to do it at all, I hope you understand!" Dee is both apologetic and a bit frantic that everyone knows she was *forced* to do this.

Liz holds up her hand to stop Dee's guilty rambling. "We *know*! However, it's urgent we figure out what we're dealing with and make plans."

Dee continues. "I injected the altered viral variant into his bone marrow and told him to wait at least five days for it to colonize. He waited the minimum time, and I *tried* to talk him into doing more tests, but he *wouldn't* hear of it! He wanted to turn *someone*, some poor woman! To be honest, I noticed I'd begun to look younger, and it wasn't *just* my daughters I was afraid for. I worried he'd notice and see me as a viable.... I *think* you get the picture!"

"Yes, and he likely would have, eventually." Tess puts her hand on Dee's arm to reassure her.

"Honestly, at one point, I considered that as an option to get him to stop, but I also knew that he wouldn't be satisfied with just one woman. Eventually, he'd turn others." Dee admits.

Tess lets out a long breath. "Yup! That's him alright!"

Sara gets impatient and interjects, "Dee, There's only *one* strain of virus in his system. It *isn't* the original, but based on your description, I'm not sure it's your variant either!"

Dee looks upset. "How could that be? Unless...*Shit!* We need to get to the lab! We must figure out where it is! Is there any chance you can get him to tell you?"

Sara pauses, awkwardly, pondering how to explain this. "Dee, you remember being shot, right?"

"Yes! Not my all-time favorite memory! I assumed I was dying, but then woke up here." She has the feeling Sara's about to challenge her scientific assumptions again.

"By *human* standards, *you* and *Jason*, died of your gunshot wounds. However, when one of us dies, we go into biological stasis, while our bodies repair themselves. We appear dead. No breathing, no measurable brain activity, no heartbeat, but also, no degeneration. You were allowed to heal and go back online biologically. Jason is another matter. We had him in custody once before, but he was rescued by two women he'd changed, but he broke them to where they were loyal to him. I believe you would call it a form of Stockholm Syndrome?" Sara pauses and Dee nods. "As an added precaution, we implanted a device that will prevent him from completely healing and coming back online. He'll remain that way until we figure out what to do with him. As you can imagine, life imprisonment is not an option when one can live to be well over a thousand years old! And *killing* us is harder than the stories make it sound." Sara smirks.

"I see, so I'm guessing that would make him a dead-end? I wish I could help you, but I really don't know where the lab is!" Dee's frustration seeps into her voice.

"I believe we can still find it. Even though you never ported there yourself, your mind unconsciously knows where it is." Liz explains.

Dee is confused. "Me? Port? You mean teleport? He said not everyone could do that and that I couldn't! Do you mean I could have popped out at any time and escaped?"

"*Don't* be so hard on yourself! Under the circumstances, you couldn't have, but you *do* have that ability." Sara points to the new bracelet on her wrist. "I assume you noticed that you have a new bracelet?"

186

"I was wondering about that. Jason called it a mark of owner-ship, and Vince said something about it, but that's all a blur now." She fingers the bracelet, examining it.

Sara sits beside her and turns the bracelet to show the opal like gem in it. "The opal in the bracelet is not something you can get in an average jewelry store. It's from a planet in the Centauri sys-tem. It's technically an opal, but has some additional impurities and a higher silication level that can be used as a psychic modula-tor. We all have what you might call paranormal abilities. Para-normal is really a misnomer. All humans have the potential for basic psychic skills, but most of them only use it on a latent level. One of the things the virus does, is bring them out and amplify them to a usable level." Sara nods at Tess. "Why don't you give her a PK demonstration?" Sara gives Tess a wide grin.

"Really, Sara? Haven't I blown out enough light panels?" Tess gives her a sarcastic grin, but when Sara raises her eyebrow and stares her down, she knows she isn't getting out of it. "Dee, watch the plate of cookies on the table." Tess focuses, and a chocolate chip cookie rises from the plate, hovers in the air and flips end over end until it lands in front of Dee.

"*Holy Cow*! How'd you do that? *God*! I know a couple of physi-cists that would *kill* to study you!" Dee's eyes are wide, and she runs through the possibilities.

Sara continues. "A bracelet, or sometimes a pendant, made with one of those stones is a modulator we can set to limit psychic activity, or at least unconscious activity, until any of our people having issues controlling their skills can master them. This one will filter out any unconscious uses, but when we teach you how to use your skills, you'll be able to, including porting. The one Ja-son put on you was intended for a special class of recent trans-formees we've been recruiting, whose abilities are far above aver-age, and atypical, so he could program it to maximum, which cut off your abilities almost completely. I'm sure he didn't want you to use them to escape or against him."

Dee rolls her eyes. "What a *bastard*! That sounds like something he'd do!"

"We'll help you port shortly, and we should be able to find both the cabin and the lab that way!" Liz grins reassuringly.

Dee relaxes, feeling a bit more optimistic. "That's a relief!" She turns to Sara, who has returned to her seat across the table. "I'll give you all I've got! My journals, the genetic sequencing records of the original and the variant. I've got video of the few trials I did with the altered virus and non-compatible blood. I have a culture growing, but...how long have I been out?"

Tess says, "About two weeks."

Dee looks a bit stunned by that, considering no time has passed for her while in stasis. "Hope it hasn't overgrown the Petri dishes I was culturing it in. I also have preserved versions of the original and the variant stored at -80C since it contains both DNA and RNA, otherwise, the RNA degrades quickly." She rambles out scientific jargon.

Sara lets out a snort. "You know! Once we get this all sorted out, you and I need to get together and talk! I'd love to learn more about the virus from you. Until recently, we've always taken it as it came. We only recently got the genetic key sequence from our Benefactors, as we call them."

"I'll be glad to go over it all with you; Sara, was it?" Dee inquires.

Liz rolls her eyes, "*Scientists*! Speaking of the virus, Sara, what are the results on your samples from Dee?"

Sara pulls herself back on track. "Surprisingly, she's only carrying the original strain. I thought for sure she'd have been infected by Jason's new strain, but she isn't."

Kari ports in, startling Dee. Liz reassures her. "Dee, this is my partner, Kari Anderson. She's been doing some research on what we believe may be the result of your... tinkering."

Dee nods and Kari sits, out of breath. "Amy and I have been working on this for a couple of days straight. There's an increase in reports of certain psychic and paranormal phenomena, as well as psychiatric reports and references to things like hearing voices. The Atlanta area *is* ground zero, but we've been having reports from other cities as well, including a couple as close as Greenville, SC. It also appears to be popping up along other travel hubs that connect to Atlanta."

Liz covers her eyes and massages her temples. "Do we have any idea if it's hitting the general, human population or...?"

"Now, that's the good news! If you can call any of this *good* news. Of the cases we've been able to track down and identify, about 45 total identified cases, worldwide; all *are* genetically *compatible*. We thought we'd found one that wasn't, but the name was familiar, and it was an LM potential from the last batch we got in from Yasamen." Kari yawns, having not slept in about two days. She paths to Tess, *Now I understand why you wish caffeine still worked on us!*

Sara let's out a huge sigh and her shoulders sag. "That is very good news. It sounds like the virus is only affecting those who carry the gene sequence, so it doesn't appear to affect the general population, meaning we're talking a few tens of thousands of possible cases, rather than the whole human race being at risk!"

Kari clears her throat. "Sara, we still need to monitor the general population. I correlated the areas where there have been cases with reports of cold or flu-like symptoms. You know how it is, ever since the COVID pandemic, anytime anyone starts feeling bad, pandemic chatter rises. There *are* reports of a mild virus going around in the same hot spots, but it's only mild fevers, aches, pains, weakness, but no respiratory symptoms or sore throats. The only cases of psychic outbreaks are among genetically compatible individuals, thankfully"

Sara regards Dee. "You said your virus affected non-compatible cells?"

Going Viral

"*Yes,* though I didn't have time to explore what it was doing to them, it was clearly infecting the samples and trying to change them." Dee tells her.

"Hmm...yet, the humans don't seem to have more than mild symptoms and no psychic breakouts. I'll have to test some of the virus I got from Jason on non-compatible blood." Sara addresses Dee.

"We can also do a full gene sequencing of the new virus and run an analysis. I've got equipment and software that will do all of that!" Dee tells her, realizing her own scientific curiosity has been peaked.

"Dee, we may need to bring all your equipment, samples and so on back here to Medical. I'm worried that your lab could be found, especially if the human authorities, like the FBI are still looking for you." Sara suggests.

"Alright, we'll need some safety measures for transporting it through populated areas." Dee contemplates the best way to safely transport the virus.

"That won't be necessary. *You're* still thinking human!" She grins. "I need to explain a few things to you. Why don't you come to my office while the others continue to investigate the outbreak." The two medical women get up and leave the room, still discussing the situation. Liz suggests that Sue and Tess go back to the office to strategize, and that Kari and Amy, get some rest until Sara and Dee know more.

190

GETTING THERE'S
HALF THE BATTLE

Sara and Dee walk together to the lab at Medical. Sara places a sample of the virus strain from Jason in a portable virus cooler, and grabs a few pieces of equipment.

Once she has everything she needs, she puts the box of supplies and equipment next to her, touching her leg, and extends her hands out to Dee. "Take my hands. I'm going to connect to your mind; you should close your eyes and think about your lab. I want you to picture it in as much detail as you can and think about how it felt when you were there. Think about the light, the atmosphere, anything you associate with it."

Dee stares at her, confused, and uncertain how this will help, but she takes Sara's hands, closes her eyes, and does as she asks. She feels a sense of movement even though she's not moving physically.

Sara releases her hands. "Open your eyes!"

Dee opens them and looks around, amazed to see that they're standing in the middle of her lab. "How? I mean, I have no idea where the lab is! And yet, we're here." She grabs her journals and hands them to Sara. "I've got digital journals on the computer there, but my notes as I worked are here!"

"You didn't need to consciously know where your lab is located. Part of your mind knew, even if you've never known it consciously. Think of it as having a built in GPS! Let me ask you this, when you remembered some of the subconscious training, did you remember anything about porting?"

"Not how to do it, or I'd have tried to get to my daughters." She says, but pauses, trying to recall what information surfaced. "I don't know if this is right or not, but I remember something about having to pass between something, dimensions? It doesn't really make sense to me. Physics was never my strong suit!"

Sara nods and pats her on her arm. "*No*, but you're right. There are multiple realities; in fact, an infinite number. If you think of each one as a funky bubble, we living inside one bubble, but there's a membrane of sorts that doesn't follow the normal three-dimensional laws of our physics. We can slip into that membrane, but travel there is not forward, backward, up, down, left, and right! There is no linear reality there. We think about where we want to go when we enter and exit where our minds take us. On some level, you instinctively know where your lab is, as you also know where that cabin is. We'll have to go there too, so I can tell the others where it is. I won't make you stay there any longer than necessary. From what I gleaned from Tess and Sue's minds, that place holds some awful memories for you!"

Dee nods. "*No kidding*! This whole situation has been an absolute nightmare!" She pauses. "Sara, I know you all are...happy...being like this, but I didn't choose to become one of you. Isn't there any way to change me back? To make me human again?"

Sara's expression grows solemn. "There's *no* cure, at least not anything *we* have to offer. I suppose it's possible our Benefactors could reverse the process, but I doubt they would, especially now."

"Why especially now? Because I altered the virus?" Dee's voice shakes with frustration and a remaining tinge of guilt.

Sara takes her by the arm and leads her over to the mattress on the floor. She sits, motioning for Dee to do likewise. "It's not a *punishment*, if that's what you think?"

Dee nods. "I wondered, as it has certainly felt that way!"

Sara gives Dee her best Yoda stare. "Being Apara is far from a punishment. It's actually a compliment and an honor! It means they

192

chose you out of all the people on Earth because of your intelligence, your psychological stability and predispositions, and your psychic potential! Fewer than 1 in 250,000 people on this planet carry the gene sequence our benefactors spiced into your DNA! It wasn't a matter of it being a random sequence they keyed the virus to; they chose those they thought could do what's necessary, and who could handle the responsibility of the gifts entrusted to them! Though I see how, with your rather traumatic initiation into this life, with Jason as your guide, that it may seem otherwise."

Dee ponders this for a minute, then says, "Hmm, I may not have asked for this, but looking at it that way, I guess I can live with it." She gives Sara an awkward smile.

Sara says, "There are other reasons, too. There were many of our people over in Jerusalem trying to stop the nuclear bomb last year. We lost over 3000 of our kind that day, and I'm still patching up some survivors! Everyone we can transform helps us make up for those losses. I know it's not what you wanted, and normally, you'd have been out of the running because of your age, and status as a parent, but I'm glad someone like you has joined us. And yes, we *need* your help to deal with the altered virus, at least until our Benefactors can send representatives to help us."

"*Wait!* Are some of *Them* coming here? How the *hell* does that work?" Dee looks flummoxed, thinking about the possibility of aliens coming here or even meeting them.

Sara laughs! "Most likely, they'll send some of their own altered representatives! Our Benefactors, while humanoid, can be disconcerting to work with directly. They're highly telepathic, with an intellectual capacity that always makes me feel like I'm a child. The hybrids are engineered representatives that are a merging of human DNA and theirs, but it's been tweaked a bit as well. They can communicate both telepathically and verbally with ease, and look a bit more human. With a little help, they can even pass as human. You'll likely get to meet them since you altered the virus. They'll want to see, in your mind, what you did, in detail, and work with you to find a solution."

Dee blanches a bit at the thought of working with aliens. "Granted, as a scientist, I'm definitely *interested*, but I'm still getting used to being, well, this! Aliens are a whole other ball game!" She laughs.

"Don't worry too much!! Be glad it'll be them and not our actual Benefactors! Even *I* have trouble dealing with them for longer than a few hours at a time! I'm hoping they'll send Isanda! I've known her for a very long time, and she's very easy going! You'll like her!" Sara pats her on the knee! "Anyway! You said you have a culture of your virus growing, as well as preserved samples? Show me." Sara's eyes sparkle reassuringly, and the two women stand. Dee walks over to the incubator and containment unit for culturing viruses safely. She grabs her protective gear, but Sara stops her. "You won't need those! It shouldn't affect us, especially since you are not infected after almost certainly being *exposed* when you were shot!"

Dee shakes her head. "It feels very wrong not using protective gear, though it will certainly save time without it!" She punches in a code, opens up the unit, and pulls out a tray with several Petri dishes filled with viral cultures, but when she takes one out, she lets out a gasp.

"What is it?" Sara stands beside her, looking for herself.

Dee's confused and stammers out, "These cultures should be practically overflowing! But they're nearly dead, or may be dead! I don't get it! They cultured fine when I set them up. There were plenty of viral particles when I injected Jason's bone marrow, but these look like they've almost entirely expired! It's possible that they ran out of infectable host cells, but I really didn't expect their growth to regress this much! Let me check the frozen samples." She goes to the freezer unit, but Sara speaks up.

"Dee, we should take them back to Medical. I've looked over your equipment and I should have nearly everything we need there, though we should bring your laptop with us. I'm sure we can scrounge up a dock and a monitor for mirroring your laptop. Does your refrigeration unit have a battery backup?" She inquires.

"Yes, it should maintain -80C for at least two hours if the power goes out." Dee looks around the room. So, I should take my laptop, the refrigeration unit with the frozen samples, and my journals?" Dee disconnects the laptop from the external monitor, puts her journals on top of it, and brings them over to where Sara has her never-unpacked box. "I thought we were going to go over them here?"

"My lab's more advanced. Is all of this from your lab in Frederick?" Sara walks around, taking a mental inventory of everything.

"No. Most is, but the monitor, sequencer, separator/purifier, and some supplies were brought in after Jason took my equipment...and *me*, that is! Why?" Dee wonders what Sara's thinking.

"I wasn't sure how your equipment compares to mine, but mine is more advanced, and I'm sure our Benefactors will bring even more advanced equipment with them. Bring the cultures, even though they're no longer viable. Put them back in the containment unit for now. Unplug that, the cooler, and bring them over here." Sara rambles off, distracted.

"We shouldn't leave this stuff here. What if someone finds it?" Dee puts the last of the equipment in the collection on a table.

"*Oh!* That won't be an issue. I've got a decontamination team coming in when we leave. They'll make sure there are no viral particles left behind, or records in the sequencer's built in memory logs. Let's get these back to medical, and then I need you to take me to the cabin." Sara extends a hand to Dee, and the two women, the equipment, supplies, and preserved viruses reappear in a lab in medical. Several of Sara's people promptly move the viruses to a better containment unit, and take her laptop. "Now, let's try this again. Take my hands and picture the cabin."

Dee does so, the reaction is quicker, and the transition to the cabin is easier. In fact, she barely realizes she's traveled. She opens her eyes, looks around, and scowls at the grungy, rustic cabin. "What do we need here?"

"Don't worry about it, unless there's anything *personal* you want to retrieve." Sara gives Dee an empathic once over as she senses a stress reaction to being back in her 'backwoods dungeon'.

"Are you *kidding*? There's nothing here... well, wait a sec." She goes into the bunk room, opens a drawer in an old dresser with peeling paint, and digs in under the work clothes Jason acquired for her. She pulls out the printouts Jason had thrown at her of her daughters. "*Only* pictures I have left of the girls."

Sara sees Dee's eyes tearing up, walks over to her, and pats her on the back showing she understands. Sara ports them back to medical, into a room that is more livable than a standard hospital room. "We'll find you a place you can stay eventually, but for now, you can use this room. It's best to have you close by while we work on the viruses. Get some rest. I'll look through your journals and when you get up, we can look at the viruses together. I want to put samples of both together in a blood and tissue medium to see what happens. If you need me, think about me *loudly!*" She chuckles and walks out. Dee enters her temporary abode and finds clothes in her size in the closet and dresser. Not her usual style, but her old clothes wouldn't fit now, as her weight has redistributed to a more youthful form.

She takes the color printouts of her daughters out, and lays them on a nightstand by a regular, twin bed rather than a hospital bed. She turns on a light near the bed, turns off the overhead, lies down, picks up the images, and looks through them one at a time. She cries, knowing she'll likely never see or hug her daughters again, but also realizes it's the way it must be.

POTENTIAL CHAOS

Sara and Dee have worked for several days with the original and Dee's altered virus. They discover that the altered virus has become a *virophage*. While it does try to attack regular human cells, it is more prone to attack other viruses; in specific, the original virus that transforms humans into Apara. After the altered virus has infected all the cells and viruses it can, it dies off, leaving the original virus altered and active in both the bone marrow, and the bloodstream.

A meeting is called to bring everyone up to date. Besides the usual representatives from Inspiration Inc, Sara, and Dee, there are several Apara from other regions where human potentials have randomly developed various psychic or Apara specific abilities such as porting. The conference room has about twenty representatives, as well as Sara and Dee, who are sitting together at the end of a long table.

Sara stands and clears her throat. "As everyone's aware, some of our potentials have been developing active abilities while still human. Most of them have developed heightened psychic abilities or other senses, though one report of someone porting, and another who causes people around them to have memory issues, have been reported. Unfortunately, I have to confirm what most of you have heard as rumors; a variant of the virus that transformed us all has been released, and is transmittable by bodily fluids, including blood and saliva, as well as limited transmission through airborne particles."

A representative from one of the African centers, Imani, interrupts Sara with a question. "The virus has been stable for thousands of years! How is this possible?"

Sara nods to her. "If everyone can hold their questions, I'm getting to all of this. As some of you know, we've had a rogue in the Southeast US, around Asheville. He's turned several women over the last year. He's now in extended stasis here in Sanctuary until we can determine how to deal with him. The last woman he turned..." She motions to Dee, "worked as a geneticist and cancer researcher in Maryland. We cut off the rogue's access to our database, which he'd hacked early on. We also prevented him from getting to some of his targets, including a couple of our recently discovered Lost Mission potentials. We can surmise that he still had some files from the original database backed up somewhere, and that contained our latest Apara, Dr. Thaddea Price. Our rogue Apara resorted to various forms of abuse to control and manipulate his victims. Jason used physical and psychological violence against Thaddea, who goes by Dee; she was 48 when he kidnapped and turned her, and he used various threats, including against her two, adult daughters, to force her to alter the virus in his bone marrow. He wanted her to make the virus generally compatible, rather than only compatible with those carrying the genetic key sequence. If he couldn't find out who's compatible, he'd change the rules and make the virus compatible with anyone." There are gasps and mumbles around the table. "Please, don't be angry at or blame Dee. She's been through enough! I'm sure most of you would have done the same thing if family had been threatened." Sara stares everyone down until they become quiet and focus on what she has to say. "I've sent an overview of our findings regarding the virus currently in the wild. It is *not* the original virus, nor is it the virus Dee created; rather, her virus altered the original virus into a second-generation variant. The new virus affects those carrying the genetic key; in other words, all potential transformees. However, humans can *carry* the virus, and usually have mild symptoms such as fatigue, low-grade fever, and body aches. Some have presented with mild anemia and we believe some are asymptomatic carriers. The point is that humans are carriers but are not altered unless they are potentials. Meaning that there's no way *we* can prevent the spread at this time. It's no doubt already spread to thousands of humans before causing random changes in our potentials."

Again, murmurs around the table and an overall emotional cloud of foreboding hangs over the room. A Korean Apara man, Kyung, politely stands and waits to be acknowledged, asking, "Have there been any cases where potentials have developed fangs or a need for blood?"

Sara frowns. "Not so far, but we're monitoring the usual channels for any suspicious attacks or deaths which could indicate someone's developed that aspect of our condition. We certainly hope it's limited to our abilities, but even that has caused some problems. Early on, we came across a woman who ported spontaneously when a car almost hit her while crossing the road. We have people working to discredit such instances, especially this one, where there is a video of the incident."

Liz speaks up. "We've alerted all of our people at social media and search engines to be on the lookout for such reports, and for videos, and do their best to limit their spread, or even delete them when possible, or 'fact check' them into obscurity! Unfortunately, as the virus spreads, it may get harder for people to write off an increase in paranormal incidents."

Sara stands there as people chatter around the table. "Okay, *everyone*! *Please* focus! You'll have plenty of time to discuss when I'm done! Dee and I are doing what we can to analyze the rogue virus so we can predict how it works and what kinds of abilities it may bring out. The problem may be that some of the Lost Mission people, who we are still trying to identify, could develop unusual, stronger, or even problematic abilities. In addition, we believe this can affect potentials of any age, not just those we might normally consider turning, though we have yet to see it occurring in any young children." She turns to an African American woman. "Michelle, you told me before the meeting that one of your identified LM potentials developed an unusual ability, can you tell everyone about her case?"

Michelle nods, "Yes, Teresa Mendoza, one of the recent Lost Mission potentials we've brought in to our offices developed the ability to create a limited, spontaneous EMP-like effect when she's angry. She caused a major traffic jam when she got cut off on interstate 75 near downtown Atlanta and stopped thirty-two cars around her, causing some of the drivers behind them to collide with stopped vehicles! We had someone explain it away 'scientifically', but when she got to work, she shorted out three computers before we realized it was her, hazed her mind and had her energy levels checked. Naturally, we couldn't let her go home in that state, so she's currently staying with one of our people in Sanctuary and has been filled in on the situation. While she's accepted what we are and is willing to join us, we haven't yet turned her because we're not sure if the virus may cause any problems."

Sara fights off a yawn. She's been working with little rest for the last few days. "Michelle, I'll talk to you after the meeting, but we need to get a sample of her altered DNA and consider her a test case for post-viral transformation."

"*Unfortunately*, we're limited with what we can do other than watching for outbreaks and doing damage control. However, there is a hybrid team, as well as one of our Benefactors, on their way to Earth to help with this crisis, but it will still be at least three weeks before they arrive on Earth."

Yasamen, from the London and Middle East offices, stands. "I'll step up our searches for LM potential matches, since they are likely to present with more obvious and problematic abilities. Does this virus impact those already among the Apara?"

"No, it shouldn't. Once one of us is transformed, one gene in the key sequence is replaced so it's neutralized. The virus still needs an intact key sequence to latch onto to invoke actual changes. In humans, it's more of an immune response to the virus rather than the virus causing genetic changes." Sara explains. "One thing we need are blood samples from affected potentials and humans so we can see how their DNA is being affected. We don't believe it leaves any long-lasting effects in non-compatible humans, but we also don't have enough data to be certain."

A Native American woman with long, braided hair stands. Sara acknowledges her: "Yes, Aiyana?

"Sara, do we know if the new virus is stable, or is there any possibility it will mutate as it spreads? And do we know if any particular ethnicities among our potentials are more susceptible? COVID hit the Native American communities quite hard in 2020."

Sara purses her lips and thinks, *I'd hoped no one would ask that yet!* But says, "We *don't* know at this point. This is another reason we need blood samples, and, if possible, bone marrow samples of any infected potentials. In Apara, once the original virus runs its course, it becomes dormant and resides in our bone marrow, only becoming active when we feed on a compatible subject. This virus, at least in Jason, is always active and present in the bloodstream. Neither his original nor the first-generation altered virus remained in his system once the second-generation altered variant spread through the bone marrow and subsequently, into the bloodstream. It's vital we know if the altered virus stays in infected potentials, and if so, how long. We may need to resort to isolating them once infected."

"There may be thousands of potentials affected. Where would you isolate that many? Certainly not in *human* hospitals!" A Caucasian man with a Scottish accent blurts out.

We're working on building a rather significant complex of dormitory-like apartments in Sanctuary, similar to where some of our Jerusalem long-termers have been living. For now, we're building about 300, but we can expand that as needed. Alternately, these facilities can be used to house new, unpartnered Apara if it turns out we don't need to isolate our potentials longer than a short period of time." Sara paths to Dee, *And you thought all those COVID briefings in 2020 were complicated! Hmph!*

Dee paths back. *I think I've learned more in the last few days than I did in my last year of graduate work in genetics and virology! By the way, Thanks for standing by me. I would like to address everyone, if that's okay?*

Sara nods and gives her the equivalent of a telepathic hug. *You don't need to do that! You know!"*

I know I don't need to, but I want to.

Sara and Dee's telepathic discussion lasts barely a couple of seconds before Sara addresses the room again. "Everyone, Dee would like to say something. Please keep in mind the extreme duress she was under. She is not to blame for this and has been through enough punishment by our rogue to last her an Apara lifetime." Sara stares down the room, practically daring anyone to have any ill will toward Dee.

Dee stands. "I wanted to say that I'm very sorry for all of this. I didn't want to do this, and I know most, if not all of you, never had children prior to becoming Apara, so I hope you understand that I couldn't sacrifice my daughters. I tried to talk him out of this, and even considered sabotaging it, but it always came back to two things: my daughters' safety, and last, but not least, I was afraid that if I tried to weaponize it against him, that I might make it even worse than what he wanted me to do. I'm working with Sara and will be working with the...Benefactors and their team in whatever capacity I can to make this right." She nods briefly and sits back down.

Sara addresses everyone, "You have all the pertinent information on your tablets. Please go brief your centers, as well as any centers in or near your regions that are not represented here today." Sara dismisses the meeting and escorts Dee back to her room.

Sara chuckles unexpectedly; Dee stops and turns toward her. "What's so funny?"

"I was thinking how you said you'd considered trying to weaponize it against Jason. Whether you tried or not, you did accomplish that!" Sara grins from ear to ear.

Dee looks confused, asking, "And how did I do that? This virus is causing havoc because of him and he still carries it!"

"Yes, *that* he does! But the virus in him now won't turn someone, which was his goal, to be able to turn others freely! While it's not out of the question that it could turn someone out there, you've made it virtually impossible for Jason to *ever* transform another person against her will, even if he were to go free some day!"

Dee sighs with relief. "*Hell*! That makes me feel a *little* better!" The two women go down the hall to Dee's temporary abode, where a visitor is waiting for her.

UNEXPECTED

As Dee approaches her room with Sara, she notices someone sitting on a bench outside her room. She senses who it is before she can see him clearly. It's her proverbial guardian Angel, Vince. Dee grins, happy to see him again. Sara excuses herself and walks the other way, grinning, as she knows both Dee and Vince need a friend after losing what's important to them.

"Hello, stranger! I didn't expect you to come around now that I'm back on my feet!" The tension drains from Dee's shoulders and she stops to chat.

"Dee!" He stands and gives a slight bow. "I wanted to come by to check on you and see how you're adjusting."

Dee shrugs. "It's been crazy since I 'came back from the dead'!" She laughs awkwardly. "There's so much happening, including a lot of it that's more-or-less *my* fault, so I've been working with Sara to do damage control."

"Yes, I heard about the virus. If only one of us had stopped the shooter, maybe it wouldn't have gotten out!" He suggests.

Dee pauses, then tentatively shakes her head. "No, by then it was probably already spreading. The blood splatter just accelerated things. Sara believes that anyone he fed on, including the woman in the alley, became carriers as it can be passed by saliva, as well as blood."

"Any chance of tracking down the carriers?" He sits back down again and pats the bench beside him, and she joins him.

"Unlikely, it's already spread to far too many people to track, including asymptomatic human carriers. There were several hundred people at the venue, and I don't know how often Jason may have fed or otherwise exposed people in the week before we went to Atlanta. So, we're playing catch up as new cases are reported or suspected. Sara's got help coming from the... aliens? Benefactors? Never thought I'd be talking about aliens as fact, let alone get to meet and work with them!" She shrugs and shakes her head in bemusement.

"Ah! *Yes*! I've met them a few times. Fascinating minds! Constantly in motion and thinking on many levels at once! They're taxing to spend *too* much time with at one sitting, though I did my best!" He remarks. "*Hey*! If you aren't busy, maybe we could go get something to eat and I can tell you more about them! You know, to prepare you to deal with them!"

"That would be *wonderful*! We just finished the big briefing with a bunch of center reps. Since everyone was coming in from different time zones, I only napped a little, and now, it seems like it should be breakfast! I was so nervous! Afraid they'd all hate or blame me. Sara had my back, though! She made sure they knew I did what I could." They stand, and Vince slips an arm under hers. "Yes, Sara looks after those she likes! She's an excellent ally to have!" He remarks. "Dee, do you like Italian food?"

"*Yes*! Very much so! Though it usually gives me heartburn, but I'm guessing that *won't* be a problem anymore. Though is anything open this early? It feels like it should be breakfast!" She asks, and he ports them away to the town of Anchiano, Italy. They reappear in an alley near an old church.

Dee's a bit disoriented by the sudden port. "Where are we?" She looks down the alley. The street in front of the building is a walking street with inlaid flagstone, and no cars aside from one or two delivery vehicles outside shops. From the sun's position, she guesses it's around noon, give or take a couple of hours. They walk toward the main street and she sees old, stone buildings with ceramic tile roofs. The air is cool, but not cold. She hears people speaking, but not in English.

Vince laughs. "We are in Anchiano, Italy, where I *was* born!"

Dee gapes at him, mouth open and eyes wide. "*Italy*? I know this porting thing can get you from one place to another quickly, but I never expected to go to another continent for a meal!" She shakes her head in disbelief, but looks around as she gets out onto the flagstone street. The sun is shining, and there's a cool breeze. She looks at a nearby tree. It's large, with spreading branches, and has a few dark berries or fruit clinging here and there, while others litter the ground. "Is that an olive tree?"

Vince laughs. "I didn't expect *you* to know that! *Yes!* The season is pretty much over now! Anchiano is in Tuscany, not far from Florence; Olive country. *Come!* There's a little café down the street I believe you will enjoy." He grins and extends his arm. She tentatively reaches out to take it, but he slips his arm under hers, and guides her down the street in a rather old-fashioned manner.

"I *had* no idea you're Italian! Your English is perfect! You didn't have to go to the trouble of taking me to Europe! We could have grabbed something close by." She realizes that even though the crisis is over, she feels oddly at ease with this man, like on some level, she already knows him. They walk along the flagstone until they come to a street café with a few tables outside. A couple of other people sit in the sun reading newspapers and enjoying a midday repast.

"Have a seat. I'll go in and order. I come here often." He holds out a seat for her on the outside patio and goes into the building. A few minutes later, he comes out with two glasses of wine. "Local red wine from Tuscany." He offers her a glass with a slight flourish.

Dee takes it and nods. "Thanks! I could really *use* a drink! The last couple of months are still making my head spin!" She says, forgetting what Jason told her about Apara and alcohol. She takes a sip. "*Mmmm!* That's *nice!*"

"Unfortunately, you'll have to drink it for the taste! The alcohol has *no* effect on us!" He cocks his head to one side and smirks as he sits. He makes a silent toast and begins sipping from his own glass.

"Ah, yes. I forgot about that. So, you were *born* here?" Dee asks as she puts her glass on the table.

"*Not* in *this* café, but yes, here in this hamlet! But it was a *very* long time ago, and much different from today!" He stretches and laughs. "It's been a long time since I shared this place with *anyone!*"

"Is it okay for me to ask how long ago? When you *were* born, that is?" She quickly takes a sip of her wine.

He chuckles. "Promise you won't, as they say, 'freak-out'?"

She rolls her eyes. "Scientists don't 'freak out', we just revise our hypothesis!"

He laughs. "*Nearly* 600 years ago!" He raises an eyebrow and watches her grin turn into a silent 'Ohhh'. "It was *quite* different back then! It certainly *smells* much better now, that's for *sure!*" He lets out a belly laugh.

Dee shakes her head with a bemused expression. "This *really* is going to take some getting used to! So, how old were you when you joined this crazy life?"

His smile slackens, and he takes a slow sip of his wine. "Like you, *dear* lady, I was not as young as most. I was in my 60s when a seemingly young woman came to me one night and offered to show me more than my imagination and curiosity could handle. *Little* did I know what I was in for!"

"*Wow!* Don't I know it! My intro to this insanity was a harrowing experience. What *little* I remember was pretty rough! I hallucinated, vomited, and was wracked with fever. It felt like it lasted forever, and I was weak, and slept a lot afterwards. And all this 'de-aging'! It's such a strange feeling knowing that, in a few years, my daughters will look older than me." She feels like she's babbling. She glances down at her hands, noticing how smooth and supple her skin own has become.

He makes a slight snort. "Personally, I *don't* remember much at all. With my age, it was decided that the world should think I'd moved on to the afterlife! Once she started the process, and let it gain some speed, she did something to me. I assume she used telekinesis to rupture a blood vessel in my brain so it would appear a stroke took me in my sleep. This didn't happen here, but when I lived in France! I was interred there, and after a time, the woman came for me, and ported me out of the crypt. An unnamed old man who'd died penniless was left in my stead! By the time she came for me, I looked almost as I do now, albeit a bit shaggier!"

"Did she tell you what she was going to do to you?" Dee asks.

He looks distant, reminiscing. "Not *exactly*! She told me she could bring back my youth, give me many lifetimes to travel, learn, create, and invent! *However*, she left the *rest* out, but I've learned to live with it all!" His eyes sparkle with sarcasm.

Surprised, Dee asks, "You were an *inventor*?"

He laughs. "My *dear* woman, I was *many* things, including an inventor and a bit of a closet *scientist*! They apparently sent her to bring me in. My mind, for the time, was...let's just say *unique*! I was the definition of a true 'Renaissance Man'!"

"And have you?" She inquires.

"Have I what?" He looks at her questioningly.

"Learned more than your imagination and curiosity could handle? Have you continued learning and so on!" She says.

"I've *never* really stopped!" He laughs loudly.

"And how does *bartending* fit in with all of *this*? Or was that a *front* for rescuing me and catching Jason?" She finishes the last of her wine, and he immediately flags down a waiter to have her glass refilled.

"You *could* say I'm taking a *vacation*! I like to think of bar-tending as a mixture of chemistry and psychology!" He grins. "I've been doing it for the last year. The woman who brought me over to this life... she and I were together for a long time, but went our separate ways a couple of centuries ago, remaining friends. I wanted to travel and explore, especially the 'New World' as it *used* to be called!" His smile and eyes dim a little, and he drinks the last of his own wine. "You know about our part in Jerusalem, *right*?" Dee nods. "She was part of the evacuation envoy; helping to move as many people out of the city as possible in case the bomb couldn't be stopped. She was only about two kilometers from ground zero and didn't make it out. Even though we were no longer together, it hit me harder than expected. So, I stepped out of the active life among the Apara to have some time to recover from that loss! I followed an old friend to Asheville, North Carolina and got a job working in a craft brewery. I have fun mixing the drinks and it's helping me get back in touch with humanity again."

"I'm *sorry*. That *must* have been hard! I can't imagine knowing someone for *centuries* and *then* losing them!" She realizes that she will outlive her own children, and a glimmer of tears show in her eyes.

"Are you *alright*, Dee?" He notices her mood shift.

"Yeah, I hadn't connected the dots until now. I'll outlive my girls. That just *seems* wrong!" She sniffs and dries her eyes.

He puts one hand on hers. "I'm sorry. I didn't wish to bring you more pain! I'd hoped to give you a pleasant trip out and a break from your work with Sara."

"It's alright. I have to come to grips with it eventually. It will be strange not being in their lives, though." She looks up and sees the waiter carrying a large tray in their direction. He puts it down on a nearby table and begins to ramble off everything he puts down on their table in Italian.

Dee hears in her mind. *Eventually, you'll learn to translate yourself, it's one of our gifts! But for now, I'll translate! The platter is full of locally made, cured meats and cheeses, as well as fresh bread made this morning. The pasta is fresh prosciutto and Parmesan tortellini with black-truffle Alfredo sauce. And lastly, freshly made pistachio cake with almond frosting!*

"That's *a lot* of food!" She picks up a fork and tastes the tortellini. "Oh, *wow*!"

"What you don't finish, you *can* take home! Since we're porting, no one's going to stop you from taking it out of Italy!" He gives her an ear-to-ear grin. "Besides, there are no national borders in Sanctuary!"

They eat and Dee enjoys the variety of tastes and textures, especially with her heightened senses. "I think this is the first meal I've enjoyed in months! Not that the food at Medical is bad, but it's practical. And what little Jason gave me to eat was usually cold or old fast food!"

Vince grins, saying. "I *thought* you might be up for a treat! I used to meet Lisa here occasionally; the woman who changed me. I used to eat here all the time, but have only been here a couple of times in the last years."

"I guess you miss her?" Dee fills a small plate with cured meats, cheeses, and bread.

Vince gives her a wistful smile, but his eyes show sadness. "Yes, back when I first met her, years before she turned me, she was one of the few women I'd met that I could converse with on a variety of subjects, from art to science. You should understand that, back then, very few women were educated! I found I had to keep company with those who were the thinkers of the time. Mostly other men, but meeting a woman who could challenge my mind back then was a rare treat *indeed*! So, when she returned years later, having not aged a *single* day and offered me the literal chance of a lifetime, I *took* it! And we had nearly four good centuries together, but the thought of visiting new lands, and learning about new things, new cultures, ideas, and discoveries, was incredibly enticing to me! But *alas*! She preferred Europe! We agreed to part ways, but stayed in touch, meeting occasionally. We still had a connection, and when that broke at her death, it left me with an emptiness in my soul! It was Sara who suggested I take a year or two and do something simple. It helps, but sometimes, the conversations with bar patrons make me miss the company of a fellow brilliant mind even more!"

Dee leans back in her chair, saying. "I know the feeling about having someone who's a mental match. My ex-husband is a professor at UCLA. When we met, we inspired each other with ideas and theories; but it didn't last."

Vince looks at her, curious. "What went wrong?"

Dee looks thoughtful. "Ego mostly, that and a couple of nubile college students who knew how to stroke it. After that, everything revolved around him and what he wanted. At the time, he was at a small, private college, but that wasn't *good enough* for him! So, he started looking for a more prestigious institution, without even talking to me about what I wanted or how it might affect the girls. He got an offer from UCLA and *told* me we were moving, and I told him no! I had my career, the girls were happy in their school, in advanced programs, and that was that!"

Vince flags down the waiter and says something in Italian. The waiter returns a minute later with a fresh bottle of wine, opens it and leaves it at the table. "There are times I wish this stuff would still take the edge off of life!" He pours some for himself and for Dee. "Have you stayed in touch with him?"

Dee lets out a sardonic laugh. "No more than necessary! Mostly about the girls. He got them a deal on tuition at UCLA, but they must live with him to get it. Our own, hm... 'connection' broke long ago and I've not found that perfect storm of intellect and personality since. And now what? I'm stuck in this crazy new reality! It's not like I'm going to be rubbing elbows with all the other academics anymore!"

"Not *all* the intellectuals are *human*, you know!" He takes a slow sip of his wine.

"*Oh! Vince!* I didn't mean any *slight!* It's all so new! I feel like my head's spinning and I don't know which way's up." She shakes her head and absentmindedly picks up a cracker with a truffle laced sharp cheese on it.

Neither of them speaks for a couple minutes. Vince mulls over his next move as though it's some momentous decision. He gets a resolved expression. "There's a reason I don't share this place with many people. It's literally a bit too close to home for me, and I've spent a very long time keeping my *past* to myself."

Dee leans forward, her interest piqued. "*Why* would you do that? You seem like such a nice guy and... I don't know! There's something about you that just feels right, or comfortable to me!"

"I hope you still feel that way after I give you a little tour. I think I'd like to share this place with you a little more in depth." He winks and finishes his glass of wine, flags down the waiter and asks him, in Italian, for something to put their leftovers in. The waiter returns with containers and a bag, as well as the check. Vince pays with his card, but brings out a fairly thick stack of Euros and hands it to the man saying something, but the only word Dee recognizes is "mother" in the rapid barrage of Italian. The man nods and says *"Grazie"* several times, bowing slightly; then he turns and goes hurriedly back into the family-owned restaurant to give his mother the money.

Vince turns back to Dee. "I didn't visit here for a while, because I wasn't aging. His mother used to wait tables while his father cooked many years ago. I told the waiter the money was a gift from my father, that he still remembers this place fondly, and wants to help them out. They got behind a few years ago during the Pandemic. I checked and they have some outstanding loans. That should help them a little!"

"That was very nice of you!" She exclaims.

"They're family! Not descendants of mine, but of cousins, and I'm able to help." He says, packs everything into containers, and puts them in the bag, including the remainder of the wine. "Come, I want to show you where it all began." He extends a hand to her, they walk back toward the alley and port out, reappearing along a walking path that leads up to an ancient farm. They come in from the side, and see an old, stone building with a red, tile roof. The building is fairly low to the ground and surrounded by flagstones. There are people milling around.

Dee looks at all the people and asks, "More family?"

He looks down and grimaces. *"Tourists!* I avoid my past for a reason, *dear* lady!" He walks her over to a gateway, and on the wall, it says:

ANCHIANO
CASA NATALE
DI
LEONARDO

Vince doesn't say anything, but waits to see if Dee can pass this last test. She gasps and turns to him. *"Vince?* As in Leonardo Di *Vinci?"* She stares at him with wide eyes and a thought that this *can't* be true.

He looks at her and grins, bowing. *"Congratulations,* dear lady! You've just joined a very elite group of people who know who I really am!"

FLABBERGASTED

Dee stares at this reasonably modern looking, young man; her mouth silently hanging open as she looks back and forth at the sign and him. "Are you *kidding* me?"

"Not at all, dear lady! Due to my relative, historic fame, I've chosen to keep my identity to myself, even among most Apara. *Alas*! It's easier that way. I don't want to be treated like I belong in a *museum* even more than my artwork!"

Dee shakes her head in disbelief. "I *knew* there was something *special* about you, but I wasn't expecting this! This is *amazing*! I remember going to Washington, D.C. on a class trip many years ago. We went to the National Gallery of Art on the Mall. I stared for a long time at a portrait you painted; a woman, but I don't remember the name! When I got home, I went to the library, and did some reading up on you! Not only your art, but your inventions, and your amazing anatomy drawings! *Those* were part of what inspired me to go into the medical sciences! We had to do a report in History class: What one historical figure would you *most* like to meet? I chose *you* because you didn't let your time or culture stop you in your quest for knowledge! But I *never* thought I'd *actually* meet you!"

He chuckles. "That, my dear, must remain our little secret! Sara knows, and my friend, Titus Russo, he goes by Ty now, he knew me while I was still human. In fact, he was the one who arranged for Lisa to sit for me! Otherwise, only a handful of others know. I think Lissa, hm... Liz suspects, but has so far respected my wish for anonymity."

Dee's eyes go wide again. "*Lisa*? As in *Mona Lisa*?"

"Yes! You can imagine how I felt when she revisited me when I was 67 and still looked like the young woman, I'd painted years prior!" He snickers, and again, slips his arm under hers. "Come, let me show you around."

At first, Dee is flabbergasted by this turn of fate. *I'm walking around Leonardo Da Vinci's birthplace with the man himself as a tour guide! This may even beat the idea of working with aliens on genetic engineering and virology!*

Her mind races as they walk the grounds together. He points out various things from his memories of living here. As they walk and talk, she slowly relaxes into a comfortable rapport with him after her initial reaction to his reveal. They walk casually around the grounds, Vince willing those around them to ignore their presence, and not to notice when they deviate from the normal tourist paths, and settle under a spreading olive tree in a field.

Vince gives her a slight chuckle. "Granted, it's not the same tree as when I was young, but I used to spend hours sitting under one quite similar, and look out over the hills. Even then, my mind was filled with ideas, and brimming with curiosity!"

Dee sits under the tree with him, imagining what he must have been like back then. "Vince, or should I call you Leonardo? Leo?"

He gives her an amused grin. "Stick with Vince! I want as few as possible to know who I *really* am."

"Why tell *me*? You *barely* know me!" Dee asks as she stares into the eyes of this miraculous man.

He ponders in silence for a few seconds, gathering his thoughts, and takes her hand in his. "I've touched your mind and felt the brilliance there. Granted, a bit bruised and tarnished by recent trauma, but it's there. I could sense it from the moment you came up to the bar in the Peach Tree Pagoda, and it felt so good to sense that in someone again! Though, at the time, I was focused on the mission: stopping Jason and possibly multiple deaths, including yours. We didn't know you'd become one of us, but I could clearly sense it when I met you."

"How did you all know *where* to find us? And you mentioned *deaths*?" Dee wonders what forces drew this man into her life.

"My friend, Ty, the one I've known since I was human, he recently found a human woman and turned her. He didn't know she was compatible when they met, but he, too, lost his partner, Emma, to Jerusalem, and was lonely. But she shares one of *my* gifts! She sketches. But *hers* are perhaps even more remarkable than mine, as they show the future!"

"You've *got* to be *kidding* me!" Dee looks perplexed.

He chuckles. "She certainly *saw* Ty coming, even knew what he is, what would eventually happen to her, and yet, she faced it with grace. She's fairly new among us, but her skill is unmatched when it comes to her visions. She saw you and Jason, and the conflict over you having to choose which woman he would turn. She saw you protecting your daughters. That part happened, but the last part, played out somewhat differently. The original sketch was of you two in the Alley, with the blonde woman. She was lying on the ground with bite marks. You were already down, shot in the chest, and Jason was being shot in the sketch. We knew it was him, but we didn't know whether you were human or if either you or the blonde were alive or dead. Chances are, from what you told me about Jason's virus variant being incapable of turning someone, that had he been able to get further than a few sips, the blonde would likely have died from blood loss when the virus *didn't* turn her. We suspect, had we not intervened, someone may have tried to rescue the woman, believing you two were attacking her." He explains.

"I wondered how you all were there, ready to help me and stop Jason, but I was overwhelmed with everything. At least *something* good has come out of all of this!" She says.

He reaches over and gently caresses her left cheek. "*Yes*, I believe it did." He leans in slowly and gives her a gentle kiss. Dee's surprised, but returns the kiss, looking awkward afterwards. "What is it? Did I do it *wrong*?" He looks at her with a twinkle in his eye.

"It's nothing! Not the kiss, that was *very* nice! But there's been a lot of theoretical talk that you prefer the company of men. So, I wasn't really expecting...." She trails off, blushing.

"Yes, well, I'll admit that prior to Lisa, most of my companionship, intellectual, and otherwise, may have been down that path. A person's gender doesn't matter to me, you see! It has more to do with the light that shines from within someone. Most people are like a flickering candle. Moments of brightness and dimness! Some people are barely a kindling ember! But there are those few who I've tried to surround myself with whose minds shine like the sun! That's what matters, not what gender they are, what they look like, or if they are rich or poor!" He pauses, taking both of her hands in his. "I've missed feeling this in someone close to me since Lisa passed, and I feel you've missed it even longer! Perhaps *we* can be there for each other? Friends, companions, perhaps even *more*?"

She grips his hands tighter and looks into his bright blue eyes. "I'm not sure I deserve your interest after all I've messed up with my tinkering! But I think I'd enjoy spending more time with you, and see where it goes?"

He takes her hand and stands, pulling her up and close to him. "Then *I* have a *suggestion*! You don't *need* to stay at Medical if you don't want to. I've plenty of room in my home, if you'd like to stay with me?"

When she hesitates, he adds, "No pressure, Dee. I've got a guest room you can use until we see where things lead, but I'd really enjoy the company of a fellow, brilliant mind, no matter where things go... or don't."

His offer makes her thoughts and emotions war within her; she thinks, *what would my girls think of me taking up with some stranger?* Then she realizes *it doesn't matter what they think! I'll always care about them, but my life is now on another path. What I do has no effect on them now.*

She looks at him and says, "I think I'd like that. I mean, living in the same home as Leonardo Da Vinci! I'd be crazy *not* to take you up on that. I'll have to clear it with Sara and get my clothes and stuff from Medical." She stares at him, still finding it all somewhat hard to believe!

"I *suspect* Sara already has an inkling about us!" He laughs gregariously and pulls her into a hug. "Sara has a bad habit of matchmaking. *She* was the one who suggested I be there when you awoke, after all. She suggested that I make you *feel* safe!"

"She was right there." Dee yawns, exhausted by her day's adventure.

He leans in, kisses her again, and the world swirls away, her eyes now closed, and she knows they've ported because the air is warmer and still. She opens her eyes as Vince releases her from the embrace.

"Took you two long enough!" comes a very familiar voice from a chair in the corner of Dee's room. They both look at Sara, sitting there, grinning like a cross between Yoda and the Cheshire Cat! There are duffle bags at her feet, Dee notices her closet's empty, and all her belongings are packed. "Thought I'd save you two some time!" She gives them a knowing look as she picks up a box from a nearby desk. "Here's your laptop, a tablet, a cell phone, and some hard copy info on the latest updates!" She faces Vince with a faux-serious expression. "I *assume* you'll get her back here tomorrow morning so we can continue our *work*?" Sara eyes him like he's a mischievous scamp!

"Of course, Sara! I'll make *sure* she gets back here when you need her!" He leans over, picks up the duffle bags, and Dee picks up the box. The two port out, but there's a lingering, telepathic message and a big mental grin from Sara, *Have fun!*

HOMECOMING

Dee and Vince appear in a living room with a high, slightly domed ceiling. She gapes in amazement as it looks like the canopy of a rain forest, full of branches, vines, tropical flowers and even wildlife.

"Oh, my God! That's magnificent! That must have taken you ages!" She exclaims.

He laughs and stands behind her, giving her a hug. "That's one advantage to being nearly immortal! I was inspired by a trip to Brazil's rainforest about 150 years ago. I only wish I could have fully captured the beauty I saw! But *alas*! There were no color cameras back then, so I had to paint it from memory."

"I'd say your memory is pretty damn good! I feel like I'm there!" She looks closer, noticing a hint of movement and realizes the birds in the trees are not paintings, but intricately painted models done to scale.

He spins her around to face him and smirks, saying, "If you think that's an amazing view, come with me." He releases her but takes her hand, leading her up a flight of stairs to a room with double doors. "This will be your room. Even if we do end up together, this can be your personal sanctuary when you need time to yourself." He opens the doors wide, and bows, motioning her in. She steps into what amounts to a small suite, with a living area, a bedroom and bathroom off to the side." Cooking you'll have to go downstairs for, otherwise, all you could need is here.

The walls have decorative pillars in relief every few feet, with hand-painted, climbing roses going up them. If they'd been any more realistic, she could have smelled them. She follows the roses up the walls and onto the ceiling. It's painted like a pergola, with the flowers wrapping around painted wooden latticework.

"Like it?" He smirks.

"Well, if I didn't believe you about who you are, I have no doubt now!" She laughs and looks him in the eye, still amazed that this man is not the lowly bartender who rescued her from Hell, but Leonardo Da Vinci in the flesh!

"Both the living room mural and this were my experiments in Trompe-l'œil. It means to deceive the eye in French. I became fascinated with the technique, and must admit, I may have gone a bit *overboard*. But this is only part of what I wanted to show you." He leads her to another set of double doors, these leading outside, to a veranda. He opens them, and motions her to go out.

She steps out to a view of rolling hills, a sculpted garden nearby, olive trees, and what appears to be a small grape vineyard some ways away from the house. Dee has the strangest feeling. "I feel like I've been here before."

"My dear lady, in a way, you were here just an hour ago. This is the same location in Sanctuary as my original home in Anchiano. I built my home in Sanctuary on the same lands I was born on, though being just Lisa and I at the time, it is far more modest than the tourist trap you visited earlier." He says, smugly.

"I'd hardly call this modest!" She stutters out in amazement.

"It is merely my home as I have made it, and now, I wish to share it with you, *Cara*." He says softly.

"Thank you, Leo...sorry, Vince. After what I've been through the last months, this feels like Heaven after a tour through Hell, and I'm ecstatic to spend this time with you, in whatever form it takes."

Vince spends the next hours giving her a tour of both his home and lands, including his artist workshop in a lofted area with a large window for extensive sunlight. He then takes her on a tour of the land, showing her the gardens, his vineyard, and a large barn like building full of centuries worth of his tinkering with inventions.

When they leave his "Hall of Amazing Contraptions", as she dubs it, he stops to pick up some dried olives which have fallen to the ground and withered in the Mediterranean sun. He stuffs them in oversized pockets and extends his hand to her. She takes it and he ports her to a still, blue lake.

"Watch..." He says, taking out a couple of olives and tossing them out into the lake. The next thing she knows, a large fish practically leaps out and grabs an olive mid-air.

Dee inhales, then lets out a laugh, blurting out, "Can I try?"

He reaches into his pocket for more sun-dried olives, and hands them to her. She tosses one, and it goes much further than she expects. Two fish leap out for the same olive and bounce off each other, the olive drops into the water and is gobbled up by a third fish. She laughs so hard she has to sit in the grass.

Vince joins her. "I've missed hearing laughter around me here at home. It's nice to hear it again." He says offhandedly.

When she calms down, she looks at him seriously. "I just hope you're not disappointed in me now that you've entrusted me with your big secret. I'm afraid you may be projecting too much hope onto me. I may not live up to your expectations." She says, watching a stray duck land in the lake to see what the fish find so enticing.

Vince reaches over and gently tips her face to look at him. "Dee, when you were slipping into stasis, I was in your mind. In that instant, I knew who you were, and are. I knew you had a mind to rival my own, and while a bit worse for wear after Jason, I believe we have the potential for grand adventures together in the future." He says and gently leans in for a kiss.

Dee hesitates slightly, thinking, after what I did, I don't deserve someone like him.... But her negative thoughts evaporate as his lips touch hers and she feels like energy is flowing back and forth between them. After a couple minutes, they separate.

He says, "Sorry. I don't want to push you too fast. It's just I feel like I know you so well after our mental contact, and I forget you may not have felt it in the same way." He stands, extending a hand down to her. When she takes it, he pulls her up. They stand there, watching the sunset, side by side. He ports the two of them back to his abode, saying, "Are leftovers okay? I haven't exactly shopped for food for two." He grins. When she nods, still somewhat stunned by the day's events, he enters his kitchen and prepares the remains of their lunch, including more wine, and more of the pistachio almond cake for dessert.

Dee is completely sated and exhausted, even though her body's clock is six hours behind Italian time, and she nearly falls asleep at the table.

"If you're that tired, *Cara*, you should rest. I'll clean up. Your bags are in your room.

She drags herself woozily up from the dining room table, yawning uncontrollably. She tries to say goodnight, but only additional yawns come out. She clumsily waves at him, and he nods back at her, knowing he made the right choice confiding in her. Now he will just have to be patient.

She stumbles to the stairs, and drags herself up them by the railing, walking almost on autopilot to her new quarters. She looks longingly at the bathroom, where she sees a large, porcelain tub with gold, lion's foot legs. The cabin only had a cramped shower, and Medical still had showers, rather than tubs, at least in her room. It's been ages since she could soak in a warm bath and unknot her muscles. She realizes that if she did bathe, she'd likely end up back in stasis, falling asleep and 'drowning' in that deep tub. She thinks, *tomorrow....* slips under the covers without changing, and is asleep seconds after her head hits the pillow.

A few hours pass, and all is quiet in Vince's provincial home. Both he and Dee are sound asleep in their own rooms when he's startled awake by waves of terror. He barely remembers to grab his robe, not wanting to encroach on Dee's privacy with his nudity, as that is how he always sleeps. He dashes into her room, and she's tossing and turning, and sobbing in her sleep.

He picks up waves of despair and fear emanating from her, and cautiously sits on the edge of her mattress, doing his best not to startle her. He gently brushes her cheek and silky black hair, whispering, "Dee! It's alright, you're safe. Please wake up."

After a minute, she startles awake, not fully certain where she is, tears flowing, and jagged sobs fighting to escape her lungs. He gently takes her by her shoulders and gives her a gentle shake to make her focus on him, saying. "Dee! *Listen* to me, you're *safe* in my home!"

Her eyes suddenly become clear, like she's seeing her surroundings for the first time, and lets out a long, jagged sigh. "Oh! Vince! It was *horrible!*" She utters.

"What is it, *Cara*? What's wrong?" Vince asks, searching her eyes for some clue to what is wrong.

"I guess it was just a nightmare, but it was so vivid!" She says, trying to regain control of her emotions.

Vince pulls her close, holding and rocking her until she's ready to tell him what she dreamed. After a few minutes, her breathing calms enough for her to get the words out, "It was dreadful! I was back home, reunited with my girls, and Lynda told me she got married while I was gone, and wanted me to meet her husband. I followed her to where he was, and saw his hair, and dreaded what I knew was coming. He turned around and it was Jason! He grinned at me wickedly, standing behind Lynda. He smirked, fangs down, and said 'Nice to meet you, Mom!" and bit Lynda! Then she sprouted fangs, and the two of them turned Celia, too! Oh, God! It was a true nightmare! Just Ghastly!"

Vince pulls her close again, rocking her, saying, "Hush, Dee! That's never going to happen! Jason is safely locked away. Your girls are safe. I promise!" He continues to rock her as she sobs and cries herself out, slowly dozing on his shoulder. He gently disentangles her from him and lays her down, pulling the cover up over her. He can still sense a mixture of horror and exhaustion warring at her unconscious mind; the one making her sleep, while the other side of the coin wants to wake her so she won't dream such horrid things again.

He takes a quilt from an old chest and settles in a nearby armchair, protectively, as though his very presence might ward off the nightmares threatening to ravage her soul. Before he dozes off, he paths to Sara, who's still awake working on the virus issue, and lets her know Dee may be late, as she needs sleep and recovery time. Exhausted himself, he nods off, not waking until she does the next afternoon.

CONNECTIVITY

Dee spends her time split between long work days with Sara at Medical and 'home' with Vince, getting to know him better. On one level, she instinctively knows him, as he does her, but she doesn't trust such intuitive, gut feelings over logical deductions. Part of her resists getting closer to him because she doesn't have a logical path for what's happening so quickly, but that is not the only thing holding her back.

She senses Vince longs for more, but is holding back, leaving the progression of their budding connection to her to take at her own pace. She appreciates him giving her the time and space she needs, and yet, it makes it that much harder, because she has to choose to make the next move.

It's a Saturday, and Sara insists she take a break. Dee spends the day at home with Vince, but he's called in to bar tend late evening, European time.

"Sorry, *Cara*, I'd hoped to spend the entire day with you, but it seems there is a bug going around, and despite my being officially on vacation this week, they need me to come in." He says, gently caressing her cheek.

Dee looks deflated, not only because Vince must leave, but because the mention of a virus going around makes her cringe. "I hope it's not *my* virus." She says.

He crouches down in front of her and leans his forehead against hers. "You must stop beating yourself up over this! You were in an impossible situation. Choices were made, yes, but you really had no choice, not with Jason's threats at play. The Hybrid team will be here soon. I'm sure they'll be able to find a solution. Get some rest. I'll check on you when I get home."

Dee nods without saying anything, and watches him port away to Asheville to tend bar for the evening. She's been contemplating her options with Vince all day, and felt almost brave enough to talk to him about it, but now that point is moot.

She climbs the stairs and cuts through her room to the veranda. For a winter night, it's relatively warm, and she stares off into the distance. Because of her enhanced, Apara vision, she sees details even in the dark. She stares off into the distance, noting how much the nearby mountain range reminds her of Frederick, Maryland.

She thinks, *there's really no going back, but how do I move forward? I know Vince wants more, but my whole adult life has been all about either my family or my career, or the competition between them.* She continues to ponder her dilemma, searching her soul to find what she really wants. After about an hour, she crawls into bed and sleeps.

Vince ports in, flustered and irritated at 9 AM Central European time. Dee is sitting in a glass enclosed patio eating cereal and yogurt, with fresh berries. Rain has moved in while she slept, but she's warm and dry inside the glass shell with a fire in a nearby stone fireplace.

Vince joins her with half a cantaloupe on a plate and a cup of cappuccino. He gently drags his hand along her back as he joins her. "Get any sleep?" He asks.

"Yes, no nightmares, if that's what you mean. How was work?"

"Annoying." He says and stabs at his cantaloupe in frustration.

"Annoying? What does that mean?"

"It means that after they dragged me in, we hardly had any clientele! It would seem someone started a rumor that COVID was back, so most people stayed home, including much of the staff! I sat there, polishing glasses and straightening up bottles for several hours until we closed, only to have the boss approach me after closing for help in the kitchen cleaning up, as half his kitchen staff called out as well." He sighs. "I'd have much rather stayed home with you, but therein lies the responsible behavior instilled in us all by our benefactors! Playing hooky goes against the grain!"

226

Dee pauses thoughtfully, asking, "Will you have to go in tonight?"

He glances at her, sensing something percolating under the surface. "He'd like me to come in, but if you need me here, it's not like I need the money!" He waits tentatively for her reaction.

"Vince, I know you got this big mind dump from me, but I feel like I need to explain myself to you." She says cautiously.

He nods, but stays quiet, listening, and maintaining eye contact.

"I know you want more, and I do, too, but...how do I put this? No matter what I look like now, I feel too *old* to start over! I have a lifetime of baggage. My whole adult life has been focused on a career or family. I tried to date after I moved to Frederick. It was the most awkward thing I've ever done! Everyone puts on their best facades, trying to draw someone in. Honestly, I don't know how to do relationships anymore!" She lets out a nervous laugh.

Vince's expression softens, knowing that Dee is open to more, but is stuck in her human reality. "*Cara... Amore*, take it from someone approaching their seventh century, you're never too old!" He smirks, then leans in and hugs her. "I realize things have happened quickly, but this isn't a dating app or website. We don't need to go through all the ritual song and dance like humans do, *Amore*. With telepathy and empathy, it's possible to know the important stuff quickly. Yes, we'll have to discover the minor details about each other, but I know you! And on some level, you know me better than you realize. Perhaps you don't know how to access that, or you don't trust that?" He cocks his head to one side, waiting for her answer.

"Vince, I'm a scientist! You're talking about gut instincts and possibly imaginary impressions when I was dying of blood loss! How can I let go of a lifetime of strict, scientific method and just trust my instincts? I want to, but it goes against all my training, and I'm not sure how to get around it." She says, torn between logic, emotions, and a desire to take an irrational leap of faith.

Vince sits back in his chair and stares out at the gentle rain in thought, then says, "I'll be right back." He ports out without even standing up, returning twenty minutes later with a small vial of blue liquid. "This may help, and Sara gives her blessings."

"What's that?" Dee asks, skeptically.

"A drug we sometimes use to either open up psychic pathways in new transformees, or it's used to share dreams. For what I have in mind, the dosage will be between those two uses." He smirks. "When you're finished, come up to your room. We'll do it there."

Dee glares at him, uncertain of his plans. "Do *what*?"

"Recreate the psychic intimacy of the night we met, without the trauma." He ports out before she can object, reappearing in her room to make things ready, including closing all the curtains and reducing distractions.

Dee wanders in the door a few minutes later, still hesitant to port around casually. She closes the door and leans against one of the faux-columns. "What makes you think this will be any easier for me to accept than what I gleaned from you at the Peachtree Pagoda?"

He motions for her to join him on the edge of her bed. "Because, you'll be fully aware and not in a crisis that makes you question everything as...hm...oxygen deprivation delusions? Isn't that what you call them?"

She joins him and settles roughly, annoyed. "Reading my mind is not fair, buster!" She scowls with feigned annoyance.

He reaches over and grabs two shot glasses with a small amount of blue liquid in each, handing one to her. "Humor me! You *know* you're safe with me. Drink that, and I'll drink mine. Then we'll lie down and wait. Consider it an experiment!" He grins, knowing that will reach her scientific sensibilities.

She purses her lips, putting little faith in shared dreams, but drinks it down and lies in bed. Vince takes his and lies beside her, taking her hand in his. After a few minutes, she drifts off and she and Vince are back beside the lake. She looks around her and everything seems vividly real. "I thought you said you were going to recreate things from Atlanta?"

"No, I'm creating a connection between us like that night, but without the trauma. This place has a link to joy in your mind! One of the first times since your nightmare began you relaxed and felt joy. I sense you've been missing it far longer than that, however."

She lets out a deep breath and relents. "What do you need me to do?"

"Come here and lean against me. Close your eyes, and let go." He tells her.

She looks at him skeptically, but does as he says, leaning against him in the grass and closing her eyes. He enfolds her in his arms, and she gets an overwhelming feeling of safety which grows warmer and overwhelms her with a feeling of love, and a sense of who this incredible man is. She perceives the depth of his intellect and a goodness in his soul she never knew from her husband.

She'd married him because they had an intellectual rapport, but the emotional was never really there. At the time, it was logical they became a couple, but there were few emotions involved, at least not from him. She realizes it was *his* deficit, not her own, but his lack of emotional capacity dampened her own, for if she felt deeply, she wouldn't have been able to stay with him as long as she did, as he could never satisfy her emotional needs. It was easier to just suppress her own emotions and live in survival mode.

The more she feels from Vince, the more her own emotions wake to life. It's turbulent at first, feeling things from her past with her husband, and the joy of her daughters. He somehow sidesteps her emotions around the last couple of months, as that trauma would sabotage his efforts.

The longer the experience lasts, the less she's able to tell where Vince's mind and emotions end and hers begin. Time stands still in that state, as two souls merge, briefly, into one.

As the drug wears off, she awakens in her bed, curled up on Vince's chest. She has a hitherto unknown feeling of peace, and a feeling of total connection and comfort with this man. She feels love, both from him, and within her own soul for him. She gasps and looks up at his face.

He has a gentle smile, and paths, *Believe me now?* He tips up her chin and makes eye contact before leaning down and kissing her, gently at first, but with more fervor as she responds, no longer uncomfortable with the idea of intimacy with him; for now, he is far from a stranger! She *knows* him as deeply as he claims to know her.

They make love under the ceiling of red roses; quite fitting for the love and passion they've found for each other.

A *PORTENTIAL* PROBLEM

It's been a little over two months since Callie joined the ranks of the Apara. She's now doing her jewelry nearly full-time in a workshop Niall set up for her at their home, in Sanctuary. Otherwise, she learns to use her basic Apara skills from various teachers, including Niall. They decide she should quit her daycare job because her new needs, abilities, and physical strength create too much of a risk, uncontrolled, around the children.

She's been frustrated lately. When Niall turned her, he told her she would likely have some unusually strong abilities, but she's been having trouble even getting her 'normal' ones, at least normal for Apara, to work properly. Not having the usual pre-conditioning is turning out to be a major stumbling block for her.

She gets permission to take a break from all things Apara and get back to her jewelry work for a while. She's in her workshop, setting up to do some casting. She just put the scale out on a workbench so she can measure the plaster for her casting molds when she gets a phone call from an old friend. She gets talking to them and heads into the main house to fix some snacks while she chats. She's thinking about weighing her plaster, turns around, and her scale is there, on the kitchen counter. *What the absolute hell?* She thinks, grabbing it, and her tray of snacks in one arm and carrying her cell with the other.

She heads back to her workshop, puts her snacks down, the scale back on her bench, settles in a rocking chair while she talks and snacks. When she's done talking on the phone, she goes back to work. She mixes out the plaster, blends it well, and puts it into a vacuum jar to get all the air bubbles out. She fills a flask with wax molds inside it with plaster, and again, vacuums it to get the bubbles out. She repeats this process for a total of nine five-by-three-inch flasks, lining them up on the other end of the table to dry. When she's on the last flask, her throat is itching from some of the plaster dust floating in the air, and thinks, *I'll have to go grab a soda from the house after this one!* She puts the last flask with the others, and turns around; There's a cold bottle of Dr. Pepper sitting right next to her vacuum machine! She thinks, *Okay, what's going on here? Maybe Niall was listening in telepathically and sent me the soda?* But then she thinks about the scale mysteriously showing up in the Kitchen when she *knows* she left it in the shop!

She reaches out to Niall telepathically, at work at Inspiration Inc., *Are you playing games with me? Trying to pull a prank or something?*

After a few seconds, she gets a telepathic reply, **What are you talking about? I've been in meetings all morning! What's going on?**

Weird stuff! She paths. **I've had stuff suddenly move from where I put it in the shop to the kitchen, and then I was thirsty and turned around and a cold soda was sitting there by my equipment where it wasn't seconds before!**

Ah! Okay! It's probably your unconscious mind using your porting ability to move stuff around! Some of us can do that consciously! For example, we forget something at home, so instead of porting home, grabbing it and coming back, we can picture it and pull it to us! If it becomes a problem, put your cent-opal bracelet on! I'll help you when I get home. He writes it off as normal, but she still finds it disconcerting.

Okay. Hate using that thing, makes my wrist tingle, but I'll get it. She paths. She ports to their bedroom, grabs the bracelet, fastens it around her wrist, and returns to her preparations for casting. Once the bracelet's on, no more mysteriously porting objects show up. She cranks up her music in her studio and gets things ready for casting the next day.

***

There's a meeting in Liz's office at Inspiration Inc. The usual crowd's there, Liz, Kari, Marc, Tess, and Peder, as well as Niall, who's been acting as liaison to his Apara sibling, Katie, in Atlanta. They aren't biological siblings like Liz and Peder, but were taken in by the same, elder, Apara woman when they were turned. In their case, it was more a sibling relationship than anything romantic, and their Apara 'mom', Tanith is one of the older Apara still active among them, on par with Sara and a handful of other senior Apara.

They're discussing the latest developments around the altered virus. Liz clears her throat. "Okay, everyone! Sara's been updating me on the virus situation. It's spreading through the human population rapidly, but only appears to cause a mild immune system reaction. Sara needs more samples to see if it's changing any human DNA or not, but we believe they're just carriers. Unfortunately, anyone who's a potential runs a very high risk of catching the virus, if exposed. We've yet to see anything that will let us predict what abilities may surface. It's like playing Russian roulette! In some potentials, they may see minor elevations in general psychic levels or even increased physical senses, while others may manifest a specific talent to a point where it could expose our existence. We know the virus has spread beyond the United States and North America. The Atlanta stop on the k-pop group's tour was one of the last stops on their tour before heading back to South Korea. We've had our centers in Busan and Seoul watching for cases. There has been an increase in mild viral symptoms among the general population, and at least three cases among potentials. In one case, a 59-year-old man was put into a psychiatric hospital for hearing voices. His telepathic sense blossomed with no control, so he's picking up on everyone around him. Unfortunately, they're treating him with anti-psychotics and other medications for schizophrenia, which is not going to do any good in his case. Sara suggests replacing the GPS core of our trackers with a small sphere of Centauri opal, and see if that reduces or cuts out the 'voices'. The other cases are relatively minor, but we're monitoring them for further development."

Marc clears his throat and asks, "How much Centauri opal do we have on hand?"

Liz sighs and says, "*Unfortunately*, nowhere close to enough if this spreads rapidly! We've been putting the strongest ones into necklaces and bracelets for new Lost Mission transformees. Our techs are working on creating small, polished pieces that can be used on some of the more extreme cases, but a lot depends on if we see a sudden spike in cases, but it's a temporary measure. We believe the hybrid team is bringing more with them since we're bringing over Lost Mission potentials; we may have to spread it thinner until they can send an unmanned shipment to us."

"How long until They get here? Katie needs to know, as she's dealing with ground zero of the outbreak." Niall asks.

"Probably about another two weeks, so expect things to get worse in the meantime, especially as it spread among the general human population quickly, albeit harmlessly." Liz takes a seat as she's so exhausted, standing takes too much effort.

They move on to other subjects, including the status of the Lost Mission potential project. When the meeting is over and everyone is heading out, Liz says, "Niall, can you stay for a few?"

He stops, turns around, and sits again. "What's up?"

"You seemed a bit distracted at one point. Is everything okay at home?" Liz inquires as she picks up her mug of sassafras tea and sips it.

"Yeah, nothing major. Callie's been frustrated with her abilities not working the way she expects them to, and now, her porting ability has developed a mind of its own. She had a bottle of soda suddenly show up when thirsty...that kind of thing. I told her to put her bracelet on for now and we'll work on it when I get home." He grins, trying to make light of this turn of events.

"Are you sure she's alright on her own? I know you've only been coming in when necessary." Liz reaches over and picks up a tablet.

"I'm *not* sure. It depends on what's going on with her and this spontaneous porting of objects she experienced today. I think it freaked her out, but if the bracelet stops it, I may be able to come in more." He says, but Liz feels his uncertainty.

"I was wondering if you'd be willing to help Katie out in Atlanta for a few days. You can always pop back home to check on Callie, or even take her with you. Maybe she'd like a chance to get out and about again? Or we can find someone who can keep her company." Liz suggests, trying to be helpful.

"I'm sure I can port down there and help Katie off and on. Callie knows how to reach me if she needs me." He trails off, a thought occurs to him. He picks up his cell phone and checks something. A smile crosses his face. "I *thought* so! An artist she likes is putting on a concert in Atlanta this weekend. I've seen a poster for them and meant to look into it. I can surprise her with tickets, if there are any left."

"That's a great idea! Here's a tablet to take to Katie with all the latest information. Sara said to tell her they are going to attempt transforming Teresa Mendoza soon. The key sequence is still intact, so hopefully, our standard virus will still work on her. If not, we'll have to see what the Benefactor's team can come up with. They're doing tests to see if the altered virus has left her system or not." Liz yawns. "Sorry, I've not had enough sleep since all of this hit the fan. Kari threatened to have Sara knock me out tonight." She grins.

"I'm going to check on those tickets and then head home to tell Callie what's going on. If you don't mind, see if Tess or Sue could make a little time for her?" He picks up the tablet and heads upstairs to his office.

He sits at his computer and pulls up several ticket sites; after a little finagling; he finds two tickets to see a couple of members of Starship perform, including their lead singer. They're doing one last tour before retiring for good, and he knows Callie would love to see them in person before they retire. He grabs the tablet Liz gave him, a few things from his office, and ports home.

He ports into the living room, finds Callie lying on the sofa, and feels frustration and pain emanating from her. Niall crouches down beside the sofa and brushes her hair out of her face. "What's *wrong*?"

He carefully scans her mentally, but before he can come to any conclusions, she rolls over, facing him, saying, *"Headache!* This thing makes my head throb! But if I take it off, I'm afraid things will start popping around the house." She lets out a small whimper as the light in the room makes pain shoot through her head.

He reaches over and tries to ease the pain. "Did that help at all?"

"Some." She squints from the bright light behind him.

"Get some rest. I'll see if anyone can come here and adjust your bracelet. It may help if they do a little fine-tuning. In the meantime, I have a surprise for you that may make you feel a little better." He grins from ear to ear as he hands her the printout for the ticket confirmation for the concert. It's in one of the medium-sized venues in Atlanta this coming weekend. "I have to go down there anyway to help Katie out, and I thought maybe you'd like to go see them Saturday evening?"

Callie's grimace melts into a soft grin. "That would be *awesome*! I hope I can get this thing..." She shakes the wrist with the bangle on it. "adjusted before then." She sits up cautiously with Niall's assistance, and he escorts her to the bedroom.

"Rest, and I'll call Sara about your bracelet. Do you want to stay here until the concert, or do you want to come with me?" He sits on the edge of the bed, stroking her face gently.

"I've got to do my casting tomorrow and finish processing it on Saturday morning or I'll have to start over." She yawns.

She slowly settles in to bed. Niall leans over and gives her a light kiss. "Sleep well! I'll grab some dinner so you have plenty to eat tonight and leftovers for tomorrow. You *know* I'll just be a port away!"

She nods off to sleep quickly, as the strain from the cent-opal bracelet has exhausted her. Later that evening, Niall slips into the bedroom to wake her. "Time to get up, Callie! You've got a visitor!"

Callie stretches and opens her eyes. *"Who?"* Her voice squeaks slightly between her stretch and a yawn.

"I don't think you know her, but she's Sara's apprentice. Heads up, she's *still* human, but I understand she's slowly leaning toward joining us!" He takes her hand and pulls her upright.

Niall opens the bedroom door and lets in a petite, Asian woman. "Callie, this is Annie Deng. Jason went after her too. She's been living in Sanctuary since he and his women tried to corner her. Sara drafted her to be an assistant, or apprentice?" He looks at Annie questioningly.

"Apprentice, thank you! She's taught me a lot and I enjoy working with her!" Annie exclaims enthusiastically. It wasn't long ago that Annie had been nearly in shock after Jason and his female cohorts cornered her in one of the larger artist's buildings in the River District, Riverview Station. Thanks to one of Tess's newer abilities, Annie was saved from that fate.

Niall moves away and pulls up a chair for Annie in case she needs it, but she stands next to the bed with a tablet and a small scanning device. She looks confused and turns to Niall. "Has she had any new talents pop up? I'm getting some strange readings here."

"Not that I can think of." He says, having relegated her objects moving around in the apartment as an unconscious use of her porting skills to bring things to her.

Callie speaks up. "What about my soda and scale?" She turns to Niall. Annie raises one eyebrow and looks at Niall questioningly.

"What is this? Soda and scale?" Annie inquires patiently.

"It's probably nothing! She's had a couple of things spontaneously port to her, it's something some of us do if we forget something some-where, if we can picture it where it is, we can port it to us through the membrane. I assume that's what she did! She was thirsty, and sud-denly, a soda from the fridge showed up." He laughs.

"Could be, but these patterns look telekinetic, but not quite." She taps the screen on her tablet. "Are you sure she ported them to her and didn't levitate them?"

Callie chimes in. "They came from a different building and the doors were closed, so they couldn't just float in!"

Annie stares at the tablet, looking at the frequency of the supposed PK signature and discovers that it's creating a discordant harmonic with her Centauri-opal, creating feedback neurologically. "Let me try this!" Annie types in something on her tablet, Callie let's out a sigh, and relaxes.

"Whatever you did, my headache just vanished! Thank you!"

"Let me know if the pain comes back. There's definitely something atypical happening with your energy, so keep an eye out. Sara told me you're a Lost Missioner, so it could be something *quite* unexpected! Keep the bracelet on if you go out, and get a hold of me or Sara if you feel worse, or if anything *wonky* happens!" Annie turns off her tablet and puts the sensor away in a bag. "Goodbye, Callie, Niall!" She nods to each of them as she goes out and waits in the living room for Niall to port her back to Medical since she's not yet Apara.

After Annie leaves the room, Niall sits on the edge of the bed again. I've got to go down to Atlanta tomorrow. Are you sure you're up to being alone? I'm sure they won't mind if you tag along. You could even go to the Aquarium or something, or we can get dinner downtown after work; you, me, and Katie. Things have been so hectic, you two have barely had time to get to know each other, and she *is* family!" He reaches over and takes her hand.

"I *know*, but I've already got flasks set up to go in the kiln tonight! If I don't cast them soon, it'll be too late. I've been working on that whole new series of pieces, and I really don't want to remake them all." She pleads eagerly until he rolls his eyes.

"*Okay*! But if anything odd happens, path me immediately! *Got* it? I'll be home late tomorrow. Katie and I have a lot to go over, but I can be home in the blink of an eye if you need me, okay?" He leans over and gives her a light kiss. "I'm going to take Annie back to Medical. Hopefully, she'll let someone turn her so she can get back and forth by herself!" He laughs and says, "By the way, there's Thai food in the kitchen if you're hungry." He heads out to the living room where Annie's waiting patiently and ports her back to Medical.

238

FOOD BY THOUGHT

Niall heads out early Friday morning, porting to Atlanta to work with Katie on identifying and cataloging any Atlanta area potentials affected by the virus. Callie gets up with him, but goes out to her workshop early to check on the kiln and her plaster molds (flasks). The flasks must be slow heated over several hours to burn out any residual wax left inside them. Some are reproductions of her preexisting jewelry line, but four flasks contain one-of-a-kind, wax models for brand new designs.

It'll still be about three more hours until she can cast, as the plaster filled metal flasks had to reach a temperature of 1350F before cooling to 1000F, when she can pour molten silver into them.

She putzes around her workshop for a while, and cuts a few pieces of turquoise she'd put aside for new, one-of-a-kind pieces. Now that she's among the Apara and has the resources for it, she's been having fun bidding on rare materials for her pieces on eBay. Having good stones always inspires her best work; that kind of creative process always makes her feel better.

She's been cabbing for about two hours and doesn't really want to go clear back to the house for food. Niall left the Thai food he'd brought back from Singapore in the fridge. She gets a lopsided grin and turns off her stone grinder. She thinks. *I wonder if I can intentionally port something from the fridge!* She closes her eyes and pictures the contents of the fridge. She pictures the boxes of Thai entrees. Niall labeled them in English to make it easier for her. She scans them mentally until she pictures the one marked Khaosoy, a curry noodle dish she really likes, and pictures it in front of her. She opens her eyes and it appears in front of her; but for a split second, she could have sworn she saw the inside of the re-frigerator as if she were looking through an irregular window in space. "Cool!" She says aloud and shoves it in her workshop mi-crowave to heat it up. She realizes she doesn't have any silverware or chopsticks in the studio, so she pictures the drawer where she keeps some reusable, stainless steel chopsticks. Pictures them in front of her on the table next to the microwave. She opens her eyes, and again, there's a brief afterimage of the drawer she keeps them in, but it vanishes so quickly, leaving only a set of chop-sticks on the table, that she isn't sure she saw it at all! She eats her food, and checks her smart phone, forgetting about the weird flashes or afterimages of the fridge and drawer.

When it's time to cast, she sets everything up. She melts the silver in an electric smelter, pulls out the flask she needs to cast, and puts it open side up on the vacuum base. She gradually brings the vacuum under the flask to full. The vacuum sucks the air out of the mold and the metal down into the nooks and crannies in the plaster. She uses a pair of small tongs to pick up the glowing crucible from the electric smelter, and pours the molten silver into the opening on the flask until it fills, leaving a small button of rapidly blackening silver in the hole on the top. She puts the crucible back in, and weighs out the silver for the next flask while her cast flask cools down a little before quenching it in water, or it splatters everywhere and can damage the silver.

Her cell rings and it's Niall checking in on her. She rolls her eyes, knowing he's worried about her being there alone. "Hey, Niall. It's a good thing you called now, and not two minutes ago, or I'd have been in mid-pour!" She says.

"Everything going *okay*? No *weird* stuff today? No *headaches*?" He got a weird feeling from her earlier, but was in the middle of reviewing new case reports with Katie and their Apara contact from the CDC.

"Oh! *Yeah! Fine!*" She pauses. "I *taught* myself a new trick!" She admits.

He's quiet for a second. "*Oh? What did you do?*"

"Well, you know what you said about porting something to you if you can picture it? I did it! I was hungry, and I ported some Thai leftovers and chopsticks to my studio!" She says, clearly proud of herself. She thinks, *Damn it! I need to go quench that flask.* She glances at it. The flask disappears, and falls out of *nowhere*, as if it were coming through a hole in space, landing with a huge, messy splash in a bucket of water she has on the floor. "*Shit!*" She exclaims, putting her cell down without thinking. She rushes over to the bucket and watches it sputter and steam as it cools and breaks down the plaster into mush.

Thinking something's wrong, Niall ports in and puts a hand on her shoulder. She jumps, and a light bulb blows out nearby. "*Damn it,* Niall! Don't do *that*! You scared the *shit* out of me!"

"I *scared* you? You're the one that said 'shit!' with no explanation and left *me* hanging!" He gives her a frustrated look.

Callie giggles, "*Sorry*! I realized I needed to quench my flask, looked over, and it went *poof*! Ported! Fell out of the *freaking* air and landed in the bucket! I didn't even *try!*"

"Callie, I'm happy that you think this is cool, but I'd rather you not experiment when I'm *not* here! What if you'd ported that hot flask onto a table and started a fire? Or ported it into your hands! You'd heal, but it would cause one hell of a *painful* burn!" He stares down at the milky white water. It's stopped sputtering, but hot steam is still rising. Callie says nothing, but grabs a pair of larger tongs and lifts the flask out of the water. A nearly perfectly formed metal 'tree' of jewelry rests in the metal flask, completely black from oxidation. She carefully picks it out with her fingers. It's hot, but not hot enough to burn her fingers. She turns to Niall, holds it up, and grins at him with such infectious enthusiasm that he breaks his scowl and gives her a lopsided smirk.

"*Just be careful*! I've got to get back to my meeting. Do you want me to bring anything home from Atlanta for dinner?" He asks before porting out.

"Hm, there are still plenty of Thai leftovers, but I wouldn't say no to some of that Korean beef you got in Duluth last week." She grins at him, giving him her best innocent puppy look.

He rolls his eyes and gives her a slight shake of his head in exasperation. "Bulgogi and Japchae it is!" He ports out, leaving her to finish her casting.

TRIAL BY FIRE

The next day, Niall wakes up early and gently nudges Callie awake. "Hey, sleepy-head! Are you coming with me, or are you coming down later for dinner and the concert?"

Callie yawns. "I should work some more in my workshop! I've got to cut all the little jewelry pieces off and clean them up, plus I cut some killer turquoise yesterday morning! Polychrome Royston!" She grins enthusiastically.

He gives her the same look every time she makes a jewelry or stone reference he doesn't get. "*Polychrome*? And that means?" He gets dressed as she explains.

"It means it has both blue and green in the *same* stone! Beautiful material! It's got some spiderweb patterning to boot!" She pauses, getting an odd expression. She opens her hand and there's one of the best cabs she cut lying in her palm; in fact, it's the one she pictured while describing the colors and spiderwebbing. Her look of surprise shifts into a grin. "Like this!" She holds it up to show Niall.

"*Huh*! Did you bring that *thing* to bed with you? Am I going to have to compete with your *stones* at night?" He jokes, laughing sarcastically.

"No, of course not! It just *showed* up! I was thinking about how to describe it to you and then it was in my hand!"

Niall closes his eyes for a second, and settles next to her on the bed. "Callie, I know you're *excited* because you *managed* to port a couple of things, but I want you to take things slowly! And preferably, let me work with you on it when we have some time!"

"*But* I didn't *even* try! I thought about it and *POOF*!"

"Hm, I may have to have Sara adjust your bracelet herself. Annie may have missed something." He comments as he picks up the stone and examines it. "You're *right*! It's a nice stone!" He puts it back in her hand and leans in to give her a kiss, and gets ready to head out.

Callie stops him before he can port out. "By the way, I have a favor to ask you…"

He sits back down beside her. "*Oh*? Will I *enjoy* it!" He gives her a lustful smile.

"Not *that* kind of favor! Though I'm sure I can think of *something* you could do in that area too!" She grins. "The big gem shows in Tucson and Quartzite, Arizona are coming up and I've always wanted to go! I figure, since we can port, we don't have to worry about flying, driving, or even finding a hotel since they're all sold out by now anyway, and I've never had the money to spend there… can I go?" She gives him her best puppy dog eyes.

"*Yes*, but *not* without me! Especially with your latest porting tendencies! Someone's got to keep you from becoming a *klepto* at the show, or you'll end up porting everything you like back home unconsciously!" He grins and makes a face at her. She promptly throws her pillow at him, but he ports out before it can hit him.

CHICKEN! She shouts telepathically and gets mental laughter in return.

She gets ready to start her day, goes out to her workshop, and works on the silver castings from the day before; she clips them off the 'tree', files down rough spots and puts them all in a tumbler with abrasive in it to clean them up. They have to tumble for several hours, so she cuts some more turquoise enthusiastically, while listening to music through her headphones.

About 4 pm, she shuts everything in her studio down. She showers, gets dressed in a nice, deep blue dress with gold trim, puts some light makeup on, and a matching lapis necklace she made. She had taken off the bracelet to shower, but forgets to put it back on. She's feeling a little more confident after a successful round of casting, her potentially profitable stone cutting, and having consciously ported a couple of things. Apara abilities, especially in novices, are often influenced by one's mental state. If you feel insecure, you're more likely to lose control or fail. At the moment, she's feeling more confident and happier, so her control is better. As a result, she doesn't notice she's left the bracelet sitting on the counter in the bathroom.

Once she's ready, she focuses on Niall, sensing his mental signature, and clairvoyantly checks that he's either alone or with other Apara. *It would never do to port in with humans in the room! Niall would have to do damage control on their memories!* She thinks. Luckily, it's only he and Katie in her office.

Katie gives her a wide grin as Callie ports in. "Callie! Welcome to Atlanta!"

Katie hugs her Apara step-sister and Callie warmly returns her hug. Niall's sitting in an office chair, watching. "You look really nice! Are you ready for dinner?" He asks.

"Yes! I've been working all day and didn't eat! Though I *did* remember to feed before coming down here!" She says before he can ask.

He nods. "How's Filipino food sound? Our CDC guy recommended a place near the venue. He suggested we share a couple of their sampler platters." He comes over and slips an arm under hers.

Callie asks Katie. "Aren't you coming?"

"Not this time, I have to meet with Sara and Dee tonight at Medical. We're planning to turn Teresa tomorrow and need to go over a few things first. Sara wants us to do it there in case there are any complications. You two have fun!" She tells them with a smile and ports out.

Niall ports them into a dark corner behind the restaurant and they go in. The atmosphere is jovial, and the odor of new and unfamiliar foods excites Callie. There's a large group of people celebrating nearby. They look like they may be a large, Filipino family. Callie feels a little sad watching them, and Niall takes notice. "What is it?"

"Looks like they're celebrating that old woman's birthday! There are many family members all around her; It just has me thinking, nothing important." She tells him, putting a smile on for show.

"Then *why* do you seem so sad?" He takes her hand, caressing it gently.

"I'm remembering family gatherings when I was a kid. Thanksgiving, Christmas, birthdays. I haven't spoken to anyone in my family since before I was turned. Not that I'm that close to any of them anymore! *Political* differences! Seeing them celebrating is kind of bittersweet, that's all." She picks at some garlic butter shrimp on her plate.

Niall checks the time. "We should finish and get to the venue. Doors open soon." He attempts to distract her by getting her mind on the concert. He knows that even if she wanted to see them, she'll have to leave her family behind eventually.

***

They stand in line outside the venue, slowly progressing toward the front door. It's chilly outside and people are eager to get in out of the cold, though the temperature doesn't really bother either of them.

"Luckily, I found two tickets in the first few rows, otherwise, behind the 10th row is general admission! I figured you'd want to get up close!" He has his arm behind her and gently rubs her lower back. After a few more minutes, they're in the venue and seated, third row center. When the performance begins, the room grows quiet. There are only two original band members, along with a younger female singer, so they're doing an acoustic show without the huge concert amplifiers and effects. Callie's enjoying the concert, though she's a little sad to know this iconic band will finally stop performing in a few more weeks when this tour's over.

The musicians play and sing for about an hour and then take a half an hour break. The venue has a bar and food. Niall grabs some snacks and drinks. They're sitting in their seats, waiting for the concert to resume.

They casually chat with some of the other fans sitting near them when both Niall and Callie get an odd, prickly feeling. They feel a large surge of psychic energy building somewhere in the venue. Niall seeks the source mentally, and it's somewhere closer to the front doors of the venue. Shouting, arguing, and sounds of physical conflict erupt.

The sound level in the room increases, as does the psychic energy surge. Callie looks at Niall and paths, *Why am I feeling hot?*

I'm not sure, but I don't like the psychic levels or overtones! He replies.

As security heads toward the disturbance, the shouts and sounds of brawling increase. There's an explosive flare of light, and the smell of smoke. Niall says, *"FIRE!"* The area by the exit has burst into flames and they're spreading unimaginably fast around the edges of the venue, almost like the walls have been doused with accelerant, making it impossible for people to get out through the main or emergency exits at the sides of the building. Screams of panic and coughing from the smoke fill the room. "We need to get out of here!" Niall shouts over the din of chaos, fire alarms, and screams.

"*Niall!* We've got to help these *people!* We *can't* leave them in here to die!" Callie pleads with him.

"I'm not sure there's anything we *can* do! I just did a clairvoyant scan and the fire is already surrounding the building, blocking *all* exits! It's like it's got a mind of its own! We have to port, Callie! Even if we could take anyone with us, it *wouldn't* be many and we *can't* expose ourselves!"

"We could make them *forget!*" She pleads.

Niall coughs from the smoke. "We need to go now!" He grabs her hand, but she pulls it away and surges into the crowd, looking for any way to get everyone out. She worries about the band as well, who have come back out on the stage, as the green room is on fire, and they're trying to keep the crowd from panicking and crushing people in desperation to get out.

She thinks, *if only there were a way out through the stage, the only place that isn't in flames at the moment!* She feels odd, like there's a pressure in her head, followed by an almost audible roar in her mind, and pain. She feels Niall grab at her, but then stops as he peers at the stage. He feels energy swirling, and watches as the stage shimmers and an irregular 'hole' appears, leading to a wooded area. People see the woods through the billowing smoke and assume the back of the venue has collapsed, giving them a way out, and rush the stage.

Niall looks for Callie, but she's up on stage, helping the elderly musicians through what appears to be a rip or hole in thin air. "*Bollocks!* That's a *God damn portal!*" He realizes that was the second surge of energy he'd felt. The first, he soon discovers, came from a belligerent, drunk man who'd picked a fight with another man by trying to pick up the man's wife. *Pyrokinetic?* He thinks. *Fuck! He must be an infected potential!*

The man in question is face down on the floor, face covered in blood from a fist to his nose, unconscious. Once the blaze had broken out and spread, it no longer needed him to add psychic fuel to the fire. As everyone runs through the huge portal on the stage, probably 15 feet across, and into the woods, Niall grabs the unconscious man, and ports him to Medical. He paths to Callie. *Are you okay?*

Yes! Fine, though I'm not sure where I am! I didn't think there was a wooded area behind the venue! As she stands there, exhausted, the portal starts to flicker and close, leaving around three hundred people standing in the middle of the woods, in the dark, no sign of the venue or the fire. "What the *Hell?*" Callie says out loud.

People are crying and stunned. A few are in shock; most are dealing with smoke inhalation. Callie senses multiple Apara porting in, and feels an odd wave of energy. All the humans drop to the ground, unconscious, while she looks on. A minute later, Niall ports in by her side. "Are you *okay?*"

"Yeah, what happened to everyone?" Callie looks around, confused by the scene.

"Callie, I don't want to upset you, but I think your little porting talent is a *hell* of a lot bigger than we realized!" He puts his arm around her and ports her to a room in medical.

Callie looks around and realizes where she is. "What are we doing here? I'm fine, but some of the people aren't!"

He grabs her by the wrists and gently encourages her to sit in a chair. "Callie, they'll be as fine as they can be, though we're gonna have one hell of a damage control job to do."

"What are you talking about, Niall! The back wall must have fallen...I think?" She stops talking, realizing that things don't quite add up. She looks at him, silently with growing uncertainty.

"I have the feeling we've *discovered* your 'special talent'." He tells her, as he crouches down in front of her chair and brushes hair out of her soot smudged face. A burnt odor clings to her hair and clothing. "What were you thinking right before the escape route *appeared*?"

"I...I..." She pauses, focusing. "I was thinking the stage was the only wall that wasn't on fire and wished there were some way to get everyone out that way."

"I think you created that 'exit' by opening up a *portal* to Sanctuary that everyone escaped through. Sara will have to confirm it, of course, but I'm not sure what else it could be." He tells her, calmly, not wishing to upset or excite her in case her abilities decide to kick in again.

"*What*? You're saying I *caused that*? I didn't think that was possible!" She reruns everything through her mind, trying to make sense of everything. She flashes on the headache, nausea, and desperation to get people to safety and how the stage seemed to shimmer and waver until she saw the woods showing from the back of the stage. She looks at him, flabbergasted.

"I think you *may* be right! I felt nauseous and had a splitting headache. I felt like I was going to have a *seizure* or like I had power flowing through me and suddenly..."

"You created a *spontaneous* portal to Sanctuary! I'm pretty sure an infected potential with pyrokinetic abilities started the fire! I found him unconscious on the floor, aura still crackling with energy, so I took him to medical. Sara's got him sedated.

Sara and Liz called in the troops, who went in and used a ton of Sara's wave generators to knock them all out. The less time they're awake and aware, the less we have to alter their memories! Though, I'm not sure how they're going to explain away everyone getting out of that fire, but they'll come up with something!" He sighs, and sits on the floor, leaning against her leg.

"So, *everyone* got out?" She asks, still coughing a bit from the healing smoke inhalation she'd suffered.

"Yes, thanks to your portal. Remind me never to bet against you doing something! You were so *determined* to save everyone you created that escape route, literally out of thin air! I'm not sure how, but I'm guessing it's connected to what you've been experiencing this week." Niall and Callie sit in a room at Medical, recovering relatively rapidly from the smoke damage to their lungs.

After nearly two hours, Sara comes in, smelling of residual smoke and looking frazzled. "There you are!" She says in a huff. "*Sorry!* But you all left me a bit of work! Had to take a team and at least surreptitiously stabilize a few old folk with smoke inhalation! We ported as many as we could into the field behind the venue as soon as their memories could be redacted. A few needed more care and were treated and placed further away from the venue. By the way, the whole place burned down! What a *mess!* Witnesses are describing it as though it had a *mind* of its own, as the flames moved quickly and refused to go out until there was nothing left of the venue to burn." Sara rants as she checks over Niall and Callie.

She gets an odd expression after looking at Callie's scan on her tablet. "Physically, you'll both be healed in another couple of hours, however..." She crouches down in front of an exhausted Callie. "You, young lady, are showing some rather odd energy readings!" She glances at Niall, pathing, *I think you're right! Annie told me she'd picked up some atypical PK signatures. Other than porting small objects to or from Sanctuary, I've never heard of anyone being able to create a spontaneous portal! But she's an LM potential, so we may be dealing with a mutation!*

Sara takes Callie's hand and tries to get a direct read on her energy, but stops. "Where's your bracelet?"

Callie looks down at her wrist. "*Huh*?" She's quiet for a minute, trying to remember what happened to it. A look of understanding appears. "I think I *left* it in the bathroom when I showered."

"That may have been just as well. With the energy you put out, you might've either *fractured* the stone, or *knocked* yourself out with the feedback." She grins. "We'll need to fit you with a different one, anyway! Something stronger, perhaps. Before we do, we need to know what we're dealing with!" Sara drags two chairs over, sitting in one, and motioning for Niall to join her, pathing him, *Get your ass off the floor!*

Sara softens her usually crotchety manner and asks Callie calmly. "I understand you've experienced items spontaneously porting to you? When did this start?"

Callie yawns and says, "A couple of days ago, I guess. It started while I was working in my jewelry shop. Yesterday, I couldn't resist trying it out, and ported my lunch from the kitchen to my workshop, then there was another small, spontaneous thing when we got up today, but nothing else until the fire."

Sara makes notes on her tablet. "Did you notice anything unusual when stuff ported to you?"

"The whole thing seems unusual!" She blurts out. "The first times, things were suddenly there." She focuses on her memories of her conscious attempts. "There was something the times I ported my lunch, though. Right before the item materialized, I could swear I saw the place it came from, literally, not in my mind! The inside of the fridge and the drawer where the chopsticks were. It was like a window opened and I could physically see the place I was porting stuff from! I figured it was a holdover from picturing it in my mind."

"Interesting... anything else?" Sara furrows her brow as she listens in on Callie's mind as she recounts her experiences.

"Yeah, one other thing. I was on the phone with Niall when I realized I needed to put my hot flask of cast jewelry in a bucket of water to cool it, but I was on the phone across the room. It disappeared, and when it reappeared, it fell into the water from above, like it fell through a hole in midair!" Callie recalls.

Sara processes the information briefly, then says, "Normally, when we port an object to us, it's like pulling an item out of water and into the air, the object passes through the surface tensions, or membrane, and is instantly surrounded by the air. What you did appears to be more like opening a window, reaching through it, getting the object and closing the window again. Our Benefactors have provided our portals using their own technology. It's not *normally* something we can do ourselves! However, between what you said about your ports on Friday, and what happened at the concert, I'd say you can not only port or pull an object to you, but open a stable portal from one place to another! One you can see through or even go through physically like we do the doors to our homes in Sanctuary!"

"Sara, her first ones were *physical* ports within Sanctuary, from one place to another, but that event at the venue was between the realities and it was massive!" Niall tells her while holding Callie's hand tightly.

Sara gives him a tights smile. "I realize that, Niall, but stress played a big factor in that! It's like the stories of humans lifting cars to save a trapped child while under stress. Stress can have a similar effect on us. We'll have to watch it. I do want to fit her with a higher-grade Centauri-opal device, but that will wait until tomorrow! I've got to get back to Liz and Katie about turning Teresa! Despite this crisis, we don't want to put things off another day." Sara stands, pats Callie on her shoulder. "Go home. Wash the smoke out of your hair and sleep. Oh yeah, wear your existing bracelet until we can fit you with a customized one." Sara walks out the door, letting it close behind her.

Niall helps Callie up. She's so tired her body feels twice as heavy as usual, both to herself and to Niall. He puts his arms around her and ports her back home to Sanctuary. "That shower can wait until morning." He helps her out of her dress, into bed, and under the covers. He goes into the bathroom and finds the bracelet exactly where she expected it to be. He returns to bed with it, but she's already sound asleep. He slips the bracelet back on her and puts her arm back under the blanket. He showers and then joins her in slumber.

ROULETTE VIRUS

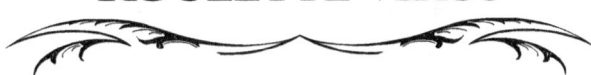

Three days after the concert blaze in Atlanta, there's a meeting at Medical, in Sanctuary. As the crisis is expanding, the room is filled with Apara from various parts of the world. The room is abuzz with talk about the outbreaks among their local and regional potentials. Sara enters and clears her throat. Everyone grows quiet and all eyes turn to her.

"*Alright* everyone! We have a ton to cover today! I know most of you have local cases you want to talk about, but we *must focus*, so if you have local cases to report, click on the app marked Roulette on your tablets and file any reports there! Please wait until we're done with the meeting, as I need your undivided attention. Someone from Medical or our rep with the CDC will be in touch with you as soon as possible! Please hold your questions until I'm done! If I have to explain something multiple times because you aren't listening, you'll be expelled and you can read the *damn* CliffsNotes!" She snaps, pulling up a list of topics to cover on her tablet.

She continues, starting with a general update on the spread of the virus. "First off, the virus is continuing to spread and has now been seen in much of Europe, Eastern Asia and Australia. There have been minor cases reported in South Africa as well. Unfortunately, it's hard to get an overview in the Middle East due to post-Jerusalem issues." She swipes the tablet to the next page in her notes. We've now found approximately 474 cases of infected potentials, worldwide, who've shown some form of alteration." There are rumblings around the room as very few realized so many cases had shown up already. "The majority of these are *minor* changes! The most common is a heightening of the *normal*, human senses; often only one, but there have been cases of all senses being heightened. In a couple of cases, the person became so sensitive to sensory input, that they were hospitalized and sedated. Cases of psychic abilities showing up, however, are also on the rise. We've seen several people having precognitive dreams, and there's been an increase in people reporting hearing voices. Interestingly, there's also been an increase in cases of synesthesia! The human disorder where sensory input gets crossed such that a person may smell a color or see a sound as flashes of color or light, for example.

As you see in the app on your tablets, we've named the virus the Roulette virus because we never know if or how it's going to affect one of our potentials. We think that once it attaches itself to a person's key sequence; it recodes part of the usual DNA and enhances one or more abilities in said potential. We haven't found a clear pattern yet, but we suspect that it's sometimes picking the strongest ability a potential has and brings it out, while in others, it's very random. Most cases, only one ability is brought out, though we've seen a handful who have had more than one show up, like PK and telepathy, or precognition and heightened hearing, for example." Sara puts a small box with a lens on the table and telekinetically turns off the lights. The box projects a 3D animation showing how they believe the virus is attacking compatible DNA. We believe this segment here causes the virus to focus on the first changes it initiates rather than moving on and doing all of them, or a complete transformation."

Kyung, the South Korean Apara rep, looks like he's about to interrupt. Sara stares him down, and he closes his mouth again. "And to answer your unasked question, Kyung, no, we still haven't seen any complete transformations, nor have we seen cases of fangs growing in, or anyone craving blood as of this morning! By the way, any new cases or unusual developments will be updated and available through the app, so please check there *before* pathing or calling me!" She snaps, clearly overwhelmed by the current situation.

"There is *some* good news. We've turned one of our Lost Mission potentials who contracted the virus before we could turn her. Unlike the normal virus, the key sequence is not altered in any of the cases we've studied so far, so we *can* transform affected potentials. That doesn't mean we will turn *all* of them! Many are probably unacceptable, and we're working on possible ways to curtail their new abilities!"

She continues, "On a more serious note, we've had about five incidents this week that could have become casualty events or exposure risks. One case involved an LM potential who developed explosive pyrokinesis. In his case, he was one of the few male LM potentials. He was intoxicated and belligerent, at the time, and got into a fight. When his anger peaked, fire erupted in a concert venue and spread unnaturally fast! Local fire investigators are still trying to figure out what kind of accelerant was used to cause the fire to spread so quickly. Luckily, thanks to one of our own, everyone escaped, though our pyrokinetic is officially listed as missing" She glances at Callie and Niall, but doesn't elaborate on how Callie was able to rescue everyone.

"Another case involved a previously unidentified Lost Mission potential with a variant on PK and pyrokinesis. She can telekinetically accelerate the molecules in metal, causing them to bend or melt. Luckily, when this ability manifested, they weren't near any major structures. She did, however, halfway melt a lamppost, causing a grass fire from exposed electrical wires and a short circuit. In both cases, we've brought them to Sanctuary, sedated them, and have energy dampeners in place to prevent any new incidents until we can determine if they will be turned or not. In another case, we believe a woman in a crowd caused multiple people around her to have nosebleeds, and one person is currently in the hospital from a stroke. Unfortunately, the woman ran off before any of us could find her, and we're still trying to track her. The last two both involved people who could somehow affect or channel electricity, leading to people getting anywhere from mild shocks to a couple of victims ending up hospitalized after their hearts stopped from a shock." Sara pauses and the Apara around the room murmur to each other.

Sara's temper grows short. "May I have *everyone's attention, please*? Only a *few* more minutes, I promise!" She raises her voice over the din, impatiently. "The situation is likely to escalate before our Benefactor's team gets here in another week and a half! I need *every* center to create social media or internet teams to scour the net for talk or stories about emerging abilities. When they find them, use the app to report location found, and any information on them, especially names, locations, presumed abilities, and any other identifying factors! We're centralizing the reporting through the Atlanta and Asheville offices. Contact Michelle Simmons in Atlanta or Marc Girard in Asheville if you can't get through via the app, but *only* if you can't get through. Your teams will need people skilled in hacking and information control. We need these reports curtailed! Meaning deleting them, limiting their reach, or debunking them publicly! Use the app for all reports unless it's an emergency! We can't have everyone calling or pathing every time there's a new incident! It will be overwhelming for our coordinators! Lastly, the same thing goes for any questions you have today! Put them in the app, and we'll answer them and send them out as notifications." Before anyone can break Sara's no question rule, she ports out.

ARRIVAL

The hybrid team arrives. Because they can traverse realities, they can transition to Sanctuary, so are never visible to humans on Earth. Their transport ship arrives near Medical, gliding down silently and settling in a clearing nearby. Their main ship stays in orbit, as does the non-hybrid Benefactor in charge. The ship they send down to medical is about 25 feet across, and is shaped roughly like a bubble whose bottom has been flattened. It has no doors or windows, as hybrids, Benefactors, and Apara all can port, making doors not only unnecessary, but without them, there is less risk of atmospheric leakage.

From the inside, the skin of the ship can become transparent in any direction to allow visual navigation as necessary. The skin of the ship itself is a composite material, but it works like camouflage, bending images of its surroundings around the ship to cloak it from onlookers. The aliens themselves, as well as hybrids, and Apara can see the ship as they see a blue glow around it which is not perceptible by humans, but is by anyone carrying a gene from the Benefactors; a gene that was included in the virus that transformed all Apara.

Sara and Liz are waiting for their hybrid guests near the landing site. Sara's face brightens when she sees her long-time hybrid counterpart, Isanda, port out of the ship, and give her a big smile. While Apara are transformed humans, the hybrids, or "Samhata", which, in Sanskrit, loosely means joined or 'forming one mass or body' were created off world by their scientists and grown from a blending of Benefactor and Human DNA. Isanda, from a distance, looks fairly human, but closer up, differences can be seen. Her proportions are slightly off, and while she clearly looks female, her proportions lean toward more androgynous lines. She has what appears to be medium length, silver hair that looks like it's full of static electricity, as it fluffs up, and moves around on its own. Closer, her hair has an almost feather-like texture; instead of a single strand, each strand branches off into fine, short strands. Her 'hair' is not like human hair, but functions as a sensory organ that reacts to psychic energy.

Her face is nearly human except that her lashes match her hair in color, her irises are slightly larger than normal, and an odd shade of purplish blue that have shifting flecks of colors that reflect her emotions. Her features are otherwise fine boned, and nearly human, almost frail or pixie-like, yet her movement, while flowing, clearly shows a quiet strength. Her skin is a medium brown as the cultures she was assigned to were largely in Central and South American native cultures.

When they speak, their voices are smoother and softer than most human voices, and often have a telepathic harmonic that Apara can pick up simultaneously, allowing them to understand no matter which language the hybrid speaks. When in the company of multiple Apara from different backgrounds, they will usually speak whatever language is most common, but could as easily speak whatever language is native to the human they are conversing with. Apara share a variant of this ability; if they go someplace where they do not speak the local language, they tap into the speech centers of the person or group they are dealing with, and their minds will automatically translate their native language into the verbal equivalent of the local language. It's exhausting at first, but over time, the Apara assimilates the new language into their own brain's speech center such that they can use it in the future without the more taxing, subconscious link created by the initial contact. Many Apara speak multiple languages they accumulate over time.

Samhatas were created as intermediaries between the Benefactors and Apara, as the minds of the Benefactors can be overwhelming after an extended period, even for the most telepathically skilled Apara. Samhatas find both telepathy and verbal language equally natural, but because they mostly use spoken language when on Earth, their speech is often more formal or stilted, and things like contractions and colloquialisms are rarely heard unless they spend extended time on Earth.

Isanda walks smoothly over to Sara, arms extended, to give her old friend a hug. As she moves away from the transport ship, several other hybrids port out, bringing various equipment with them to deal with the current crisis. Once out of the ship, they port again almost instantly, taking the equipment into Medical so they can set up their crisis center, and return for more equipment and supplies.

Isanda gives her old friend a concerned look. She uses English because Liz is also there, but could easily speak in Sara's ancient, native Mayan dialect. "Hello, old friend! I have been reviewing the information you forwarded to me in transit. We hoped to avoid this, but with the genetic age beginning on Earth, it was inevitable."

Sara lets out a long sigh. "Yes, I've known for a while that it could be a risk if any of us ever ended up in human hands and studied, but this caught us off guard."

Isanda lightly touches Sara on the shoulder, and her hair swirls around even though there's barely a breeze present. "I understand the scientist who created the altered virus is with your people now? I would very much like to meet her and examine her memories, so I know exactly what she did."

Sara nods. "Of course, she's with an old friend of ours." Sara paths a wordless thought privately, indicating that she's with Leonardo now. Sara knows Liz suspects Vince is more than he seems, but she promised him centuries ago to keep his real identity between them, and the few others who know who he is.

Isanda met him shortly after he was turned and found it fascinating that such a man could be so different compared to the other humans of the time. "I would very much enjoy seeing him again as well! Such a sparkling mind!" She turns to Liz and her hair flutters with enthusiasm. "It is very pleasant to see you again Lissa Pederson. I assume you and Kari Anderson are well?" She

regards Liz with an unblinking glance and Liz feels subtle telepathic probing and emotional waves coming from Isanda.

"Yes, we're both well, though the last couple of years have
been difficult." Liz admits.

"Yes, the nuclear incident... I have not been involved with those
teams myself, but have heard of the devastation and loss of life. Such a
tragedy to lose so many of your people with many thousands of years
of cumulative experience gone in an instant." Isanda's eyes seem to
soften, and her irises shift to a darker shade of purple with flecks of
shimmering green, which in Samhatas indicated deep sadness.

The three women walk toward Medical together, rather than porting. Isanda listens to the crunching sound of the ground under her
feet, her gait is slower, and slightly labored compared to Sara and Liz.
"*Apologies!* It always takes me time to adapt to Earth's gravity after the
long trip here, but I prefer to adapt by walking. My fellow Samhatas
prefer to port as much as possible until they adapt."

"Not a problem. I feel like I've been on the run since this whole crisis
began, so it's good to slow down a little." Sara walks next to Isanda in
case the gravity becomes too much, and she needs to support her.

As they approach the entrance to Medical, Sara sees young Annie
Deng waiting anxiously for her at the door, and a corner of her mouth
curls up in amusement. She projects a thought to Annie, even though
Annie is still human. *We'll be there soon! My! You are so anxious!*

Hearing this in her mind, Annie goes back inside and waits
quietly, sitting at the bottom of the long stairway from the Atrium
up to the main Medical center.

Isanda touches Sara's arm lightly, asking, "Is that a *human* here
in *Sanctuary*? Is she one of the *infected*?"

"Human, yes, infected, no." Sara paths the explanation of how Jason
tormented her, making her remember every time he fed from her, then
forget until the next time, and how he'd planned to turn her, bringing
her suppressed memories permanently to the surface again.

"I see. Yes, I have heard of this rogue. He reminds me of some of the original ones from your time. Is she going to become one of you?" Isanda asks.

"I believe so. We're giving her time to adjust after her trauma. She's been my assistant here for several months, but she's slowly leaning toward letting someone transform her." Sara says, and Isanda senses emotional overtones from Sara.

Isanda paths privately to Sara. *Have you become so attached, my sweet Abha? All these years you have stayed above that! And now? I think you are waiting for something more than her decision!*

Isanda startles Sara by addressing her by her ancient name. *Nobody but you has called me that since the time of the Maya. I found Sara is much easier for most; and yes, I'm quite fond of her. It would be nice to have a companion again. She was so nervous and traumatized when she found out about us, but when it's time, I'll offer to turn her and take her in.* Sara paths.

Isanda's eyes shimmer with a mix of green and silver overtones in the purplish blue. She paths, *I am sorry I could not stay here with you, Abha, but I had to return to our Benefactor's world. I have missed you, and understand your wish not to be alone. She will learn much from you, Abha! I will continue to think of you as that bright young Mayan girl from long ago, but will only use your real name between us!*

The two very old friends walk the rest of the way, neither speaking nor pathing, alongside Liz. As they enter the Atrium in Medical, Annie eagerly stands as she sees Sara and the others come in the door.

Sara comments to Isanda. "When Annie found out you and the others were coming, she got *very* excited. She's quite eager to meet someone who isn't from this planet!"

Isanda's lips twist into an odd smile, and her eyes get glints of yellow in them, a sign of amusement. "Well, we must *not* disappoint her then!"

Liz paths to Sara. *I'm going to go check on things back in Asheville, but will be back later.* Liz ports out, leaving the two women on course to meet a nervous and excited Annie.

ANCIENT HISTORY

Sara and Isanda approach the stairs and Annie tries not to stare, but can't help it. She grew up watching every Star Trek series she could, and meeting someone from another planet, even if she is part human, is like a first-contact situation from the show. Sara and Isanda come to a halt in front of Annie.

"Isanda, this is my apprentice, Annie Deng." Sara motions to Annie, who's shaking in anticipation.

Isanda nods to Annie; her hair flutters around her head lightly, and her purplish-blue eyes light up with flecks of yellow-gold, which make them look a little like a cross between Lapis and amethyst. "Hello, Annie Deng! I meet so few humans anymore, it is an honor to meet you. As I believe the expression goes... any friend of Sara's is a friend of mine!" She reaches out to shake her hand. Having spent more time than most hybrids on Earth, Isanda tries to use more relaxed language than some of her subordinates.

Annie glances at Sara for reassurance that it's okay to shake her hand, and after Sara gives her a subtle blessing, she reaches out and takes it. Her hand is warm and very soft, with odd overtones of electricity or energy, something that catches Annie off guard as she's not used to feeling anything psychic aside from Sara's paths and the one time when she 'felt' Tess's astral-self with her when Jason came after her. Nervously, she shakes her hand and timidly says, "Pleasure to meet you, Isanda. Sara has been looking forward to your visit. She told me it's been a *long* time since you've been here."

Isanda's eyes shift a little darker with highlights of green and silver again. "Yes, I spent a very long time here when Sara was new to the Apara. That is how I met Sara. She became Apara while I was on Earth and we became *good* friends." Isanda paths to Sara. *Does she know your story? How you became Apara?*

No, no one I work with now does, only some of the old ones who keep to themselves. Most only know me as being 'old as dirt' and from some ancient civilization. Sara sends her a mental grin. *I think it's best most don't know how old I actually am or the circumstances of my turning. That was a different time and place.*

Isanda reaches into a small slit on her sleeve and pulls out a small, naturally faceted, purplish gem that shifts between blue and purple as the light hits it from different angles. She reaches out and puts it in Annie's palm. "Annie Deng, this is a natural gem from the same planet we find the Centauri-opal. It also has special properties. It will enhance your latent psychic abilities and make it easier for you and Sara to communicate." She observes Annie's excitement at having a trinket from another planet.

"Can I *keep* it?" She looks up at Isanda's eyes, which flash overtones of yellow mixed in with the green and silver.

"Yes, of course you may." Isanda blinks slowly as her kind doesn't need to blink as often as humans, and sometimes she has to consciously remember to do so, or risk disconcerting someone like Annie.

"Thank you!" Annie's excitement is obvious. She turns to Sara. "Maybe I can ask Callie if she can make it into a necklace for me?"

"I'm sure she can! She's coming by later this week so we can experiment with her new ability." Sara explains. "We need to get upstairs and check on the new lab they're setting up. Meet me tonight around 8 pm and do rounds with me."

"Yes, ma'am... Sara!" She turns and skips off through the outer atrium door, galloping over to one of the nearby dormitory buildings where she lives.

Isanda touches Sara on the arm. *It will not be long before she is ready for you, Abha! Do not keep your past a secret from her if you wish her to be in your life! What happened to you was not your fault; you know that!*

Yes, I know, but that was long ago, in another life! Sara paths as they go up the stairs.

Agreed, Abha, but it is the reason you are who you are now. The healer who never lets herself get too close to those she cares for, and will not allow any healing for herself because of guilt. Isanda senses the pain lurking in Sara's mind.

Sara stops and stares at Isanda's eyes, which are now more purple than blue, with dark green flashes. *It is still impossible for me to forget what I was back then, before you found me and took me in!*

Isanda puts her hand on Sara, ports them the rest of the way to Sara's cluttered office and closes the door. Isanda sits in the only clear chair in Sara's office. *You were made Apara by one who'd been turned by one of the first ones, with the unkeyed virus. He used a violent, blood ritual to turn you, then starved you; he sent you among your own village like some ravenous demon, as punishment for them not worshiping him as some kind of demigod. Your actions were NOT your fault! You were insane with hunger and trauma from your turning. Can you not forgive yourself even after over four millennia?*

I still have nightmares every few years! The obsidian knives they held above me, cut me with, and shared my blood, then the priest gave me his own blood and turned me, but not before giving me that drink which made me hallucinate awful things before I'd turned enough that he could cut my heart out! They told me I would rise again as a demon servant! An evil plague to punish my village! Sara's visibly shaking as she remembers the ritual that brought her into this very long life.

She reminds you of your first victim, doesn't she? Isanda reaches over and lightly touches her cheek.

After a minute of not looking at Isanda, Sara faces her. *Yes! She does! Her innocence and eagerness remind me much of my childhood friend that I drank until her heart stopped!*

Yes, and you have spent thousands of years atoning for that and other deaths your transformer was responsible for by being a healer! First for your own people until your lack of aging made them fear you, and then in other villages. Now, you continue your work among the Apara themselves. Isanda reminds her. *I remember that night when they unleashed you on your village! I sensed the fear and panic among your people and came to investigate. I found you curled up in a large, hollowed out tree outside your village, covered in blood, and snarling with near madness, when I tried to coax you out! I took you in, calmed you and took you to the Benefactors for treatment.* She reminds Sara.

Yes, I remember. They replaced the virus with the keyed version and did their best to heal my mind and soul. They even tried to make me forget what I'd done, but they couldn't keep it from resurfacing. Sara sits in her own chair after tossing a baby Yoda toy onto her desk.

Abha! It is time to let the past go! You have atoned for longer than many civilizations have lasted. Show Annie Deng that you are proof that Apara choose not to be monsters. She looks up to you, but also cares for you much as I did then, and still do now. Isanda makes her look her in the eye.

But you left! The pain buried by millennia in Sara's soul rises to the surface, making Isanda flinch.

I had to, Abha! I had to go back and share all I'd learned here on Earth. And as long as I stayed, you were not healing from your trauma! Isanda's eyes shift again, showing deep red flecks of anguish.

"You *could* have come back sooner!" Sara says out loud, quietly.

Isanda continues telepathically. *Yes, I could have, but I couldn't bear to face your pain so long ago! It was still there when I came back during the Renaissance period and it's still there now! Let it go, Abha! Give yourself the healing you've given to so many others!*

Sara looks up with tears in her eyes, something very few have ever seen. Isanda holds Sara, comforting her as nearly four millennia of suppressed pain boils over and slowly escapes.

As Isanda sits there, comforting her longtime friend, her mind multitasks and paths to the others on her team to get everything ready, but not to disturb her unless it's absolutely necessary.

Secrets & Slights

After a couple of hours, Sara and Isanda leave the seclusion of Sara's office and head to the newly set up lab. Isanda paths to Sara, *Abha, I will need access to all the information you have on the new virus, plus those affected by it. Tomorrow, I would like to meet the woman, Thaddea Price, so I may review her memories and get her insights!*

Sara nods. *I'll let Leonardo and Dee know. I'm sure he'll wish to come along with her. He's become quite protective of her, and I'm sure he'd like to see you as well.*

Isanda says, *As would I! I missed him when I was here last, around 30 Earth years ago.*

Sara stops and glares at her, astonished, and speaks aloud. "You were *here* 30 years ago? Why *didn't* you come *see* me? I did not know you were on Earth!"

Isanda gently touches her shoulder and gives her an odd look; not sad, not angry, more like a mix of apologetic and admonishing. *Abha, I am sorry! I was only here intermittently. I was stationed on our small base on Jupiter's moon. We were working on a special project, and then the background radiation surge began, and affected unborn children here. I rarely got back to Earth because they were so busy looking at the new mutations showing up in newborns. I was also worried that it would make things harder on you at the time!*

Sara stares at her, radiating annoyance, and feelings of being slighted by Isanda. *Can you at least tell me what your special project was? What was so important?*

Isanda looks Sara in the eye. *Some Benefactors, foreseeing a greater need for highly skilled Apara in the future, set up a small project where we altered children's DNA in utero.*

What?! I should have been told! Should have known so we could look out for them when they came of age! Sara paths, wondering why Isanda and the others didn't trust her with that information.

Isanda cups Sara's cheek with her hand. *Abha, it was a controversial project, even among our Benefactors, so it was kept quiet. Unfortunately, it didn't work. We worked with a small number of unborns, altering their DNA, so when they might be changed, their talents would be greater than average! We experimented on only ten subjects. Four died before they could be born or shortly thereafter, only three showed any major gifts and two were mentally unstable, including one that likely developed severe schizophrenia later in life. Right after that, the radiation waves hit the Earth and began causing mutations in the 'Lost Mission Potentials', ending the need for our experimentation. I was sent back home, and then the ship dealing with those special potentials was lost! I haven't been back since then.*

What happened to the others? Sara has her hands on her hips.

Three showed no major talents, so were never tagged. The one remaining who seemed both stable and talented died in an automobile accident when she was still quite young. Isanda continues walking toward the lab, hoping Sara will let it go.

Sara follows her, still sulking over Isanda not visiting her or filling her in thirty years prior. They enter the room, which is full of futuristic looking equipment. A team of seven other hybrids are making the lab ready for action. No one is speaking because telepathic communication is more efficient between them than verbal. As Isanda communicates with her team, Sara ports out to her office, grabs a tablet, and returns to Isanda, who looks at Sara expectantly.

Sara hands her the tablet. "Dee's... Thaddea's records are on here. We've consolidated all of her digital and handwritten notes, readings, genetic sequencings, and video from her microscope for you. I thought you might want to familiarize yourself with this before meeting her. By the way, she prefers to be called Dee." She turns around and ports out before Isanda can say anything more.

268

Isanda's eyes glimmer with flecks of dark red and green. She knows her arrival on earth has opened up old wounds in Sara. They had once been very close, but Isanda had to return to their Benefactor's home world after being on Earth so long, and Sara never got over that loss. She'd visited off and on over the millennia, and every time she'd come back, she'd hoped Sara might have found happiness among the Apara, but she'd thrown herself into her healing work, and rarely let anyone get close to her because of how her time among them had begun. She considered visiting thirty years ago, but knew it would reopen those wounds like picking at psychological scabs. Being the hybrid expert on genetic manipulation, she had no choice but to come for this crisis, and knew it could be complicated and difficult for Sara. She's pleased to see the connection growing between Sara and Annie, but is concerned that her visit could interfere with Sara's progress.

Isanda takes the tablet, goes over everything in Dee's notes, and data so she's ready to meet with her the next day.

MEETING OF MINDS

Dee wakes up to the smell of strong coffee, warm bread, and fresh fruit. She opens her eyes and sees Vince sitting in a nearby chair, reading an Italian newspaper. A breakfast tray is sitting on her nightstand: a cup of cappuccino, a croissant and a bowl of yogurt with granola and fresh berries in it. She sits up and stretches. "Good morning."

"I didn't want to wake you, but you do have a meeting to get to." He brings the tray over and places it on her lap.

"Oh! *Yes*! I *do*! I'm losing track of the days around here! So many *years* of routines and it's strange not to have them right now!" She digs into the yogurt, savoring the sweet, fresh blueberries and raspberries, mixed with the savory granola and slightly tart yogurt.

"I figured you should eat before we go." He sits on the edge of the bed, leans over, and gives her a good morning kiss!

She looks up at him and says, "I never thought I'd end up with anyone after my divorce. I was fed up with his ego and threw myself into my life with the girls and my work. I certainly didn't see *anyone* like you coming into my life." She takes another spoonful of the yogurt mixture and washes it down with a sip of cappuccino.

"I know you had a hard road into this life, but personally, I'm glad you were turned, because we'd never have met otherwise." He smiles softly, and gently rubs her arm.

"Yeah, sometimes good things do arise out of the ashes of nightmares." She finishes her breakfast, puts the tray aside, and gives him a berry-flavored kiss.

"I want to talk to you about your meeting today. You'll be meeting with a hybrid named Isanda. I've known her for around 500 years. She and Sara have been close since Sara was turned."

"*Wow*! How long ago was *that*?" Dee inquires.

Vince laughs. "*Dear* lady! As I have my *secrets*, so does Sara! If she wants to tell you, that's her choice! All I can say is that Sara is one of the *oldest* Apara I've ever met!"

Dee lets out a snort of disbelief, saying, "Considering her Star Wars obsession, that's very *odd*!"

"Seriously, when dealing with Isanda, watch the flecks of color in her eyes; they reflect her mood. She *may* want to look at your memories about the virus. *Let* her! I trust her, but I saw Sara yesterday, and got some weird overtones from her about Isanda. Perhaps there's some strain between them. I don't want you to get caught in the middle of everything!" Vince gives her a hand out of bed so she can get ready for her visit to Medical.

Dee is ready to go an hour later. "*Uh-uh!* You're not going anywhere yet!" Vince shakes a finger at her.

"What now?" She glares at him in frustration.

He gives her a lopsided grin with one fang showing. "You may have *eaten*, but you need to *feed* before you head out, or you'll get tired quickly, not to mention, *cranky!*"

Dee sighs, saunters over to him, puts her arms around his neck, and pulls him closer. He exposes his neck to her, and she gently feeds from him. When she's done, she heals his wounds, and leans against him, her ear over his heart. "I'm not sure I'm ever going to get *used to that*. I still feel like I'm doing something *horribly* wrong." She searches his eyes for reassurance. He pulls her close, hugs, and rocks her gently.

"You will, *eventually*. For now, you'll feed from me or from bagged blood until you can get over those feelings. We don't hurt our feeders, and I won't *let you hurt* anyone, I *promise*. Remember, the reason we have to feed on blood is so we're dependent on them, *not* above them! Too many of the first ones ordained themselves, gods or demigods, over humans! Don't think of it as a punishment that we must depend on humans for our survival and stay hidden from them as well; they did it to remind us we are here for *humanity* and that we *need* them. It's symbiotic, not parasitic. We

feed off humans, but we protect them and this planet in return!"
He holds her away from him about a foot and looks her in the eye.
"*Now*, you're ready to go!" He gives her a kind grin, takes her
hand, and the two of them port to the Atrium in Medical. Sara is
there, waiting; tapping her foot impatiently.

"About time you two *got* here!" She snaps, only half-sarcastically.

Vince paths to Dee. *Told you! Something's up!*

They follow Sara up the stairs to an upper level and pause outside
of a door. Sara turns to Dee. "Okay! This is your first time dealing with
any of *Them*! Try to stay calm and focused. Don't get ruffled if they
seem to read your mind because *they do.* It's second nature to them!
I've told them to stick to verbal English as much as possible, as you're
new, so if they go into pathing mode and you can't keep up, or get a
headache, politely ask them to speak aloud!" She addresses Vince. "I
assume you're going to stay with her? Please be her backup, in case
you notice her getting overwhelmed."

"Yes, Sara, though I'm sure Isanda will watch out for her as
well. She's always been good with the new ones." Vince reminds
her, eliciting a mildly annoyed look over her shoulder at his comment before turning around and opening the door. She paths privately to Dee. *And whatever you do, try not to stare!* She paraphrases yet another Star Wars line.

They go into the room with the Samhata team. At first glance,
Dee thinks they all look much alike. She can't help but take a long
look, trying to do it without actually staring. After all, this is the
first time she's ever met anyone not from Earth. But then again,
she's only been Apara a couple of months. She's still adjusting to
the reality of belonging to a network of 'vampires', living right in
front of everyone, in broad daylight. *After that, alien-human hybrids
should be easy enough to accept.* She thinks.

Isanda looks up and puts her tablet down. She walks over to
greet the newcomers. "Hello, Leonardo! It has been quite a long
time since I have seen you! You look quite well!"

"Yes, thank you, I'm *fine*, but please, I go by *Vince* now! My work and name became even more famous over the years and I prefer to be *incognito*!" He says, then motions to Dee. "This is Dee, the scientist you asked to meet today!"

Isanda bows her head slightly and extends her hand in a typical human greeting. "*Dee*, I am Isanda. I have been going over your journals, records, and research. I have not gotten to the virus samples themselves yet. I'm quite impressed with what you did with the virus under the circumstances!"

"You mean with the *damage* I did?" Dee asks, feeling a bit insecure.

Sara gives Dee an annoyed glance at her sudden self-blame, and Vince pull her closer in support.

Isanda glances at Sara, having heard her thoughts. "Sara is right! You *must not* blame yourself! As I am sure Sara would agree, when one is flung into an unknown and frightening situation, one often acts on impulse, or does things one later regrets!" She paths to Sara without turning to face her. *Isn't that right Abha?* Sending a mental, knowing look along with her path.

From behind Isanda, Sara gives what can only be described as a dirty look at her old friend. Dee notices, and hears a mental comment from Vince. *See?*

Isanda easily picks up on all the private pathing, but chooses to ignore it. "Dee, I have questions for you after going through your journals. I must make certain I understand exactly *how* you altered the virus. Please, come sit with me." She turns and paths to Sara and Vince. *She is safe with me! You two should go about your days and leave us to our science!* The overtones of her path are quite clear. Isanda did not want the distraction of Vince's protective hovering, nor did she want to be distracted by Sara's prickly mood.

Sara and Vince leave the lab, and Vince stops Sara. "Okay, you know *why* we were tossed out! What the *hell* is going on with you? I haven't seen you this *moody* since they killed off Han Solo!"

Sara turns toward him, pursing her lips. "It's none of your *damn* business!" She says and ports out.

Vince approaches Liz and Kari about Sara's odd behavior. He senses it's more than her being overwhelmed by the crisis and worries that it may lead her to make mistakes. He ports out, pathing to Dee, *Going to talk to Liz about something. Path if you need me!*

Dee doesn't answer, but sends a mental acknowledgment that she got the message, then gets back to work with Isanda.

Isanda queries her about some of the tools she used to edit the virus's DNA. "What is a CRISPR kit?"

"It's our current, primary tool for finding and editing genes. It's an enzyme derived from proteins taken from a certain type of bacteria. It can be used to track down specific genes, edit them, or even turn them off or on without removing them! It's the basis of nearly all of our current bioengineering technology." Dee explains.

"I see...yes, we once used a similar technique, but I need to make sure I understand what you did and how you did it. Compared to our Benefactor's genetic technology, CRISPR is still quite *primitive*, so I was surprised to see you even approached your goal, even though it missed the mark in the end." Isanda flips the pages on the digital document. "You were certainly on the right track. It wasn't so much your tools or a lack of skills, it was likely an interaction between your CRISPR technology and the... I believe you called them Base5 and Base6 in your notes?"

Dee nods. "Yes, I found two amino-acid bases I've never seen before in DNA. I assume they are from out there?" She asks, pointing toward space.

"Yes, your supposition that those are non-terrestrial bases is correct. There are no similar ones found in life on Earth. They came primarily from the Benefactors own DNA that was sampled, giving you some of your abilities and traits, such as porting, indefinite life span, and rapid healing, for example. Most of the rest were based in latent *human* psychic tendencies. Other non-terrestrial DNA was also sampled. A mixture of that and elements from some Earth Viruses were combined to make the transformational virus that creates the Apara. I have a theory about what went wrong, but we need to look at your stored samples now." Isanda says without any judgment in her tone. The two women enter side room where the viruses are stored.

They bring out a sample of the original virus, the altered one, and the one taken from Jason. Isanda uses short, clear rods, one for each sample, and touches each to one of the stored viruses, turning the tips of the rods blue once each one is sampled. She labels them by turning the other ends of the sampling rods green for original, orange for Dee's altered virus and red for the one taken from Jason. Dee follows Isanda back into the lab and the three rods are put into matching slots in what looks like a crystal ball with swirling colors. Isanda explains, "This is our equivalent of a genetic sequencer and analyzer. In a few minutes, we will have a full sequencing of all three versions, as well as the analysis and projections for how each works based on simulations."

"*Wow!* I had a relatively fast machine, and it still took twelve hours to give me a single sequencing print out!" Dee watches the swirling colors.

Isanda watches Dee puzzling out the swirling lights, and listens in on her public thoughts about what they may be. "Come, sit. I will explain." She says kindly but enthusiastically. Dee may be a relatively primitive scientist compared to the Samhata and Benefactors, but she enjoys seeing the curiosity and mental acrobatics Dee's doing to understand what she's watching.

"How does that even work? It looks like some funky variation on a snow globe or Lava lamp with swirling liquids in different colors." Dee keeps glancing back, fascinated by the dynamics of the motion and colors in the globe. Part of her can nearly perceive structure and pattern in the hypnotically, swirling patterns.

"That is a type of computer. I believe your people are beginning to play with the idea of photonic computing? Where light is used

instead of electrical, digital, or binary signals. As you may have noticed," She says; pointing to the bracelet Dee still wears. "Much of
our technology is based on crystalline science. It can be used with
light and energy instead of electrical, on-off signals, or binary. The
crystals are an artificially grown, liquid form of a crystal. The crystals
are on a nanotech level, and are programmed to analyze the genetic
material in the inputs. The swirls and colors of light are from a dy-
namic form of artificial intelligence in the collective crystals in the
quartz sphere. It works much faster, and is much more complex,
than even the most advanced computers on Earth, though some
Apara scientists are dribbling out similar technology. This will lead
to similar technology, so, by the time the Benefactors are ready to
make official contact with Earth, there may be computers here
which will can interface with their technology."

"That's fascinating, though I suspect the technology itself is
way over my head!" Dee laughs. "I understand some of the concepts, but I'm so used to thinking in terms of hard drives, circuit
boards, RAM, and so on. I would love to learn more about it!"

"You will have time to learn, Dee. When this is done, and you
are settled in, I will have some of the Apara in our scientific community contact you." Her eyes flash with golden tones, signifying
that she is pleased with Dee's reaction to this new experience.

"That would be wonderful! Science has been my life, well, aside
from my children, that is." She gets sad shadows in her eyes when
she thinks about how she'd love to share this new life with her
girls, especially Lynda, who is following in her scientific footsteps.

Isanda tilts her head to one side, and her eyes flicker back to flecks of
dark green. "You understand that is not possible, do you not?"

Dee looks at her with a confused expression. "What's not possible?"

Isanda gives her a long nod and a thoughtful look. "That you
cannot share your new life with your daughters. *However*, I believe
Sara and the others are working on something that may help them
in their future studies."

Dee looks at her, confused. "Oh? Like *what*?"

"I do *not* know the details, but they want to make sure you have peace of mind regarding your daughters, so you can fully embrace your new life." Isanda wonders what it must be like to be a mother and to be in Dee's situation.

"I guess I'll have to ask Sara about that when she comes back." Dee comments, distracted by this new tangent.

"Give Sara time to tell you herself. She is distracted. So, it may take time to do what she has in mind." Isanda looks over as the swirling ball of colors shifts to a slower swirl of mostly blue and silver white. "Ah! The results are complete." She says and takes the tablet Sara gave her over to it, and opens an app that allows the tablet to interface with the alien tech.

Dee watches the process, fascinated, as complex charts and information pop up and disappear on the tablet. "Is that thing communicating with the tablet?"

"Yes. The tablets here are hybrid devices. They may look like a basic iPad or similar, but have much more memory and computational power in them. This app..." She points to an icon on the screen. "Is importing the data from the sphere and translating it into a form your computers can use, as well as into an information matrix which is translated into Earth languages. When it is done, it will transfer the information to another unit so we may view it in three dimensions, and watch the simulations the sphere creates."

Dee shakes her head in amazement, and the yellow flecks of amusement come back into Isanda's eyes. Isanda looks at her thoughtfully and touches Dee's shoulder. "This process will take significantly longer than the analysis. In the meantime, I need to ask your assistance with something."

Dee pauses, remembering what Vince told her. *She may want to read my mind, and I should let her.* She thinks.

Isanda nods. "I see Vince already told you what I may ask of you! Your notes are quite thorough, but it would help me

278

immensely if you would allow me to wander through your memories and see exactly what you did. You don't have to do anything other than relax and let me in." She does her best to sense Dee's reaction to this potentially invasive request.

After a minute, Dee nods curtly. "*Vince* trusts you, so I'll extend you that same trust. What do you need me to do?"

Isanda guides her over to a room off the main lab where there are two reclining chairs that look like they belong in a science fiction movie in a spaceship. They're white, and looked like hard material, but when Dee touches the seat, it conforms to the pressure from her fingers, and an odd, tingling sensation runs over the surface of her fingertips. "The seats are made of a material which will conform to your body and provide comfort. The tingling is a layer of energy that will connect you and I to make it easier for me to review your memories without strain on either of us. In some ways, it will be as if I am you in your memories."

"It took me weeks to sort through all this. Are you going to *review it all*? Do I need to let Vince know I won't be home for a while?" Dee looks concerned.

Isanda laughs a light, little laugh that gives off telepathic harmonics or echoes of laughter in Dee's mind, catching her off guard. "Oh, *no*! Have you not noticed how you can have dreams that happen over hours, days or even longer, but you wake up, realizing you have only been asleep a few minutes? Time is not the same in the mind. It will take a few hours, but you will be back home with *Vince* tonight!" She says, glad that Vince has found someone after Lisa left this life. She thinks, *If only Sara can finally take that step!*

Dee carefully climbs into one of the reclining seats and feels the material change shape to accommodate her body's contours; however, the energy layer kicks in, creating a buffer between the chair and her body, not unlike a mag-lev train floats above a monorail. "This is going to take some getting used to! Are you sure that energy is safe? I'm not going to get electrocuted or get radiation burns?" She says, half joking.

Isanda gives her a sideways look and raises one feathered, gray eyebrow, trying to gauge whether Dee is being serious or not. "Even if it did, it would cause no lasting *harm to you!*" She nod at Dee as she lifts herself into the other seat. There is a control panel on hers with a hand shaped indentation. She puts her hand into it, the lights in the room dim, and the energy field grows, but instead of feeling uncomfortable from the increased energy, it helps Dee relax and enter an almost hypnotic state. She's not asleep, but her mind is relaxed and open. She's aware of everything, but her mind is passive. She perceives a feather light telepathic touch as Isanda touches her mind.

Do not be afraid! It will feel like you are reliving parts of your past, but if I venture into something you cannot deal with, path 'stop' and I will. Isanda paths to Dee.

Dee feels Isanda settling into her mind, as though she's an overlay on her consciousness. It's not painful, but it does feel odd, like she's not sure where she ends and Isanda begins. She closes her eyes, and the energy surrounds and engulfs her like a soft, silky blanket.

Flashes of memory from her time under Jason's control surface in her mind. At first, they are random and vary from mundane to terrifying. Isanda flashes on her memory of the young woman with long black curls Jason made her feed on after she was turned, and she utters a mental *STOP!* Isanda backs off of that memory immediately, not only from Dee's command, but because the emotions surrounding it are hard for Isanda to bear.

Not only is she getting the visuals from Dee's memories, but she's getting all the emotional and psychological responses, as well as the physical sensory input. Eventually, Isanda focuses in on the memories of the time Dee spent in the lab. She replays as much of that as she can, flinching slightly when Dee relives the bone marrow needle in her pelvic bone, and again when Jason

280

brought her daughter, Celia. She avoids similar memories, focusing on Dee's medical studies, methodology, and memories of her observations and theories about the virus.

The longer this goes on, the more Dee feels almost like Isanda is living inside her during her experiences, as though she's a mental ghost along for the ride, watching her every move. It it's like they're in sync.

After about three hours, Dee slides back into awareness of herself and her surroundings. She opens her eyes and the lights are still dim. She feels gentle fingers massaging her temples. "Relax here for a few minutes. Coming back to conscious and current awareness can be disorienting." She says out loud, knowing that the physical sound will help break her out of the disassociation from physical reality, as they'd both been in tight telepathic communion for the last three hours.

Dee yawns. Her limbs and head feel heavy, but she asks, "How long?" Her own voice sounds almost unfamiliar to her as there's a residual telepathic echo, as though she were hearing herself through Isanda's ears.

"About three Earth hours." Isanda says, softly as she slowly adjusts Dee's seat into a more upright position.

"Seemed like weeks." Dee feels a little queasy as she becomes more vertical.

"Relax, and breathe slowly." Isanda walks away and then comes back. She puts a glass in Dee's hands. "Drink."

"Blood?" Dee asks, smelling it, she notices it has odd overtones of unfamiliar scents.

"In part. There are other compounds added which are restorative. This process is hard on your body and mind, especially as you are relatively new to this life." Isanda raises the lighting slowly, careful not to overwhelm Dee's senses.

"Did you get what you needed?" Dee asks, slowly sipping the warm blood.

"Yes, I believe so. The protein spike you spliced into the permanently activated virus, combined with unforeseen effects from the CRISPR enzymes, turned the virus into a virophage, as you theorized." She tells her, but thinks, *Though I suspect there is yet another element involved, best not to mention it until I can verify.* She continues out loud "It changed the original virus in an unexpected way. While it did not make it infect and change unkeyed humans, it did create a protein spike on the second generation which attacks regular human cells, enough to cause an immune reaction so they become carriers for about a week. However, with keyed humans, the virus changes the person's DNA. I will need to do some experiments and observe it in real life, but based on my own genetic engineering knowledge, I would suggest the virus still binds with the compatible DNA and then the spike randomly targets one of the usual areas in each cell. Either the first or most viable change is copied back into the virus, creating new viral particles. These change the rest of the cells to match. Most of the time, there is only one enhanced talent, sense, or skill, but occasionally, more than one reach a critical level. The transformation essentially gets 'stuck' and doesn't go through the rest of the process, changing the keyed human to full Apara."

Isanda explains it as simply as possible without sounding condescending. She knows Dee is an expert by Earth standards, so does not wish to talk down to her. She's seen the ideas and theories Dee toyed with, and is impressed with her skills, considering Earth's relatively primitive genetic sciences.

"In other words, I royally *fucked* things up!" Dee blurts out.

Isanda looks at her oddly. "You did complicate matters, but I believe I can create the biological equivalent of an 'anti-virus'. It will be similar to your virophage and will bind to the altered, second-generation virus and render it inert. However, a lot depends on how stable the virus is. If it is capable of spontaneous mutations, unlike the original, it may require several generations of anti-particles to completely eradicate it."

"You can do this? How would you distribute the anti-virus? We've had a lot of trouble getting people to take vaccines in the last few years, so if this is something that would be distributed to humans, I doubt it will be successful, not to mention, having to get FDA approval!" Dee explains, remembering the early 2020s anti-vax hysteria and conspiracies.

Isanda helps Dee out of her chair and leads her to another room with more comfortable seating, and normal, albeit not bright lighting. Another Samhata comes in with a tray of protein-rich foods such as nuts, cheeses, and meats, as well as bread and crackers. "You should eat as well. The process we went through uses much energy, both psychic and biological." She pushes the tray toward Dee. "As to the anti-virus particles, it would not require vaccinations. Our ship will distribute it by seeding clouds with the particles, as well as directly into some water sources. In areas with poor water resources such as desert lands, we can release an airborne particulate that will reach most environments. The goal is to neutralize the virus, both in humans, and any that may be in the environment."

Dee nibbles on snacks, saying, "What about those that are already infected? Will it *undo* the damage?"

Isanda lets out a long breath and Dee senses her frustration. "No, it will not. Unfortunately, there is no simple way to do that. For one thing, if we created a blanket suppression for such enhanced abilities, then it could very well hinder anyone the Apara choose to bring in as new transformees from developing their own skills. The anti-virus will, assuming there are no mutations, prevent any additional infections. Your people will have to find those already infected, especially those who may be problematic, and evaluate the best course for them."

Dee leans back in her chair. "What do you mean, the best course?"

"I realize a lot of the process that goes into choosing new Apara is unfamiliar to you. When potentials are evaluated, they look at several factors: life situations, psychic potential, intelligence, and perhaps most importantly, psychological stability and adaptability. My understanding is that while you possessed all the qualities one would normally consider positive for transformation, your life situation when you were in your prime transformation age range precluded turning you. I believe you were married and pregnant in your mid-20s?" Isanda asks and takes a few bits of the finger food.

"Yes. I graduated high school and college earlier than average, and got married. I got pregnant with Celia and had to finish my doctorate between Celia and Lynda." Dee recounts.

"Because you were married and a mother, you were unavailable. Otherwise, you would have been prioritized as a potential trans-formee. But when family is involved, it's considered too traumatic to turn someone and take them away from them." Isanda's eyes flicker with highlights of green and some dark red as she thinks about the trauma she felt in Dee's memories from how Jason turned her and treated her, as well as her having to leave her family behind.

Her mind drifts to Sara, and how her first victim was not only a good friend, but a young woman Sara had feelings for. Sara was one of the 'two-spirited', though her friend was less inclined toward such feelings. Sara was singled out for the ritual because they believed there was power in such souls and they often included homosexual acts in some of the religious rituals in Mayan cultures.

The Apara man who transformed her saw her 'two-spirited' nature as something he could tap into to create a powerful tool against her own particular tribe for not bending knee and worshiping him. He told his acolytes that the ceremony would create a powerful demon servant. Isanda often wondered if that part of the ritual, and being singled out because of her nature, prevented her from choosing a partner of her own. Their own relationship contained some intimate elements, but Isanda felt more like a surrogate mother or caregiver for Sara.

The relationship lines among Apara, as well as among Samhata, are often blurred due to how each group 'reproduces'. Apara turn humans to create new Apara, and the creation of new Samhata, as needed, is a much more impersonal act than among humans, or Apara, as their Benefactors create new Samhata in a lab, and raise them at an accelerated rate, rather than Samhata procreating and raising children as humans do, or bonding with a partner as many Apara do.

Dee ponders the possibility that someone would have turned her had she not fallen for her ex-husband and had children. Part of her resenting her failed marriage, though she would not have wished her motherhood undone.

Isanda is still lightly in mental sync with her. "Are you well, Dee?"

Dee snaps out of her deep thought. "I guess so. I was thinking about what you said; that I would have been prioritized if I hadn't been married with children. How likely would I have been turned if I hadn't married?"

"I cannot say for certain. Much depends on their need for new Apara at the time, and the need for specific skills. You were considered a top priority because of your intellect and psychic rating. There was a good chance you would have been brought in had you not married or had children. The period when you were in your prime transformation years were more than a little unstable after the terrorist incidents and wars in that period. They were actively bringing over new Apara to stabilize the world situation." I was not here then, but I kept up with the situation." Isanda heads to the door as it opens. One of her team has brought two mugs of tea for the women. "Here, you must be thirsty after the cheese and cured meat.

Dee takes the mug in her hands, smells the rising steam from it. It has a slightly nutty and sweet odor. She takes a sip and exclaims, "*Wow!* That's good! What is it? Some sort of herbal blend?"

"It is something I brought with me from our Benefactor's world. It will help relax your muscles and perhaps help your mood. Though I dare say you have every reason to feel depressed after how the rogue treated you, and being forced to leave your family behind. Still, this new life has much to offer. I hope you will learn to see the light of the future and...what is the expression humans use? Grab the gold ring with both hands? Sorry, I am not used to using such expressions. But I trust you understand my point?" Isanda sips her own tea, yellow flecks sparkle in her eyes, though there are still flecks of green as well.

Dee nods and puts her mug down on the table in front of her. "I'm trying. It helps that Vince came into my life. I certainly couldn't have hoped to have a more *fascinating* and *inspiring* partner in my life!" She smiles subtly and Isanda senses the budding love in Dee's heart for her old friend Leonardo.

"I'm glad he found you as well! He needs someone who stimulates his mind and inspires him." Isanda looks down at her tablet briefly, looking distant for a split-second right afterwards.

"I'm not sure I'm up to that job, but I *do enjoy* his company! And he certainly challenges and inspires me!" Dee admits, thinking about her adventures with the man she'd once considered the historical figure she'd most like to meet. She's still dumbstruck when she realizes that not only had she met him, but is now living with him, sharing ideas, creative endeavors, as well as sharing a bed. Dee glances down at the tablet, and, nods to it, she asks, "Is everything okay?"

"Yes. My team just let me know they have started the viral tests on compatible blood samples, so we should soon know if my hypothesis about how the virus works is correct. I assume you wish to know once I get the results?" She says, sensing Dee's curiosity swell.

Dee's eyes grow wide. "Oh, yes! Please let me know when you know *anything.* And if there's anything I can do to help make things right, tell me."

There's a knock on the door and Isanda smiles. "I believe that is your partner. He's anxious to get you back home and have some time together with you." She paths to Vince. *Come in, Leonardo! She's ready for you!*

LOOSE ENDS

Vince enters, and walks behind Dee's chair, rests his hands on her shoulders, and kisses her on the top of her head. "Are you ready to go home?"

Dee yawns. "Yes, I'm exhausted after all of this!"

He extends a hand down to her and pulls her up. "Then let's get home! I brought in food from Italy for dinner! My relatives wanted to thank my 'father' for his recent donation!" Vince pulls Dee close in a side hug. He turns to Isanda. "We'll catch up later." He paths an aside privately to her, *I need to spend time alone with Dee tonight. It may be a difficult one for her. Liz, Sara, and the others have finalized the situation around her kidnapping. Her name will be cleared, but she will also be officially dead to the world, and that is often hard the first time it happens for any Apara, but especially in her case, when there are offspring involved.*

Upon 'hearing' his path about the night ahead for Dee, flickers of green and red return to her eyes. While she's never had to deal with that kind of self-grieving process, she knows what she felt from Dee when she thought she'd attacked her daughter and when Jason attacked her older daughter, Celia. *May it go well with her, old friend!* She paths.

Vince ports Dee home and the living room is filled with candles. He's set up a place for them to eat by the fireplace, where a roaring fire is burning. He brings out two plates and puts them on the low table while Dee settles onto the large pillow on the floor on one side, enjoying the warmth from the fire. Vince returns to the kitchen and brings out a bottle of the same wine they'd had in Italy, along with two glasses.

Dee watches as he comes over with the wine and sits on his own pillow, pouring them two glasses of wine. He raises his wine glass in a toast. "To a long future together!" He catches her eyes with his, and she joins him in the toast.

"Vince, what's this all about? What's the reason for going all out like this? Surely not just because your *relatives* wanted to thank you for helping them." She eyes him suspiciously.

"Enjoy your meal, Dee." He tells her, without answering.

With that, she puts the pasta from her fork in her mouth, lays the fork down on her plate, and looks at him with a raised eyebrow and pursed lips. "*Spill*, Da Vinci! I know something's going on! You've been hard to read since you picked me up!"

He lets out a sigh and puts his own fork down. "You know how I went to see Liz today?"

"Yeah, though I got the impression you were going to talk to her about Sara's attitude." She cocks her head to one side, waiting for him to answer.

"I was, something's up with her. Well, between her and Isanda. Sara even told me to 'mind my own damn business' earlier today! *Very* unlike her!"

Dee's eyes go wide. "That *does* seem out of character for her. However, I get the *feeling* you're trying to distract me from the real reason we're sitting here having gourmet Italian food and wine. *Spill!*"

"*Alright*! After talking to Liz about Sara, she filled me in on something they've been working on that has to do with you." He pauses, waiting to see how she reacts.

"What about *me*? I've settled in with you. Does she have an issue with *that*?" Dee asks, confused.

"No! Not at all, in fact…" He reaches under his pillow and brings out a passport and a driver's license. He holds it in his hands a few seconds before cautiously handing them to her. "With everything that happened around your disappearance, they've set you up with a new identity, especially with your de-aging." He smiles anxiously, but she can still sense there's more to it, and somehow knows he's trying to avoid upsetting her.

She takes the passport and license. The license is for North Carolina with Vince's portal home address on it. In both, she sees photos of herself with her de-aged appearance, and the name on both is Thaddea Leonard, not Thaddea Price. "Leonard?" She looks up at him curiously.

"Since we're together, they're using my last name; well, my assumed last name!" He grins.

"I'm amazed no one's figured you out! It's not that *huge* a leap to go from Vince Leonard to Leonardo Da Vinci!" She shakes her head as she looks at her new ID, noting that it has the date of her turning as her birthday, with a year that would make her currently 26 years old. "This is all *so strange*! I am who I've always been, but I'm *not me* anymore. I get why it's necessary, nevertheless, it's like who I was is gone, and I'm a ghost of myself!" She laughs sarcastically.

"It's a life change, and with any life change, there's a *grieving* process. Technically, you died!" He gives her a lopsided grin, and she senses there's more he has to tell her.

She puts the IDs down on the table and drums her fingers next to them. "What *aren't* you telling me?"

Vince gets a resigned expression. "*Alright*, Liz found a way to wrap things up on your old life. Clearly, they're never going to find the *fugitive* Dr. Thaddea Price. They also don't want your family to be left with any doubts, so they found a way to...to give them *closure*."

"*Exactly* how are they going to do that?" Dee's voice gets higher pitched as her anxiety level increases.

"Now that they have everything they need from your lab and the cabin, they've staged a fake death for you. They found an unidentified woman who recently passed away who was similar in stature to you, and left her body in your lab and set it on fire, making sure that there was too much damage to identify the original corpse through dental records or DNA. They then 'salted' the remains with your actual pre-transformation DNA they cultured from samples taken from your home. As far as the world and your family are concerned, you died in that lab blaze." He pauses, reaching out an empathic tendril to see how Dee's handling it.

"*But if they think I died in a bio-lab blaze, how does that clear my name*? I would have thought that would make me seem even *more guilty!*" Vince knows she's trying to stay calm but is getting more and more upset. He hears her thinking, *What are my daughters going to think? They'll wonder if I was a terrorist for the rest of their lives!*

"*Dee*, they've made *sure* your name's been cleared! They added and backdated some files on Jason's laptop at the cabin, showing a plot where he kidnapped you to force you to create a bio-weapon, threatening to kill your daughters if you didn't help him. Then they set the cabin on fire, but made sure the computer's drive was salvageable. The FBI has it, and we have someone on the inside who is making sure that the evidence clears your name." He reaches over and puts his hand on hers. It's going to make the news tomorrow that you were the victim, not a terrorist, and when you didn't do what he wanted, he killed you and burned your lab to cover his tracks."

Dee cups her hands in front of her mouth and nose, her hands trembling. "*So*, they've made sure all doors are *closed* for me? *Not* that I was going to go back to see my daughters, but this really makes everything *so* final, doesn't it? I'm *dead* to them now! I can't imagine what they're going through! And yet, here I am, having a gourmet dinner with you while they grieve!"

"Dee, it had to happen! Don't you want them to have closure? To move forward with their lives? Or did you want them to wonder for years if you really are a terrorist, where you might be, or if you were even alive? They did this *for* you as well as for your family!" He explains, stroking her arm.

"I guess part of me hoped to find some way to say goodbye to them! To find a way to encourage them to go on with their lives! And for Lynda to keep going with her studies! I planned to get her an internship in another department up at Detrick!" Tears well up in her eyes as she realizes that her old life is *truly* gone; that in some ways, Dee really is dead now, and she's grieving her former life.

Vince moves closer to her, pulls her head against his shoulder, and feels her break down into jagged sobs as the reality of her old life being over sinks in. "This had to happen, *tesoro mio!* You can't keep clinging to a life that's gone! Your daughters will grieve and eventually move on, but so *must* you! It's psychologically necessary for you to do so! I am *here* and will help you through it all!" He holds her close and rocks her gently. He lets her cry herself out before relaxing his embrace. He reaches for one of the cloth napkins he has on the table and uses it to wipe away some of the moisture on her face.

"*Everything's* been such a whirlwind! I tried not to think about this! Part of me always hoped the girls would think I might still come home, though, rationally, I know that's impossible! *Hell!* They definitely wouldn't *recognize* me now, would *they!*" She takes the napkin and blows her nose in it. "*Sorry!*" She puts the damp, snotty napkin on the floor next to her.

"*You're* worried about a *napkin?*" He takes her by the chin and shakes his head.

"I still feel so guilty about *everything!* Not only the virus, but *leaving* them! I *know* it's not *my* fault! But somehow, it still *feels* like it is! I should have known something was fishy and avoided Jason in the first place!" She sniffs to clear her nose, and looks up at him with puffy, bloodshot eyes.

"You *couldn't* have avoided him. He could have ported in and taken you even if you'd gotten in your car and driven out of state! You *certainly* couldn't have *overpowered* him!" He pulls her close again, but holds her more gently this time.

"I *know*, but I still feel guilty about so much! Even being *here* with *you!* I feel like I'm shirking my motherly duty by being here with my *lover* while my daughters *grieve* for me!" A fresh torrent of tears erupt and roll down her cheeks.

Vince scoops her up into his arms and ports to the bedroom with her, laying her down on the bed, and gently brushing her hair out of her eyes. "Get some rest! Dinner can wait."

"I'm not sure I'll be able to sleep. *Not* after all of this!" She rubs the salty tears away from her eyes and looks up at Vince.

"Dee, with as *ornery* as Sara was earlier today, do you really want me to drag her over here to give you a sedative?" He gives her a wicked little grin, but she notices concern and pain in his eyes as he knows what she's going through.

"*No*, but I keep thinking about what will happen to them now! I *never* made a will, so everything will have to go to probate! Their dad will have to cover their education until that's settled, and I'm afraid the girls might take a break until things are settled and lose momentum in their education!" She swallows, imagining their potentially bright futures turning dull and uncertain.

Vince sits on the edge of the bed. "Well, I have one other bit of news that may help put you at ease about that."

Dee's breathing's ragged, and she chokes out, "W...what?"

Liz had one of our people who fronts as a human lawyer draw up a will, leaving everything equally to your girls, added your signature, and witnesses. In addition, you have a rather significant life insurance policy that will now pay out handsomely!" He grins.

"No, I didn't! I had a small one. Only about $35,000, at most." Her voice sounds raspy and muffled from her tear clogged nose.

"Yes, you *did* have that, and by the way, now that your name is cleared, it will pay out! Like your new 'Last Will and Testament', arrangements have been made. Do you think $500,000 split between them might help them continue their education, and get a good start on life?" He looks at her softly.

"Oh, *my God! Yes!* Lynda could finish her undergrad at UCLA and then work toward her doctorate! And Celia's majoring in anthropology. She could finish her education as well. But how did

Liz manage that?" Dee relaxes with Vince's revelation. She lets out a long yawn, feeling the emotional exhaustion hit her hard.

"We have business fronts of all kinds, including insurance, *Amore*. We also have virtually unlimited financial resources, so it was just to set the right things in motion, and *voila!* I know it's not the same as having their mother in their lives, but we thought that might help." He smiles. "Go on, sleep! I'm going to put the food away and join you shortly, *tesoro mio!*" He turns off the lights and cleans up their barely touched meal, saving it for when she's feeling better.

Afterwards, he calls Liz. "Hello, Liz, it's Vince."

"Did you tell her?" Liz asks.

"Yes. It was a bit touch and go, but it helped her to know her estate and the added 'insurance' payout would help her daughters start their adult lives. I'm sure she'll have some ups and downs for a while" He remarks as he finishes cleaning up a few things, and blowing out all the candles that hadn't burnt out on their own in the living room. He closes up the glass shield in front of the fireplace to keep any sparks from popping onto the carpet nearby.

"Vince, I know you *think* you can see her through this, but remember, Tess and Sue are both available if she needs to talk. Normally, I'd say Sara as well, but after what you told me about her rather erratic behavior earlier today, I think Tess or Sue might be better for the time being." Liz says, and Vince hears Kari's voice in the background. Liz chuckles. "And Kari will gladly be there for her as well!"

"Thanks. Have you figured out what might be up with Sara?" He asks as he walks back toward the bedroom, waiting just outside the door to finish his conversation.

"I'm not sure, but I've heard that she and Isanda used to be quite close. You might ask her?" She tells him.

"I have a sneaking suspicion it may have started with Isanda. I got some odd overtones on their interaction earlier today. I suspect Sara might be angry at her or feel hurt?" He leans against the wall, but peaks through a crack in the door to look at Dee, who has succumbed to exhaustion, and is snoring from a very clogged nose. He shakes his head and pulls the door quietly shut.

"I'll see if I can find an excuse to talk with her tomorrow; maybe I'll pick up something from her. Get some rest, Vince, you sound like you've been as much through the ringer as Dee has. Goodnight." Liz hangs up.

Vince quietly opens the door, carefully joins Dee in bed, careful not to wake her. He knows she'll need her rest if she's going to get through this without complications.

A SMALL TALENT

Isanda studies Dee's memories, as well as her notes. Her team attempts to replicate the altered virus that Dee created, but cannot make a viable one despite following the procedures to the letter. Isanda's hair flutters around like she's touching a Van de Graaff generator on a windy day. While her hair usually reflects ambient psychic energy, it also can show signs of internal frustration.

Sara intends to walk past the lab, ignoring Isanda, but she sees her hair, and knows something's off. She sighs, turns, and checks on her old friend, putting aside her irritation with her for now. Isanda is so focused on the riddle in front of her she doesn't notice Sara's presence.

Sara hesitates briefly, but gently reaches out, and strokes Isanda's shoulder, causing her hair to flinch, and settle as Isanda turns and sees the concern in Sara's eyes. "What's wrong? I *thought* you had this figured out?"

"I thought I had, too, though I wondered about one thing that did not quite fit, and now, it appears my suspicion must be correct." Isanda remarks, and Sara senses her disbelief at her own conclusions.

"Is the virus a bigger problem than we thought?" Sara pulls up a chair and sits next to Isanda, finding it hard to be angry at her when she's upset.

"That is still unclear. The problem lies in *how* Dee created the altered virus. According to our tests, it shouldn't be possible." Flecks of white and silver dance in her irises, showing confusion and frustration.

"Were Dee's notes incomplete?" Sara picks up her own tablet and pulls up Dee's digitized notes.

"Not exactly! She recorded everything meticulously. It all matched with what I saw in her memories. The only problem is, even doing the exact things she did, we cannot replicate the virus!" A nearly physical wave of frustration flares out from Isanda and washes over Sara, making her gasp. *Sorry, Abha! I did not mean to lash out!* She paths, sticking to Sara's old name in her mind.

"What happened when you tried to replicate the virus? Did it come out differently?" Sara peaks over at Isanda's screen to see what has her so disturbed.

Isanda laughs an odd laugh. The sound comes out almost like a multi-note, discordant sound, showing extreme frustration. "It does *not* work! We could not create a viable virus. The protein spike is not compatible. It will not integrate into the new virus, and without it, it cannot infect and alter the original virus. What she has created *should* be impossible!"

"Is it possible she forgot what she did?" Sara skims the notes on her tablet and watches the video of the attempted alteration. "It clearly works in the video documentation of her procedure."

"I know. It worked, but there is no way it *should* have!" Isanda gets an odd expression and her hair flutters like a twitching cat's tail. She goes over to what vaguely resembles a microscope with a flat screen on it, slipping in the rod with the orange tag on it, and zooms in. Isanda zooms in even more, squinting her eyes as she focuses on where the protein spike begins and ends in a single viral particle. She runs her hand along the edge of the scope and the screen flashes briefly. Several locations, including where the spike attaches to the remains of the original virus, glow bright orange. "*Oh!* That is *unexpected!*" She sits with a thud and looks at Sara.

"What's unexpected?" Sara perceives disbelief combined with comprehension roll off of Isanda.

Isanda picks up her tablet and goes into the potential database, pulling up the original Benefactor evaluations on Dee's potential. She skims it in their original written language so she can be sure to get the proper interpretation. After a few minutes, she puts the tablet down on the table and her expression shifts to one of comprehension. "The Benefactors who evaluated Dee as a child believed she would show strong talents in healing, which fits with her chosen career, and some form of telekinesis."

Sara looks at her old friend, still uncertain what she's thinking. "Oh? How does that figure in with the virus?"

Isanda motions for Sara to come over to the scope and look at the image with her. "Those bright spots are what have been puzzling me. They should not be possible! Under natural conditions, they are not compatible genetic fusions! The orange tells me how they became possible! Dee *telekinetically* altered the virus. Her technology did part of it, but I believe she has the ability to alter or adapt the virus through a combination of her healing and telekinetic abilities. She thought it into the form she wanted it to take unconsciously. Which explains why the virus altered Jason's original virus. When I was in her mind, one of her overwhelming fears was that he would test the virus on one of her daughters. She was afraid he would turn one or both of them, and torment them... rape them...yes, that is the word from her mind. She must have unconsciously made this virus change his original virus into something that *couldn't* turn anyone else, especially her daughters!"

Sara mutters a string of ancient Mayan curses under her breath, eliciting a sidelong stare from Isanda. "I've never heard of anyone with that ability. If she were one of the Lost Mission potentials, I might not be so surprised, but Dee was born long before their time!

"The base abilities exist in many of your people, but she adapted them to her career! I read through some of her previous work and this is not the first time she's produced an altered virus or DNA chain that could not be replicated! Her telekinesis, when combined with her healing tendencies, is on a microcellular level." Isanda's expression shifts to one of comprehension and awe. "This explains why her virus collapsed once it finished its job. The genetic bonds were not stable long term, but its alterations to the original virus are what we need to look at now. We must determine if the second generation altered virus is stable and what we can do to neutralize it."

"I wonder if she can use her skills in other ways?" Sara comments, distracted by a passing idea.

Isanda looks at her former charge, chuckling lightly. "You will forever be the same! Always looking at unusual angles. You are free to explore that with Dee if you wish, but right now, my team and I must focus on finding a solution to our larger problem." She strokes Sara's face lightly with one hand. "Please do not go back to being angry with me." She says aloud, sending the name *Abha* telepathically. "I have missed our cooperation and our friendship. I should not have avoided you, but I felt you needed to move on! I cannot be here all the time! You know that! All Samhata must return home periodically, to teach what we have learned here, but also to renew our energies among the Benefactors, if not, we weaken mentally. It is perhaps a flaw in our design, though I doubt our Benefactors see it that way! They never intended for us to live permanently on Earth!"

Sara sighs, and leans into Isanda's gentle touch. "You made me feel safe and sane when you found me. I have been afraid to lose that feeling, so have never looked elsewhere." She sits, emotionally exhausted, as she finally faces what she's avoided for millennia; She thinks, *It really is time for me to move on, to stop pretending to be the strong, ancient wise-woman healer who needs no one but myself! I've hung on to the strength that Isanda gave me so long ago, pretending she was there, keeping me strong! I've been so afraid to stand on my own, thinking I would be nothing without her, but I'm not! I haven't been pretending! I am a healer, and it's time I heal myself, and possibly Annie in the process.*

Isanda breathes a sigh of relief, golden flecks light up her purple-blue irises like two royal Lapis Lazuli stones. Knowing no one but Sara can hear her she speaks aloud. "It *is* time, Abha. You do not need me to give you strength, as you have always had it, even before you became Apara! I remember you, even back then, being the strong-willed

298

girl who chose her own path among the Maya! Cadmael feared and re-
sented the power inside you. That is why he chose you for the ritual!
Not only because he felt he could use your power, but because he felt
the need to break your power as a symbolic breaking of your people! I
believe he felt that if they saw he had broken you, that he must be a
powerful god! A god worthy of their fear and worship!"

Sara swallows, knowing what Isanda says is true. "Will you stay
for a while? I would like Annie to get to know you well!"

Isanda's hair curls under her head and settles, its shade shifting slightly from silver to slightly purple. "Yes, Abha, I will stay
for a while, but you must promise me something!"

"Anything." Sara nods.

"Tell Annie of your past! She nearly shared a similar transformation to yours. I believe it will let her feel more comfortable
with you to know that you share this!"

"I will. But, first, Vince contacted me to ask if you need to see
Dee today. She had a difficult night last night." Sara relays.

"I am aware. Vince pathed me about it when he came for her. I
will not need to see Dee today, but perhaps tomorrow after I have
explored my findings more." She touches Sara on her arm gently,
and Sara feels energy bridge the fine gap between their skin. "I
am very glad that your people have finally stopped Jason Templeton. When we have done what we seek to do with the virus, we
must contemplate what must be done with him. Perhaps even Dee
may be some part of that?" Isanda leans over and hugs Sara. "I
think you and Annie will be very good for each other! You will
now be the caregiver, as I was for you, but I think the two of you
will soon grow to complement each other as equals!" She nods.
"Go! I need to meet with my team about my findings!"

Sara nods and ports out.

HEALING MENTAL TOUCH

A few days pass. Isanda and her team are busy analyzing second-generation virus samples from around the world to determine if there are any mutated variants. Once they know it has not mutated, they search for a neutralizing agent that will make it biologically inert.

Sara has told Isanda that she will speak with Annie, but wants to wait until the crisis is over so she can give Annie her undivided attention when she turns her. Isanda accepts this, but makes Sara swear an oath to go through with it.

Dee is home, dealing with her grief. Her logical, scientific mind tells her she doesn't *need* to grieve, reminding herself that she hasn't *really* died; that she's *still herself*, so should get on with her new life. Her emotions and body decide otherwise, as she finds it very difficult to gain the momentum to do much other than sleep, eat, and feed. On the fourth day, Vince comes into the bedroom after working in his workshop to find Dee asleep, blanket up over her head, hiding from the world. He sits on the edge of the bed and gently strokes her back through the heavy quilt. "Are you going to sleep your first *century* away?" He nudges her shoulder with one hand.

Dee groans and curls up tighter under her quilt. "Leave me alone! I *want* to sleep." She mutters.

"*Tesoro mio! Grieving* is normal, doing your best imitation of a hibernating bear is not! You've barely eaten in four days, and you didn't feed fully either! Did you have more nightmares last night?" He asks, knowing that she did as they pre-empted his own dreams, and he ended up watching her watch her daughters cry and grieve in a graveyard. They couldn't see her, but she could see them. Both of them had bite marks on their necks. She panicked, and looked up at who she thought was her ex-husband, only to see Jason. He glared at Dee and smirked, then laughed at her. As his laughter echoed in her ears, the girls wailed louder, and opened their mouths and they both had fangs.

She sobs under the quilt. "It's nothing." She says, though it sounds muffled from under the blanket.

"It wasn't nothing. I saw your dream last night!" Vince gently rubs her back through the blanket.

She rolls toward him, and pulls the blanket down so she can see him. "You *read* my mind while I slept?" Her voice has tinges of betrayal in it.

"No, *Cara*! I was sound asleep! Your dreams overrode my own! I was dreaming about riding a horse through the fields of my family farm as a boy when the dream shifted, and I was watching you, watching them! I saw what you saw. You *know* your daughters are safe. Jason is in induced stasis." He reassures her.

"I was so afraid he'd use the virus on them! That he'd do to them what he'd done to me, and worse!" Tears flow again, her eyes still red and puffy from her last crying jag.

He lies down next to her on the bed, so his face is at the same level as hers. "This is not healthy grieving, *Cara*! You must deal with this before it pulls you down into a deep, psychological pit!" He tugs the blanket down so he sees her entire face and strokes her cheek with the back of his hand. Dee says nothing, and her eyes look like a light has extinguished in her soul. He knows she won't willingly talk to Tess or Sue. He suggested it several times, but she balked, so he makes an excuse to take her to Medical. "Isanda and Sara want you to come by today. They have more questions for you." He tells her, knowing that the one thing that might get her out of bed is the need to make things right after her tinkering.

Dee wants to curl up and go back to sleep, but slowly drags herself into a seated position, knowing she promised to do *whatever* she could to make good on her mistakes. She drags herself out of bed and walks heavily, like some stiff zombie, to the bathroom. She splashes cold water on her face and gets ready.

When she comes out, Vince is standing there with blood. "You're not going anywhere until you've fed properly!" He extends his hand out, giving her a bag of blood. She half-heartedly bites into it and drinks it, not caring that it's running down her chin. Vince gives her a pained glance. "You are being messy! That's not like you at all!" He leans over and licks the blood off her chin and gives her a kiss. She accepts it, but barely responds.

"Not like a little blood is going to shock anyone at Medical." She says with a disheartened sigh, and grabs her tablet. She stands there waiting for him to port her to medical like she's waiting for a bus.

Vince slips his arm through hers and ports her directly into a small room with a sofa, a couple of chairs, and a table. There are two women in the room, but it takes Dee a few seconds to realize that it's Tess and Sue. She gives Vince an angry glare and tries to port out, but nothing happens.

"Sorry, *Cara! No* porting! You must sort this out. I'm worried about you and feel like I'm *losing* you." He tips her chin up, forcing her to look him in the eye. "Tess and Sue helped you before! I *believe* they can help you again!" He takes her arm, gently pulls her over to the sofa, and sits her down. He squats down in front of her, making her look at him rather than off to one side, avoiding his gaze. "I can stay if you want me to, but one way or another, you're going to talk this through with them. I can't lose you to this wallowing despair!"

"This was all a *trick* to get me here? Isanda and Sara *didn't* need to see me?" She sulks.

"Sara will be along shortly. She's dealing with something with one of the infected potentials. Apparently, their gift draws too much power and was giving them seizures." As soon as he tells her that, he realizes he's made a mistake. Hearing that her virus is causing another person distress only adds to her ever-worsening guilt. "*Cara! Stop* it! You can't blame yourself for everything!"

She looks completely dejected. "*Go!* I'll talk to them." She waves him out unenthusiastically.

Vince leaves the room, but paths to Tess and Sue. *I hope you can do something for her! I'm finding it increasingly difficult to get through to her. She's sinking deeper into despondency every day! I miss my Dee! That brilliant mind that shines like the sun! Please help me find her again!*

We'll do our best, Vince! I promise! Tess paths.

Vince heads off to find Sara or Isanda, two of the few genuine friends who know who he really is.

Dee sits silently on the sofa. Despite her de-aged state, she looks older and worn.

Tess and Sue have been working together since Sue was transformed, but after Tess was drawn into Dee's nightmare by Sue, they've been working even more in Tandem on Sue's therascapes. Tess's raw people intuition, combined with Sue's education, practical experience, and ability to go into the minds of others through dreams as a form of therapy works very well when dealing with Apara with psychological issues.

They've recently been working with Jason's former captive transformees; most recently, with Alice. Before she was turned, she'd been a timid young woman one might have otherwise overlooked, and that was the way she preferred it. When Jason and Philipa found her, she'd been at the movie theater seeing a new romantic-comedy. Movies were one place she could go and still be practically invisible. The darkness in the room and everyone focused on the screen was one of the few places she felt comfortable in public, because she could literally blend into the furniture.

Jason and Philipa chose seats on either side of her that night, and when the movie was over, she found she couldn't get up to leave, or even cry out in distress. Once most of the people had left, she got up with the two strangers and walked along with them as though they were friends of hers. Once outside, they walked around the back of the building where Jason used his mental control on her to make her strip in front of him. He then took advantage of the situation, as well as feeding on her. When done, they ported Alice to the fallout shelter, where he and Philipa tormented her for days before finally turning her.

Both Alice and Philipa were psychologically damaged, though Philipa's was a very different kind of damage. She'd been taken from a psychiatric hospital in Virginia, where she was being treated for paranoid schizophrenia and violent tendencies.

In some ways, she was the perfect partner for Jason, because her obsessive tendencies made her devoutly loyal to him, and her violent streak made her useful. Her issues, however, were deep-seated and long term, and she's been kept in an induced, near stasis like coma since being freed from Jason.

Alice has been dealing with severe PTSD and a form of Stockholm Syndrome. Sue and Tess worked together, going into her mind and helping her relive the situation with a different outcome, giving her the illusion of power. They helped her understand that she is not to blame for what happened to her. Now, as an Apara, she knows that she doesn't *have* to worry about anyone taking advantage of her again.

In addition, Amy runs a self-defense program for Jason's victims, and has helped empower Alice physically as well as psychologically.

Somehow, Sue's dream therapy literally reshaped her neurochemical balance, boosting serotonin, reducing cortisol and other stress-related hormones, and helping pull her out of a near catatonic depression; something they hoped to repeat with Dee.

In Dee's case, they've been in her mind before, and saw how she could warp her self-perceptions into a literal nightmare. While she was not in the same situation as she had been, her grief reaction to her official death is been worse than expected.

While she understands why she had to fake her death on a rational level, years of maternal instincts make it hard for her to release the feelings of guilt for *abandoning* her family, as well as her research. She was so close to making a breakthrough in treating several forms of cancer with her altered viruses.

Her official 'death' made her realize she'd never be able to complete her research. While Dee found herself happy with Vince, her human world death overwhelmed her, and plunged her into a deep depression. Vince contacted Tess and Sue, knowing they'd helped her before. He could sense her withdrawing more and more each day, and while it has only been a few days since her official death, he's terrified by her mental downhill slide.

Tess paths privately to Sue. *I don't like the vibes I'm getting from her at all! If she'd been human, I'd worry about suicide!*

In a way, that's what she's doing, shutting down. Her body may not die, but part of her wishes she could. Where's Sara? I thought she'd be here by now. Sue paths.

She'll be here shortly. She's done with the emergency in medical but said she needed to grab something from Isanda. Tess paths as she watches Dee apathetically slouching in her chair. staring at the table in front of her blankly.

Sue decides to begin, with or without Sara. "Dee, I know you don't want to be here, but I feel you know you *need* to be, am I right?"

Dee sighs, briefly looks up as Sue, and then away again. "Does it matter? I'm here, aren't I?"

"Yes, it matters. As long as you understand why you need to be here, we may be able to help you!" Sue explains, using a firm, but gentle tone. She feels Dee's annoyance at Vince for bringing her here under false pretenses, but part of her understands why he did it.

"I get it. I just...." She sighs. "I've spent years of my life focused around my work and my girls, and now, both are out of my reach. Even though my girls are adults, there's so much I can't be a part of even though I'm alive!"

Sue narrows her eyes, trying to sense Dee's base emotional state through the tumult of emotions running through her conscious mind. "What are you most afraid you'll miss?"

Dee gets a pained expression. "*Everything*! Their college graduations, them getting married, and having children! I'll *never* hold my grandchildren, if they have any! I won't be there when Lynda gets her PhD. I can't be there if they need me!"

Tess paths to Sue. *And this is why they don't turn people with families! No matter how rational and scientific her mindset, it still comes back to emotional bonds!*

"You can always follow their social media. I know it's not the same, but at least you'd know when major life events occur!" Sue looks up as the door quietly opens, and Sara comes in with a Carafe and several mugs on a tray.

Dee looks up at Sara briefly and then back at Sue. "I think that may be worse! I'd see a glimpse into their lives, but I'd feel horrible I can't be an active part or there for them when they need me! I feel like I've *abandoned* them *both*! I know, I *know*! *None* of it is *my* fault, and the insurance payout will help them financially, but I hate that they're grieving my loss when I'm *right here*! What *right* do I have to be happy or have a new life when they're made to *suffer!*" Tears run down her cheeks, and Sue, out of habit, pushes a box of tissues across the table.

Sara fills the mugs from the Carafe. Warm, slightly nutty and sweet steam rises from the mugs, and Dee looks down at a cup longingly. "Isanda asked me to bring this. She knew you'd taken a liking to it!" She says as she puts the first mug in front of Dee.

Dee nods, sniffling. "Please tell her thank you."

Sara smiles and passes the other mugs around to Sue and Tess, and lastly, takes a mug for herself. "This is a drink from our Benefactor's world. Isanda used to make it for me long ago, and she brought some back with her.

Dee sips hers and relaxes, despite her frustration. Sara paths to Sue and Tess. *There's a little something extra in her mug that should make it easier for you to slip in, Sue.*

Sue closes her eyes, focusing on Dee. A minute later, Sue, Tess, and Dee are all sitting together in front of a café in Frederick, Maryland as though they are all old friends getting together for an afternoon coffee. Dee is a bit disoriented at first, but clearer-headed as she relaxes into the dreamscape, drinking her coffee, which has an unusual, nutty side taste. Sara's not in the dream, but monitors the process for research, as well as monitoring brain chemicals and stress levels in Dee.

"So, Dee, I understand you have two daughters?" Sue sips her drink while watching Dee's reaction.

"Yes, Lynda and Celia!" She says and slips her fork into a piece of rhubarb-strawberry pie in front of her, savoring her seasonal favorite.

"You should bring them along next time! I'd love to meet them." Sue says, taking a stab at her chocolate cheesecake.

"Oh, I'm afraid that *won't* be possible! They're out in California with their father, studying at UCLA." Dee says with a wistful look in her eye.

"You miss them, don't you?" Tess prompts.

"Yes, very much! But going to UCLA is what's best for them, and it made it possible for me to come here and run my research project at Detrick. For once, I'm not working under someone's supervision. It's *my* research." She says and takes a long sip of her coffee.

Sue chimes in. "It must be very satisfying to run your own project. I'll bet your daughters are proud of you."

Dee shifts uncomfortably. "I *hope* so... though, I sometimes worry they think I've washed my hands of them by sending them to live with their dad once they came of age."

Sue nods her head slowly. "Sounds like maybe you've got some regrets?"

"Not exactly. Part of me feels bad moving on with my life now that they're adults, but I put much of my life on hold raising them, especially after their father and I split up! I deserve a life of my own, too, but I still feel like I should be there for them!" Dee picks at her pie with her fork, eyes looking distant as she thinks about her girls.

"Dee, look at me." Sue tells her.

Dee looks up at Sue and the world around them shimmers and blurs. When things stabilize, they're still at the café, but Dee knows she's not really there. "Oh, *God!*" She says and cries.

"You've been grieving about losing that connection with your daughters for a while, not just since you've become Apara, but since you let them go off to California to college to pursue your own life! That's where your guilt comes from! Not from your becoming Apara, or your official 'death' in the human world! Those things exasperated the guilt you already felt for moving on and putting your own life on the front burner after so many years putting Lynda and Celia first. Add to that, Jason dangled their well-being over your head all those weeks, forcing you to put them first again. Part of you became *so* obsessed with protecting them, but when it was over, you could relax, and then Vince helped you move on in other ways. However, your official death put the last nail in the proverbial coffin, and brought all those guilty feelings you suppressed since the girls moved off to college, especially once Lynda left. With her following in your footsteps, and you can't be there for her, you're youngest, it's part of what triggered the greatest guilt!" Sue says, almost on autopilot, as her therapist's intuition kicks into full gear.

Dee's eyes are unfocused as she thinks about what Sue said. After a brief time, she looks up again. "I *feel* like I should have been there for them. Maybe I should have moved out to California *with* them?" She gives an ironic laugh under her breath. "If I had, then maybe Jason wouldn't have gotten to me and we wouldn't be in this mess with the virus!"

"Dee, Frederick was outside his comfort zone. Once he set his mind on you because of your skills, he'd have gone anywhere he needed to in order to find you! And if he'd gone out there, who's to say he wouldn't have used your daughters there and then to get you to comply! It could have gone much worse if you'd been living with your daughters when he took you! Trust me, I know Jason all too well!" Tess tells her. "I've dealt with that man since the first day I worked for Inspiration Inc! If he decided he wanted to get to you, he'd have gone to California to find you! Nothing you could have done would have stopped him!" Tess pauses, then adds, "Besides, you'd never have met Vince had you remained human! I know it's a small consolation, but still, you wanted your own life again, and he's definitely the icing on that cake!"

Dee nods, realizing that as much as she would never *choose* to give up her girls, she wouldn't want to lose her amazing man, either! She sags down in her chair, hearing rolling thunder as rain starts to fall. While they don't actually get wet, the rain washes away the dream, and the women wake up back in the room in Medical.

There are tracks from tears on Dee's cheeks, but she's more relaxed and present than she'd been in days, and the repressive aura of despair has dissipated. "I was blaming everything on what I've become, and what I've done, not realizing my guilt started at least two years ago when Lynda left for California. I can't believe I missed that!"

Sue leans forward toward Dee. "You spent years of your life devoted to your family, even while working, they were front and center in some ways. There's nothing wrong with moving on with your life now that they're adults! There's no shame in that, nor should you feel guilty!"

"I know, but I'll still miss out on so much in their lives!" She sighs.

"You may not be there physically, but you *can* watch from afar! And I'm sure they know you love them! I happen to know that part of the evidence on his hard drive included notes about using your daughters to make you comply. They'll know you risked everything for them and that will be with them their entire lives!" Tess reminds her.

Sara sits with them now that the dreamscape is done. "You girls did well, but I need to talk to Dee now." Tess and Sue both feel the mental 'run along now' push. They get up and walk over to Dee, hugging her before porting out.

Dee takes a deep breath and lets it out slowly, regarding Sara. "What did you need to talk to me about?"

"I wanted to let you know that you unknowingly protected your daughters in another way Sue and Tess are unaware of." She pours Dee some fresh tea.

Dee takes a sip. "Hm, it's even good cold! So, how did I protect them?"

"Isanda and I have been going over your notes, memories and results, as well as trying to replicate your virus as a means to create an antivirus and discovered something quite unique." She gives her a lopsided smile. "There's *no* way what you did in the lab created the virus *by itself.*" She senses Dee's objection and holds her hand up to stop it. "No matter what they did, they couldn't replicate *your* virus. The protein spike *isn't* compatible!"

"Then *how*?" Dee looks at Sara, mouth open in confusion.

"When you were evaluated as a child, your genetics suggested two psychic strengths: telekinesis and healing. We believe you used a combination of the two to splice the spike protein onto the virus, but your fear that he would turn your daughters is what changed the virus into a virophage. Your desire to protect your daughters made the virophage change the original virus in a way that prevents him from turning them or anyone." Sara leans back in her chair, a satisfied expression, knowing she's surprised the scientist with a psychic twist. "Most likely, you've been doing this since you were still human. Isanda found a few of your research papers where you managed to create genetic alterations no one else was able to replicate." She waits for the true meaning of all of this to sink in.

"I know I created some sequences my supervisors said were impossible, but I assumed they'd missed something! You're suggesting I psychically *spliced* the DNA?" Dee gives her a look of disbelief.

"Yes, and more! You were able to unconsciously program the virus. I think, if we work on this, you may be able to control it consciously! Maybe even help people with genetic defects or damage?" Sara suggests.

"*Really?* How?" A spark of interest and excitement flares from within. *Maybe my scientific life isn't over?* She thinks.

"I'd like you to consider working with me on some tissue samples from some of the humans with radiation damage. Perhaps your abilities could repair the cellular and genetic damage. Perhaps your research may have eventually created a cure for cancer, but I'm betting your abilities may be able to cure it directly, or even reprogram T-cells to attack the cancer or reprogram the cancer itself to revert to normal tissue. Think of the possibilities!" Sara says enthusiastically.

Dee contemplates the possibilities her gifts may bring, but gets a deflated look. "*Oh!* But *how* can I do any of that *without* my credentials! They *died* with my human identity!"

Sara laughs, "*Isn't it obvious, Dee?!* We created a new identity for you, with a *real* passport and license! Do you think it's out of our power to create academic *credentials* for you? I promise, your life among the Apara will be far more scientifically fulfilling than your human scientific life! If you want to research, we can set you up with a proper lab, funding, and more. You can research, or actively save lives with your gifts! I must introduce you to Vanessa Manheim! She was one of Jason's earlier victims. He didn't turn her, but left her to die. However, the important thing is, she was a nurse."

Dee asks, "*Was?*"

"Yes, that is her official degree. However, since becoming Apara, and training here at Medical, as well as with a couple of Apara who work in the human medical field, she'll soon be at a skill level that surpasses most human doctors. We'll make arrangements for her to get new credentials as a medical doctor. She plans to open a low-cost clinic that specializes in clients for whom traditional treatment has failed. Granted, we will have to set up some safeguards, or she'll end up in the spotlight as a 'miracle-worker', but she wants to spend a few years giving back to humanity through her healing skills." Sara says, sipping her alien tea.

Dee is pensive, saying, "Maybe, if I can make a difference, I'll be able to cope with all this better. I've felt lost. Between dealing with the mess I made with the virus, and not having my daily routine and research, I've felt out of place and useless." Dee explains.

"We can, and will, help you find purpose again. I promise you that much. Perhaps, with a little practice, you can even undo some of the viral damages if you can master your skill." Sara suggests.

"Do you *think* so?" A look of hope crosses her expression as she realizes maybe she can fix the damage she caused on Jason's behalf.

"We've had to bring the more extreme cases into the fold, or at least to Sanctuary, as they are a danger, either to themselves, humans, or an exposure risk to us. However, many are not suitable for actual transformation. We're looking at several options, but the best would be if we can revert their DNA to its natural state. I don't know if it's possible, but if you can unconsciously turn the virus into a weapon against Jason, I suspect you can tell someone's DNA to turn off an ability." Sara pours the last of the tea into Dee's mug. "Don't you think that would be a worthwhile goal?"

"Yes, I do! I'll feel better too, knowing that I may be able to fix some of the damage my virus has caused." She agrees.

"Dee, many of those exposed by the virus are suitable and needed after our losses, but you could make an enormous difference for the rest!" She lays a hand on Dee's shoulder. "Sometimes, when all looks like chaos, order and purpose arise from the ashes! Let go of the past and help *us* move forward! Things will sort themselves out! I'm certain of that! Be an active part in the process and I promise, we'll keep you busy!" She chuckles.

Dee looks resolute, and says, "I'll do my best! But first, I need to go home though, and apologize to Vince! I've been *awful* to deal with the last few days!"

No sooner does Sara send a wordless path to Vince than he appears in the room. "I hear you're feeling better?" He crouches down in front of her and gives her a crooked smile and a raised eyebrow.

"Yeah, I am. Can we go home now?" She asks, and he knows she's accepted her new life when he senses her thoughts about a long night together. No guilt allowed! He leans in, kisses her, and the two port out again.

FULL CIRCLE

Tess and Sue wait for Sara in her office, curious about Sara's cryptic need to talk to her, as well as her scientific recordings taken during the psychological dream healing process. After a few minutes of waiting, Sara opens the door and stops. "And *where* am I supposed to sit!?" She says sarcastically to the two women.

Tess gets up from Sara's chair. "There you go Sara! I was just keeping your seat warm!" Tess grins, knowing how cantankerous Sara can sound, even though *she's all bark and, well...okay, 'some bite'*, she thinks.

Sara rolls her eyes for show. "I guess you want to see the *readings*?"

"Yes, that too! How's Dee?" Sue asks.

Sara sighs. "She'll be fine! *Just fine.* Thank you for working with her! I had a little something to add that helped her find a new purpose among us!"

"Oh? Did we *miss* something Sara?" Sue asks.

"No, *nothing* psychological!" She paths a wordless, conceptual path explaining the whole thing about how Dee could use her abilities to alter the virus the way she unconsciously wanted to.

Tess leans against the wall. "*Wow!* That's quite a unique talent!"

Sara nods. "Yes, it is! And she developed it while *still* human! But it kicked into high gear once she was turned and under stress. Her maternal, protective instincts brought it out. Now, as to the results! I need to look them over, but I will tell you there were noticeable changes in her neurotransmitter balance as your session reached resolution. Your abilities work on at least two levels, Sue! Telempathic dream therapy, but also, you directly affect neurotransmitter levels and neurological feedback loops!"

"Feedback loops?" Sue asks.

"Yes, think about how people get into so-called, vicious cycles! They get depressed, feel bad about themselves or guilty about something and get more depressed! It creates a neurochemical cascade that creates a downward spiral into depression, or other mental states, such as paranoia. Somehow, your ability is able to stop, and at least begin to reverse it! Quite a useful talent!" Sara smirks and straightens up the Star Wars knickknacks on her desk, patting a baby Yoda figure on its plastic head.

"Yes, but it's still touch and go, and I'm not sure how effective it will be with more severe cases!" Sue suggests.

"We'll have to keep experimenting, that's all. Perhaps, soon you can try with Philipa?" Sara gives her a look that says that is *more* than just an offhanded suggestion!

"*Maybe*, she's a whole different ballgame! Dee, Alice, and the others I worked with all has situational problems, things that could be traced to events or decisions that hurt them psychologically, but Philipa's are more biological or chemical imbalances and their roots are likely genetic. I'm not sure my talents will be able to fix those." Sue twists her long, auburn hair in her fingers nervously.

"Well, be that as it may, we won't know until you give it a try!" Sara nods curtly and smirks! "Who knows! If Dee really can alter DNA, maybe she can help with that part." Sara suggests offhandedly.

There's a knock on the door. "Come in, Isanda." Sara smiles, no longer angry at her long-time friend.

Isanda comes in and nods at the other women in the room, but looks at Tess for a few seconds. "Isanda, these are two of our newer Apara. This is Sue, who's been working as a therapist. She was a psychologist while human, but her abilities augment her professional training." Sara paths an overview of Sue's abilities rapidly. "And this young woman joined us about a year and a half ago. It feels like she's been with us *much* longer. This is Tessa Waterford."

Isanda bows her head slightly, then turns to Sara. "The one who worked with your people while *still* human? I had not heard that she joined you. I thought she was incompatible."

Tess chuckles. "Yeah, they *thought* that! But it turned out I was *misfiled*! I was in an accident when I was three, and my bio-tag got destroyed, so I was in the inactive database. Luckily, I still reacted to their subliminals in a job ad, and showed up on their doorstep, looking for a job!"

"She's with Marc Girard. I'm not sure you've ever met him, though he's from roughly the same time period as...*Vince*! Our Tess has some of the strongest abilities and potential I've ever seen! Every time we think she's peaked out, they keep expanding." Sara explains.

Isanda's eyes grow wide and flecks of several colors appear. Her hair does an odd little set of rapid flutters. She stares at Tess and attempts to read her. Tess feels the psychic pressure Isanda's mental touch creates, and blurts out, "*Please* don't do that! Now I'm nauseous!" Tess blurts out.

"You could *feel* me?" Isanda sounds surprised.

"Hell, *yeah*!" Tess makes direct eye contact with her and gets the strangest feeling of déjà vu. "Why do I feel like I know you?"

Isanda approaches Tess. "I am not quite sure, but I have the same impression! Would you permit me to touch your mind? It may help me to understand that feeling."

Tess looks at Sara for reassurance and gets a nod from her. "All right." She says a little anxiously. She knows Isanda is one of the purported hybrids; a mixture of human and benefactor, but Marc told her that if she ever met one of them, to act normal, and *not* freak out meeting her first non-terrestrial!

Isanda gently touches Tess's shoulders with her hands. Tess feels an odd sensation as her normally impressive shields completely shut down and allow Isanda peruse her mind. Normally, that would unnerve Tess terribly, but she feels completely at ease, as though this strange woman is somehow familiar to her, and she knows she's completely safe.

Isanda's eyes are closed as she works her way into Tess's mind. Sue and Sara watch in fascination. They sense fluctuations in Tess's aura as Isanda sifts through her mind. Suddenly, she opens her eyes again with a look of surprise. "It *is you!*" Isanda says aloud. "We *all* thought you were deceased!"

It takes Tess longer to snap out of the mental communion. "*Whoa!* What the *hell?*"

Isanda says, "You said they listed you in the *inactive* files, as in *deceased?*"

"Yeah, so they tell me! Everyone thought I wasn't compatible, but they couldn't make me forget when I found out about Marc being Apara, so I *had* to work *with* them." Tess rambles out, still disoriented.

"But clearly, you were compatible! How old are you? What is your birthday? I'm 30. My birthday is October 10th. Why?" Sue gently guides her clearly disoriented friend into the chair she's just vacated.

Isanda looks at Sara. "It's *her!* The *only* one who *showed* promise and stability!"

Sara's expression shifts to one of comprehension. "You're *kidding*, aren't you? Tess was one of yours?"

Tess looks up at Sara suddenly. "One of her what?"

Isanda turns toward Tess. "I have known you since before you were born. Though Tessa was not your name then, was it?"

"No, my birth name was Marie Elizabeth Scott, but my aunt changed my name when they adopted me after the accident...I...I *remember* you...your *mind* and...your *eyes!* They always sparkled gold and purple when we visited!" Tess stammers out, uncertain where the memory is coming from.

"Isanda gives her a subtle nod. "*Yes!* I considered you the closest I can have to a daughter. Though you had parents, I helped to make you what you are."

Tess gets a confused expression. "Somehow, I *know* that, but I don't know why or how..."

Tess becomes dizzy and Sara must steady her. "Look at me, Tess!"

Tess does, but has difficulty focusing. "She needs to rest. Her mind is not used to that contact now, and I think you may have rattled a few mental cobwebs." She remarks to Isanda.

Sue, who is very confused, chimes in. "Sara, *what's* going on?"

Sara paths the explanation to Sue so as not to overwhelm Tess with the truth yet.

Isanda adds, *Our project was shelved indefinitely when the Lost Mission mutations began and not revisited.*

Sue looks back and forth between Sara and Isanda. "Did you *know* about this, Sara?"

Sara shakes her head. "Not until a few days ago, and even then, only theoretically! She mentioned the one promising subject had died young, but I didn't connect the dots!" She admits. "I'll be right back. I'm going to put her in a room and get Marc over here. She'll be fine, but I'd like her to stay here until her head clears." Sara ports Tess to a room with a comfortable bed, not a hospital bed, but the room that Dee used before she moved in with Vince. She gets her settled and reaches out to Marc. *Now, don't freak out, but I need you to come to Medical!*

Is everything all right? Is it Tess? Marc paths and the overtones of panic wash over Sara like an enormous wave at the beach.

Calm down! I told you not to freak out! She's fine, a little disoriented, that's all. She's resting, but I'd like you to come sit with her until she wakes. I'll fill you in when you get here! She paths and feels a hand on her shoulder. She turns around, and it's Marc with an expectant expression.

"Fill me in *now!*" He hovers over Tess in the bed. He senses something odd about her energy, but not what.

"Isanda communed with her telepathically." Sara tells him.

"What the *Hell*? *Why* would she do that? Tess isn't even involved with the virus situation!" Marc is rather flustered and distracted.

"She had good reason to do so, and now I *know* why your *dear* partner is *so special!*" She sits in a chair at the base of the bed.

Marc turns and looks at her, mouth agape. "What the *hell* are you talking about?"

"I'm talking about the reason Tess is so different from other potentials and transformees! Why her abilities are *so* strong!" She grins at him as she watches his mouth close, and a look of disbelief appear.

"Are you telling me *They* had something to do with Tess's abilities? How can that be?" He stares at Sara, waiting for an explanation.

"You'd better sit down!" She chuckles, and waits for him to pull up the other chair and sit down next to Tess's bed. "I had no idea about any of this. Didn't even know Isanda was in this part of the galaxy back then, but she and her team were on a *sensitive* mission around the time Tess was conceived and a few years afterwards. Seems Tess was a guinea pig in her project!"

"A *what*? A *guinea pig*? Are you telling me they experimented on her?" He asks, getting more upset by the second.

"Apparently, she was part of an enhanced human experiment to create higher grade potentials. The project was shelved after they thought she'd died as she was the only viable subject out of ten they tinkered with." Sara explains.

"*Tinkered* with?" Mark takes several deep breaths to get himself under control.

"Yes. She was genetically engineered to have a higher psychic potential should she become Apara. The project was, as I believe the expression goes, 'off the books'. I didn't know about it myself! They never even told me they were doing it!"

"When you say viable, what do you mean? Was she the only one to survive their tinkering?" He's getting angry at the thought they could have caused her death by toying with her DNA, even though he never would have met her in that case.

"Not entirely; some died, some showed no major potential, and two that did show potential were considered psychologically unstable. Tess was the only one that 'hit the mark', and they believed she died! So, now you know why her abilities are so strong." She says with a huff.

"Is there anything *They* can do to help her control them?" He asks.

"I'll talk to Isanda. I just found out about this, myself, and my first duty was to take care of Tess when she got overwhelmed. Now, if you can sit with her, I'll have a talk with Isanda and get some details!" Sara ports back to her office, leaving Marc to watch over Tess.

When she ports in, only Isanda is there. "Sue went back home when Colin came by looking for her, as she was tired after working with Dee. I was looking at the readings you took. She has an impressive talent!" Isanda says, as though nothing is off.

"*Okay*, Isanda, I *need* you to tell me everything!" Sara says as she sits.

"*Everything*?" Isanda blinks and flecks of gold and bright green flicker in her eyes.

"Yes, as in, I need to know exactly what alterations you made to Tess's DNA! She was the strongest potential we'd seen in decades, if not longer, and she still has some control issues. Now that I know you all monkeyed with her DNA, that finally makes sense! Maybe, if you tell me what your team altered, it will help me help her!" Sara says with a huff.

Isanda blinks slowly several times. "Sara, there was no monkey DNA used in the experiments!", she says, taking Sara's comment literally.

"Damn it! You know what I mean! You tinkered with her DNA and now I demand to know what you altered! She's had a rough time because of it." Sara says, exasperated.

Isanda looks uneasy, with odd tones of red Sara has never seen before washing over her irises. "I will have to consult my records."

"*Come on,* Isanda! I know your memory! Fill me in!" Sara says with frustrated, empathic overtones.

"Very well, but this is going to take some time." Isanda says and explains all the ways she altered Tess's DNA and what the intended goals were.

SURPRISE!

Mark watches over Tess as she sleeps, and notices that her energy fluctuates erratically, but slowly settles into more normal patterns. At one point, he can tell she's having a rough dream as she becomes restless, and her eyes move rapidly under her lids. She tenses up briefly, and yet another light panel needs replacing in medical as it flares, cracks and goes dark. He sighs, taking her hand, hoping that will help calm her. Sara sends Annie to check on Tess for her, as Isanda's explanation is time consuming.

A few hours later, Tess stirs. She opens her eyes a crack, and closes them again, groaning. "Lights... *too bright*!" She mutters.

Marc turns them off except for a smaller table lamp and sits back down, taking Tess's hand in his. "How are you feeling?"

Tess lets out a deep breath and opens her eyes a squint. "Like *shit* warmed over! Ugh... correction! Like an experiment gone awry!" She rolls over to face him. "Where...?"

He reaches over and brushes her long blondish brown hair out of her face and kisses her on her forehead. "Still in medical! Sara called me in to keep you company until you came to."

"Ah...okay...." She looks at him. "Did I imagine it all?"

"Did you imagine what?" He asks, concerned.

"The alien...hybrid...I *know* her!" Tess tries to focus, but things are still muddled in her mind.

"Apparently so, but Sara will fill us in shortly, I hope." He strokes her palm with his thumb.

"Where is she? Get her?" Tess takes in a long breath and nearly dozes off again.

Marc reaches out to Sara. *She's waking up. I sure hope you have some answers for her!* He paths.

Coming! She replies. Two minutes later, she stumbles through the door carrying her tablet and looking wiped out.

"*Well*? What did you find out?" He asks, grasping Tess's hand a little tighter, causing her to stir once more.

Sara gives him a look and rolls her eyes. "*Plenty*! Let's wait until she's fully coherent, so I don't have to repeat myself. She should also feed and eat." Right on cue, Annie comes in with a tray containing various protein-rich foods and a bag of blood. She puts it on a small rolling table and pulls it up next to Marc. "Thank you, Annie! This may take a while. Feel free to take the rest of your shift off."

Sara resumes her seat at the end of the bed. "You're in for a few surprises, Marc! You definitely know how to pick'em. Tess here is literally one in about 8 billion!"

They wait a few minutes until Tess yawns, scrunches up her shoulders, and opens her eyes. Marc grabs extra pillows and puts them behind Tess's back.

"I wanna go home and sleep some more..." Tess yawns again.

"Not yet, love. First, you need to eat and feed, and then Sara needs to talk to us.

Tess looks at him, and then Sara. "This is about... Isanda, isn't it?"

"Yes, and *about you*." Sara says bluntly.

Tess looks off into thin air, unfocused for a second, then back at Sara, giving a laugh of disbelief. "I'm a *fucking* science experiment! Now I know how Sue felt!" Tess blurts out, sounding slightly drunk.

"So, it seems. Take care of your physical needs first. I'll tell you what Isanda told me, but some things are still unclear." Sara puts her tablet down on the end of the bed.

"Unclear?" Tess asks.

"Yes, I know what they intended, but whether the alterations were fully successful remains to be seen.

Mark helps her with her food until she stops him. "I can't eat more!" She puts her hand out to stop the next 'serving' he's trying to jam in her mouth as though she were a baby.

He nods, but hands her a bag of blood. She uses a fang to slice off a corner, and drinks it through the hole in the bag. "Okay?"

After she's had time for the blood to process into her system, Sara asks, "Are you feeling clearer headed?"

"Yeah, *yeah!* Give me the CliffsNotes version so I can go back to *sleep!*" Tess yawns.

"Sorry, no shortcuts with this." Sara looks from Tess to Marc. "Tess, you were one of ten subjects in a genetic engineering experiment that took place *in utero*. While you were conceived normally, you mother's OB/Gyn was one of us. She picked out five mothers-to-be whose children showed genetic promise. Do you know if your mother had an amniocentesis?"

"I do not know! I was *three* when they *died*! Complex medical procedures weren't exactly on the mother-daughter discussion list!" Tess quips sarcastically.

Sara nods quietly. "No, I guess they wouldn't be, but I'm guessing they did. Was your mother older than average?"

"Yeah. My parents were in their mid-thirties when I was born. They both had careers, so family waited. At least that's what my aunt told me." She was younger than my mom by about seven years." Tess feels Marc grip her hand briefly and returns the gesture.

"All the women who had that procedure became a pool from which Isanda's team chose their guinea pigs! Five from your mother's clinic and five from one in Virginia that was also run by one of our people. They didn't know what the experiment was, but were asked to keep detailed records of development and any eventual complications. Long story short, four died before or shortly after birth, all male, three showed no signs of increased psychic potential, and three did, all female. Two of those were psychologically unstable. One of them was likely to develop severe issues later in life, the other, they believe, would be prone to autism and possibly bi-polar disorder. You were the only one out of ten that was considered fully successful. Early indications showed a higher psychic potential, and genetically speaking, no signs of potential mental abnormalities. Isanda worked with you in your first three years. They periodically picked you up, evaluated you. and went through the usual procedures, including embedding *some sublimi-nals in* your mind. Then the car accident occurred, and they thought you had died. Because of the high failure rate, and the advent of LM mutations, they shelved the project and she and her team went back home. It was not a fully authorized experiment, so it was not 'on the books'. I was never told! Didn't even know Isanda was in the galactic neighborhood, and I've known her for... well, since I became Apara." Sara admits.

"Okay, so what exactly did they *do* to me?" Tess asks, feeling more awake and focused, though she's not 100 percent sure she wants to know.

"I know what they *attempted* to do. Some of it fits with your skills, and some, well... Isanda would like your permission to take tissue and blood samples to see if all the alterations in your DNA came to fruition when you were turned." Sara watches Tess's reaction. She doesn't seem upset, and then says. "What the *Hell*! Might as well get *some* answers! If I'm gonna be a *freak*, even among the Apara, at least I'll know why!"

Sara pulls up a document with notes she made while talking to Isanda. "Your shielding ability and heightened PK were both target talents. With the shielding came general telempathic ability, too. Your people reading skills are likely an unforeseen offshoot of your telempathic abilities, possibly combined with a bit of precognition, which lets you predict how people may react to different experiences."

"What about the *out-of-body* stuff?" Tess asks.

"She's not sure what caused that, though they were aiming to give you stronger clairvoyance and remote viewing abilities, so it could be connected to that!" She suggests.

"And what about all these abilities being too strong to control? Was that part of the package?" She blurts out, and Sara winces at Tess's frustration.

"The reason you don't have better control is because they never got to finish your pre-conditioning because of your accident. They'd given you some basics about feeding and using some of your normal Apara abilities, but didn't get to your enhanced abilities. Isanda has offered to work with you while she's on Earth. She may be able to help you harness your skills more efficiently." Sara feels stormy waves of emotions bombard her from Tess.

Marc knows Tess is frustrated and wraps one arm around her to calm her.

"*Gee*, how nice! Doctor Frankenstein is going to help the science experiment control herself!" Tess slumps back into the pillows on her bed.

"*Tess! Stop* it! This confirms what I've known since I met you! You are so, very *special*! It doesn't matter to me how you got that way, but if you've been given these gifts, you should learn how to use them to the fullest!" Marc tells her, stroking her cheek gently.

Somewhat mollified, Tess calms down. "Sorry, Sara. I shouldn't be taking this out on you! You had no idea, but it's all a bit much!"

"I know, believe me, I wasn't expecting this. I, too, knew you were special when I met you, but didn't have any idea *how* special." Sara admits as she scrolls to the next page.

Tess notices her scrolling and asks, "Is there *more*?"

"Yes, though we haven't seen any evidence to support these alterations yet. She says that you should be able to use your PK to create energy projections. For example, you should be able to create a ball or wave of energy that can be directed. Sorry, she found this hard to explain. It can potentially be used as a weapon if you need it, or to push away objects that are heading toward you, more like a physical force shield." Sara makes a note to get to Isanda explain this better.

"You don't suppose that's what's happening when I blow out light panels and stuff?" Tess asks, looking pensive.

Sara pauses for a second, thinking, then nods. "You may be right. I'll ask her when I see her."

"Anything else, Sara?" Marc asks, sensing Tess is starting to reach her limits, and will soon need to crash for a few hours more.

"Yeah, she said you should be able to recognize other potentials and intuit what their talents might be. This was meant to help us choose who we should turn by being able to sense what someone's skill set may encompass before turning them." Sara checks off that one.

"That could be pretty useful with the lost mission people, and maybe even with this virus! I may be able to help you weed through the affected potentials if I can anticipate their breakout or transformation skills" Tess yawns.

Marc paths to Sara. *If there's anything else, you'd better hurry up or she's going to doze off on you!*

Sara gives him a glare for his snarky path. "There is *one* last thing they attempted to program into you, though this could be a touchy subject."

Tess looks at her, feeling the exhaustion overwhelm her again. "Just tell me! What's going to happen? Am I going to swap genders or shoot laser beams out of my eyes?" She chuckles as she sees Marc's look at the thought of waking up with Tess as a man. She hears a mental *Quelle horreur!* from his mind and giggles at the image his mind creates. She snorts and says "You know you'd love me *anyway!*" and gives him a huge grin! To which Marc rolls his eyes."

Sara shakes her head, but is glad to see Tess regain some of her sense of humor. "The last thing isn't a *psychic* gift, but you might consider it *a gift*, none-the-less. Tess, before you joined us, had you ever thought about having children?"

Tess, who's taking a sip of water, nearly chokes on it and begins coughing uncontrollably. After she settles and catches her breath, she blurts out, "*Kids? Me?* Maybe... kids aren't something I ever felt I *had* to have, and after Ox, I wasn't even sure I wanted to deal with *other* men!" She chuckles, then turns to Marc. "But you cured me of that thought!" She leans over and kisses him on the cheek.

"They toyed with the idea of Apara reproducing biologically, as well as by turning people." Sara pauses and tries to sense what both Marc and Tess are feeling.

"Would the kids be born with *fangs* and need *blood*?" Tess asks, getting an image of a baby biting her when she breast feeds it. She grimaces.

Sara reassures her. "No, any children would be born *essentially* human with a couple of minor exceptions. They would come into their abilities as they approached their teens, and if they are hurt or even killed, they would recover quickly or even go through a variation of stasis. When they reach adulthood, their abilities would reach their full potential, and their need for blood would kick in."

Tess shakes her head in disbelief. "So, are you telling me I could have a child?"

"*Yes*, if what they did worked!" She says.

"Does this mean I should be on birth control?" She wonders, thinking of her rather active sex life.

Sara grins. "No, it is not something that will happen accidentally. It will require some supplementary treatments to make your body ready, and bring forth ovulation, but yes, it's *possible!*" Sara says, almost envying Tess this possibility.

Mark shakes his head. "But I *can't* father a child! All Apara men are *sterile!*"

"That's not *entirely* true. Your sperm are fertile until they flow into your testicular fluid. That's what stops their viability. If the two of you ever choose to procreate the old fashion way..." She smirks. "Isanda has a formula for a medicine that will make your fluid less hostile to your sperm, and allow you to become a father!"

Marc leans back in his chair, almost holding his breath, remembering how he watched Collette's children from a far, and even watched over them after she'd died. "I could *really* be a father?"

"Yes, if the two of you so *choose*! Isanda has promised to instruct me how to make it possible, but there are *no guaranties* that the genetic engineering even *worked*, but if the two of you want to try, I'm more than happy to help you, on one condition..." She trails off with a lopsided, Cheshire Cat grin. "I get to be *Godmother*!"

"We'll have to talk it over Sara, but if we decide to do it, you're a shoo-in for that job!" Tess tells her and grins at Marc, while wondering about all the possibilities this could create.

Sara nods. "That's it, unless there have been any unexpected effects. I need to take those samples Isanda asked for, but then you should go home and rest, *young* lady!" Sara grabs a kit for taking blood and tissue samples. The blood sample is simple enough, but when she needs to take the tissue samples, she explains, I need some of the undifferentiated epithelial stem cells from your intestines. It'll be easier if you close your eyes. I'll numb it so you don't feel any pain." Sara takes out a longer needle and slips it into Tess's abdomen, guiding it gently into a cluster of the needed cells. She carefully withdraws the needle and waits for the track to heal before releasing the numbing effect. "That's it, you're all set!" She leans over and cups Tess's face. "Go home and get some sleep!" She packs up the samples and goes back to Isanda with them.

Marc smiles thoughtfully. "Sounds like we have a lot to think about!" He grins and ports her straight home and into bed. "*Sleep!* Doctor's orders!" He tucks her in and heads down to his office to work, but has trouble focusing because his mind keeps wandering to the children he may have had with Collette, but knew it was not an option, so he cherished hers at a distance, as though they were his own.

BREAKING THE OUTBREAK

About a week has passed when Sara calls a meeting. Liz, Kari, Tess, Marc, Sue, Niall, Dee, and Vince all meet in the conference room at Medical, with Sara and Isanda arriving after a few minutes. Sara addresses them, saying, "Alright everyone, we've made *some* progress. With as many Apara as we now need to update, we'll hold a wider meeting via teleconference later, but as you are part of Liz's inner circle, she'll be delegating tasks to you first." She moves her gaze from person to person in the room. The lights turn off and a three-dimensional holographic projection of the virus appears above the conference table. "That is the second-generation virus found in both Jason and the general population. We don't have to worry about the first generation. The only viable samples of that are in the deep freeze here in medical!" She nods to Dee. Isanda and her team have analyzed the new virus and found that it has not mutated, which is fantastic news. They've also discovered a vulnerability."

She waves her hand in the air and the image zooms in on the DNA in the virus. Sara continues, "As Dee discovered, four bases make up our DNA and most life on Earth, except for a few viruses which sometimes insert a fifth, foreign base. Normally, we have: adenine (A), cytosine (C), guanine (G), and thymine (T). Normally, A always bonds with T and C with G. However, the original and altered virus have two additional bases which are *not* Earth based; for the sake of simplicity, we'll call them 5 and 6. These two usually bind to each other, but 5 can occasionally replace A and 6 can replace G. When Dee's altered virus changed the original one, it created a ring around the spike protein with receptors for base 6. As long as those receptors remain open, the virus remains active, but if we release particles of base 6, they quickly bind with the receptors, causing the spikes to withdraw into the virus, making it inert." Everyone watches as the three-dimensional presentation shows the particles binding with the foreign bases and sucking in the spikes, which causes the virus to shut down and disintegrate.

Dee watches, fascinated, but asks, "I assume they're going to seed the clouds with particle 6, but will this cause any harm to the environment?"

Isanda speaks up. "No, these particles only last up to a month outside an Apara's body. Ironically, while you are not affected by sunlight, after roughly a month, UV light from your sun will cause any residual base 6 particulates to completely break down into atoms which will disperse harmlessly into the environment."

"How will you be seeding the clouds or otherwise reaching planetary saturation?" Dee asks.

"Our main ship will transition back into your primary reality's space, but use cloaking technology to avoid detection. They'll use cloaked probes that are normally used for collecting environmental samples during planetary exploration. In this case, they will be releasing a fine dust of base 6 into clouds around the world. Since the bases do not exist on Earth, none of Earth's detection systems will recognize them as foreign compounds in the drinking water. We will let the rain distribute the bases as much as possible. In dry zones, we will seed the bases into sand storms and directly into drinking water sources. A month should be sufficient to destroy the virus itself, but, if necessary, we will do a second round. Last, we will repeat this here in Sanctuary, as the virus has spread here through those infected and brought to medical. We will only treat a 200-mile radius, as all infected individuals have been confined to, and Apara cannot be carriers." Isanda explains.

Sara clears her throat. "We believe once the virus is eliminated both in nature and in any carriers, that stage two will be up to you. We must track down as many of the affected potentials and evaluate them. If they are minor changes, such as stronger

332

physical senses or minor psychic talents that are within human norms, then we'll make note of the individuals, and let the abilities be. What we must focus on are the major or potentially disruptive abilities; things like porting, pyrokinesis, uncontrolled PK, or uncontrolled telepathy and empathy. Many of the latter cases will no doubt show up as an increase in psychiatric intakes for paranoid schizophrenia or delusional behavior. In other words, hearing voices. Here, they really are hearing the mental voices or feeling others' emotions."

Sue speaks up. "If they're institutionalized, how do we get them out? Won't it seem suspicious if a bunch of psych hold subjects suddenly disappear?"

"Yes, it would, but we have extraction teams being prepared. The teams have skills in redacting multiple memories quickly, as well as other members that have tools to purge the individuals from any computers or extended databases. Once extracted, then *you*, Tess, Kari, and others psychiatric skills will evaluate them. It will have to be done quickly. If they are suitable for turning, then we'll do so, but the vast majority will probably be unsuitable, because of age, psychological issues, or incompatible life situations. For those people, we'll have memory redaction specialists, including most of Isanda's team, standing by. They'll make sure the individuals can be reintegrated into their lives as efficiently as possible." Liz explains. "Marc, you and I will be coordinating with other centers like we did before Jerusalem, and Niall with Katie with our CDC rep."

Marc nods. "Sounds good."

Tess opens her mouth as something occurs to her, blurting out, "Wait a second! We can't put people with strong, active abilities back into their own lives and expect everything to go back to normal!"

"Absolutely *right*! We're going to curtail their abilities or stop them all together, but right now, we're still researching our options." Sara tells her.

"What *are* our options? When I got my abilities after Marc gave me the psiamp, I got dragged into your world whether I wanted to or not because you *couldn't turn them off*." Tess blurts out.

"Tess, you were *one* person and a rather unique one, as we *now know!*" She gives Tess a pointed stare, which makes her feel like all eyes are on her, knowing that she's more of a freak than ever; however, at this point, only a handful know Tess's DNA was tinkered with, nearly all of whom are present. Sara continues. "We're looking at several options, though the two most promising are an infusion of Centauri-opal dust into the affected individual's spinal column. It's harmless to humans, but should embed itself into the bone and tissue and disrupt the higher levels of psychic energy needed for such strong talents. Otherwise, Dee and I are working on a project involving reverting their affected DNA back to normal, but it's still in the early stages. Failing either of those, we may have to request additional help from Isanda's team and our Benefactors, whose minds may be strong enough to suppress more powerful abilities on a subconscious level." Sara let's out a long sigh, but Tess is mollified.

Tess sighs. "Sounds like a hell of a big job. Should Kari, Sue, and I put the lost mission project on hold for now?"

Liz chimes in. "*Absolutely not!* We *need* to ID as many of them as possible! They will be among some of the strongest and most unpredictable talents if infected! The more of them we know about, the easier it will be to check in on them, and determine if they've been infected."

"Sounds like we're gonna be too busy to even sleep." Tess jokes.

"We're working on finding others with usable skills to help you. Unfortunately, you are still one of our best when it comes to intuiting if someone will transition well, and the combination of you, Sue's psychiatric background, and Kari's long experience are hard to beat, so, yeah, there's going to be a lot of pressure on you for now, so, unfortunately, I wouldn't make any *other* plans until this calms down."

The group begins chattering among themselves, and Sara bangs her mug on the table to get their attention. "Isanda's team, as well as our on-ship Benefactor are producing the base 6 dust and should have it ready to start dispersal tomorrow. Tess, I need you to contact Amy and make sure her team is keeping track of new outbreak reports? They should begin to taper off in a few days, especially among the non-potentials. Once the cases drop, that's when we'll need to go into hunt and evaluate mode." Sara stares pointedly at Tess, Kari, and Sue.

Vince has been quiet the whole time, sitting with Dee, holding her hand. He clears his throat. "Sara, what can I do?"

"For now, do what you've been doing, support Dee! She's going to need emotional and psychological encouragement as we work on our genetic reversion project. Dee, you're one of our newest here, and we know how much you've gone through. You'll need to tell us if you feel overwhelmed or ask for *help* when *you* need it. We're going to be so preoccupied with the whole process, we might not notice if you're struggling." Sara stares her in the eye until she nods.

"I will, Sara. I know how important this is." Dee feels Vince gently squeeze her closer. He paths, *I am here for you, Amore!*

Liz stands and says, "All right, everyone! This is the proverbial calm before the storm as we wait for the dust to take effect, and see if it works as expected. So, take the next couple of days and get some rest, because once we start tracking down the altered potentials, it's going reach a frantic pace!"

Everyone talks among themselves for a few minutes, discussing what they can do to make this work. But eventually, everyone ports home to take some personal time and recharge before the big push.

SMALL CHANGE

Dee and Vince port home and he pulls her into his arms. "Okay, this is officially a *no moping zone*." He leans in and kisses her.

"I'll do my best, but if I don't keep busy, my mind starts wandering to all sorts of things..." She grins at him.

He pulls her closer. "Then I'll have to keep you occupied and very, very happy!" He gives her a lusty grin and chases her off to bed.

Once Dee's asleep, Vince quietly gets out of bed and goes down to the living room. He pulls out his tablet and searches online for her daughters. He has trouble finding anything until he remembers that Price is her maiden name. She went back to using it after her divorce. He finds one of the people search sites that lists possible relatives for a Thaddea Price in Frederick, Maryland. There's an asterisk after her name on this particular site, meaning the subject is deceased.

Vince sighs, and scrolls down to possible relatives. Her ex-husband's and her daughters' last name is Finkle, so he begins to search in earnest for Lynda and Celia Finkle, finding various pictures of them, including pictures with Dee, and saving them to his tablet.

He finds several pages for them on social media, and while skimming through Celia's page, he reads one of her recent posts.

> **I think Josh is planning something! He was all excited back in November about plans for us to go to Spago in Beverly Hills for my birthday, but then we got the news about mom and everything got put on hold! So now that everything has finally calmed down, he wants to go there Saturday night! I'm *so* nervous! I think maybe he's gonna ask the big question! If you know**

him, please don't tell him what I suspect! I don't want to freak him out and scare him away! Lol!

Hm, but can I get them done in time? Will it make her happy or sad to see her daughter get engaged? I'll start on the portraits tonight and work on them while she's with Sara the next couple of days. I'll have them ready for her by Saturday afternoon. Maybe I should give Tess and Sue a heads up in case it backfires? He ponders.

He ascends a flight of spiral metal stairs to the loft area that is his artist workshop. It's large, but cluttered. There are sketches for inventions he's toyed with over the years, as well as a corner filled with marble and a floor covered in marble dust. There's a large window that connects with a skylight, where natural light comes in during the day. He has that area partially walled off to keep the marble dust down, as it has a nasty tendency to get into wet oil paints and dim the vibrant colors. It's nighttime now, so he'll have to settle for daylight bulbs instead of natural light. He puts his tablet down on a nearby bench and opens three of the best pictures he found of Celia and begins painting her portrait. He looks up when he notices the first shift in light from the impending dawn. He moves the half-finished portrait over toward one wall and puts it facing the wall, just in case Dee sneaks upstairs and looks around. He washes up, getting all the paint off his hands, changes clothes, and makes breakfast.

Half an hour later, Dee stumbles in, still yawning. "You're up early. Do I smell waffles?"

"Yes, *Cara*! With fresh strawberries and cream! Did you sleep well?" He asks and puts a plate of fresh waffles in front of her.

"After last night? *Hell* yes! You, my dear, are an artist in *so* many ways!" She gives him a very contented smile, inviting him to bend down and kiss her anew. She wrinkles up her nose and says, "You smell like turpentine! Have you been painting this morning?" She asks and stuffs a large fork load of waffle, whipped cream, and strawberries in her mouth.

"*No!* Sorry about that! I went upstairs to look for something and knocked into a flask some brushes were soaking in and it splashed on me." He joins her with his own plate and settles at the table. "So, what time is Sara expecting you?" He asks.

"She said she'd be there by 5 am, Medical time, and there's what? Six hours difference from here? I don't know how you manage the time difference!" She yawns again.

"Yes, six hours. Medical is roughly in the mountains of Western Virginia, around what would be Charlottesville." He comments casually.

Dee chuckles. "Right between Frederick and Asheville! This whole alternate Earth thing, though! Seriously, how does anyone keep a schedule when you all live all over the world?"

"It helps that porting doesn't give one jet-lag!" He laughs loudly. "You'll get used to it. You're still used to always sleeping at night and being awake during the day, but we adapt to having our homes in one place and our work somewhere else! Now, back to getting you to Sara. It's 8 am here, so what time is it in the Eastern US?"

"2 am? So, I need to be there in three hours?" She guesses.

"*Bingo!* So, we'll have to kill three more hours...." He gives her a lustful grin.

"As much as I'd love that, I'd probably fall asleep after and end up sleeping way past 5 am, not to mention being distracted as *Hell!* I'm going to read over some of the info Sara sent me, but there's always tonight... or is that this afternoon?" She shakes her head, trying to figure out all this time zone confusion.

"I'll hold you to that!" He grins mischievously. I need to hit a couple of markets this morning–I'm out of fresh blueberries, which is why I did waffles instead of your usual cereal and yogurt!" He quips and puts their empty plates in the sink. "Would you like some more cappuccino?"

"Would love some, but *God!* I miss the caffeine buzz!" She grabs her laptop from the desk and settles in on the living room sofa. She reads over various theoretical papers Sara gave her, and before she knows it, it's 10:48 am Central European time. She gets ready and grabs her laptop. Vince isn't back yet, so she ports herself to Medical. She's quite happy with herself when she ports in right outside Sara's office as a tired-looking Sara comes dragging down the hall.

"Morning, Dee. I sense you are doing well today." Sara opens her office, turns on the lights, and a little figure on her shelf with a light sensor plays the first couple of lines from Darth Vader's March. Dee laughs. "My youngest would really like you! She's totally obsessed with Star Wars, too!" Dee gets a wistful expression.

"*Dee!*" Sara looks at her sternly.

"I'm *okay*! I *know* I can't go back. I just... I don't know, my first impulse was to take a picture of your office and text it to Lynda, but I won't do it! I swear! That's a can of worms best left closed." She sighs.

"Wouldn't work anyway. Don't get upset, but for now, your phone will only call other Apara's phones. Liz's orders."

"She doesn't trust me?" Dee looks a little upset by this revelation.

"It's *not* that! She *knows* you understand you can't go back, but it's like you said, your first impulse was to snap a picture and send it to her! Sometimes those play out before we know it, and then we'd have to go wipe her memory and edit her phone records. Come, I've got several samples from altered potentials for us to work on. Did you read the info I gave you?" Sara pats Dee on her arm as they walk down the hall and into the hybrid lab.

"Yeah, this morning. Some of it was over my head, though. Hey, isn't this Isanda's lab?"

"Yes, they're all up on the main ship preparing the probes, so we get to play with the *good* equipment!" Sara's eyes twinkle with mischief. She leads Dee over to a screen sitting above another swirling sphere. This one has two holes or sockets on the front. Sara takes out another transparent stick with a touch of green on the end. "This contains a tissue sample from one of our affected potentials, post-infection. This one contains a sample we got from his home of his pre-infection DNA." She puts one in each socket and the screen lights up showing a DNA print from each sample on each side of the screen.

"Look at the one on the right. This is his original DNA. You don't have to memorize it, but absorb this image into your mind."

"Okay, now *what*?" Dee asks impatiently.

"Focus on that image in your mind, and focus on the left sample." Sara blocks the image on the left with a large sheet of paper.

"How can I focus on it if I can't see it?" Dee snaps.

"You don't *need* to see it. You want it to look like what you see on the right. Don't try, just do!" Sara says with one of her Yoda-like stares.

"Dee shakes her head at Sara's Star Wars reference, but pictures the image she'd seen, and reaches out to the sample on the left, trying to will it to be like the image in her mind. After a few minutes of trying, she feels a bit light headed and gets a shooting pain in her skull.

"*Stop! Relax.*" Sara demands and takes down the sheet of paper, so Dee can see the left sample.

"They're not the same!" She says with a huff.

"No, they aren't, but I didn't expect a perfect result on your first try!" Sara swipes the left side to the right and a different image comes up. "This is his DNA before you began..." She swipes it again. This is the DNA after your attempt. She swipes down twice and it overlays the after on the before." Sara nudges Dee. "See?"

"They are different! Did I do that?" Dee zooms in on the minute changes in the DNA. "Whoa! That's freaky! *How*, exactly, did I do that?" She sits with a thud.

Sara laughs. "There are times when understanding how actually stands in the way of *doing*! You think it can't work, so it doesn't, you try too hard so nothing happens! When you changed the virus in your lab, you weren't trying to change it with your mind, you thought you were using your CRISPER enzymes, and they did do *some* of the work, but not what you wanted the virus to become or do! That came from in here!" She taps on Dee's forehead, making her go briefly cross-eyed.

"All my life, I've striven to understand the hows and whys behind science! How things work! It goes against the grain to only look at the end result and not how to get there! It's like telling me to go to Peoria without a map!" Dee shrugs.

"You're making something that your mind finds simple into something too complex. Do you think about how to open or close a door when you do it? Do you measure the calories your body needs to create movement or how much force you need to push the door? *NO!* You just *do* it! Part of you knows how to do this, because you've already done it when you made the virophage, and it changed Jason's virus as you'd hoped, making him *impotent,* in a way!" She grins at Dee, knowing she got her point.

"If only I could have made him *truly* impotent! I have the impression he's brought a lot of misery to a lot of women, even before he became Apara!" Dee shakes her head thinking of how close she may have been to becoming his outlet for sexual release. She shivers thinking about it, and about the threats he made against her daughters, and making *her* watch! "There are times I wish he could burn in *Hell* for what he's done, but he can't even *die!* At least not easily!"

Sara grins broadly. "Hey! You get good at this and maybe you can help make him even less of a threat!"

"What do you mean?" She eyes Sara.

"I mean that the last time we had him in custody, we used a chemical neutralizer that stripped him of his abilities. With what we're attempting to do with our altered potentials, if you can master that, maybe you can revert some of Jason's DNA? Cut off the *root* of his power! He was telepathic before we changed him, and used those abilities to influence women to sleep with him, *among* other things. What if you could turn off his abilities permanently?" Sara grins. "*Think* about it!"

"Oh, if I could do that, it would be *amazing,* but... but it would be like playing with fire! We could inadvertently get burned in the process! What if I accidentally make him *stronger* instead of weaker?" But Dee looks pensive as she imagines the possibilities.

"It's an idea, and maybe a little inspiration, for you to make this work. Want to try again?" She motions to the screen.

342

Dee gets a determined expression, but relaxes. She looks at the original DNA sequence one more time and closes her eyes. When she opens them, Sara's smiling and motions toward the screen.

"Not perfect, but it's close!" She pats Dee on the back as she reviews the changes.

"That's incredible! I only missed two pairs! Maybe you're right! It doesn't matter if I understand the mechanism as long as it works!"

The two women work on this the rest of the day, trying samples from several altered potentials. Dee gets close to a complete reversion of the DNA by about 1 pm, but as she tires, her attempts become less complete. "Time to quit for today! Get some rest! Make sure you eat and feed! Heavy psychic work drains you in more ways than one! You did extremely well! It doesn't matter if it wasn't perfect. We have time for improvement. I want you to come back at the same time tomorrow and we'll work on it some more!" Sara tells her.

They continue this process for the rest of the week. Dee is often so exhausted when she gets home that she feeds, eats whatever Vince puts in front of her, and crawls off to bed, reassuring him she really *is* exhausted, and not falling into a deep depression.

A GIFT BORNE OUT OF LOVE

Saturday morning comes around. Vince makes sure Sara doesn't request Dee's presence today, and he lets her sleep in knowing that they would have to deal with more than the usual 6 hours' difference tonight. Around 11 am CET, Vince lays two wrapped packages under the bed. He lies on the bed next to her, marveling at how beautiful she's become. Her dark hair reminds him of Lisa, but she's so different in spirit! He leans over and gives her a light kiss. She stretches and her eyes flutter open, but close again as bright mid-day sun spears at her eyes as it peaks through a narrow part in the curtains.

She yawns. "What time is it?" She opens her eyes again and his bright blue eyes sparkle with amusement.

"It's after 11 am! *Before* you complain, you *needed* the rest!

She relaxes into her pillow again. "Has Sara called? *Shouldn't* I be there practicing?"

"No, *Cara*! It's Saturday! I *insisted* today is a free day!" His smile is full of mischief.

"A *free* day? I'm not sure we can *afford* a free day with everything coming!" She complains and pulls herself up into a seated position, leaning against the headboard. She glares at him, sensing something odd. "You're *up to something*! I can tell! What is it?"

He smirks. "I know we're not married, but we're partners, and my family has a tradition where a husband gives his wife a gift. It's usually done after their first night together, but *alas*! That ship has definitely sailed, and my gifts took a little time to craft."

"*What* did you do? You know you don't have to give me any gifts!" She blushes, caresses his face, and runs her fingers lightly through his beard.

"I remember you said you admired the portrait of mine hanging in the Smithsonian National Gallery. It was of Ginevra de Benci, for the record." He reaches down and brings up the packages, both wrapped in silken fabric. "*These* are for you!"

"You *didn't*? Did you make copies of that portrait for me?" She asks, touched that he remembered her earlier admission.

"*Heaven forbids*! I painted something much more meaningful, *Amore!*"

She fumbles with the silk fabric, unwrapping it from the first painting. Happy tears cascade down her cheeks that Leonardo Da Vinci took the time to paint her a present! She pulls the last wrap of fabric from the first painting, and sees the portrait of her daughter Lynda with her long, black, curly hair, and flowers surrounding her. Dee gasps, "It's absolutely *stunning*! I can't believe you took the time to do this!"

"Don't stop now! Open the *other* one!" He laughs.

Nearly trembling, she unwraps the red silk fabric around the second, matching frame, and sees that he's captured Celia's likeness and personality. "They're amazing! Thank you! How...how did you ever... it's like a sliver of their souls are in those paintings!"

He laughs and puts his arm around her. "You *inspired* me! There is part of you in each of them!" He pauses and then gets an ear-to-ear grin. "That, and I googled them! I found plenty of pictures online! Instagram, Facebook, and the age of the selfie really makes it quite easy to see who they are! There's definitely a lot of you in Lynda, but even Celia, she has your smile!"

Happy tears are now a minor waterfall cascading down her cheeks. "This is *so* amazing! Thank you again!" She gives a sudden gut borne laugh.

"What's *wrong*?" He asks, sensing a mental snide comment.

"The only negative thing is, I can't show these off to anyone! They'd take one look and know *exactly* who you are!" She laughs uncontrollably at the absurdity.

"I promised Sara a look! You can at least show her. I had to promise her something for giving you a day off!" He quips.

She takes a few deep breaths and forces herself to calm down. "Maybe, in spite of all the horrible weeks with Jason, he inadvertently did me a favor making me Apara. I'd never have met you otherwise!"

He wipes a few strands of tear-soaked hair out of her eyes, saying, "And had you been turned 20 or so years ago, I might not have realized how lonely I was, as it wasn't until Lisa left this life that I truly knew that emptiness."

Dee throws her arms around him and holds him tightly. "I wish I had something to give you, but anything I could, would pale in comparison!"

"But you've already given me the best gift, Cara! Yourself! You've brought back something I haven't felt in centuries, and I don't plan to let it, or you go anytime soon!" He leans in and kisses her and they spend a couple of hours showing each other exactly how much this new bonding has come to mean to them.

Afterwards, they go for a walk in his rather expansive garden outside their home in Sanctuary. They reach the center, where one of his stone creations, a carved mermaid in waves has been turned into the centerpiece of a fountain. They sit in front of it on a carved stone bench.

"*Cara*, I have another gift for you. We're going out to dinner tonight, and no, not to my relative's restaurant in Italy. It's a place on the west coast of the US, so I'm afraid it will be a bit of a late meal for us!" He grins.

"You really don't need...." She says, but he stops her mid-sentence.

"Yes, I *think* I do." He grins mischievously, doing his best to keep the actual surprise a secret. They spend the day together. He forbids her from touching her laptop and her work. He takes her out to a clothing shop in Italy and insists she pick out something nice to wear to dinner. He takes her where she can get her hair cut and styled, as it has grown out since she'd been turned.

3 am European time rolls around and Dee comes out in her new clothes, hair styled, and even has makeup on. "I feel silly getting all dressed up like this! It's just *not* me!"

"Sure, it is! There is far more to you than science, my dear! *Humor* me!" He grins and extends his hand to her. She takes it and they port, reappearing in the alley of a busy city somewhere.

"Where are we?" She asks, feeling disoriented.

"Near the restaurant..." is all he'll tell her.

"*No!* I mean, what *city*?" She asks, somewhat annoyed at his lack of forthcomingness.

"Come on! We'll be late for our reservation!" He takes her hand and drags her out onto a busy street and down to a restaurant. She notices they must be in California because of all the California license plates, but not where. They go in, are seated, and order their meals. About halfway through their meal, she hears a familiar voice, and looks up to see Celia and her boyfriend enter the room.

"*Oh, no!* We've got to *leave!*" She tells him urgently.

He looks around casually, leans over, and whispers in her ear, "Relax, she'll never *recognize* you! Not at your current, apparent age, and with all the makeup."

She switches to pathing, afraid Celia might recognize her voice, or that she might draw attention to themselves chewing him out. *You KNEW they'd be here, didn't you?*

He doesn't reply, but she perceives the equivalent of a smug, mental smile.

Dee watches as Celia and Josh settle in two tables over. She thinks *Celia looks so happy!* She's a little surprised Celia doesn't seem heartbroken over her death, but she is glad Celia is happy. That's what's important.

Dee picks her meal, surreptitiously glancing Celia's way from time to time and listening to their conversation with her heightened hearing. She draws out her meal, wanting to be there as long as her daughter is, even though she knows she can't go over and do what she really wants to; tell her she's alive, loves her, and give

348

her an enormous hug. Her emotions war within her. Happy to see her oldest daughter there, in good spirits, and moving on with life, but sad that she can only observe.

Vince watches patiently, eating his meal, and ready in case Dee can't refrain from her desire to hug Celia. After a while, Dee notices Josh start emitting anxiety, and wonders what's wrong. Before she can react, he pulls out a small gift-box and presents it to Celia, asking her to marry him.

Dee's mouth drops open as Celia squeals a delighted 'YES! Of course!" and leans over to kiss him. Waiters nearby, who Josh had informed that he was going to propose, begin to clap, and bring out a cake with 'Congratulations on your Engagement' written on it.

Once that happens, people at nearby tables join in the applause, and Dee does as well, trying not to cry.

Vince paths, *Are you enjoying your present, Cara?*

You knew? How? She paths, glad for that ability as she's too choked up to actually get the words out verbally.

Yes. I thought, this way, even if she doesn't realize you're here, you can be part of this milestone in her life. He grins and reaches across to take her hand. *As to how, how does anyone know anything these days? Facebook! She suspected that was why he was going to bring her here! And since you've refused to look at it, afraid it would make you sad, I knew you would be surprised!*

Thank you! Dee paths, and carefully reaches out empathically to touch her daughter's mind and feel her joy. *This is a wondrous gift, Vince! I'll never forget it!*

Afterwards, they port back to their home in the Sanctuary equivalent of Italy, and Dee feels oddly whole again. Exhausted, but happy, she falls asleep in Vince's arms, still dwelling in the lingering empathic glow of her daughter's joy.

AFTERMATH

Once the Hybrids have created enough of the base 6 amino acids, they'll seed the Earth with them. Luckily, they don't have to seed it with enough to match every viral particle. Once the manufactured base attack the virus, causing it to collapse and disintegrate, they are freed up from the virus and can affect other viral particles. About a week after the hybrids complete distribution, Sara, Amy, Marc, and Liz meet at Medical.

Liz looks exhausted. "So, are we seeing any changes yet?" She asks.

Sara pulls up a page on her tablet and hands it to Liz. "The good news is the number of new, reported virus-like illnesses has dropped off significantly. There's been a drop of about 25% in the last week. Isanda said it would take some time for the bases to deal with all the viral particles, but if it hasn't dropped to near zero within a month, they'll consider another dispersal."

Liz turns to Amy. "And what of reports indicating abilities showing up among potentials?"

"Those have dropped about 18%, but we knew there would be a lag as those already infected may not express their new abilities right away, plus, only the strongest incidents are going to get talked about. Someone's hearing improving or other sensory improvements might not get any attention." Amy explains.

"I assume the various centers around the world are still sending reports to the app?" Liz asks Marc.

"Yes, in fact, we've had to get Ty and Val to expand the storage space allocated for that database on our servers. Most are minor, but there have been some that are more... problematic." He admits as he scans a spreadsheet of reports ranging from someone complaining that their sense of smell has increased and it's driving them crazy, as they live near a sewage treatment plant, to reports of more dramatic abilities, like someone who wipes hard drives when they use a computer; a few more pyrokinetics, and three more cases of spontaneous porting this week alone.

"How are we coming with our intervention teams?" She asks.

Sara sighs. "We're working on them, but it takes time to train our teams to go in, evaluate the subjects, and teach them how to inject the Cent-opal dust into the spine properly, unless, of course, they are deemed suitable for turning. I'm afraid Tess and Sue are getting a little burnt out with their share of the load."

Marc let's out a stifled guffaw, "I can vouch for that! Tess has been absolutely *surly* lately from her work load and lack of sleep."

"Okay, and what about those that can be brought over?" She asks.

"So far, only about fifteen have been brought over, though there are more we feel *should* be transformed at our dormitories at Medical. It's going to take time to find people willing to sponsor or take them in and be their mentors. This is happening way to fast to properly pair people up, even with Tess, Sue, and Kari using their skills to do so. There's a transformation 'wait-list' now." Sara sighs.

Liz looks around the table at her consulting team. "Do the best you can, with priority on the most problematic emergent talents, and hope that new cases drop off soon."

The meeting ends, and Marc, Kari, and Sara leave, but Amy lingers. Liz notices she's not gotten up. "Is there something *else*?" She asks, almost afraid of the answer.

"Yeah, I heard from Charlie this morning. He's coming back for a visit next month and wants to 'hang out'." Amy informs her.

"*Oh?* You know that once he left here, he fell off the proverbial map?" Liz asks.

"So, I heard. Checked out of the hotel and vanished; no record from any airports, nothing from passport control anywhere, no credit card usage, social media, and so on. Like he's vanished from the planet. His hotel was paid for through a hard to trace, off-shore shell company. Are you sure one of the Hybrids didn't abduct him?" She says with an exhausted but sarcastic twinkle in her eye.

"Did he say anything *else*? Did he *ask* about Marc or I again?" Liz asks, feeling like Charlie may be a more serious issue than anyone realizes.

"Nope, he said he'll be coming back and wants to hang out. Dave nearly lost it. He does *not* like Charlie at all! Says if he can't read someone, he sure as *Hell* doesn't trust them!" Amy recounts.

"Let me know when you set a date to meet him. We may want to set you up with a subcutaneous tracker, just in case. This is all setting my precog tendencies on edge." Liz admits, concern in her eyes.

Amy nods and says, "I agree. People don't just disappear like that without a trace, especially internationally! I know he was heading back there, but there's nothing! *Oh*, I talked to Ty and Val and they did a check on the roster for the debris team for the Jerusalem Reclamation Project. He worked there for a short time in May and June, but his name dropped off any rosters in July. They did a deeper search and found to him, Liz, that he was listed as MIA after a cave in."

"*Helvete*! Liz exclaims in Norwegian. "We've got some contacts in the Army. I'll see if they can find out what happened."

"Thanks, I'll let you know as soon as I know anything." Amy says and leaves.

"Likewise, Amy." Liz says, distracted by this latest mystery. She sits back at her desk and sends messages to various contacts in the military, and in Israel, to see if they can find out what Sgt. Charles Abrams might be up to.

It's a Match!

Charlie's lounging around with Janna watching a movie they've seen about fifteen times since they became part of 'Operation Bloodsucker', as he calls it when his bosses aren't around. Not being allowed access to live broadcasts down in the bunker, they're stuck watching a limited library of films and television provided to them by their superiors. Charlie nearly dozes off in boredom when a voice comes over an intercom. "*Abrams*, report to the briefing room immediately." Uri the spook's voice is somewhat agitated, so he gets up, throws on his fatigues over his casual clothes, and runs down to the briefing room.

He arrives at the door and it's guarded by two rather large guards. One looks at him, then says, "Sgt. Abrams? You're expected, go on in." He moves out of the way, opens the door, allowing Charlie through, and the guard moves in and stands inside, in front of the door, and closes it. Charlie feels anxious with these guys guarding the room, wondering if they are there to keep others out, or him in, for some unknown reason.

Uri looks up when the door opens and motions Charlie to come in and sit down. Dr. Zelkind is there, as well as a couple of other scientist-looking types.

Uri settles in at the conference table and clears his throat. "We've been studying the phone data you acquired and the phone numbers in our subject's cell phone do match the ones for this Lissa Pederson and Marc Gerard. Somehow, they are definitely connected to our subject and the events surrounding the Jerusalem bomb. By the way, sorry to hear your ex has gotten involved with these blood-drinking *demons*." He trails off.

"Thank you, Sir. I don't suppose you've found any way to cure them of their condition?" Charlie asks, knowing that Amy could be taken out if it came down to a full-scale attack on this Inspiration, Inc.

"No, Abrams. It's far too early for that. We're still determining the details of transformation, though some of the text conversations and emails we've extracted from Ms. Ledbetter's phone have given us some insight." He remarks.

"Oh? What kind of insight, Sir?" Charlie inquires.

"As we suspected, it appears to be a virus that causes the change. Some of her text and email conversations suggest that the only reason it worked on Elias is that he is *genetically compatible* with it. It only works on a small fraction of people." Dr. Zelkind explains.

"How do we find out who's compatible?" Charlie wonders aloud.

"That, Abrams, is the problem. We believe that they have some kind of overview or a way to test for compatibility. Once we know more, you may be sent on a new mission to get that information from your ex." Uri says, giving him a malicious grin.

"How am I supposed to get anything out of her if she's one of them, Sir? She's stronger than I am, and apparently, holding a gun to her won't be a major threat!" Charlie exclaims, torn between his distaste for these monsters and old feelings for Amy.

"We're working on other tools to neutralize their advantages." Uri explains cryptically. "Once we have those tools perfected, your ex will be no match for you.

"Still, I doubt she'd betray them. She seemed very...well, Sir, she seemed quite satisfied with her job. I got the distinct impression she feels she was doing good, not evil. I mean, she didn't come right out and *talk* about specifics, but I'd hazard a guess that she feels her job lets her make a difference." Charlie tells them, wavering briefly, in the absolute belief that vampires *must* be evil. Somehow, he can't reconcile that Amy might be evil. Deluded, possibly, but he can't see her as evil.

"Abrams, these beings are, no doubt, quite adept at deception. She's no longer the woman you had a relationship with, she's one of *them*! Don't make the mistake of assuming you even know the woman any longer." Uri emphasizes, sensing Charlie's wavering about whether these beings are the enemy.

"Yes, Sir. Thank you for the reminder." Charlie says, knowing that the last thing he needs is to give them a reason to doubt him, as they're unlikely to let him go if his focus and beliefs stray too much from their agenda. He knows way too much for them to ever let him leave if they consider him even slightly disloyal, and he knows that means either becoming a prisoner himself, or being *killed* off as a liability.

"Besides, when we're ready to send you in, you *won't* be alone. Your team will go with you, as well as Elias. If you find your emotions getting in the way, I'm sure the others won't hesitate to pursue whatever recourse is necessary." Uri says, with a *double* implication: They'll do whatever is needed to get the information from Amy, and if he becomes weak in his resolve, they'll surely take care of him, as well. He thinks, *I've got no choice. When the time comes, I'll be the one to confront her, and hopefully, I'll be able to leverage whatever connection we have left to get her to cooperate, because if I can't, the others won't hesitate to torture her to get what we need.*

Uri can tell that Charlie's mind has wandered, and asks, "You with us, Abrams? Are we clear?"

"*Yes*, Sir!" Let me know when, where, and what to do!" He says, ignoring his nagging doubts and playing the good soldier.

"*Good*! Now, we know that they have other abilities besides reading minds and teleporting. Elias has shown that he can move objects with his mind! Something that could be a useful weapon, so it's vital we find a way to block that ability. In addition to reading minds, Elias has shown us that he can mentally control others to some extent, making them compliant. He believes it's something they do when feeding. At least that's what his intuitive knowledge tells him. It's another reason you need to be very clear-headed about your ex, Abrams. She may well have been influencing you through some sort of mental compulsion." Uri turns to Dr. Zelkind. "Doctor, isn't there something else you wanted to mention?"

"Yes, Uri, absolutely. In addition to going on a mission to get data, there's been a viral outbreak that's been seen around the world, and may be related to them." She admits.

"Oh? *Viral*? As in the virus that makes them what they are?" Charlie inquires.

"We're not *quite* sure, but your ex has been researching cases of a virus which may be associated with outbreaks of unusual phenomena, as well as an increase in hospitalizations for delusional symptoms such as hearing voices. From what we can gather, a virus is causing those who are compatible to develop unusual abilities. We're in the process of investigating similar reports here in Israel. So much has been missed here, as our priority's been the recovery of Jerusalem and radiation related health crisis, so minor viral outbreaks have gone unnoticed. We already have an increase in psychiatric incidents due to the figurative fallout from the bomb. There have been a lot of stress and trauma reactions, as well as grief related diagnoses, but we're able to access health records, and are running them through an algorithm looking for anyone who might be affected." Zelkind explains.

"To what *purpose*? Do you think you can use some of their skills?" Charlie wonders, missing the obvious goal.

"No, Abrams. If the virus is only bringing out these abilities in compatible subjects, we can use that to find others we can transform, and use them against our enemy." Uri interjects.

Charlie realizes what this implies; they will go from using military and intelligence volunteers for potential transformees, to abducting civilians that are likely compatible, and transforming them without their permission. He gets a proverbially bad taste in his mouth as some part of his mind nags at him that his clear cut, black and white idea of good guys and bad guys may be inherently faulty. Even with warning bells going off in his head, he asks, "Sir, are you suggesting changing these people whether or not they volunteer?"

Uri narrows his eyes and clicks his tongue against the roof of his mouth prior to responding. "We'll be *helping* them control these new abilities, and in return, *they* will show their gratitude by helping *us*, especially if, as we suspect, these beings may have had something to do with this virus in the first place."

"Do you think the virus is a bioweapon, Sir?" Charlie asks, taken aback.

"Possibly! It *may* have been designed to expose those people who are compatible by marking them with these aberrations they're developing. Or, it's *quite* possible it's something they were *hired* to release. One other bit of information we've gleaned from your girlfriend's phone is this: She and the others have been referring to their 'Benefactors', who we believe may be their financial backers or those who hire them as mercenaries. There is also talk about hybrids. We're wondering if that is what the virus does, creates a cross between them and humans. Perhaps these mysterious abilities they're supposedly developing are only a *first* stage in some kind of worldwide attempt to increase their numbers through an *airborne* variant of the virus in their blood. Whatever the case, we're going to take advantage of this and find some that we can convert and use against them." Uri elucidates, sounding even more unhinged and paranoid than usual; just the sort of thing one might expect from a 'spook', too long in the business.

Charlie pauses a second, uncertain how he feels about being part of an operation that intentionally experiments on civilians, but replies, "I get it, Sir. I'll do my best to keep my focus on the big picture."

"Good! Now, as to why we've called you in. We noticed one set of messages between Amy and someone named Tess that has us concerned. She apparently felt uncertain why you wanted to get back in touch. We want you to establish more regular communications with her. Mention nothing about her work or her bosses unless she brings it up. Make her think you're interested in her, and that you're coming back in a month for another visit, and would like to get together." Uri suggests.

"*Tess*? Oh, Sir, she is Amy's friend. I think she's with that Marc fellow, and speaking of seeing people, I don't know how well Amy will take it if I act like I want to pick up where we left off. She admitted to me that she's seeing some guy named Dave. I *assume* he's one of *them*, as she mentioned she *works* with him. I don't know how she'll take it if she feels like I might be treading where I shouldn't, Sir. You *don't* know Amy. She doesn't take shit from *anyone*!" Charlie shifts uncomfortably as Uri, Dr. Zelkind, and the other, silent observers watch him.

"Understood, but I think that will be the least suspicious approach. It was the long gaps between contact that made her suspicious of your intent. For this to work, we need her to feel... *comfortable* with you again." Uri says, implying a potential for getting close to Amy again. "We'll set up times for you to get in touch with her. By email at first, and then, by one or another form of chat. Communications will be monitored... so we can check them for any potential information from her side, of course!" Uri wants to be sure Charlie knows that he will be monitored, in case his allegiance *is* wavering.

"Of course, Sir. I understand. Standard infiltration technique. Lure the enemy target into a false sense of security and then get them to confide in you, or otherwise acquire the information from them." Charlie clammers out, realizing that Uri has been looking at him suspiciously.

"Yes, Abrams. We'll brief you more as needed. Start thinking about what you can say to her to get her to trust you, and perhaps, even *welcome* your interest again." Uri says and nods to the guard at the door, who opens it and allows Charlie to leave, following him out. Charlie returns to Janna in his quarters, but the meeting continues.

Uri addresses the others. "He's somewhat uncertain in his resolve, don't you think?"

Dr. Zelkind clears her throat. "I think you're staring at him like a hawk was making him uneasy. He's been on board from the start."

The two other scientists chat between themselves and one of them timidly says, "We *agree* with Uri." And then, is quiet again, as though he fears reprisal should he speak up *against* the agent.

Uri dismisses the two men, who scurry out of the room as though Uri were a cat that let two mice escape, but may change his mind before they can get away.

"Zelkind, I do believe Sgt. Abrams may have a conflict of interest which is making him unclear in his thinking, and that makes him a liability. We need him *for now*, to make contact with Ms. Ledbetter again, and meet with her, but once that phase of our plan is done, I suggest we find another use for the sergeant. A *scapegoat*, perhaps?" Uri says without further elucidation and the two leave the room, followed by the two guards, and walk down the hall.

CLEAN UP

Back at Medical, most of the usual inner circle are meeting with Michelle from the Atlanta center. Amy is away doing security training in Australia. It's been about three weeks since the alien amino acid base was dispersed around the planet and they are evaluating the status of the problem.

Sara stands at the head of the table, and despite her relatively short stature, commands the attention of the crowd by clearing her throat. "Now that I have everyone's attention, we have some excellent news. Cases of the Roulette virus have dwindled to a trickle. There are no longer any new cases being reported in most of the world, and only a relatively small number appearing in a few more isolated regions where the bases have been shown to break down faster because of the climate. These are primarily near the equator. As a result, our Benefactors will do another pass in the region 35 degrees north and south of the equator, with more emphasis on the North as it contains far more land and population. Hopefully, with that, we'll be able to end the virus once and for all. Now, on to the *not* so good news! Our studies show up to 35% of all living potentials may have been infected, meaning there are many people out there to check. We'll have to determine if their emergent abilities are worth doing anything about, and if not, we'll need to do annual follow-ups for the next five years in case those abilities expand." Sara pauses.

Before she can continue, Liz chimes in: "Sara, what resources do you think we'll need to follow up on these people? I have to consider this when we calculate how many new Apara we need, so we have enough to keep up with our world duties and managing the damage from this situation. I'm very concerned we may not have enough viable transformees out there to do it all!"

"I hear you, Liz. And honestly, I'm not sure. Isanda and some of the hybrids will be staying on planet for the next few years to help us, but that is more in a *technical* capacity. Even so, they may use some of their technology to help us track more of the Lost Mission potentials that aren't in any of the world, genetic databases." She explains, looking frustrated at the enormity of the situation, even though they've nearly stopped the virus itself. In addition, I've noticed a pattern which has me concerned. There have been barely any reported potentials under the age of eighteen displaying psychic or other talents from the virus, and no cases under the age of fifteen."

Tess tentatively raises her hand, saying, "But isn't that a good thing? I mean, maybe they're immune?"

"Unfortunately, that's unlikely. Cases of the virus itself were registered at all ages and in both potentials and non-potentials according to our contact in the CDC. I'm concerned about this for a reason: while we very rarely turn children, it has been done with very promising subjects who would have died before they become adults. In their cases, turning them heals whatever ails them, but their abilities, physical changes and need for blood do not show up until sometime between their 16th and 18th years of life."

Everyone hears an under-the-breath exclamation from Kari: *"Faen i helvete!"* She curses in Norwegian, then speaks up full voice. "Sara, are you telling us we may see children manifest abilities once they near adulthood?"

"*Indeed!* So, this will not be over for quite some time. We'll need to monitor child potentials until adulthood for any breakthrough abilities as they enter their teens, but *especially* as they near adulthood." Sara huffs out.

Marc's face shows signs of strain as he asks, "what of those adult potentials who are not currently manifesting? Is there any chance some of those have been infected, but their new abilities haven't manifested yet, but eventually will?"

"Unfortunately, it *is* possible. Sometimes, psychic abilities, in humans, come out under stress, especially things like telekinesis. Think *poltergeists*! I've spoken to some of our IT folk who program search algorithms, and they're working on a set of them which will watch for ongoing reports of anything that could indicate a breakout talent, it will then cross reference any names with our databases, and send us alerts as soon as a flag is raised."

Sara sits and slouches down in her chair, then turns to Tess. "I need you, Kari, and Sue to continue your Lost Mission work. Please make sure to inform Sue of *all* we've discussed. She's been training several other Apara to take on some of the counseling burden, so couldn't be here today."

There's a quiet knock on the door. Had they not all had excellent hearing, they might have missed it. Sara smiles subtly. "Come in Annie."

Annie comes in, still a bit timid, but no longer afraid of the other Apara. "You said to meet you at 8 pm for rounds. It's 8:22." She looks at everyone in the room, nodding greetings, but smiles a little wider when she greets Tess, as she will always have that special connection with her after her help escaping Jason's.

Sara sighs, glad to see Annie's face in the doorway. "So it is, Annie. I'll be along shortly. Can you wait in my office?"

"Yes, Sara." She says, and skips off down the hallway.

Liz leans forward, and cocks her head to one side while looking at Sara. "Annie sure has become attached to you, Sara. Isn't it about time you have that little *talk* with her?"

Sara let's out a long sigh, glances from Liz to Isanda, who gives her a raised, feathery eyebrow, and paths, *Yes, Abha, isn't it about time?*

Sara answers both of them, out loud, "Perhaps it is." She ports out, leaving the others to talk among themselves and disperse from the meeting.

A PLACE FOR ANNIE

Sara ports in right outside her office and carefully opens the door so as not to startle Annie. "Hello, Pepem." Sara has recently begun calling Annie by that nickname, which means butterfly in her native Mayan. She hopes Annie will soon be willing to come out of her human cocoon and become that butterfly for her. Tonight is the night Sara will finally attempt to coax her out of her safe, silken reality and challenge her to soar with her. But first, Sara *must* share her story with Annie, as she promised Isanda she would do.

"Hi, Sara! I'm ready for rounds!" Annie says excitedly, always happy for her special time with Sara. She feels safe with her, more so than with nearly any other Apara, with the possible exception of Tess.

"No rounds tonight, sweet Pepem. I was wondering if you would like to come to my home for supper and a chat?" Sara asks, nearly holding her breath as she waits for her answer.

"*Yes*! Of course! But what about all the patients?" She asks.

"That's what staff are for! I've asked them to give us the night off. I have something I need to talk to you about." She says and extends her hand to Annie. Annie takes it without hesitation and they port out. They reappear near a cozy home in the woods, a small pond outside, a stream entering the pond as a tiny waterfall, and exiting once again as a stream.

They port in on the opposite side of the pond. The sun is low in the west, sparkling reddish through tiny gaps in the trees, making sparkling reflections in the pond in front of them. Beyond her home, several deer are grazing on berries, and in the other direction, Annie startles at the sound of unfamiliar birds.

"Wow! It's beautiful here! This is where you live?" Annie says, looking around her in all directions.

"Yes, Pepem, this is and has been my home for a very long time, though I have had many houses over the years, all have been built here. As you can imagine, I modernized every now and again." She watches in amusement as Annie goes over to the pond. Annie crouches down and peers into its shallow water.

She lets out a gasp, "Sara! You've got fish and frogs in there!" She exclaims as if she's discovered some strange new life in a fantasy realm.

"*Come*! There will be time later to explore my realm!" She quips and guides Annie across a small bridge over her pond. She steps off the bridge and onto inset, flat, greenish stones that make a walkway up to her door. The lower half of the cottage is made of the same semi-polished stones. Most are various shades of green, but some are almost yellowish, brown, or mixed colors. As she studies them, she notices some have carved symbols in them that look like something she'd seen in her Art History class in college. She has the feeling it was quite ancient, possibly Pre-Columbian.

"Sara, are those stones jade?" She asks, as a certain familiarity nags at her.

"Yes, they *are*. They are from my homeland." Sara says, as though it were an unimportant fact.

"Where *are* you from? You've never told me." Annie asks, as Sara nudges her into the house.

"Today, it's known as Guatemala, but I was there long before it was ever called that." Sara comments without further elucidation as Annie passes through her doorway and is in awe at what she sees. Above the jade part of the walls, are more modern constructed walls and yet, she feels as if she has traveled back in time. Painted directly on some walls are brightly colored, Mayan-style scenes. In other places, there are jade carvings in the same style. There is a border above the jade boulder walls made of multicolored jade inlay in an intricate pattern going around the room. The floor is made with the same flat slices of jade that made up the walkway, although these are mortared in as a proper floor. Her furniture is simple, but comfortable, with one exception; a shelf made of hardwood and sheets of obsidian. On the shelves are various Mayan artifacts, and in the center, in what appears to be a place of honor, is a carved, blue-jadeite figure of some sort of bat like being with fangs.

"You're *Mayan*?" Annie asks, surprised because she had no idea, as Sara has no accent, and her Star Wars obsession makes her seem somewhat more contemporary.

"Yes, I am." Sara says, standing nearby, watching Annie explore the artwork and artifacts in her home.

"This collection is amazing! Are these all Mayan artifacts or are some modern recreations?" She asks, carefully touching a Jadeite carving and noting it's very cool, as real jadeite often is.

Sara chuckles and comes up behind Annie, laying one hand on her shoulder. "Yes, and no. They are authentic *Mayan* work, but the works you see span millennia, including recent times.

Annie makes a sudden gasp and turns to Sara. "Did *you* make all these?" She motions with her hand to not only the carvings but the paintings and mosaics.

"My father was a stone worker, and despite being a daughter, he taught me the art. He had *no* sons, but wanted my sisters and I to teach our sons the trade someday. However, I was the only one of my siblings that pursued the art, while my sisters went back to weaving and cooking. But then again, I was never quite a typical female, even back then." Sara recounts.

Annie rolls her eyes. "Boy! Can I relate to that! When I was a kid, my mother expected me to learn how to be a good daughter and learn everything her mother taught her." She gives a sad laugh. "I was more interested in climbing trees and roughhousing with my brothers! Much to my mom's dismay!" She turns back to the figurines on the shelf. "Did you bring all this jade with you from Guatemala?"

"Yes, but not all at once! While I did not have strength enough to carve when I was younger, my father showed me how to tell which stones held the secret Mayan treasure! I would take a piece of jade with me down to where more was found and clink it against the boulders. Unless a boulder has been broken and exposed, it's hard to tell jade from any other rock because of the 'skin' or 'crust' on it. However, banging raw jade with a known piece of jade produces a unique, ringing sound. My father would send me out to find the pieces and gave me some red pigment to mark the jade stones, then he would send men down to collect the ones I'd identified. I never got it wrong!" She reminisces.

"So, you brought all the jade for your wall and your floor here to build this place?" Annie asks somewhat awestruck as jadeite had a place in her own cultural background as well.

"No, Pepem! After I became Apara, it was something I would do that made me feel normal again. I would bring them here, where I chose to live, and put them at the base of a waterfall nearby. Once they stripped off the crusts and exposed the jade beneath, I started a pile to work from. With my new strength, I became quite adept at carving, as my father had taught me. My homes have changed over time, from an almost hut like dwelling, to wood and other materials, but when I built this place a few hundred years ago, my water worn jade pile was so large, and there were tools I could use to split it into sheets, at least some of it, that I decided to make my home largely from materials that came from my original home." She moves a little closer to Annie as she looks over the figurines on the shelves. Annie pauses at the blue jadeite one that looks like some kind of half man, half bat creature.

"I've never seen blue jade before! But why use such a beautiful stone to carve such a demonic-looking creature?" Annie asks.

Sara picks up the figurine and looks at it. "Come, sit with me and I'll tell you a story about this creature." They go sit on a sofa covered in brightly colored, woven cloth. "This creature is called Camazotz. It is a bat-demon or bat-god depending which mythology. It was not really written about until this millennia, but the origin of this creature comes from my time. The reason it holds that 'place of honor' as your mind refers to it, is because it has everything to do with what your generation would call my origin story." Sara gently hands it to Annie to hold. "Some believe the creature is based on the large bats from the region, but it isn't, not *originally*. You know how we've told you that Jason came after you because you were compatible?"

"Yes, and you told me how the Benefactors make people compatible by choosing those they feel would make good Apara, and adding the genes to their DNA for the virus to latch onto." Annie recounts.

"Yes, well, it wasn't always that way, Annie. Back in my time, there were still Apara whose virus was unkeyed, and they could turn anyone they gave their blood to. Unfortunately, some of the Mayan rituals made it clear to some of the Apara at the time, that blood is power. They discovered that their blood could raise others to their evolved status. Unfortunately, the power went to some of their heads, and they deemed themselves demigods or even gods among men and expected the rest of us to worship them. Cadmael was one such Apara gone wrong." She pauses.

"You mean he was kinda like Jason, don't you?" Annie surprises her with her insight.

"Yes, little Pepem, but much, *much* worse. Jason may have a huge ego and a lot of issues, but Cadmael came to my village from a good distance away, searching for new people he could convince he was some sort of god. He came to my village, but no one would worship him. They had their own gods to believe in, and he was not one of them! I was there, with one of the men who was bringing back baskets of smaller jade rocks for carvings, when Cadmael demonstrated his power by telling the people what they were thinking and then telekinetically lifted a woman in the air. People began to scream at him, but not in fear. My father's man told everyone to take jade from his basket and help him repel the evil one who tempted them to abandon their own gods. I threw the first stone and hit him squarely...well, where it hurts!" Sara gives her a knowing grin. He, and a group of female handmaidens, some human and a couple he had turned, were forced to retreat, but apparently, I had made an impression. He sent one of his handmaidens into town, dressed as a commoner, and asked around about me, the Jade worker's daughter who was *so* bold. I was not like most other girls, as I said before. I was one of what many indigenous people refer to as the two-spirited. I was seen as having both aspects of a woman and of a man because I would do work for my father, but also because I preferred other women. It took a while, but I was fifteen when he came for me. My whole family was down in the jade quarry, if you can call it that. There had been a great storm and much new rock had been exposed when a hill collapsed."

"You mean some kind of avalanche or rock slide?" Annie asks.

Sara nods. "Yes, and it exposed some new jade including fantastic colors like that blue. We were all working: my mother, my father, my two sisters, two men who worked for my father, and of course, me. Cadmael was only one man, but he was not human, and while I, my mother, and sisters hid, he used his fangs to kill the men and then came for us. He had one of his Apara handmaidens hold my mother while he drained my two sisters, and then finally found me hiding up in a tree. He used his mind to make me come down. I fought him, but to no avail. Once he had me, his handmaiden drained my mother, leaving me alone."

"Oh, my *God*! That's definitely *worse* than Jason!" She gasps.

"It didn't end there either, Pepem. I have not told this story to anyone in a very long time. Isanda knows, as do a few closer friends, some of whom rarely ever show themselves much these days as they have grown tired with their age and keep to themselves after long service. I want you to know my whole story. I want you to *know me*." Sara says, and has to fight tears.

"Sara, you *don't* have to tell me if it hurts you to remember." Annie tells her, putting one hand on her shoulder.

"No, young one, you should know. I will not go into the gory details, but Cadmael had a reason for killing my family and taking me. It was all part of his revenge on my village for denying him, and my dual nature was seen as powerful in some rituals because two spirits would be sacrificed instead of one!" Sara says with a sigh, choking up as she allows herself to remember.

"They were going to sacrifice you?" Annie gasps in horror at the thought of the obsidian knives she'd once seen in an anthropology book.

"Yes, and no. The ritual he performed was one of his own making, and was used to cover my transformation. Long story short, he gave me a drink made of distilled essence k'aizalaj okox, a type of mushroom with psychedelic properties that made me hallucinate, claiming I was being possessed by demons. He performed a ritual where he and his Apara acolytes and handmaidens all fed from me. When I was just this side of death, he gave me his blood, turning me. There was a prolonged series of ritualistic behaviors I would rather not discuss. It was meant to create a frenzy among his cult, and give my body time to transform enough that I would *appear* to die when he cut my heart out, and rise again, later, as that!" She points at the blue jade statue.

Annie looks at her with shock, and asks, "But Apara can't really turn into *bats*, can they?"

"No, they cannot, but his handmaidens prepared a costume to make me look more frightening. He presented my drained, heartless, and lifeless body to the village and told them he'd killed me and my family. He took me away with him, telling my village that I would return as a demon that would punish them for their impudence. He starved me when I awoke, and unleashed me, dressed in a black robe with bat-wing-like sleeves, on my village. I was mad with hunger. Ironically, the first person I met was my *best* friend, though I saw her as possibly more than that. I watched her eyes grow wide with horror as she saw me, a ghost of the dead in all black with fangs; the foretold demon servant sent to be the angry god's wrath. I couldn't stop myself. I was starving, and before I knew it, I *killed* her. It did, however, snap me out of the madness when I realized it. He hoped I'd attack many, but I stopped after the one person I most cared about besides my family. I found an old, hollowed out tree and hid there, afraid, and ashamed of what I'd become and done. Isanda was in the neighboring village working as a teacher and healer when she felt my friend's terror and then mine. She found me, took me in, and took me to the Benefactors. They did what they could to help me. They even tried to wipe it from my mind, but it didn't work." She looks into Annie's eyes to face whatever condemnation might be there, but she senses only sympathy and love from the girl, no horror or blame, other than that Cadmael did that to her. Annie reaches over to Sara and draws her into a hug, making Sara's tears drip down onto Annie's shoulder.

"It's *okay, really!* I *know* you're *not* a monster! *None* of the Apara, aside from Jason and maybe that Philipa are.

Sara wipes away the tears with her sleeve. "That's what I was *supposed* to be." She explains, once again pointing to the blue, jade monster. It's made from a piece of rare, blue jadeite I found right before Cadmael found us. I went back when I was well enough, found it, and carved the creature I saw in his mind while he drained me. It was a creature he'd invented to frighten those he wished to rule."

"But why *dwell* on that, Sara? That's not *who* you are! Everyone knows you're a *healer*, not a monster!" Annie tells her, cupping her cheek with one hand.

"I keep that there, in its special place, to remind myself that I choose another path. A path where I've been trying to make up for the deaths that I was responsible for." She explains.

"But I thought it was only one person?" Annie looks confused.

"I count my *family* and my father's servants as well. If I hadn't been the strong-willed child, Cadmael would never have chosen me to be his messenger, and they would have lived." Sara let's out a long sigh and almost slumps down in emotional exhaustion. "I've lived a solitary life for so long. Working as a teacher and a healer for longer than many civilizations have survived, and I'm tired of being alone."

Annie's mouth drops open in surprise as she realizes why Sara needed to tell her of her past. "How long have you been *punishing* yourself?" She asks.

Sara laughs almost hauntingly. "Around 4 *millennia*, child! Isanda and I were together for a few centuries as she taught me and helped me make amends, but when she left to go back to the Benefactor's world, I came here. This is my refuge where I retreat whenever I'm not working. Very few others have been here in all that time." She looks Annie in the eye, wondering if she dares to ask Annie the question that's knotting up her insides. Before she can ask, however, Annie gives her a soft smile.

"Sara, you *don't* have to be alone anymore. I'll be here for *you*, even if you need me for *millennia* to come." She says and tips back her neck, inviting Sara to make her hers.

Before she does, however, Sara uses her hand to get Annie to look at her. "There's one other thing you should know before I bring you over; my real name is Abha, and only you and Isanda are allowed to call me that, my little Pepem. Now, it's time for you to make that change from a caterpillar into a butterfly." She reaches over and holds, rocking her gently to help settle the last wisps of anxiety in Annie's mind. Once she feels her let go, Sara gently feeds from her, and gives Annie her blood, turning her. Now neither of them has to be alone or afraid again.

SECOND THOUGHTS

It's been nearly a month since Charlie began communicating with Amy regularly. He feels like their conversations are becoming more normal and natural, and believes he's regained her trust. After a lengthy chat on Facebook, he leans back in his chair and thinks, *I sure hope I can get through to her. I really don't want to see Uri's thugs try to get anything out of her. No matter what she is now, she's still Amy; that much is clear to me now, and part of me still cares for her.*

He yawns and heads to bed, where Janna's waiting for him with a quizzical look. Charlie gets into bed, saying nothing, and pulls Janna against him, stroking her now medium length hair. She let it grow out since they were transferred to the Israelis; he likes it, and her this way. She shifts a little uneasily and rolls toward him. "You do remember what she is now, don't you? How all of this is *just* a mission, *right*? Or do I have to worry that I might lose you to some blood-drinking monster?" Janna searches his expression for some indication of what's going on with him.

Charlie looks at her, taken aback by her implied accusation. "*Janna!* I'm with *you* now! I could *never* be with one of them, but..." He trails off, trying to find the words. "I don't know how to explain it, but no matter *what* she is, she's still Amy, and part of me is loath to do anything to hurt her. I'm hoping I can somehow convince her to cooperate."

"That's a long shot, and you know it! She's one of *them*, and no matter how she may seem in your chats, there's no way she'll *fucking* side with us over the others like her! I wouldn't trust her if I were you. *Hell*, I don't even trust our *own* bloodsuckers! Elias gives me the willies, but some of the new ones they've brought in and transformed are...I don't know...I keep getting the feeling they'd turn on us in a second!" Janna admits.

"I'll admit, I wouldn't have chosen some of the recruits they've transformed. They were either already questionable types, or they were brought in here without warning, terrified out of their minds, and conditioned by some of Uri's guys to comply. I can't help but think some of them will crack under pressure, and the others feel like they're just waiting for their chance to turn on us and drink us dry!" He confesses. "Honestly, and please don't repeat this to Uri or the others, but sometimes I wonder if we haven't misjudged these beings. Uri and his other spooks are all making some big assumptions, and I can't see Amy joining up with some kind of supernatural mercenary group that does contract terrorism. It's not something she'd do under any circumstances!"

Janna gets an odd expression, like she's not sure she just heard what she thinks she did. "You'd *better* keep that *crap* to yourself or Uri will have you hanging out with the laundry!" She admonishes him.

"I *know*! But I don't like how they've handled things lately! How would you feel if you were a civilian, and they drag you out of your home, subject you to conditioning to make you compliant and then turn you into some sort of vampire soldier?" He blurts out, but then gently leans his forehead against hers. "Janna, *don't* worry; they *need* me to get to Amy and get this database they've been talking about! They're not gonna *off me* just because I don't completely agree with their methods!" He caresses her cheek and then pulls her closer. "Got an early morning briefing. Sounds like the shit's about to hit the fan! Get some rest! Everything's gonna be fine!" He reassures her.

The next morning, while Charlie showers, Janna slips out of their quarters and heads to Uri's office. An assistant looks up as she enters the outer office. "Good morning, Medic Baker. Uri's expecting you, go on in."

She nods to the assistant and opens the door, slipping in. She closes the door behind her and lets out a sigh. "I only have a few minutes while Charlie's showering, but it's as you feared. I think he's been influence by his ex. I'm not sure you can trust him to do the right thing for her."

"Go on back to him, Baker. We've already got a contingency plan in place. By the way, you'll be staying here to make sure he has a reason to complete his job." Uri gives her a lopsided smirk and waves her out.

OPERATION DATABASE

Once Charlie's been briefed by Uri and Zelkind, he prepares to be ported back to Asheville. This time, they've set up an Air B&B rental for him to use so he can lure Amy there and be alone with her. He feels uneasy about leaving for the States, however, as Janna sprained her ankle in the gym and won't be on this mission with him. He says goodbye to her and takes his duffle bag with him to the briefing room, where Uri and Elias are waiting.

Uri raises an eyebrow as Charlie comes in the room. "Abrams, here are the tools you'll need. Elias will go with you and be ready to come in as soon as you subdue Ms. Ledbetter. Once her powers are neutralized, she should be as subject to Elias's mind control as any human. We know she's got access to the database from her texts, so once she's under control, your team will go in when no one's in the building, access the information, and then upload it to our cloud."

"And when it's over, I'm to bring Amy back with me? Then you can try to *cure* her, right?" Charlie asks anxiously.

"Yes, of course! Not like we can let her tell them all about you and us! There are only two options, and I'm assuming you don't wish us to do her any harm, *correct*?" Uri asks, watching Charlie closely to see how he responds.

"*Right*! I mean, I *know* what she is, but I'd prefer to see her cured than taken out." He admits, feeling uneasy like he's just answered a question incorrectly on a major test.

"You'll be on your own with her until you've drugged her. We've learned from having several of these beings here now that they can sense others like themselves nearby. Are you *sure* you can do what's *necessary*?" Uri inquires dramatically.

"Yes, Sir! *Absolutely!*" He says, but thinks, *It's up to me to get Amy to comply without hurting her, and get her the help she needs to become human again.*

Uri makes brief eye contact with Elias, who's standing behind Charlie and sees him shake his head slightly as he reads Charlie's thoughts. Even though Charlie has the anti-pathing implant, he's unaware that Uri can turn it on and off as needed, so has been somewhat sloppy with his thoughts around Elias and the other vampires. Elias sends Uri a telepathic message, as they've been practicing even though Uri's not one of them. *He's definitely compromised. Still has feelings for her. I'll be ready to step in and do what's necessary if he doesn't.*

At that point, Charlie slings his duffle bag over one shoulder and picks up the 'tool kit' for dealing with Amy. He feels Elias grasp his shoulder and braces himself for that inevitable disorientation teleporting gives him and does his best not to wretch when they arrive in the house they've rented. It's isolated, at the end of a long, winding dirt road, at the top of a small mountain in Fairview, an area southeast of Asheville. It will be a good place to deal with Amy without having any witnesses to come to her aid should things go awry.

OPERATION CHARLIE

Liz sits at her desk pouring over reports on the effort to track all infected potentials who have manifested new abilities. Whenever possible, they evaluate them at a distance. If they aren't Apara material, the hybrids will do what they do best; abduct the subjects while they sleep and work on their minds. So far, the use of the dust from Centauri-opals has worked well, though sometimes, the amount injected isn't sufficient, and a second abduction and treatment becomes necessary.

Those that can be turned are being assigned handlers to bring them over, but as always, it takes time to ease them in. Tess, Sue, and Kari have been overwhelmed by the effort, but they've also been training others to help them with the preliminaries of the evaluation process, allowing them to focus debriefing on preparing the potentials for their new lives among the Apara.

Liz is disturbed to discover that several older people who've shown new abilities have been diagnosed with dementia or Alzheimer's. Those are some of the most difficult cases, as any that *are* brought into the fold will have to die as far as their friends and families are concerned. However, that may be kinder than subjecting their families to years of dealing with atypical dementia symptoms that won't respond to any of the treatments.

She moves on to some new statistics suggesting that up to 65% of all potentials under the age of eighteen, may have been infected by the virus before the hybrids destroyed it. The hybrids can use their technology to scan the subject's current DNA and compare it to their original surveys of it, post gene-tag, of course. Anyone who shows a significant deviation from the original genetic survey is flagged to monitor, and will eventually be picked up and implanted with a subcutaneous sensor which will alert the Apara and hybrids of any increase in psychic activity.

Liz is so engrossed in her work that she doesn't realize Amy is standing in the frame of her office door until Amy clears her throat. Amy's been working hard on Liz's suggestion to learn to dampen her emotions around other Apara, so Liz didn't get the usual wave of emotions that often precedes a visit by newer Apara.

After Amy clears her throat, Liz looks up, a bit surprised that Amy has managed to sneak up on her. She gives her an exhausted smile and waves her into her office. Amy closes the door and the two women move to the meeting area.

"So, Charlie's coming back to town and wants to get together. Have you all found out anything more about where he's been?" Amy asks.

"Not a lot, though we know he's in Israel. Despite of their attempts to mask their IP address when he emails or chats with you, Ty's narrowed it down to somewhere in the more arid region to the east of Jerusalem." Liz says and yawns.

"When's the last time you *slept*?" Amy asks, concerned that Liz is looking rather haggard.

"I think it was about two days ago." She gives Amy an ironic grin.

"*Liz!* I'm surprised Kari hasn't *made* you get some rest!" Amy blurts out, concerned.

"I think it's been *three* days for her!" Liz grins and attempts to change the subject. "So, what were you saying about Charlie?"

"He may already be back in town, though I've done searches on airline itinerary and haven't found him, and nothing comes up from our tap into the passport system. I suppose he could be coming in through some kind of secret military channel, but that's not normal for someone supposedly doing physical labor as he claims. It's more like what they use when some level of secrecy is involved, like for spies or special forces." Amy rambles out as she thinks out loud.

"Where are you going to meet up this time? Are you going to use the bar at South Slope? If so, make sure Vince is on duty. He's cut back his time there since Dee came along." Liz is happy Dee has someone to help her adjust, though she has the sneaking suspicion there is far more to Vince than meets the eye. However, she doesn't have the energy to pursue such puzzles at the moment.

Amy says, "He's holding up in an Air B&B rental for the next week and wants to make me dinner Sunday night."

Liz narrows her eyes and furrows her brow, as her intuition balks at this idea. "I'm really not sure that's wise. We don't know what's going on with him.

"I can *handle* Charlie! Don't worry! I've *always* been able to handle him, and now, if things get out of hand, I'll use my Apara skills to deal with him!" Amy suggests, sounding confident she can handle any human.

"What about taking Dave with you?" Liz suggests.

"I don't think that would go over too well. Dave is likely to lose it if Charlie gets at all too familiar with me, if you know what I mean! I've told Dave I may have to get a little close with him, so he'll let his guard down, and then *maybe* I can read him."

Liz stretches and yawns again, a bit distracted by all she's been working on, with sleep deprivation on top of it. While Apara don't have to sleep as regularly as humans, many try to get some regular sleep, but they are quite capable of short stints of no sleep during emergencies, as long as they feed extra to compensate. "Alright, keep me posted. If I don't hear from you, I'll send *Dave* in after you!" She gives Amy a mischievous grin.

"It'll be *fine*, Liz! It's not like he could know what I am or any-thing!" Amy says as she leaves Liz's office. Liz gets a shiver of premonition, but not specifics, so she writes it off to stress and exhaustion, turns off the light in her office, closes the curtains, and takes a nap on her sofa.

DOUBLE-BLIND

It's Sunday evening at about 6:45 pm, and Amy pulls up to the small house on the top of a mountain where Charlie is staying for his visit. It's the last property at the end of a long, winding dirt road. She hates such roads, but has no choice but to drive, as she won't be able to explain how she got there if she ported in outside as she could have done in town. Luckily, the weather's been relatively warm for February, so at least she doesn't have to brave any ice or snow to get there. She sees smoke coming out of the chimney and flickers from the fire dancing on a large window as she approaches the front door. She pauses before knocking; her intuition is screaming at her something's wrong, but she does her best to silence it, reminding herself, *It's only Charlie! I've always been a match for him and now, he doesn't stand a chance!* She takes a couple of deep breaths, a step forward, and rings the doorbell.

Charlie opens the door, smiling, and the aroma of kielbasa spaghetti sauce inundates her senses. "Hi, Charlie." She says, waiting to say anything about the food until she gets closer, as a normal person might not have noticed it from outside.

"Come on in! Dinner's almost ready." He tells her.

She comes in, takes off her coat, gives a good inhale for show, and feigns surprise. "*Charlie!* Did you make your *infamous* kielbasa spaghetti? I sure hope you made plenty of garlic bread, too!"

"I sure did! And I brought back some great wine. A friend of mine there suggested I get it at the Duty-Free shop." He says, and a twinge of guilt hits him as he thinks about the real reason for the wine. One tool Uri gave him is a concoction made from deuterium-water, micro-quartz dust, and a dose of low-level gamma radiation, as it was explained to him. Their scientists discovered it would disable 'these creatures' temporarily, as it shorts out their nervous system until their bodies can eliminate it. The bottle contains a hidden compartment near the inside of the opening. Charlie can trigger it to release the compound into her glass, but not his own, without looking suspicious. The slightly vinegar taste of the wine should help to balance out the slightly sweet taste of the deuterium-water, and mask it from Amy's senses.

Amy sits at the kitchen table while Charlie finishes cooking and the two of them chit-chat about old times. The entire time, Amy tries to read him, but still cannot get anything other than some slight impressions of anxiety and guilt, which could be related to anything, including if he were aiming for some makeup sex.

The two former lovers, both thinking they have the upper hand, observe each other hoping to find some chink in the other's armor they can peer through and figure out what's really going on, but both of them are unable to pierce the other's façade.

"Why don't you go on out to the dining room. Dinner's pretty much ready." Charlie tells her. She goes out and sits at one of the two place settings. A couple minutes later, Charlie comes out with two, heaping plates of steaming spaghetti with a spicy, kielbasa spaghetti sauce, topped off with freshly-grated Parmesan and Romano cheese. He places one of them in front of Amy with a flourish. "Dinner is served!" He chirps enthusiastically, placing his own down as well. "I'll be right back!" He heads back to the kitchen. When he returns, he's carrying a large basket of garlic bread and a bottle of red wine with both English and Hebrew writing on the label. He smiles charmingly at Amy and triggers the trick bottle to dispense its payload, pouring her a glass, and then himself, an unadulterated one. He joins her at the table, thinking, *I hate tricking her like this, but better to take her without a fight and not mistreat her, than let Elias or some of Uri's thugs shoot her or something. At least if I'm doing it, I know I won't hurt her. I just hope she cooperates.*

Amy enjoys the meal. It's been their *special* meal ever since he first made it for her when there was a beef shortage where they were stationed, but he was able to get some kielbasa at the base commissary.

"Aren't you going to try the wine?" He asks, taking up his glass.

"Oh, I *will*! You *know* I love this recipe." She grins enthusiastically.

He returns her smile and lifts his glass. "Then, I'll make a toast! To old friends and kielbasa spaghetti!" He raises his glass and she does likewise, taking a sip of the wine and rolling it around on her tongue.

"Hm, that is good! Kind of a mix of sweet and sour..." She comments.

"Yes, my friend...Uri recommended it." He almost screws up by stumbling over Uri and friend in the same sentence, but makes a recovery, and moves on.

The two of them continue to chat, and are laughing about something from back in their service days when Amy gets a wide-eyed look, grows still, and begins trembling. Her heart's racing irregularly as the deuterium concoction hits her nervous system. As she realizes something's very wrong, she looks up at Charlie's face and sees eyes full of sympathy and guilt. She hears him speak, but it sounds like she's down in a well, distant and echoing, "Breathe through it, babe. The worst will be over soon."

Amy tries to path Dave for help, but she can tell it's not going through. She stammers out, "What... what have you done?"

"Amy, I *know* what you are, and I'm gonna get you *help*, but first, you have to *help* me." He tells her, honestly believing he has her best interests at heart, even though he's got a nagging feeling Uri and the others might not. Hearing that, everything goes black and Amy slips into unconsciousness.

COMPELLED

When Amy comes to, she's lying on an overstuffed sofa in front of the fire. Her head aches and she feels beyond weak, almost frail, like the time she got sick from drinking tainted water while out on patrol. Her limbs all feel heavy, but it's not just the weakness. Something heavy weighs on each of her wrists, ankles and even a across her neck. She slides her hand up to her neck and discovers a metal band around it. There are matching bands on each of her extremities. She opens her eyes, and Charlie's there, next to her, looking concerned but resolute.

She notices there's someone else in the room with them, a man with short, dark, curly hair, brown eyes, olive skin and fangs. Her mind mulls that over slowly, as if her thoughts were going through molasses. *An Apara with Charlie? What the Hell?* She thinks.

Charlie gently brushes her hair away from her eyes. "It's gonna be alright, Amy, but I *had* to do this! I don't know how you got involved in this mess, but I'm gonna get you *out* of it!" He notices her try to get up, and says, "Don't! You're still under the influence of the drug I gave you, plus these..." He lifts one of her limp arms by the cuff. "Will make sure you don't use any of your tricks or teleport out of here."

At that point, she can't deny it any longer. Charlie knows her secret. *How the hell could he know?* She thinks in slow-motion panic.

She struggles, but eventually gives up and asks, "What the *fuck* is going on, Charlie? You *drugged* me?" She sounds indignant and hurt by his betrayal.

"No choice. We *need* something from you, but knew you'd never get it for us willingly." He tells her cryptically.

"*What*? What, *exactly*, do you want from me?" She slurs out.

"We need you to access your company's database and get us a list of compatible people in Israel and the surrounding region, as well as any of your agents there. Do this for us and I promise you won't be harmed." He tells her, his eyes pleading with her to comply voluntarily.

"*How* did you find out?" Her voice fades to a whisper, feeling weaker for her effort.

"Doesn't matter, but I, and others do, and they know some of your… 'friends' were involved in the bombing of Jerusalem." He tells her, hoping that will be a revelation to her that will make her disavow her vampire associates and help him instead.

"*Involved*? No! We… they *tried* to stop it!" She utters weakly, at which point, Elias comes forward and steps in.

"*Lies!*" He spits out at her. "We *know* your people teleported the bomb into Jerusalem! It's the *only* way it could have gotten by our sensors! Don't give us any *bullshit* about it being brought in in parts and assembled there! Someone would have noticed! There would have been chatter or some kind of communication that would have tipped us off!" He continues, sounding somewhat rabid as spittle spews from his lips as he speaks, and peppers Amy's face as he leans close to her, trying to intimidate her.

Amy fights through the haze in her mind as the deuterium concoction is slowly pushed out of her system. "*No!* You *must* believe me! *We're* the *good* guys!" She squeaks out, her head now feels like it's on fire as her synapses are slowly cleansed of the heavy water toxin, and are waking to life, only to be cut off by the metal bands.

Charlie walks around the seething Elias and takes Amy's hand. "You *may* believe that, but we *know* better! Maybe they told you they were the good guys to get you to join them, but *for God's sake*, Amy! They're *vampires* and they changed you into one! You're *not* thinking rationally!" He rants at her as though he can make her see sense if he's forceful enough in his argument.

"Got it all *wrong!*" She says, and then feels an odd sensation; tingling on her scalp and a feeling of mental violation as Elias reaches into her mind and forces her to be quiet.

He grips her chin and forces her to look at him. "You *are* going to help us. We *know* you have access to the database in question." He snipes out and his eyes go briefly distant. He turns to Charlie, "Target location is now empty. There are no more heat signatures in the building, so we should go soon." He sneers out.

"Amy, see reason! Work with us! I promise, you'll be *first* in line for the cure when they find one! You can go back to being *you* again!" Charlie pleads.

Amy glares at him as her mind clears, and a maelstrom of emotions hit her; from anger to fear, and even a touch of disappointment that Charlie no longer trusts her. "You *dumbass!* I *am* me! *You're* the one who's acting like an *idiot!* You *must* listen to me!" She instinctively reaches out to compel him to listen and believe her, but is *rewarded* by a sharp pain from the right wrist cuff. "What the *fuck?!*" She complains and rubs her arm with her left hand. She glares at Charlie and the other man; angry at Charlie, and loathing toward the stranger, whom she assumes is in charge.

Elias steps closer and taunts her to her face, fangs bared threateningly. "Every time you attempt any trickery, not only will it be neutralized by the bands, but you'll get a painful reminder *not* to do it again! The pain will *increase* with each attempt and will eventually spread to all of the bands." He explains with overtones of sadistic glee.

"I'm *not* going to help you!" Amy tells them defiantly.

Elias motions to Charlie to get out of the way, showing his fangs hasten his movement. "*You will,* whether or not you want to, Ms. Ledbetter. You see, not only do the bands prevent you from using your powers, they leave you wide open and *susceptible* to mine." He plows in with full. telepathic force, overwhelming Amy, and quashing any resistance; She lets out a small, pitiful squeak as she loses the battle, leaving her in a suggestive state.

When he's done, he stands up straight, gloating with triumph. "She's *ready* for transport." He tells Charlie.

"What the *fuck* did you do to her?" Charlie demands.

"She'll recover, Abrams, but we don't have time for all your gentle persuasion *bullshit!* We have to go now, while the building is empty." Elias reaches over, puts one hand on Amy, the other on Charlie, and ports them both into the parking lot of Inspiration, Inc. "She should have a keycard in here." Elias says, tossing Amy's wallet to Charlie.

"Why didn't we teleport in?" Charlie asks.

"We're *supposed* to make this part look legit. They've probably got access logs or alarms on this *almighty* database, so we need her *on record* as going in there after hours, as though she's working, so they won't get suspicious." Elias explains as though Charlie knows nothing about stealth tactics.

Charlie finds the keycard and opens the front door. "Babe, where's the computer with the database access?" He asks her, and she looks at him blankly, saying, "Second floor, near the end of the hallway."

The three of them find the server room. Elias commands, "Amy, unlock the door." She punches in her access code as if on autopilot. Elias gives the computer a once over, but can't see any options for passwords, and the keyboard and mouse are unresponsive to his touch. He stalks back to Amy demanding, "How do we get access?" He demands.

"You can't. Only authorized individuals can. Bio-specific sensors." She answers, robotically.

"Well, then, I guess you'll be doing this part. Get us the information we need. All the names and information on any compatible Israelis and others in that region, and any operatives in the same area." He commands.

"I don't have access to the list of Apara in Israel, only to the potential database." She tells him, accessing the server on autopilot, calling up what information she can.

"Can this information be saved to a flash drive?" Charlie asks, hoping his voice reassures her unconsciously.

"Yes, but I'll have to enter my passcode again and use retinal ID to do so." She rattles off.

"Then *do* it. Here's the drive." Elias hands it to her. She unlocks the system with her fifteen-digit passcode and her retinal ID, then slides the drive into a USB port and starts the data transfer. When she's done, she removes the drive and hands it to Elias. "Are you sure there's no way you can access the operative list?" He queries.

"I don't have access. Only higher-level Apara like my boss and some of her senior staff, have access." Amy tells them.

"Guess we'll have to wait for stage two, then." Elias grumbles and tosses the drive to Charlie. "Upload that to the base cloud, will ya, Charlie?" Elias says, as he checks out the room, looking to see if there's anything else of interest.

After a few minutes, Charlie says, "Uploaded. Let's get out of here and get Amy where they can help her." But Elias looks back at Charlie with a raised eyebrow.

"I think *not*, Sgt. Abrams. I'm afraid *you've* become a bit of a *liability*." Elias triggers a gas release from the device Charlie used to upload the USB data. Charlie crumples to the ground, unconscious. Elias walks over to Amy and turns her to face him. "I can see what he sees in you; such a shame that pretty face and body is about to get all messed up, but as they say, all's fair in love and war, and *this is war!*" Elias mumbles as he ports the two of them downstairs, dumping Charlie's limp body in the storage room he's ported them into. "One last task for you, Ms. Ledbetter; I assume you'll be missed if you don't show up for work in the morning?"

"Yes, it's technically a holiday tomorrow, so all the human potentials are off, but the rest of us are working, and I'm expected to be there." Amy answers mindlessly.

"Is there anyone else who will worry about you? Or anyone who expects you to check in tonight?" Elias inquires.

"Yes, I need to check in with my boss, Liz. She'll be expecting me to do so." Amy tells him.

"Anyone else?" Elias asks with an impatient tone.

"Liz sent Dave on a mission, so he wouldn't barge in and confront Charlie, but he is expecting me to text when I get home." She blinks slowly as she speaks.

"Contact your boss. Tell her everything is fine and that you'll be coming in late. Tell her you need some time to go through everything again in your head before coming in." He suggests. "Sound as normal as possible and reassure her all is fine. Then text your boyfriend and reassure him. I don't want anyone coming looking for you." He gives her a slimy, one-sided smirk and hands Amy her cell phone.

Amy call's Liz. "Hi, Liz. I'm just checking in."

Liz replies, "Anything to report?" She sounds exhausted and unfocused.

"Nothing major happened except I ate too much spaghetti. Not sure what's going on with him. Guess we'll just have to wait and see." Amy says, sounding normal.

"Sounds good. Keep me in the loop if things change. I've got to run; Kari says if I don't get some rest *now*, she's going to buy nothing but lutefisk for dinner for the next week! Even I can't stand that shit!" She chuckles and hangs up.

"Now, text Dave." He tells her.

She does, and he replies briefly that he's busy dealing with some protests in Hong Kong with the local Apara team, but should be back on Tuesday.

He lets Amy slip out of her compelled state of mind. "What the *fuck*? Where are we? Inspiration, Inc? In a *storage* room?" She looks behind her nemesis, sees Charlie sprawled on the floor, and realizes even if he wants to, he'll be no help in that state. She's relieved, however, to see that he's alive and breathing.

Elias walks away from Amy, but leaves her semi-paralyzed, but aware. "Oh, Ms. Ledbetter, there's one more thing..." He turns around and shoots her in the chest before she can respond. She staggers backwards, collapses to the ground a few feet from Charlie, blood pooling beneath her now prone form. "That should keep you out of trouble until it's too late."

Elias walks into the main basement and closes his eyes. Three more soldiers in beige-tone fatigues show up, two men and a woman. They're all carrying backpacks and boxes. "Alright, you know what to do. Rig the place to blow tomorrow at 11 am. I'll put all the suppressors and sonic locks in place around the building"

They all work on their assigned tasks, finish about 2 am, and port back to Israel, leaving an unconscious Charlie, and Amy, who has gone into stasis, in the sealed, basement storage room full of office supplies, while timed explosives tick down to detonation silently a short distance away.

MONDAY

It's Monday morning, and it's President's Day. While officially a holiday, only the human potentials are off. With everything going on post-virus, there's far too much Apara business to take a three-day weekend, and many even work during the daytime hours on weekends, or continue working from home after hours. Everyone ports or stumbles in as usual, except for a small number, like Amy, who told Liz she'd be in late.

Everyone settles into their usual routine, and yet, there's an uneasiness nagging at some of the Apara in the building, like Liz and Marc. That uneasiness also hits Val, even though she's in New York, working with Ty. They are at the New York City center shoring up security and training their staff to do searches to find local potentials who may have been infected and altered by the virus. She feels oddly distracted, like her mind is nagging her to focus on something besides her work.

Other than that, no one knows the basement of the building has been rigged with a new form of plastic explosive that leaves no residue. There are no wires, and the timing mechanism is a plastic, digital card that has two electrodes on the back that are pushed directly into the block of explosive. The device is usually incinerated beyond recovery once the explosive is detonated. It is usually used in 'hit jobs' by military forces that are meant to be untraceable, and look like an accident, such as a natural gas explosion.

***

Across the world, Elias and his team are waiting anxiously for 10:00 am Eastern US time to come around, when they will port back and wait for the explosion. They all have gear that matches the local fire and rescue uniforms. Elias reminds them of their mission. "Once we teleport in, I'll activate the sonic locks, and the anti-ability network we've tied into their electrical system, effectively trapping them inside. Uri and Zelkind assume that most of them trapped in the explosion will appear to die by human standards. We are to extricate the bodies and remove them, transporting them back to our base. There, they'll be allowed to recover and be interrogated and stand trial for the Jerusalem bombing. In particular, we are looking for these two individuals. He holds up a tablet with pictures of Marc and Liz from the company website. These are the two that were in direct contact with our subject, so we believe they are the ones responsible. Even so, the more of these guys we get, the bigger a blow we deliver to their organization."

"Sir, what's the plan if any get out of the building alive?" The female soldier asks.

"Your guns contain tranq darts filled with a fast-acting version of the deuterium compound. Hit anyone who gets out with one of those, and they'll go down fast! I *know*! They tested it on me!" He gives them a lopsided sneer of annoyance at that part of his duties.

The woman continues, "What about human casualties? Will there be any humans in the building or are they *all* like us?" She asks, concerned about collateral damage.

"It's a holiday here, though we know there are people in the building based on the thermal detector we left there. As you know, we, and they, are slightly warmer than average humans." He gives an odd laugh. "Considering vampires are supposed to be cold, that's quite ironic if you think about it." He taps on the tablet and pulls up the infrared thermoscan. If there were any humans in the building, they would appear red or reddish orange, but as you see, all the bodies in the building are coming up yellow as they are warmer, except for one, of course, that we can't scan for, because he's underground." Elias gives them all a knowing look as he refers to Charlie Abrams, who they intend to die in the explosion, in case they need a scapegoat should officials question the cause.

One of the men chimes in. "Sir, why didn't you kill Abrams outright?"

"We need it to look like he died near the source of the explosion. On the chance anyone questions the cause. If they find him there with a bullet in his skull, that will be a *moot* point!" He explains impatiently.

10 am rolls around and Elias says, "It's time. Anyone who's coming in should be there by now. Let's go!" and the four soldiers disappear, reappearing in the woods near Inspiration, Inc, part of the Blue Ridge Parkway, and Biltmore Forrest. They move in as stealthily as possible and trigger the devices they've installed in the building to lock the Apara in.

***

Right after they set the trap in Asheville, Val goes wide-eyed, and her breathing and heart-rate increase. She stares off into space, oblivious to everyone around her. The people they are training are uncertain what's happening, but Ty reassures them. "She's having a premonition. I need some paper and pencils." He demands.

"Sorry, but we went *paperless* earlier this year." Says one trainee.

"*Hell!*" Ty curses and is about to ask a trainee to stand close to Val in case she passes out, which has happened occasionally, so he can port out for Val's supplies. Before he can, however, she lets out a loud gasp and grabs her tablet from the table. She's trembling and closes her eyes. She holds the tablet to her chest and lets out a distressed whimper. When the vision passes, she sways unsteadily, and Ty eases her back into a chair. Her breathing slows and she snaps out of the fugue, looking up at him, unable to speak. She paths him one word: *BOMB!* And hands him the tablet. On it, etched into the LED screen, is a picture of their building back in Asheville, exploding with flame and debris everywhere.

"*Merda!* He exclaims and sends an urgent path to Liz, but cannot feel her. Afraid they may be too late; he whips out his cell phone and calls. He holds his breath when the phone rings and he waits for her to answer. When he hears her pickup, he lets out a gasp and starts talking before she can even say hello. "*Liz! Listen* to me! Get everyone *out* of the building!" He commands and fiddles with the tablet to text her the image Val created electronically. He knows this picture is an evolution in Val's abilities, but he'll deal with that later. "Look at the picture. It's from Val. She made it somehow after her vision!"

"*Helvete!*" Liz swears, trying to path everyone to get out of the building, but an energy backlash gives her a sharp headache. "*Herre Gud!*" She gets up and runs out to Kari. She discovers she can path if she's within a few feet of her. The color drains from Kari's face as she comprehends the danger they're in. They try to port back to Marc's department to save time, but can't.

"What the *Hell*?" Kari exclaims. "I *can't* port!"

"Liz's eyes go wide as she tries and cannot port either. They run down the hall toward Marc's office, telling everyone in the offices on the way to evacuate through the front door as porting doesn't work. When the first person gets to the front door, Liz hears a piercing sound and a scream.

"What *now*?" She asks, as she, Peder, Marc, and Kari run to the lobby and see one of their newer recruits lying on the floor near the exit, with blood coming out of her ears. "Take her back to the lobby!" Liz shouts over the painful, sonic din emanating from a small silver device that has been attached to the metal and glass door frame. She approaches it, but her own ears begin to experience unbearable pain, so she backs off.

"We've been set-up! You three go upstairs and warn everyone. Check the windows. Maybe we can get out of that way...we'll have to jump, but we can do damage control with witnesses afterwards." Liz checks on the bleeding woman, who's regained consciousness, but is disoriented, and having trouble hearing.

The others go upstairs to check all the windows in the offices, but all have the same sonic device that activates when anyone moves within three feet of it. Liz calls Kari on her cell. "Get *everyone* down here!" She demands, and people bound down the stairs, and gather in the lobby. Some of them with more sensitive hearing are still covering their ears with their hands as pain shoots through their heads.

Peder comes back down the steps. "Liz, the *Atrium*! We can get out that way!" He suggests, somewhat out of breath. Peder heads for the door to their basement, where they have storage and a rather unusual atrium, one that technically exists in Sanctuary rather than the 'real world'. This Atrium is through a portal to Sanctuary, with a domed in garden, similar to the one at Medical. It's a place where the Apara can go during work if they need to meditate or clear their minds of telepathic static. Peder grabs the handle and nothing happens. The door won't open. He stares at the gap between the door and the frame and discovers why. "*Damn*! It's been welded shut from the *other* side, all the way around! What the *Hell* is going on?"

One of the newer Apara asks, "Who could have done this?"

Liz answers, "No idea and we don't have time to dwell on it, we must get out of here!"

A few minutes later, Tess, Colin, and Niall come running down the stairs. Tess hollers to Liz, "Marc's making sure that everyone's out, and checking *all* possible exits. I think he said something about the *crawl space*?"

Liz hears panicking; for the first time since Jerusalem, she feels a near paralyzing fear in her gut.

***

Outside, the Israeli Apara team move into position. Elias hears some of the sonic alarms go off and takes out the tablet, pulling up the thermoscan and frowns. The woman asks, "What is it, Sir?"

"Almost all the heat signatures have migrated to one room. Something must have tipped them off." He says, muttering a string of Hebrew curses under his breath.

"What should we do?" Asks one of the men.

"Get into sniper position in case they find a way out. As it is, it doesn't really matter if they know or not, they're still trapped, and quite frankly, they deserve to *feel* some of that fear *our people* felt before the nuke went off!" He spits out.

The team separates, their rifles loaded with deuterium darts, and they wait, far enough away to be out of the explosion's range, but close enough to hit their targets with their sniper rifles.

***

In the dark, basement storage room, Charlie rouses. He can't see a thing in the darkness, but pulls out a flashlight from his jacket pocket, and looks around the room with it until he sees Amy's body lying on the floor with blood painting the fabric on her chest.

"Oh, *Hell!*" He exclaims, slowly standing, still unsteady from whatever they used on him, but he stumbles toward Amy. He stares down at her body, trying to figure out if she's breathing or not, gets dizzy, and nearly falls on top of her. He braces himself and lands next to her instead. He reaches over to check her wound, but it's already mostly healed, and he feels a weak pulse. He lets out a relieved sigh, knowing she's 'alive' and tries to rouse her.

"*Amy! Wake up! Please!*" He urges her. He checks her pulse again, this time on her wrist instead of her throat, but the bracelets are in the way. "*Shit!* Elias has the controls for those things." He complains to thin air, but pulls out his pocket knife, and begins carefully prying the locked, metal bands open. He gets the two off of her wrists, and one off of her ankle, but stress and sweat make his hands slip when he tries to open the one on her other ankle, and he knicks her foot by accident.

He hears a small, weak 'ouuuch' coming from Amy, and she stirs awake. He tries again and gets the leg band off of her. Now the only one left is the one around her neck. "Amy, can you hear me, babe? It's Charlie! You *need* to snap out of it!" He leans close to her ear when he speaks. He feels something wet and sticky under one hand and looks down to see his hand is resting in half-dried blood from her wound. When he looks back at Amy's face, she's staring at him with half-dead eyes.

She stammers out, "*Fuck you*, Charlie!"

"I'm *sorry*, Amy! I...I wanted to get you *help!*"

She inhales a couple of times, then whispers, "Don't think... that's... gonna... happen." She says, her words coming out staccato.

Charlie uses his flashlight to look around the room again, and sees that the light fixture on the ceiling has been broken, the lock on the door has literally been fused, likely with a welding torch. He turns back to Amy. "We're trapped. They've fused the lock on the door."

Amy lets out a weak, impatient breath. "Wrist... *give* me your wrist."

Charlie looks at her aghast, realizing what she's asking him. "I... I *don't think so*, Amy..." He trails off, shaking his head in a mixture of fear and denial.

She narrows her eyes and tries to compel him, but gets a shock from the one, remaining band around her neck. "At least get this *damn* thing off me!" She pleads.

He looks at her for a minute, uncertain what to do, knowing she may get some of her abilities back, and not sure if he can *really* trust her. After all, even if she is Amy, she's *one* of them.

"*Damn* you! This is all *your fucking fault!*" She blurts out! I'm *not* going to hurt you! I just...I don't think they'd leave us here, locked in, if they thought we had *any* chance in Hell of getting out and warning my friends!"

"Our mission was *only* getting the information about compatibles in Israel." He reminds her.

"*No*, Charlie. That was *your* mission. I...I don't think they want either of us to... to make it out of here." She tells him, her intuition is screaming at full mental volume. "*Please, I promise!* Get this off of me and I'll do whatever I can to get us *both* outta here!"

After another couple of seconds, he does as she asks, and approaches her with the knife. "You need to stay still. I don't want to slip and have you bleed-out on me." He tells her as he works the tip of the titanium pocket knife into the thin gap where the ring joins and locks. It takes about 10 minutes and he nearly slips and cuts her twice, but he finally removes it and tosses it across the room.

Amy tries to sit up, but is too weak. "Charlie, I *know* you're not sure you can trust me, but I *really need* your wrist. I'm so weak from blood loss and I'm barely outta stasis, man! *Please!* I *promise*, I'll only take what I absolutely need to." She looks at him with pit-ifully pleading eyes until he tentatively extends his arm to her.

"Thank you." She whispers weakly. She bites into his wrist, and there's a brief but bearable pain. She draws on his wrist for about five minutes. It's a much slower feed than the neck, which is for the best, as she might not be able to stop herself quickly enough had she drunk from a major artery. She senses he's get-ting a little dizzy when his heart skips a beat. She forces herself to stop even though her body is screaming for more. It's enough, however, as she's able to pull herself up into a sitting position again. "Are you okay?" She asks Charlie, who's a little pale, more from the experience than the blood loss.

"Yeah, but now what? We're still locked in. If the door had opened out, I might've been able to ram it, but it opens in." He tells her with a shrug.

"Help me up and over to the door?" She tells him.

He slowly gets himself into a standing position, still a bit wob-bly, both from whatever they drugged him with and now, the blood loss. He braces himself using one of the supply shelves nearby and reaches down, pulls her up, and against him. She wraps her arms around his neck to keep from falling, but gives him a half-pained smile and says, "Don't get any ideas, dude! You're still on my shit list for all of this!"

After a few minutes, she feels stronger and more stable now that the blood has converted and replenished her own. She puts one hand on Charlie's arm and tries to port. "*What? Why* can't I port out?" She asks in frustration.

"I don't know. The bands were stopping you; maybe they're still too close to you or you're still weak?" He suggests.

"Guess I'll have to do this the old-fashioned way." She staggers toward the door and examines the lock in the dark, not needing a flashlight because of her Apara night vision. She reaches down and gets a good grip on the fused door knob, and uses all her strength to twist it right off the door. "Your knife, please!" She says, and he stumbles over to her with his dimming flashlight in one hand, and his knife in the other. She takes it and jams it into the works of the doorknob, knocking the other knob out the other side. She gets a grip on the hole where the knobs used to be and rips it toward her, breaking what's left of the locking mechanism and the frame. She loses her balance, but Charlie catches her, and rights her again. They walk out of the door and stop as they see blocks of something clay like in several places around the basement and look at each other.

"*Damn!*" Amy says, realizing what she's seeing. "I've got to warn the others!" She tries the door to the stairwell, only to discover it welded top to bottom, so she tries to path anyone upstairs; Tess, Liz, even Marc, but can't reach anyone even though she hears shuffling around on the floor above them. "I can't path with anyone either, use telepathy, that is." She tells him, not sure he understands the term.

Amy looks around for her cell phone and sees it on the floor, discarded and quite dead. "*Fuck!* Do you have any idea why I can't reach them? We should be plenty far away from those bands!" She says in frustration. She looks at Charlie, who's grown quiet but looks quite shocked by whatever he's thinking.

"If their plan was to blow up this place the whole time, then they wouldn't want *anyone* in here to get out. I heard rumors about some of the gadgets they've made that counteract your abilities, including something that could stop *all* of your abilities at once." He tells her.

"*Great*, we're *screwed*, then, aren't we?" She snipes at him, and looks around the room. When she gets to a certain angle, she hears a piercing whine and grimaces.

"What is it?" He asks.

"I just heard a high-pitched noise. It's like when your ears ring but louder and more irritating." She says, shaking her head unconsciously to stop the irritation the sound is making.

"It's a *sonic* lock! They used them on... they transformed some of the local virus victims in Israel and they used these sonic locks to keep them locked up until they could be controlled. They're probably using those to keep your people inside. It's particularly damaging to your ears because of your sensitive hearing." He tells her awkwardly.

"They *know* about the virus? And the psychic outbreaks? How is it they know about all of this? How *did* you know about me?" She stands there, hands on hips, distracted from escaping for a moment.

"I cloned your phone when we met at the bar. They extrapolated from there about the virus and other stuff from your texts and emails." He explains, uneasy about how Amy may react to his admission.

She narrows her eyes and stares at him, seething with anger. "*How* did they know about us in the first place? How did they know about *me*?"

He's reluctant to tell her, but knows she's his only hope now. "We found one of your people in an old cave; well, an undiscovered tomb, under the Jerusalem after a cave in I got caught in. The rest is complicated, but I made the connection between your bosses and ...well...they were looking for two people named Lissa and Marc with 828 numbers and I mentioned you worked for people by those names in Asheville, and well...." He halfway expects her to attack him in anger, but instead, she throws her dead cell phone across the room and against a wall in the direction of the sound. When it hits the wall, she realizes it echoes oddly.

She trots over to where the phone is lying, smashed at the base of the wall, wincing at the sound as it gets louder. She realizes there's an air duct for the central air system. She listens, and can tell that is where the sound is coming from, but she can also hear people talking. She shouts at the top of her lungs through the vent until she hears Tess's voice echoing down the shaft. "*Amy*? Is that *you*?"

***

Back in the lobby, it's 10:32 am and the anxiety level is palpable to everyone, even with the dampening effect of whatever is hindering their abilities. Liz is pacing the floor trying to come up with a solution, when she hears Niall exclaim, "*Callie!*" and everyone looks at him as they feel a sudden wave of hope.

He pulls out his cell phone to call her since he can't reach her telepathically, but when it doesn't go through, he looks and it says: NO SERVICE. "I don't have any coverage? What about the rest of you?" He asks urgently. Everyone checks, but their cells are all showing the same thing, 'NO SERVICE".

"*Utrolig! For Faen!*" Liz curses again in Norwegian. Whoever's behind this must be jamming our cells, too. The land lines are out, as well as the internet!"

Niall hits a wall with his fist in frustration. "If I could only get a hold of Callie, she could create a portal and get us out." He tells them.

"There has to be *some* way to reach her!" Kari exclaims.

Tess is leaning against a wall in the lobby, worried about Marc, as he's not come down yet. She knows he's trying to get up into the crawl space above the third floor to see if he can get out on the roof, but it's taking so long. As she stands there, she hears something and focuses. She bends down, listening, and hears Amy's voice. "*Amy*, is that *you*?"

Tess hears: "Oh! *Thank* God, girl! I'm trapped in the basement with Charlie! You've got to get us outta here and everyone outta the building, even if you can't get us out, you've got to save everyone else!" She rambles. "There are explosives down here, set to go off... She moves over to one. "at 11 am! What time is it now?"

There's a moment of silence, then Tess says, "It's 10:37."

"Get *yourselves* out! Don't worry about me!" She hollers up the air shaft.

Amy hears Tess talking to others, but the high-pitched sound increases and she can't hear what they're saying. The next thing she knows, she hears Peder's voice.

"Amy, we're trapped, too, but I know how *you* can get out!" He shouts into the vent. "Go down past the storage room to a hallway there, and it'll take you to a set of double doors to the Atrium. Do *whatever* you have to, but get out *that* way! It's a *portal* door to Sanctuary!"

"Got it! Heading that way!" She replies but hears Peder yell again.

"*WAIT!*" As soon as you're out, you should be able to port! Get to Callie, Niall's partner! She can create a portal to us. Tell her to aim for the lobby!" He waits for her acknowledgment.

"Atrium, portal door, port to Callie, get her to make portal to lobby! Got it!" she says and then motions to Charlie to follow her and they run as fast as they can down to the double doors.

Their captors used a mini-welder to fuse the door locks again. Amy, now feeling stronger because she's fed, but also because of her own adrenaline rush, grips both handles, and twists them simultaneously. She hears the metal creak and whine as force is applied, but they don't give way. Amy paces briefly, then backs up from the door, getting a running start. She flies into a Karate kick her mom would be proud of, breaking the weld. The doors not only open, but one door literally flies off its hinges. She yells at Charlie. "Don't just stand there like a *dumb-fuck* with your mouth hanging open, come on!"

The two run through the doors, and Amy grabs a small boulder from the landscaped garden and throws it through the glass of the atrium. "Get as far away from that portal as possible! If it does blow, you'll get blowback through it! I've got to get somewhere fast and you'll only hold me back!" She tells him and watches as he runs as quickly as possible away from the portal door.

Amy focuses on Callie and ports, reappearing in Callie's workshop where Callie is busy working at a large, electric polisher with her headphones and goggles on, unaware she has company. Amy rushes over to her and puts her hand on Callie's shoulder, startling her, and making her lose her grip on the pendant she was polishing; the spinning buff on the motor grabs it and flings it across the room. Callie pulls off her headphones and goggles in a huff and turns off the machine. She looks at Amy, annoyed. "Ever heard of *calling* first?" She asks trying to spot where her pendant flew.

"No *fucking* time! I need your help! *Everyone* does, including *Niall!*" Amy blurts out.

"What's wrong? How can I help?" Callie asks, suddenly aware that she can't reach Niall or feel him in her mind.

Amy paths a rapid, wordless explanation of the situation to her and Callie gasps. "I... I'll try, but I haven't done anything this big since I accidentally opened the portal during the fire! What do I need to do?" She asks frantically.

"I was going to say calm down, but I think the adrenalin may help you more! Picture Niall! He's in the lobby with a lot of other people. Imagine them right in front of us." Amy tells her, practically willing Callie to succeed.

Callie can almost see them, but loses her focus because of anxiety several times. Amy demands, "You've got to do it NOW, Callie! There's less than five minutes before the place blows!"

That boost to her adrenalin levels does the trick, and at 10:56, a swirly, silvery-clear disturbance forms in an open space in her studio. She watches as the view to the lobby resolves, and a very relieved Niall, and others push forward and into her workshop, knocking over things in the process. "That's it, Callie, keep it open until everyone gets through." Amy tells her, relieved that the portal idea is working.

On the other side of the portal, Liz, Kari, and Tess are bringing up the rear when Tess lets out a gasp of horror. "Marc's *still* up there! We've *got* to get him! He doesn't *know* there's a bomb or that we've found a way out!"

Liz and Kari look at each other, knowing they barely have seconds before the bombs explode. Liz gives Tess a sympathetic look, the two women grab her, and drag her through the portal into Callie's studio. Callie nearly collapses from the effort, the portal starts to close, fading, and shrinking, but doesn't close completely before there's a bright flash of light and a thundering roar, with smaller bits of debris and hot embers slipping through the last, small openings in her portal, peppering her studio and the Apara she'd rescued.

Liz and Kari hold Tess tightly between them, preventing her from trying to run back to the now-faded portal or porting out to find Marc. "*Tess! Stop!* There's *nothing* you can do! He was high enough up that even if he was in the building when it blew, he'll likely go into stasis, but should survive; but if you port back there now, and whoever did this is waiting, you'll be in *danger*, too!" Liz says as she rocks Tess in her arms to console her, and keep her there.

"I...I *can't feel* him." Tess chokes out.

"I *know*, Tess. I can't either, but we'll *find* him. I *promise!* And we'll find the people who did this!" She glances over Tess's shoulder to Kari and paths, *Get Sara*. Kari vanishes, and Sara, Vanessa Manheim, several other medics, and Annie, newly turned Apara arrive to triage any injuries.

Sue ports in shortly thereafter, as she'd been working at Medical with Millie and Miranda when Collin pathed her from Callie's workshop. Liz catches Sara's eye and Sara nods. She comes over quietly, doses Tess with an infuser of sedative, and Liz ports her home to her bed, knowing she'll sleep a good while, and can be kept under if need be.

Liz feels something move around her ankles and between her legs. It's Mabel. She picks up the cat and slips her onto the bed with Tess. Mabel senses that Tess is distressed from certain odors wafting from her pores. She goes over to a very unconscious Tess, paws at her, kneading her stomach gently before settling there, and falling asleep.

Liz ports back to Callie's studio to help get everyone calmed down and dealt with, thankful that their casualties have been low.

She spots Amy across the room and ports over to her rather than weeding her way through the crowd. "Are you okay?" She asks, noticing the blood stain on her shirt.

"Yeah, mostly. I need to feed some more, but then I need to do something." She says, cryptically.

"What?" Liz asks, having trouble imagining doing anything at the moment due to the shock of the situation.

"Charlie was involved in this, though, in the end, he helped me out. It seems there's an Israeli group of some kind that *knows* about us. They found one of ours in some tomb under Jerusalem when they were working on reclaiming the land before rebuilding. They think..." She pauses, catching her breath, "that *we were responsible* for the bomb. That's why Charlie kept asking about you and Marc. Your names were in the remains of an Apara's cell phone. They believe you two are the ringleaders."

"That's *insane!* We were there to *stop* it!" Liz says, frustrated by this new revelation.

"Like so many secret government and military organizations, they're *driven* by paranoia. They'll often jump to the most paranoid conclusion because it's better to overreact to a threat and be vigilant than be unprepared. From what little Charlie told me, they've developed weapons against us. Things that can neutralize our abilities. I think we're in for a long fight with these people." Amy suggests. "And Liz, they have at least one Apara working with them." Amy tells her and paths the image of Elias and how he'd compelled her to retrieve information from their servers once she'd effectively been neutralized by the drug Charlie slipped her.

Liz closes her eyes, and takes a slow, controlled breath. "I don't recognize him, but I'll get the word out to all the centers. Just what we don't need! Another rogue Apara!" She pauses, then asks, "Speaking of *Charlie*, where is he?" Liz asks as Kari comes up behind her partner and puts her arm around her, glad they're both safe.

"That's what I've gotta do! I got him through the portal door to the atrium, broke the glass and sent him running. Not like he can get away in Sanctuary, but he's also not aware that there are predatory animals that are not afraid of humans here. I need to find him before he runs into something he'll regret." Amy says, and vanishes, forgetting her needs at the moment as she imagines some large cat or wolf pack getting to Charlie. She may be pissed at him, but she doesn't want to see him hurt or killed, though she halfway wants to beat the crap out of him herself!

Kari gives Liz a long embrace, then steps back halfway, still holding Liz lightly. "What about *Marc*?"

"I don't know, Kari, but if what Amy told me is accurate, and they get their hands on him, this could go very badly. Unfortunately, we can't focus on Marc right now. Get everyone dealt with and home. If they don't have a sanctuary residence, see if there's room in the dorms at Medical. We don't know how much these people have on us and our people. The priority is to make sure we're all safe from these guys. Alert the other centers as well, especially the one in Tel-Aviv. I've got to get a message to our Benefactors and fill them in." Liz tells her, patting Kari on the arm as she walks away from her embrace, turns to face her, and vanishes.

Kari notices the look on Liz's face before she ports out is one of someone who's been through one too many crises, but still has to keep going. Kari turns around and makes the rounds to check on everyone, making arrangements for non-sanctuary residents to have somewhere safe to settle until more becomes known.

BETTER ONE THAN NONE

A couple minutes before the explosives will tear through the Inspiration, Inc. building, Elias mutters a loud "*Fucking Hell!*" as he notices a sudden cool signature on his thermoscan, watches it grow larger, and then all the hotter, Apara signatures disappear through it. As the last few are going through; he hears a gunshot from one of his snipers and sees a body fall to the ground from the roof of the building.

He yells, "Recover!" to one of his team. They port out, grab the body and port back right before the cool signature fades on the thermoscope and is replaced by a washout of heat as the building explodes in a fireball.

Debris from the building flies out, damaging nearby cars and buildings, alarms can be heard nearby, as well as barking dogs reacting to the noise. Though they are all still dressed in fire and rescue gear, Elias tells them, "No point in sticking around. The others found some way out, though I'll be damned if I know how! Still, better one, than none." He says and takes a good look at their captive, who's gone into stasis. He pulls a cloth out of his jacket pocket, wipes the dirt and blood from the seemingly dead man's face, and begins to chuckle. "Well, if we had to get only one, at least it's one of the ringleaders!" He reaches down and grabs Marc's body by an arm and signals the others to port out, as sirens can be heard from a multitude of approaching emergency vehicles.

REGROUPING

It's been three days since the explosion and there's been a lot of damage control to do. The building was completely destroyed and unsalvageable. Luckily, thanks to some Apara in the local emergency services, the cause was listed as a natural gas explosion, so the fact that it was terrorism does not become public. It is a far better option than it becoming known that it was international terrorism, as it would only draw scrutiny.

Liz decides that instead of rebuilding on the old location, that it's advisable to move their new offices to town where it will be harder to do anything unnoticed. The new building, when built, will have a porting filter to prevent any unknown Apara from porting in. They had one while Jason was active, but once he and his associates were captured, it was turned off, allowing the Israeli Apara access to port in, with or without Amy's keycard.

Luckily, since Ty set up the physical servers containing information on potentials in Sanctuary, with only access point terminals in the Human world, very little was lost other than a handful of physical files that hadn't been added to the servers yet, and Tess had copies of most of it on her home computer. Even all of their tablets had been backed up recently, so even without a headquarters, the search for new Apara can continue.

The existence of a militarized, covert group using humans, forcibly turned Apara, has shaken the Apara world. A lot of changes will have to be made, including security upgrades for all centers. Plans are made for every center to have multiple 'emergency exit' portal doors installed, giving them escape routes in case porting is blocked in a future attack. Eventually, they plan to create duplicate buildings in Sanctuary, linking them to the Human earth buildings with the same portal technology as most of their homes use. As long as these new, militant Apara are unaware of Sanctuary, if they break into a Center, it will be empty.

In addition, any Apara not currently living in a Sanctuary-anchored home must move to one. With future attempts, portal doors can be cut off to protect any of their people, but defending a normal, human residence is not practical, nor likely to be successful.

Since the militants hacked Amy's phone, they will also be providing secure cell phones to all Apara. While they will connect to human networks, they will be creating their own communications network using a non-standard frequency well above normal, making it harder for others to jam their phones using targeted interference. The hybrids are setting up cloaked communications satellites for this purpose.

Amy tracks down Charlie, miserable and confused, hiding in a cave during a torrential rain storm in Sanctuary, and brings him to Liz in a temporary office at Medical. After getting dried off and clean, he's more than willing to tell her anything he can considering his team left him and Amy there to die.

When questioned further about the group he was working for, he tells them they're called *Naqam* or "Vengeance" in English, as that is what they want to attain. Some of the higher-ups know that the real bombers were an international group of social terrorists, bent on forcing humanity to return to a simpler, decentralized way of life, but having the Apara as a new and terrifying foe gives them something to fight against as a united force.

Eventually, they plan to expose the Apara, at which point, it will give their people a common enemy to blame and pursue with holy vengeance as a goal. What better way to rally a religious, yet demoralized people than to have 'blood-drinking demons' from Hell as your enemy?

Charlie tells them, while he never actually saw where he was, other than in a desert region, with arid-looking mountains in the distance, he tells them that they were underground and were shielded by some sort of EM barrier. He tells them that the unit is led by a rather disagreeable Israeli agent named Uri, but he didn't know a last name, and that they'd turned at least six people they found through the viral outbreak, including two over the age of 60, and wanted to find more so they could create their own army of beings equivalent to the Apara.

This is why they wanted the list of potentials in Israel and surrounding areas. Charlie also tells them that Marc is very likely being held in that base, and he'll do whatever he can to help find him.

Amy and Dave take a larger team of her guys to the rubble of Inspiration, Inc. two nights after the explosion, after the human rescue workers had given up for the night. There have been no reports of any bodies found in the rubble by human rescue workers. Amy and her team are there with equipment as well as their extra senses to search for the only potential victim, Marc Girard, but there is no sign of him other than a smashed cell phone, half burnt, lying in the parking lot, but no body or parts are found, so they assume he must have been taken. In addition, Alice is brought in, along with Dimitrios, who took her in as both apprentice finder and partner. They don't find Marc, but they do find a deuterium dart that didn't hit any target, providing Sara and her people with a clue into how they disabled Amy. It turns out that the combination of deuterium, micro-quartz dust, and gamma exposure approaches what the Centauri-opal do, only much cruder and harder on the Apara exposed. It works like a neurotoxin instead of an inhibitor, but does get flushed from the system after a few hours, at least in its current formulation, but Sara warns that if they tweak it the right way, this new weapon could become a serious tool to reckon with. It will take a while before they can make it deadly, but a slight change in the formula can change things from a few hours to a longer-term loss of one's abilities.

Tess is kept under for a week while they search for any trace of Marc, but in the end, they must wake her, and break the news to her.

Sara, Liz, and Sue are there when she opens her eyes. She looks at her friends around her, a little confused as to why they're all staring at her expectantly while emanating waves of regret and worry. As Tess looks from one face to another, a gnawing feeling hits her, and she notices she can't feel Marc at all. She sits bolt upright, looks around the room for him, but the others hold her there so she can't port away to look for him.

"*Tess*, it's going to be okay. We'll *find* him. It's just going to take some time." Liz explains.

Tess's mind wars with itself over whether she's sad, devastated, or outright furious. She looks at the women with her and says, "*Damn* right! We're *gonna* find him, and I get first shot at the *assholes* who did this!" Suddenly, three light panels on the walls all go out and smolder, Mabel runs out of the room, skittering down the hallway from the wave of anger that expands like a quake from its epicenter, Tess.

FOREIGN WORD LIST

FRENCH

Quelle horreur	How awful
Voila	There, there it is

ITALIAN

Amore	Love, my love
Cara	"dear" referring to female friend affectionately
Grazie	Thank you
Merda	Shit
Tesoro mio	My treasure

HEBREW

Naqam	Vengeance

MAYAN

K'aizalaj okox	A type of psychedelic mushroom

NORWEGIAN

(for) Faen, Faen i helvete!	Damn, Hell, literally: The devil in Hell
Helvete	Hell
Herre Gud!	Dear lord! Oh, God!
Javel	Southern Norwegian expression that has several meanings, include 'Well?"
Julebord	Traditional Norwegian business Christmas party
Karamellpudding	Dessert similar to flan
Utrolig!	Unbelievable!